THE CASE OF THE DEAD DOMESTIC

TAM MAY

The Case of the Dead Domestic

Adele Gossling Mysteries: Book 6

Tam May

Published by Dreambook Press.

Click or visit:
https://www.tammayauthor.com

ISBN: 9781734671445 (Print)
ISBN:9781734671452 (ebook)

Quotes in the text are as follows:

Chapter 3

Aesop's Fables, "The Ass, The Fox, and The Lion"

https://www.infoplease.com/primary-sources/fables-fairytales/aesops-fables/aesops-fables-88.

Chapter 9

Proverbs: 14:1, English Standard Version

Chapter 11

Luke 6:38, New International Version

Chapter 17

Henry Wadsworth Longfellow, "There was a little girl", *Poetry Foundation*, https://www.poetryfoundation.org/poems/44650/there-was-a-little-girl.

Chapter 22

Willian Jennings Bryan, "Cross of Gold speech", *Teaching American History*, https://teachingamericanhistory.org/document/the-cross-of-gold-speech/.

Chapter 24

Shakespeare, *Measure for Measure*, Act V, Scene I, https://artsemerson.org/2018/10/02/everyday-quotes-from-shakespeares-measure-for-measure/.

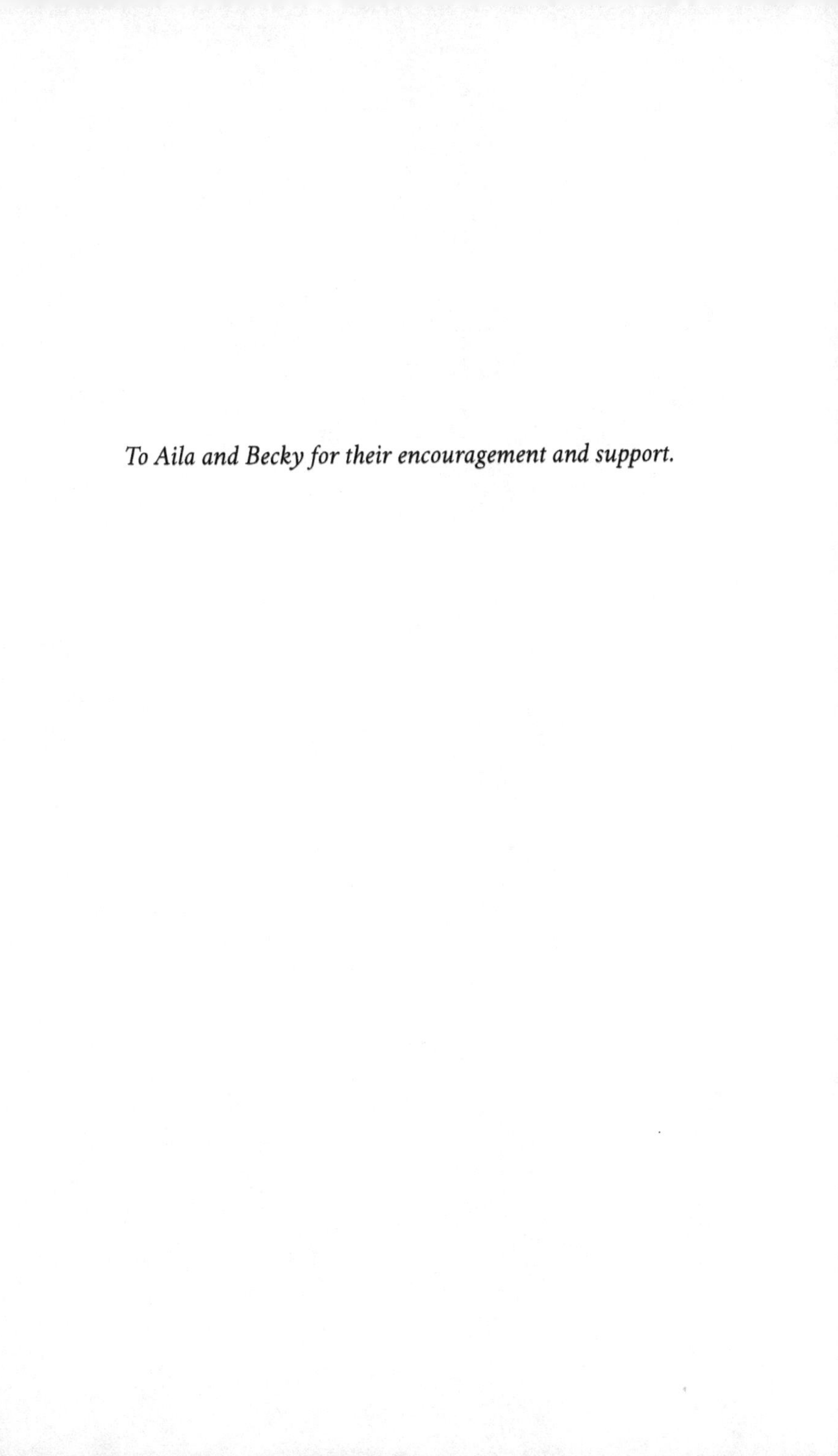

To Aila and Becky for their encouragement and support.

CHAPTER 1

If you're interested in reading more early 20th century mysteries, my free offer at the end of this book is for you! So don't forget to check that out when you get to the end. Happy reading!

When Adele Gossling first drove down Bridge Street the summer of 1902 in her Beaton Roundabout, people in town were apprehensive. Arrojo citizens knew their Victorian ideas were going to get a kick in the pants and, indeed, people like Mrs. Faderman made her the target of their discontent with the new century's free-thinking ways.

Four years later, Adele again upset the town. She had replaced her noisy Beaton Roundabout with a sportier and faster Beaton Touring Car the year before. It was "a Christmas present to myself," leaving Mrs. Faderman and her brood to pity her for not having a husband and children to give her presents. Adele's suffragist ideals had only strengthened over the years, and her ideas of progress expanded from politics to commerce.

The latter was evident when, soon into 1906, she cornered

Miss Lake, who had sold her the house on Caliber Lane and the old shoe shine shop for her stationery store. She managed to get the land between Adele's Stationery and her friend Nin Branch's herb and curioso shop at a bargain. She then convinced Nin to throw in half the money for the land.

"It's a perfect opportunity to expand," Adele insisted. "If we don't buy it up now, someone else will."

"I've no desire to go beyond what the Generous Ones dictate," Nin said. "One shouldn't go beyond one's fate."

"This is hardly about going beyond one's fate," Adele argued. "We're already six years into the new century, and the nation is starting to look less like it belongs in the Middle Ages."

"Maybe the nation does, but not this town," Nin snorted.

"Even this town," Adele said. "The Briars added a lunch counter to their store last year and even Raleigh is looking into adding a lumber shed to the back of his."

"That's not progress," Nin said. "That's nothing short of a miracle."

"Exactly." Adele smiled. "Think of the future, dear. One day, you might — well, we might marry and have children —" To this, her friend gave her a sour look. "You would want your children to inherit as you inherited from your mother, wouldn't you?"

The mention of her mother always brought a solemn gaze to Nin's face. "Perhaps you're right. Even the Generous Ones look ahead and not backward."

Nin's portion of the land remained weeds and wild flowers. At first it looked as if Adele's would as well until one crisp morning. Mrs. Raleigh was sweeping the front entrance of Raleigh's General Store and saw Adele step out of her shop with Vera Mead of Mead Builders & Contractors with a long piece of paper rolled under her arm.

As with most small towns, this minor disruption in monotonous country life created a buzz of gossip that ran up and down Bridge Street.

"Miss Gossling had no cause to open that shop in the first place," Mrs. Abberton grumbled, shifting her hat forward so it wouldn't crush her false curls. "She ought to have married by now!"

"Young ladies are so choosy nowadays," Mrs. Lynn lamented. "Why, I remember when Mary got married —"

"Miss Gossling is no longer so young, Caroline," Mrs. Abberton reminded her. "Just over thirty, I believe."

"She ought to at least have taken Derby," grumbled Mr. Raleigh. "Hardly right to go outside of town when we've a perfectly good builder right here in Arrojo."

"She has no town loyalty," agreed Mrs. Cricket. "Never has had."

"I wonder what was on that paper?" Mrs. Abberton squinted down the street as if Miss Mead were still standing there.

"Whatever it is, I hope it won't compete with our goods," Mr. Raleigh declared, and his wife, as always, uttered a "Yes, indeed!" in agreement.

Their questions were answered a week later when Adele hung a sign in the window of her shop that read *Coming soon! All your typewriting needs here!*

Beatrice, one of the pupils at the Wrigley School for Girls, tossed her head. "That ought to make some people's skin crawl!"

"Bea, if you're to be my assistant, you must learn to speak respectfully about people in town," Adele chided. "They're customers now."

"They've had plenty to say about you since you came here," Beatrice pointed out. "They think you keep ruining Arrojo's good name with your sleuthing."

"I do not sleuth," Adele said. "I help."

"Sometimes where angels fear to tread," Nin added. "Luckily, we're not angels."

"Nonetheless, Bea, I insist you be cordial to everyone who

comes in, including Mrs. Faderman and Mr. Raleigh and even the mayor himself."

"Oh, bum it!" The young woman's hand flew to her hair. She had been allowed to pin it up only that year. "I should stop saying that, shouldn't I?"

Nin gave her a placid look. "You ought to have stopped saying that two years ago."

"'A young woman watches her tongue in the presence of others,'" Beatrice mocked. Her manner was so much like Mrs. Wrigley's that both women laughed.

"Only in the right place at the right time," Adele said with a wink.

"When are they coming?" Nin asked.

"Next week," said Adele. "It's going to be awful noisy for at least a time."

"I don't mind." Nin shrugged.

"I can't wait to see people's eyes pop out of their heads." Beatrice rubbed her hands together.

"In the meantime, get your eyes on those new orders," Adele instructed. "We need them sorted and delivered by this afternoon."

Beatrice gave her a flouncing salute and retreated to the back of the shop.

"I told you it wasn't a good idea to hire her," said her friend as she watched the girl disappear.

"She's clever, Nin," said Adele. "You know how much she's helped us with investigations."

"Much to your brother's chagrin," Nin remarked as she put the kettle on for coffee.

"I've spent the last several years doing most things much to everyone's chagrin, including Jack's," Adele said with a laugh. "It's never bothered me."

"What does he think of your expansions?" Nin eyed her.

She sighed, putting down the pile of bills she was going over. "He's afraid my shop has taken over my life."

"You mean it's taken over your sense of decorum," Nin said. "Beatrice is right. Town disapproval is still high around here."

"Not for the shop, though," Adele objected. "For my work with the police."

"They think you're using the fact that your brother is the deputy sheriff as an excuse to meddle with the dirty side of life," Nin agreed.

"I won't be pinned down to the sort of life that doesn't suit me." Adele slammed shut the account book. "Not for Jack or anyone else."

"Not even for a country sheriff who's sweet on you?" Her friend raised her eyebrow.

"Not even if Teddy Roosevelt Jr. was sweet on me," Adele shot back.

"Considering he's a good ten years younger than you, I doubt you need worry about that," said Nin, and they both laughed.

The bell above the shop door rang, and a woman with brilliant red hair and sparkling green eyes stood in the doorway. The skirt on her cherry-colored walking suit swayed as she entered, the pleats opening and closing with her careful step.

"I am Arabella Parnell," she announced in a voice to match her lofty pose.

"Pleased to meet you, miss." Adele held out her hand.

The woman seemed reluctant to take it. But when she did, Adele could feel through the gloves the kind of grip that could only belong to a woman who had done her share of a day's hard work.

"You are Miss Gossling?" the woman asked.

"At your service." Adele bowed.

"Aren't you a maid at the Dilworth house?" Nin eyed her.

"I am Mrs. Dilworth's assistant," the young woman said in a nasal tone that was clearly artificial.

"Is that what she calls you or is that you putting on airs?" Nin asked.

Adele could see the young woman ready with a vicious retort, and she quickly offered Miss Parnell a chair. "We've just brewed some coffee, if you'd like a cup."

"No thank you," said Miss Parnell. "I haven't much time."

"Neither has Miss Gossling so you'd better come to the point." Nin sniffed. Beatrice, who had come from the back of the shop, stared resentfully at Miss Parnell's shining hair, as its strawberry shade matched the brilliance of her own.

"Mrs. Dilworth is giving a party for her son," the woman continued. "She, of course, wants the best stationery available for the invitations."

"I'm flattered she thinks my shop offers the best," Adele said.

"One can hardly fail to see that in this one-horse town," said Miss Parnell. "We heard your work is exquisite."

"Thank you again," Adele said. "I'll need enough time to place the order, you understand."

"The party is next month." The woman leaned forward. "Is that sufficient?"

"More than sufficient," Adele said. "Does Mrs. Dilworth — or, rather the young man — have any special requests?"

Miss Parnell extracted some patterns from her bag. "This should give you an idea."

Adele studied them. "You appreciate I've been in business now for some time, Miss Parnell."

"Your shop's reputation is known all over the county, Miss Gossling." Miss Parnell nodded.

Adele tried not to look pleased. "Then you'll trust me to make a suggestion?"

"I will take your suggestion back to Mrs. Dilworth."

"Why would you need to do that if you're her assistant?" Nin asked. "I assume if she sent you to buy the invitations, she expects you to use your own judgment."

Miss Parnell gave her a ferocious look. Then, in a more cordial tone, she asked, "What is your suggestion, Miss Gossling?"

"These patterns are lovely," she complimented, "but the colors are a little — feminine — for a young man's party. Perhaps I could suggest other colors, if the young man would approve."

"Mr. Dilworth leaves such decisions to his mother and me," said Miss Parnell. "He's just graduated from Stanford, and, naturally, he can't be bothered by such things."

"Can't be bothered by his own birthday party?" Beatrice raised her eyebrows.

The elongated countenance left Miss Parnell's face for a moment, and its vivid lines matched the belligerence of the touch Adele had felt through the silk gloves. "I'll thank you to keep out of this, child!"

"Who are you calling 'child'?" Beatrice stormed. "I'm fifteen!"

"Bea, have you finished with those orders?" Beatrice immediately retreated to the back of the shop. "I apologize for my assistant. She's new to her work."

The woman sat back, and her elegant look returned. Adele couldn't help but admire her beauty, which was almost as stunning as her friend Nin's. "Hired help can be so challenging."

"You would know," Nin mumbled.

"What are your recommendations, Miss Gossling?" Miss Parnell asked.

"This season, young men are going with nautical blue paper and gold print." Adele glanced at her. "A little daring maybe —"

"That sounds satisfactory."

"You're not taking it back to Mrs. Dilworth?" Nin asked.

"She'll do whatever her son likes," Miss Parnell said.

"And you think her son would like gold on blue?" Nin persevered.

"I've worked for the family for several years, Miss —"

"Branch."

"I'm very quick to know people's likes and dislikes," Miss Parnell said.

"You seem to know your work well, Miss Parnell," Adele complimented.

The young woman was clearly pleased. "Mrs. Dilworth appreciates me. Why, she even thinks more of me than her own daughter."

"Has she said so?" Nin challenged.

"Well, not in so many words," Miss Parnell admitted. "But I've worked with enough people to know when I'm being appreciated."

"It sounds as if you have a good position," Adele remarked.

The woman twirled the edge of her belt in her hands. "Well, one doesn't want to be a domestic all one's life!"

"Then you *are* a maid?" Nin eyed her. "I thought so!"

"I'm a lady's maid *and* an assistant, Miss Branch," Miss Parnell barked.

"There's nothing wrong with domestic service," Adele said kindly. "I've known many women like you in the city."

"I heard you came from San Francisco." She leaned forward. "I've lived in the country all my life, but I love the city!"

"Oh, you've been there?"

"Many times," she said in an airy voice, "I adore the shops."

"You only go for the shopping?" Nin asked.

"What else is there?" She blinked.

Adele couldn't help but smile. "San Francisco has a lot of culture, too, if one wants to educate oneself."

"I'm not much interested in that," Miss Parnell said. "I get along with what I know."

"If you don't intend to be a domestic servant all your life, what do you want to do?" Beatrice asked.

"Oh, I didn't say I wanted to *do* anything." Miss Parnell laughed. "One doesn't have to do anything to be something. At least, not a woman."

"But it's preferable she both do and be," Adele argued.

"I heard you were a New Woman, Miss Gossling." The young woman looked steadily at her. "You've a right to live your life as you see fit, just as I have a right to live mine."

"Indeed." Adele closed her order book. "Miss Parnell, if you're ever interested in doing more than be, I have friends who can help you. It may not bring you millions, but it would get you out of domestic work."

"That's very kind of you, Miss Gossling." Miss Parnell bowed. "But I've my own ideas about getting out of domestic work."

"I'm sure you do," Nin said in a flat tone.

The woman glared at her. Then, in an easier tone, she said, "And just to show my appreciation, I'll send over one of the invitations once Mrs. Dilworth has signed them."

"What for?" Beatrice asked.

"Why, so Miss Gossling can attend the party, of course." The girl leaned her head back a little, glancing for a moment at Beatrice.

Adele laughed. "I don't think Mrs. Dilworth would be appreciate it if a shopkeeper showed up at her son's birthday party."

"Oh, but you're so much more than a shopkeeper." The girl almost blushed. "You're practically famous in these parts."

"I'm sure you're exaggerating, Miss Parnell," Adele said, smiling.

"I didn't mean for your shop." The woman waved her hand. "I meant for being a lady detective."

"She's not a lady detective," Nin insisted. "And you're bluffing."

"About the invitation, you mean? I assure you, Miss Branch, I am not." The woman stretched out her parasol. "I told you I'm Mrs. Dilworth's assistant. She's asked me to make out the invitations."

"But you said she's to sign them, didn't you?" Beatrice pointed out.

"Mrs. Dilworth relies on my discerning taste, child," said Miss Parnell. Beatrice gritted her teeth.

"I'd like to see you try it," Nin said.

"You won't get it past the postmaster," Beatrice growled.

Miss Parnell narrowed her eyes. Then, her airy tone returned. "I'll need your address, of course, Miss Gossling. I don't want to send it here."

"You may as well give it to her, Adele," Nin said. "You won't get anything anyway."

Adele studied the determined jut of the young woman's chin, her eyes set evenly. It was clear she did not mean it as a lark. "Do you promise to get your employer's permission before you send it?"

"She'll sign the invitation," said the woman. "That's permission enough, isn't it?"

Adele still felt hesitant as she gave her the Caliber Street address.

"I might even get one for *you*." Miss Parnell glared at Nin.

"It would be to your advantage if you did," Adele said. "Miss Branch is the daughter of a prominent Rosa Gris belle."

"Was the daughter," Nin said softly, her eyes growing gray.

"Really?" Miss Parnell looked at her with interest. "I heard a different story about you, Miss Branch."

"What story?" Nin asked in a dangerous tone. "That I'm the town witch? That I murder people with dolls and herbs?"

"Well, not quite that," said the young woman. "It would be masterful if you did, though. There are some people in this town worth a few pins stuck in them." With that, she waved her handkerchief and was gone.

Nin called after her, "Don't think I couldn't!"

"You ought to cast a spell on her to shut her mouth, Miss Branch," Beatrice said. "All that nonsense about invitations and being part of the family!"

Adele stared at the young lady walking down the street,

sweeping the ground with her parasol as it swung back and forth. The sight of the breezy young woman made her shiver.

~~~~~

When the invitations arrived at Adele's shop, Mrs. Dilworth sent Mrs. Butler, her housekeeper, to fetch them and pay Adele. When she inquired about Miss Parnell, the older woman said with a sour expression, "Miss Parnell was otherwise engaged."

"That lynx will do the fun work but not the brunt," Nin growled. "She's one to get above her station too quickly."

"I guess we'll see, won't we?" Adele asked, thinking of the promised invitation.

A week later, just as she and Jackson retired to the parlor after dinner, Tomas, their caretaker, handed her a few envelopes. She recognized the gold etchings on navy blue right away.

"Good God!" She stared at it. "She really did it!"

"You know I like a civil tongue, Del," Jackson said, his handsome face etched like a wooden carving.

"You mean you like women to speak modestly," his sister snapped. "I've a good mind to teach Ruth and her daughters to swear."

"Don't you dare." Jackson laughed. "Tomas will take the family away, and you know we can't do without the Cordobas."

"I've a reason to speak strongly," she insisted. "Take a look at these."

Jackson read the invitations. "But we've never even met this Gene Dilworth."

"Nor any of the Dilworths," Adele said. "Sheriff Hatfield must have, since they moved here on the mayor's recommendation."

"I believe he went out to the house to introduce himself when they first came." Jackson nodded. "But that was merely a formality."

"Well, these invitations aren't just a formality," Adele insisted. "They're a bet, really."

"A bet?" He stared at her.
~~~~~

"Miss Parnell said she would get me an invitation to Gene Dilworth's birthday party, and Nin accused her of bluffing."

Jackson looked over his pipe at her. "And who is Miss Parnell?"

"Mrs. Dilworth's lady's maid," Adele said. "She says she's her assistant too."

"A lady's maid promising you an invitation to what looks like one of the few social events of the season in Arrojo?" He laughed. "I know you're all for mixing classes, Del, but this is too much."

"I didn't say I wanted the invitation." Adele said. "I made her promise to get her employer's permission. I thought she was boasting, just like Nin."

"Well, it seems she wasn't," said Jackson. "And Mrs. Dilworth signed the card, so she must have kept her promise."

"She's included an invitation for Nin as well." Adele waved the third envelope.

"Was that part of the challenge too?" he asked warily.

"Hardly." Adele laughed. "You know how Nin feels about social events."

"Perhaps she has an excuse not to go, but I think it would be in our best interest if we did." Jackson leaned back. "The Dilworths are the most prominent citizens we've had in a long time, and every prominent citizen will be there for sure."

"Vanessa Faderman Cook will probably frame her invitation," Adele said, picking up the lacework.

"And she'll tell her mother we were there," Jackson said. "If Mrs. Faderman knows, the whole town will know."

"And then maybe they would behave more congenially toward the deputy sheriff's sister who is always sticking her nose into police business?" Adele eyed him. "That's what you're getting at, isn't it, Jack?"

"We've been here four years, Del —"

"I've been here four years," she corrected. "You've been here only three."

"They're all still afraid of you," he continued. "Your standing is little better than your friend Zephyr's."

"Just because Zephyr goes around town with a child's wagon collecting junk doesn't make her inferior to Mrs. Faderman or anybody else," Adele protested.

"You've got to show them your ideas aren't in conflict with theirs," her brother said. "What was it you told me when you first took this house? You wanted peace and small pleasures? Has it been so peaceful the last four years?"

She shoved the lace needle in the loop. "All right, maybe I haven't had much of either, but who knew Arrojo would become the crime capital of the world!"

"Hardly that, Del," said Jackson. "You didn't have to involve yourself in all of them."

Adele put the lacework down and sighed. "I couldn't help it, Jack. All those women dead and no one to fight for them —"

"What do you think Hatfield and I are doing?" he snapped. "And they weren't all women. What about that trapeze artist last year?"

"It was the circus manager's wife who interested me, not him!" she retorted.

He puffed on his pipe while Tomas, who had entered to take away the coffee cups, looked from one to the other with concern. When the man had gone, he said in a quiet voice, "I still think we ought to go."

"I didn't say I didn't want to," said Adele. "I'm rather curious, in fact. The Dilworths have kept themselves, well, so exclusive. They don't seem to get out even in Arrojo society."

"They've only been here three months, Del," he said. "It wouldn't surprise me if they're throwing this party for their son as a way to introduce themselves into society."

"Introduce themselves!" she scoffed. "This isn't Nob Hill!"

"No, but we both know how society people think." It was true they had enjoyed the life of the well-to-do when their father, a prominent San Francisco lawyer, was alive, though they both preferred the more retiring customs of the country now.

"I'll go if I can get Nin to go," she said squarely.

He chuckled. "I think you'll find trying to persuade your clairvoyant friend to mingle with society is going to be much like trying to get a cat into a canvas bag. But you've never shied away from a challenge." He picked up the paper and was soon buried in the front page news.

CHAPTER 2

Jackson's prediction proved wrong. To Adele's surprise, Nin was more than amenable to the suggestion of joining them for the Dilworth party. "It might be interesting," she said.

"Miss Parnell really annoyed you, didn't she?" Adele watched her.

"It isn't that," her friend insisted. "The Generous Ones have made my sleep light since she came into your shop that day. And they speak."

"Speak?" Adele stared at her.

Her friend nodded. "They spelled out, 'trouble' in a cloud this morning."

Adele shivered. "For whom?"

Nin shrugged. "I don't know."

"I don't think Jack will find it very amusing," Adele said.

And, indeed, as he drove Adele's Beaton Touring Car to Nin's flat above her shop, he looked none too keen. "I'm not going in my official capacity, you know."

"I don't think Nin meant that kind of trouble," Adele said.

"Still, I'll be glad both you and the sheriff will be there, even if it is as guests."

"Hatfield and his mother aren't coming."

Adele stared at him. "I should think Mrs. Dilworth would be dying to have a woman with a title at her son's party."

"They were invited, of course," said her brother. "Hatfield said Lady Augusta has been a little wheezy lately, and the doctor wants her to take it easy."

"And he won't leave her alone," Adele said with a smile. "I've always admired his devotion to her."

"He's as devoted to her as he is to the law," Jackson echoed as he pulled the car to the curb where Nin was waiting.

Nin had gone all out for the party with a turquoise gown that swirled easily around her lovely figure to create a most feminine appearance. The square neckline framed her slim midriff perfectly, and combs with fresh flowers intertwined in them decorated her dark hair was swept in a pompadour. Adele could tell even Jackson was smitten.

"You'll be the belle of the party, Miss Branch." He cast an admiring gaze toward her while helping her into the car.

"I've no intention of being the belle," Nin said, her face glowing red.

"You might find yourself in that position, whether you want to be or not," Adele said. "You can look quite stunning without half trying, dear."

Nin slouched in the seat. "You both make me want to take these damn combs out of my hair."

"Don't you dare," Adele said with a laugh as Jackson started the motor. "Keep them in to show up Miss Parnell, if nothing else."

"I doubt she'll be present if she's only a lady's maid," Jackson said.

"According to her, she's practically one of the family," Nin said in a mocking tone.

"I wouldn't take too much stock in that, Miss Branch," Jackson said. "Domestics who step out of line are very quickly put back into it."

"It isn't stepping out of line, Mr. Gossling," said Nin. "Mama once told me if a servant believes herself on intimate terms with the family, it's because someone put that in her mind."

"You could be right," Jackson said as he pulled up to the Dilworth house.

In spite of the Dilworths' standing in the community as friends of Mayor Willett, their house, Adele noted, was much like any other one would find in the country. There were no elaborate architectural wonders, no high steps, and few broad windows. She recalled the intricate decorations that had greeted them four years before at the Blackstone party, including a red carpet and paper lanterns on the veranda. But here, all was plain, almost like a night at home.

As they ambled down the hall, Miss Parnell appeared completely outfitted with a ball gown, fan, gloves, and even a dance card dangling from her wrist. She held the arm of a girl who looked Beatrice's age, dressed elegantly but simply and whose face showed the same awkwardness as Nin's at the social event.

"I'm so glad you've come, Miss Gossling!" Miss Parnell called out.

"As you kept your promise, we could hardly refuse," Adele said, glancing at Nin.

Miss Parnell turned to the young woman beside her. "Hazel, this is Miss Gossling who owns the stationery shop in town."

"You've been told to call me Miss Dilworth." The girl glared at her.

"I don't think I know you yet." Miss Parnell's eyes swept over Jackson, whose good looks and sturdy build always impressed women.

"Jackson Gossling, miss," he said with a bow.

"Oh, the policeman!" Hazel exclaimed. "But you weren't on the list."

"Dear, don't be rude," the young woman said with a laugh. "Your mother asked me to watch over you, and I would hate to report you were crude to her guests."

"I don't consider being called a policeman 'crude,'" Jackson said dryly. "It is, after all, my profession."

"Jack is the deputy sheriff of this town," Adele said quickly, feeling her anger grow as she glanced at Miss Parnell. "I was under the impression Mrs. Dilworth had approved our invitations."

"I invited them," Miss Parnell said to Hazel. Without looking away from Jackson or removing the dazzling smile from her lips, she put a firm hand on the small of Hazel's back and gave it a light push. "Go back to the party now."

"You can't order me around, Arabella," the girl snapped. Then, as if remembering her manners, she curtsied. "I'm sorry if I offended you."

"Don't apologize for speaking the truth," Nin said.

"Miss Gossling's shop provided the invitations to the party," Miss Parnell continued. "I thought it only right to invite her."

"Oh, how I'd love that." The girl sighed. "I mean, I've been asking Mother for my own stationery — I'm sixteen, I ought to have it, oughtn't I?" She looked to Adele for confirmation.

"I had my own when I was fifteen," Adele said.

"And you wore out the blotter with all your letters," Jackson said with a smile. "I always wondered what you had to write about so much."

"Wouldn't you like to know, dear brother?" She gave him a sly look.

"Yes, we're great letter writers, we women," said Miss Parnell, eyeing him. "I've written several myself that, shall we say, were best not seen in the light of day?" She took his arm. "Perhaps I'll tell you about it sometime."

"Perhaps," Jackson said, politely drawing a little apart from her.

"You ought to ask Adele to order you some stationery," Nin piped up.

"Miss Branch, my friend," Adele introduced her.

"Oh, yes!" Hazel's eyes brightened. "I've heard about you." Nin's face darkened, but then the girl added, "I'm interested in plants and things, you know. I'm going to be a horticulturalist."

"You must come to Nin's shop one day," Adele said. "She can teach you everything about herbs."

"I'd like that." The girl smiled.

Miss Parnell again laid her hand on the small of Hazel's back. "Come along, dear." With a bright smile over her shoulder, she said, "I'll see you all later!"

As they watched the two women move into the ballroom, Jackson said ruefully, "So that's the infamous Miss Parnell."

"She acts like *she's* the belle of the ball," Nin grumbled.

"You'll soon usurp her, Miss Branch," Jackson said.

Nin tilted her head. "You know, Mr. Gossling, I have half a mind to."

Jackson laughed. Then, glancing at his sister, he added, "I believe someone has one-upped you, dear sister. I've never seen you look so silently furious."

"I see she didn't keep her promise," Adele snarled.

"I hardly think that matters now that we're here," said Jackson. "We seem to have the approval of young Hazel at least."

"She hates Miss Parnell like the devil," Nin said.

"I don't like it, Jack." Adele took hold of his arm. "I think we ought to go home before the Dilworths see us."

"You're making too much of it, Del," he protested. "I'm sure Miss Parnell wouldn't invite us without her employer's say-so."

"Don't be too sure," Nin said. "I rather think Miss Parnell is like a leopard. Hiding among the pretty things, whose danger you don't see until it's too late."

"I still think we ought to leave," Adele said.

"You know we can't, Del," said Jackson.

Adele's stomach tightened as Mayor Willett and Mrs. Willett turned from greeting a couple and stared at them from the entrance to the ballroom.

The clear annoyance on their faces summoned up her stubborn streak. "Good evening, Mayor, Mrs. Willett," she said pleasantly

The woman's wide lips parted with surprise and her eyes, too close together, looked almost ready to meet at the bridge of her nose. "Miss Gossling! Why, what are you doing here?"

"*We* were invited," Nin said pointedly.

"Well, this is a surprise." The woman recovered as quickly as any politician's wife faced with an irksome situation.

"I wasn't aware you knew the Dilworths," said Mayor Willett in a tight voice.

"Not really," Adele admitted. "Mrs. Dilworth ordered the invitations from my shop."

"Oh!" The woman looked clearly defeated as to what to do next.

"And you think that gives you the right to take one for yourself and your friend?" The mayor clutched his handkerchief with one hand, his fingers shaking with rage. "I thought you had some decency!"

"My sister just told you we have invitations, sir," Jackson said in a strained tone as he took out the cards from his vest pocket.

The mayor's face turned white, but the shaking fingers subsided. "Is this social or professional, Deputy?"

"You could say both," Jackson said. Adele looked at him with surprise.

"What would he be doing here professionally?" Nin asked in her blunt way.

"I think the mayor is concerned with all the valuables here

tonight that might present a temptation to thieves," Jackson mumbled.

"That makes our presence here more valuable than yours." Nin eyed the mayor.

Mayor Willett wiped his face with his handkerchief. "I was just saying to Rhodes the other day, 'The sheriff ropes them in, but the deputy keeps them in line.'"

"Sheriff Hatfield has never failed us, sir," Jackson said in a decided voice.

"Ah, yes, but, sir, one can't deny he isn't exactly a gentleman." He coughed. "And you, well, you're Otis Gossling's son, after all."

"Yes," Jackson said quietly, "I'm his son, for better or worse."

"Hugh met your father once, you know," Mrs. Willett chimed in. "A city banquet, wasn't it, dear?"

The mayor chuckled. "That was a long time ago, of course. I was still running the factory. But I was most impressed with him, Deputy, most impressed."

"He was a very impressive man," Adele said, feeling a small ache in her heart.

"He told me at the time you had only a few years left of schooling and were going into law study." The man's hooded eyes regarded Jackson like a vulture. "Why didn't you, Deputy?"

"That's hardly a question to ask on such an occasion, Hugh," Mrs. Willett said with a nervous laugh.

Adele could tell her brother was uncomfortable, as he rubbed his hands against his crisp trousers. She took his arm and said in a vivacious tone, "One can approach fighting crime from many angles, Mayor. The lawyer and the lawman are out for the same end."

"Justice," Nin chimed in.

"Ah, well said, Miss Gossling," he said. "You always did have a pretty way of saying things." He laughed heartily.

Adele smiled, seething inside at the description of her words as "pretty."

"Dilworth!" Mayor Willett called over his shoulder. "Come meet one of our finest lawmen."

A stout man with a slick mustache approached them. "Lawmen? Here?"

"Come to make sure the ladies' jewelry stays where it ought," said the mayor with a laugh. "Otis Gossling's son. You remember Otis?"

The man's face eased. "Certainly I do. So you're his son." He studied Jackson. "I trust you'll make yourself inconspicuous, Deputy?"

"He can hardly do that when everyone in the room knows who he is," Nin said.

"And who are you?" The man turned to her.

"I'm Adele Gossling, the deputy's sister, and this is my friend, Miss Branch," Adele supplied.

The woman who stood behind him stepped forward, tall and slim, her arms and neck bony. Adele felt the woman examining them as if trying to remember where they had met.

"It's good of you to bring your sister and her friend, sir," Mr. Dilworth said. Lowering his voice, he added, "I wouldn't want the ladies alarmed at your presence, but if it's a social call —"

Nin clutched Adele's arm. "Miss Parnell invited us."

"Arabella?" The woman blinked. "I don't recall —"

Adele gave her brother a "You see?" look.

"We're glad to welcome Mr. Gossling and his sister, aren't we, Orna?" her husband prompted. "And their friend, of course."

"Miss Branch comes from a most distinguished family," Mrs. Willett piped up. "She's Atha Branch's daughter."

"Oh, yes, we know the Branches." Mrs. Dilworth instantly warmed.

"I don't," Nin said shortly. "I've never met them."

There was an awkward silence. A young man with the same bony neck and goose eyes as Mrs. Dilworth approached them, his hands behind his back.

"Gene, come and meet the deputy sheriff of Arrojo," his father said.

The young man bowed to Jackson and looked at Adele and Nin with interest as Jackson introduced them. "How charming to bring your sister and friend along in your work, Deputy."

"He didn't," said Nin. "We brought him along with us."

"Arabella invited them, Gene," said his mother.

A flash of anger made the round eyes narrow. "Did she indeed?"

"But we're grateful the deputy sheriff is keeping law and order for us, aren't we?" His father glared at him.

"Oh, certainly, certainly," said the young man. "Though I hardly think you'll find any of my guests the sort to sprinkle poison in a champagne glass."

"Crime finds itself even among the best people, Mr. Dilworth," Adele said.

She realized her remark, though made with lightness, was not the most soothing to people who considered themselves above reproach because of their financial and social state. An awkward silence followed.

Mrs. Willett said in a loud voice, "Oh, Pauline! You were just asking about Mr. Gossling the other day, weren't you, dear?"

Adele hid a smile as her brother winced. Pauline Willett was rather sweet but homely and shy and had, like some of the other young ladies in town, followed Jackson around when he first arrived, trying to pique his interest.

"How do you do, Miss Willett?" Jackson made his functional bow.

The young woman, whom Adele had never seen offer a word without prompting from her mother or father, curtsied in an old-fashioned way and smiled with her mouth shut.

Miss Parnell came toward them, still holding on to Hazel's arm.

"Arabella," said Mrs. Dilworth in a pleasant but slightly put-off tone. "You never told me you invited the deputy sheriff and his sister."

"Didn't I?" Miss Parnell, Adele noticed, did not even flutter an eyelash of discomfort. "I'm sure I did, ma'am."

"Did you?" Mrs. Dilworth blinked.

"Why, you signed the invitations," she said calmly.

"I'm sure you did then." Mrs. Dilworth patted her arm. "I don't know what I would do without you, Arabella."

Miss Parnell smiled, but Adele noticed a wounded look crossed Hazel's face.

"Even if she hadn't, Mr. Gossling would have brought us anyway," Nin said. "We've helped him and the sheriff solve more than one crime."

The Dilworths stared at her while Jackson's eyes became sharp. But Gene Dilworth burst out laughing.

This eased the tension, and the young man turned to Adele. "Your invitations were grand, weren't they, Mother?" He glanced at her.

"Yes, very elegant," his mother said.

"Miss Gossling invited me to her shop, Mother," Hazel piped up. "She says she can show me stationery appropriate for a girl my age."

"I've just received some of the new fashionable diaries," Adele added. "I know all young ladies love diaries."

"Oh, indeed!" The girl's eyes shone.

"So you can write about all your heart flutterings, Hazel?" her brother mocked with a smile.

"Oh, keep quiet!"

"You're very generous, Miss Gossling," Mrs. Dilworth said in a measured tone. "Perhaps Arabella and I will visit your shop next week." She turned to Miss Parnell, putting her arm around her shoulder. "Didn't you tell me you've been wanting a stamp, Arabella, dear?"

Adele caught the look in Hazel's eyes as the girl's hand

reached for the curls spilling over her shoulder. She twisted one around her finger in a harsh way.

"It was your daughter who asked, not Miss Parnell," Nin said.

Mr. Dilworth coughed. "Well, we'll just have to see, won't we, dear?" He took his daughter's arm. "For now, how about a dance?"

Her mouth a little pouty, the girl allowed herself to be led into the ballroom.

An older man with ginger hair and a mustache to match passed them, holding his hands out to Mrs. Dilworth. "Orna, my dear!"

"Late as usual, Virgil?" Gene Dilworth asked.

"Fashionably late," he corrected.

"You could have made more of an effort," the young man said crossly. "It is my birthday, after all."

"Had I known there would be such charming ladies about, I would have come much sooner." He eyed Adele and Nin appreciatively.

"These are the Gosslings, Virgil, and Miss Branch," said the woman.

The man bowed. "Charmed, I'm sure. You'll do me the honor of a dance later, I hope?" Adele and Nin both gave him a withering look. "I see Hazel is in one of her moods."

"She's sulking because Mother won't let her have a diary," the younger Mr. Dilworth said flatly.

"You're quite right, Orna," he said. "My sister didn't allow her girl to have one either. They write too many childish musings in those things."

"She'll be a lady soon, and ladies need their own correspondence," Adele remarked. "I wish you would reconsider about the stationery, Mrs. Dilworth."

"Well, perhaps I was being a little severe," the woman admitted, waving her fan. "I'll send Arabella to your shop to see to it next week."

"I would be delighted," said Miss Parnell.

"If you'll pardon me, ma'am, may I suggest you send Hazel to buy her own stationery?" Adele asked, trying to sound delicate. "A young woman's first stationery is a very personal thing —"

"I think I've proved my taste to you, Miss Gossling," said Miss Parnell.

"You do have excellent taste, dear." Mrs. Dilworth smiled. Adele flinched as Miss Parnell gave her an almost triumphant look.

CHAPTER 3

While Miss Parnell was still basking in the light of her employer's compliment, Mrs Willett approached them, holding Pauline tightly by the wrist. "Gene, I believe this is your dance."

The young man fumbled for words. "I'm terribly sorry, ma'am, but I promised to introduce Miss Gossling and Miss Branch to some friends of mine. So if you'll excuse us —" Without another word, he took Adele's arm and Nin's and pulled them into the ballroom. Adele glanced back at her brother, but he only gave her a salute and a devious smile. She made a note to reprimand him when they got home. Miss Parnell followed close behind, waving her fan in an agitated way.

"That wasn't very charitable of you, Mr. Dilworth," Adele remarked as they made their way through the large room filled with lights and swaying skirts.

"Call me Gene," he said warmly.

"What did you expect him to do?" Miss Parnell asked. "Mr. Dilworth is the king of the party, and the girl has the face of a startled hen." She chuckled a little.

Nin glared. "It was a nasty thing to do. And if you don't mind

—" She yanked free of Gene's arm. "I don't like anyone taking my arm without asking permission first!"

"I'm sorry if I acted rudely." He looked so truly humbled that Nin could only nod. "I regret I had to cut Pauline like that, but we've been friends since we were children, and I know she understands."

"What was passable as a child isn't as an adult," Adele said.

"Really, Miss Gossling, aren't you making far too much of this?" Miss Parnell fanned herself. "I've heard you're a great defender of women's rights, but —"

"Any woman has a right to be honored for who she is, even if she isn't pretty," Adele retorted.

"You wouldn't know about that, would you?" Nin gave her a sly look.

"I don't care to be insulted!" Miss Parnell glared at her.

The young man shot her a look. Then, in a more congenial tone, he asked, "If I promise to make it up to Pauline by promising her the next two dances, am I forgiven?"

"It's not up to us to forgive you," Adele said. "It's up to Pauline."

"Oh, she'll forgive him all right," Miss Parnell snorted. "It would be a feather in her cap to dance even once with Mr. Dilworth."

He gave her the same look, then said to Adele, "May I at least try?"

"You may," Adele said with a nod.

"I really would like you to meet a few friends of mine." He led them to a corner where a group of young people were gathered. Two men were among them, dressed in black suits as crisp and clean as Jackson's.

"May I introduce Maxwell Lee and Nathan Cress?" he announced. "My two best friends from school, who kept me from getting kicked out more than once." Everyone laughed. "Miss Gossling and Miss Branch, gentlemen."

"Charmed!" Mr. Lee had the kind of liquid features that made Adele think of the melodramas she had seen at the Arrojo Theater. His eyes were elliptical and dark like a wolf's, matching his slick, dark hair. He feasted his eyes on Nin.

Mr. Cross was clearly of a milder nature as he gave a jerking bow, his blond hair falling over his face as he did so. His modest smile made Adele like him.

A ragtime dance began, and the crowd of young people quickly dispersed, leaving only Adele and Nin and the three men.

"You must dance this with me, Miss Branch." Mr. Lee took her hand.

"I don't like to dance," Nin said sharply.

"Oh, but you must!" he persisted. "I'm sure you're a lively dancer."

"I'll dance it with you, Mr. Lee." Miss Parnell folded her fan and hooked it onto her belt, holding out her hand. "No use forcing the lady to dance if she's not interested."

Ignoring her, Mr. Lee said, "If you don't know the dance, I'll be happy to teach you."

"Max really dances very well," Gene chimed in.

"I didn't say I didn't know it." Nin suddenly held out her hand. "All right. I'll dance it with you, Mr. Lee."

Adele watched with amazement as her friend let the roguish, smiling young man lead her into the crowd of dancers.

"Miss Gossling?" Gene bowed and held out his hand.

"You have another lady to ask, don't you, Gene?" She gave him a pointed look.

With a wince, he shuffled over to where his parents had taken a seat with the Willetts, and Adele watched as he sheepishly bent toward Pauline, who was clearly glad to accept his invitation to dance.

Mr. Cress chuckled. "I see you're holding Gene to high standards."

"He slighted Miss Willett once, and I intend to see he doesn't do it again," Adele said.

Mr. Cress applauded. "Bravo! Would you like a glass of punch?" He glanced at the refreshment table. "Or perhaps you'd care to dance?"

"I'd rather have the punch," she admitted. "I'm parched."

He laughed and led her to the crystal bowl. "Gene can sometimes be a little inconsiderate, but it's really out of carelessness, Miss Gossling. He isn't a mean sort."

"And Mr. Lee?" She eyed him.

"Max is a good sort too," he said. "He's — well, you've seen him. He's been pampered by women all his life. His father died when he was a baby, and his mother and aunt had no one else."

"I think I understand." Adele nodded.

"I realize some ladies think him a rascal, but he really has a heart of gold and a strong sense of loyalty," he said.

"I see you do too," she said warmly.

He led her to a chair. "My father always said, 'Betray a friend, and you'll often find you have ruined yourself.'"

"I admire people who defend their friends even when they're in the wrong." Adele sipped the punch, which was too sweet and too sour at the same time. "Provided their wrong doesn't hurt anyone else or break the law."

"That's a great compliment indeed." He bowed. "May I ask, why did you make Gene dance with Miss Willett?"

"Because he promised her," Adele said simply.

"And you believe people should keep their promises?"

"Don't you?" She eyed him.

The young man laughed. "Most certainly. Any promise, big or small, should be kept."

"We're in agreement, then." She smiled.

He looked at the dancers, silent for a moment. "If I may say so, Miss Branch is ravishing."

Adele felt proud watching the way others glanced at Nin as

she swung gracefully around the dance floor, handling the ragtime dance with the grace of a waltz.

"You were right about Mr. Lee," she said. "He's an excellent dancer. Not to mention he's keeping a proper distance between himself and Nin."

"I told you Max has a heart of gold," said Mr. Cress. "I can't say that man over there appreciates it much, though."

Adele followed his gaze and realized he was looking at her brother. Jackson, stationed against the opposite wall, stood with his arms crossed, his head moving to the gliding figures.

"He's playing the watchdog," she said dryly.

Mr. Cress laughed. "I was about to say he looks ready to arrest Max."

Adele burst out laughing. "You couldn't be closer to the truth, Mr. Cress. That man is the Arrojo deputy sheriff."

"Deputy sheriff!" Mr. Cress scrutinized him. "I wonder how he got his foot in the door with the way Gene's parents are always courting the best of society."

Adele felt more amused than annoyed. "He's not as lowly as you think. His name is Jackson Gossling, and he happens to be my brother."

"Oh!" The man's face turned red again. "I seem to be tactless tonight."

She laughed. "And while we don't make a habit of advertising it, our father was Otis Gossling. Perhaps you've heard of him?"

"Well-known criminal lawyer in San Francisco, wasn't he?"

"Yes," Adele said in a quiet voice, tracing the edge of the velvet arm of the chair with her gloved finger. "He was."

"So Otis Gossling's son is working for the other side of the law," Mr. Cress mumbled. "Well, well."

Adele's shoulders tensed. "What do you mean, the other side of the law?"

"Oh, nothing, nothing." He rose awkwardly and held out his hand. "Miss Gossling, you must save me. Before I say something foolish again, you must consent to dance with me so my tongue will be silenced."

Adele laughed and accepted his gracious hand. The music changed to a waltz, and she found her partner to be true to his word, as he was both silent and a good dancer. She caught Nin's eyes as she passed. Her friend looked as if she wanted to kick her partner in the ankle.

"If you don't mind my asking," Mr. Cress said over the orchestra, "how *did* the deputy sheriff come to this party? He's not here in his official role, I hope?"

"Official role?" Adele echoed.

"I mean, there isn't any suspicion of thieves around, are there?" he asked. "I've been to such parties, you know, where plain-clothed men were hired to watch the guests to make sure nothing was taken."

"Jack came at my invitation," she assured him. "Or, rather, at Miss Parnell's, I should say."

The man stopped just as the music ended and stared at her. "What has Miss Parnell to do with it?"

"It's rather a funny story," she said as he led her to their corner. "She was sent to my shop to order the invitations and she — well, she promised to get my friend and me invitations. I suppose it was a sort of lark."

"Her lark must have put you in a rather awkward position."

"I made her promise to get Mrs. Dilworth's permission." Anger rose in her. "It was obvious when we met the Dilworths that she didn't."

He snorted. "I'm not surprised, Miss Gossling."

She glanced at him. "Why is that?"

"Gene told me she can be rather impudent." He slid his shoe around a marble square on the floor.

"Mr. Dilworth told you, or you observed it yourself?" Adele asked.

He wiped his face with his handkerchief. "Maxwell and I have been spending a lot of time here since we graduated, so we've seen how she behaves with Gene's mother."

"And Gene's sister?" Adele inquired.

"She does tease her devilishly," said the young man. "Pardon me for my language."

"It was accurate," Adele said. "Poor Hazel!"

"Gene doesn't like it," he said. "Oh, I know he taunts Hazel all the time, but, really, he cares deeply for her."

Adele leaned forward. "Has he tried to talk to his mother about it?"

"I'm afraid it wouldn't do much good. Miss Parnell has her almost under a spell." He rose. "Shall I get you another glass of punch, Miss Gossling?"

"Please." She bowed.

While he was gone, the music began for the next dance, and couples took the floor. She spotted Miss Parnell under a chandelier that illuminated her fair beauty even more. Her attention was not on her partner but the window, and it didn't take long for Adele to realize why. Mr. Lee was standing there with Nin, who had, in her usual custom, opened the window and was looking out while the breeze brushed back some of the shorter strands of hair over her forehead.

Adele watched with amusement as Mr. Lee seemed intent on telling her a story, his hands moving in wild gestures. Nin nodded without smiling. Then, Mr. Lee took Nin's arm again and led her to the dance floor. Adele could tell by the look on her friend's face that she was anything but pleased. Miss Parnell watched them on the dance floor, her figure as pointed as an arrow.

"I think Miss Parnell would be pleased if my brother did arrest your friend," Adele observed when Mr. Cress came back with the punch.

As Mr. Lee whirled Nin around on the dance floor, Nin kept

up with each step, though her expression grew more and more annoyed.

"Every girl likes to dance with Maxwell at these things," he mused.

"He is accomplished," Adele admitted. "I hope *he* keeps his promises to dance with a woman."

"He always keeps his promises," Mr. Cress said. His tone was suddenly hard. "It's the ladies who sometimes don't keep theirs."

"Modern young men are so cynical about women," she teased.

He laughed. "Modern older men, too. You know I'm practically twenty-six."

"Then I have the advantage of you," she said. "I'm almost thirty."

"I won't reveal your secret," he promised. "And for all of Miss Parnell's cheek, I'm glad she invited you, Miss Gossling."

Adele glanced at the dance floor. "A woman goes farther with boldness than she does with complacency."

"How far one goes depends on one's honesty, Miss Gossling," said the young man in a firm tone. "And one's sense of decency."

"And you think Miss Parnell has neither?"

He shrugged. "I really couldn't say."

"And you don't want to know her well enough?" Adele guessed.

"Do you?" He turned his dark brown eyes on her.

Adele watched the young woman, whose gaze left Mr. Lee as she danced with the mayor. Her blond hair shone like wax without the slightest curl out of place, and her face was bright with vivacity. Whatever she was saying to Mayor Willett was making him laugh.

"I'd like to pick apart what she values in life and change it," she said, remembering the conversation in her shop. "I believe I could."

"I wouldn't put your admiration into someone like her, Miss Gossling," he said quickly. "She's dangerous."

"Oh?" Adele looked at him.

"I mean, the way Gene's mother is taken in by her," he said. "Allowing her to come to this party, for example, instead of staying in the servants' hall with the others where she belongs."

"I understood Miss Parnell was Mrs. Dilworth's assistant," Adele said. "I've often seen assistants and companions at parties such as these."

"She's a lady's maid!"

"No one seems to know or care," Adele observed as she watched the young woman retreat from the dance floor with the mayor on her arm and approach a group of people. Her lips never stopped moving, and her bright eyes traveled from one person to another.

"Yes, everyone's taken by her," Mr. Cress said. She heard him add with a murmur, "If they only knew what lay underneath."

Miss Parnell left the mayor with the group of people and, lifting the edge of her train, exited the ballroom. "It looks as if she might make her retreat after all, Mr. Cress."

"Then you shall have to take her place as the ballroom charmer, Miss Gossling," he said with a smile.

The waltz ended and Nin hurried toward her with Mr. Lee close at her heels.

"Delightful, delightful!" the dark-haired man said with a wide smile. "You're the best dancer in the room, Miss Branch."

"You could use some practice," she said. "You stepped on my feet three times."

"Oh, I beg your pardon," said the man. "Perhaps you'll teach me some of your graceful moves someday?" His eyes became flat.

Nin smiled sweetly. "Don't count on it, Mr. Lee."

Mr. Cress laughed. "I think Miss Branch could use some punch, Maxwell."

"So could I, for that matter." The man sauntered over to the table, now crowded with thirsty dancers.

"Swine!" Nin growled. "He was drooling all over me."

"May I suggest, Miss Branch, if Maxwell becomes too much of a fiend, you kick him in the shin?" Mr. Cress's tone was light.

"I'll do one better," she said. "I'll make him dance the next one with Miss Parnell."

"I'm afraid you're too late for that," he said. "Miss Parnell seems to have realized her place and made a hasty retreat."

"Thank God!" Nin sank into a chair.

Mr. Cress burst out laughing just as Jackson approached them.

"I never knew you to be so intimate with the latest dances, Miss Branch," he said in a stinging tone.

"I don't live under a rock, Mr. Gossling," Nin declared. "Perhaps if you weren't such a stickler for propriety, you could have saved my feet by cutting in." She bent down and rubbed her heel.

"I got the impression you preferred to dance with Mr. Lee," he said just as the man approached.

"I'm afraid I've never waltzed well," Mr. Lee said as he handed Nin the punch. "It goes rather slow for my taste."

"And you go so fast, no one has time to notice your mendacity." Nin looked straight at him. Adele noticed her brother's satisfied smile.

"Well, if you can stand it, I'd like the next dance," Jackson said to her.

"Then I must take Miss Gossling as my partner," Mr. Lee said, clearly put out. "You don't mind, do you, Nathan?"

"I do, actually," his friend said in his light tone.

"Why don't you ask Miss Parnell, Mr. Lee?" Adele glanced behind him. "It looks like she's returned."

"She's been dying to dance with you all night," Nin added.

"I'd rather dance with *you*, Miss Branch." Mr. Lee bowed.

"Would you? How unkind, Mr. Lee." Miss Parnell approached them, her skirt swirling with her fan. Adele noted her face looked matted, as if she had applied fresh powder to it, and her hair was tamed with a bejeweled comb holding up the back in a twist.

Jackson gave his usual noncommittal smile, what Adele called his "lawman look". Mr. Cress seemed to be staring at something far off, his mouth a thin line of amazement. Mr. Lee's eyes grew menacing as his head tilted.

"Since Miss Branch has so generously given up her time with you, Mr. Lee, it's only right you should ask me to dance, don't you think?" She raised a coy eyebrow at him.

Mr. Cress recovered first. "I imagine Gene's going to cut the cake soon."

"Yes," Mr. Lee said in a thick voice. "We mustn't miss Gene cutting the cake." Wrinkles appeared on his forehead. "If you'll excuse me, I think I'll go see where he is." He gave a curt bow all around and swiftly moved into the crowd.

They were all silent for a moment. "Well, he was in a hurry, wasn't he?" Nin declared.

"He probably promised another lady a dance," said Miss Parnell in an airy voice. "Mr. Lee always keeps his promises to a lady, doesn't he, Mr. Cress?"

"Mr. Cress and I were just discussing that." Adele was suddenly aware of a strange shadow that had taken over the room.

The young man's face was no longer frozen and white, but his voice sounded weak as he answered, "It's important to keep one's promises."

Jackson cleared his throat. "Well, Miss Branch, it looks as if the next dance will be ours after all."

"Only one, Mr. Gossling." Nin's voice was vague as her eyes grew dim, staring in the direction of Mr. Lee. "Only one."

"And then you must dance with me, Mr. Gossling," Miss Parnell said.

Jackson nodded, though Adele knew he hardly relished the idea, as he led Nin to the dance floor.

"You like dancing, Miss Parnell?" Adele asked.

"Oh, I adore it!" She patted the back of her head. "But these new dances, they do make one tired. I had to refresh myself so all my hair wouldn't spill over my shoulders."

"Your comb is very pretty," Adele complimented. Secretly, she thought it was gaudy and pretentious. The piece spread almost all along the back of her head, crowded with rhinestones and rubies.

"Thank you, Miss Gossling." She seemed genuinely delighted. "I only wear it on special occasions, of course. It wouldn't do to parade real stones in one's hair on the street."

"Is this one of your finds from the San Francisco shops?" Adele asked.

"This was given to me as a gift," she said. After pausing, she added, "By a rather amorous young man."

Mr. Cress's hand flew to his collar as if it were straining him, and his expression was strange. Quickly, Adele took his arm. "I believe this dance is ours, Mr. Cress."

"What? Yes, oh, certainly." The man relaxed, and she could feel his arm pressing close to her hand.

The music was a ragtime dance again, but Adele could barely concentrate on the steps. Mr. Cress's pleasant features were now as tight as if someone had poured cast iron over them.

"Is there anything wrong, Mr. Cress?" she asked.

"What? Oh, no, certainly not." He looked at her. "What could be wrong?"

"I'm sure I don't know," she mumbled.

"It's just this party," he said. "I'm afraid I'm better with books than dancing."

"Then we have something in common." She smiled. "Even when I came out in society, I preferred sitting in the garden and reading a good book to fighting ants at a picnic or getting my dress drenched in a rowboat."

The iron melted, and he looked more at ease. "I knew you weren't like these other girls, Miss Gossling. I rather approve of a serious-minded young woman."

"And one who keeps her promises?" She eyed him.

"And one who isn't a hypocrite!" His tone was rough.

When the music ended, she and Mr. Cress danced the next two dances. She noticed Jackson had now coveted Nin as his partner, and even when Mr. Lee approached to cut in, Jackson swirled her away with a decisive rejection. But she knew her friend well enough to know the society of the evening was beginning to wear thin on her. Nin's reclusive nature did not stand the noise, and crowding well and she looked almost ready to faint.

CHAPTER 4

Even before the dance ended, Adele excused herself and located Nin, leading her and Jackson aside. "We need some air."

"It is rather stuffy in here," he admitted.

"Like the inside of a coffin," Nin agreed, all too eager to get out into the cool night air.

Just as he was about to join them, Miss Parnell appeared and, taking a firm grip of his arm, said, "Mr. Gossling, you can't refuse me again."

"I wasn't going to, Miss Parnell," he said politely.

"Jack never makes a promise without keeping it," Adele murmured.

"What are you talking about, Del?" He stared at her.

"Oh, nothing."

He shook his head and she could almost hear him muttering "riddle talk" as he followed Miss Parnell to the dance floor.

She and Nin found two empty chairs on the veranda and collapsed into them. "Jack was right," said Adele. "You are the belle of the ball."

"I didn't intend to be," Nin said with a blush. "Anyway, I don't think *they* like it." She flicked her head toward the group of young people in the corner not far from them whom Vanessa Cook, née Faderman, led with the same authority as her mother.

Vanessa approached them with the others following her much like the ladies followed her mother. "Mama will be happy to see you showing some community spirit at last, Miss Branch."

"I rather think she considers a church bazaar more community spirit than a party," Nin said dryly.

"Oh, Mama never objects to a little fun," she said.

"I'm surprised she isn't here," Adele remarked.

"None of them are," Nin added.

"Why, this is a party for the young people, Miss Gossling," Fern Cricket said. "Why would they be invited?"

"Because Mr. Dilworth is the mayor's friend." Adele felt her anger rise.

"Well, confidentially," Vanessa began and everyone bent toward her, "Mama doesn't quite approve of the Dilworths."

"I don't think your mother said that, my dear," her husband said in a tentative voice.

"Of course she did, Joe," his wife snapped. "She said, 'I've no patience for people who court the mayor and can't keep their servants in their place.'"

"I found Mrs. Dilworth to be commanding enough," Adele said.

"Not where that maid of hers is concerned!" Cora Leighton glanced at the dance floor with distaste. "A lady's maid dressing up and dancing just like one of the guests!"

"Shocking," Emeline, Mrs. Cricket's younger daughter, agreed.

"Acting as if she *belongs*." Laura Abberton Helm stiffened her broad shoulders.

"Why, if you did that dear, I'd —" Eric, her husband, smiled sweetly. "But of course, you wouldn't. You have much more sense."

"Not to mention no daring at all," Nin mumbled.

"I think you're all being very unfair!" This declaration came from Pauline, whose thin face deepened with annoyance. "Mrs. Dilworth has a high regard for Miss Parnell."

"Too high, if you ask me," Vanessa growled.

"She thinks Miss Parnell is much more intelligent than — well, her breed."

"You mean the serving class?" Nin eyed her.

"Miss Parnell has an education, unlike most of them," Pauline went on. "She reads all the time. She's always begging Mrs. Dilworth to give her books."

"Anybody can open a book, dear," said Laura. "If you weren't so stuck on Gene, you would see that maid hasn't only ingratiated herself onto the mother but the son as well."

"That's not true!"

Adele had to admire Pauline's fierce tone. Nin, too, leaned over and whispered, "I didn't think she had it in her. Too bad it's wasted on such as snobbish as Mr. Dilworth."

"Just because Miss Parnell is working as a domestic servant doesn't mean she can't better herself," Adele said.

They all turned to her, some with surprise, some with wariness. Cora spoke first. "Yes, well, we would expect *you* to say that, Miss Gossling."

"It's not the education I object to," Vanessa said. "It's what she's doing with it."

"What do you expect her to do with it, conceal it?" Nin asked.

"It makes her think she's worth more than she is," Vanessa insisted.

"Perhaps you're not far off there," Nin admitted.

"I'm glad you agree, Miss Branch," she said. "I would hate to think you approve of the lower classes dancing with the higher classes."

"Higher class, lower class!" Adele growled. "It will all even out in the end. You'll see, Vanessa."

"Well, for now, a lady's maid at a party isn't democracy."

Unlike her mother, Vanessa soon lost ground and was whining like a child. “It’s not even decent!”

“I’m choking in all this decency.” Nin rose, taking her friend’s arm. “Even the wind isn’t helping.”

“We’ll go somewhere else, then,” Adele said. “Where the opinions are less narrow.” She glared at Vanessa as they strolled to the edge of the veranda.

As they turned the corner, she could see both Mr. Cress and Mr. Lee with their cigars glowing in the darkness.

“Lord!” Nin murmured. “I don’t want to see that wolf!”

Adele quickly pulled her back toward the glass doors, thankful the men hadn’t caught sight of them. “There are plenty of balconies,” she said. “Come, dear, let’s find ourselves a quiet one.”

They mounted the stairs and went down the hall to an open doorway. There was powder and other cosmetics on the dressing table as well as towels hanging on the wall.

“Very obliging of Mrs. Dilworth,” Adele observed.

“Including the balcony,” her friend said, nodding toward the glass doors thrown open to reveal a marble patio with a few wicker chairs.

The cool breeze had calmed and they each took a wrap, also provided by Mrs. Dilworth, from hooks on the walls. Out on the balcony, Adele was startled to see so many rooftops in the distance. She hadn’t realized Arrojo had grown so big.

She was just about to remark upon this when harsh voices sounded below them. The voices belonged to Mr. Cress and Mr. Lee.

“Oh, hell!” Nin growled.

“Don’t worry, they can’t see us,” Adele whispered.

“They won’t if we turn off the lights.” Nin darted to the wall and the glowing gaslights were extinguished in a moment, leaving them in complete darkness except for the stars. “I’ll stay in here.”

"Do that," Adele murmured.

"Of all the colossal nerve!" Mr. Lee puffed hard on his cigar.

"She doesn't care," Mr. Cress's voice croaked. "She just doesn't care."

Footsteps sounded on the floor below them and two heads appeared. One belonged to Gene Dilworth and one was the unmistakable strawberry curls and jeweled head of Miss Parnell.

"I've asked Arabella to leave the party," Mr. Dilworth announced.

"Why should I?" The woman was defiant. "Your mother said I could stay as long as I liked."

"You forced her to say it!" Mr. Lee growled.

"I did nothing of the kind," she said. "Mrs. Dilworth has always been like a mother to me."

"Mother has a daughter, thank you very much," Mr. Dilworth snapped. "This really is too much, Arabella."

"I only want to help celebrate your birthday," she said in a coy tone.

"Is that why you wore that?" Mr. Cress flung his hand at the comb in her hair and she backed away. "You've no right!"

"I believe I have a right to wear anything that's mine," she said.

"You made a promise," Mr. Lee said in a darting tone.

Miss Parnell looked amused. "You talk as if I stole it."

"You didn't steal it, Arabella," he growled. "It was worse than that. Much worse."

Mr. Dilworth held up his hand and they both looked calmer. Then, in a quiet tone, he asked, "If you won't retire, will you at least take off that comb?"

She stared at him. "Why in the world should I?"

"Because you promised!" Mr. Cress shot out.

"Because it upsets us," Mr. Dilworth said, his voice growing almost dangerously quiet. "Can't you see how you're upsetting Nathan? You're upsetting all of us!"

This seemed to almost touch Miss Parnell. She laid her hand

on his arm. "I'm not trying to upset anybody. But it's all over and done with. Can't you realize that?"

"What's done is done?" asked Mr. Cress in an ironic tone.

"If you choose to put it that way." She opened her fan. "I hear another waltz. Come, one of you give me a birthday dance."

None of them moved. Mr. Lee threw the last of his cigar in the lawn. Adele could see his features clearly under the light above. They looked about ready to erupt. "If you don't take that comb out of your hair, we'll make you."

"Make me?" She gave a small laugh. "Oh, you do talk like a prize fighter." Her tone changed. "I wonder if your Miss Branch would approve of that. She abhors anything that smacks of masculinity."

"You leave Miss Branch out of this!" Mr. Lee thundered.

"Defending her honor?" The woman's eyebrows rose. "That's very dangerous, very dangerous indeed."

"For the last time," Mr. Dilworth intervened, "are you going to take that comb off or not?"

Adele could not hear her answer but between flashes of light and dark, Adele heard a scream. Mr Cress and Mr. Dilworth were holding Mr. Lee's arms behind his back. The latter's face was hidden in the dark.

Miss Parnell leaned against the bannister, her hand on the back of her head. Her sobs rang out.

"Get hold of yourself!" Mr. Dilworth, now completely calm, said. "You don't want to attract attention, do you?"

Rather than answer, the woman ran into the house.

"You fool!" he snarled at Mr. Lee.

"I lost my head," said his friend, shaking out his jacket and smoothing down his hair.

"At least it will get her away from the party," Mr. Cress said as all three men retreated from the veranda.

Adele slowly went back into the room.

"What happened?" Nin asked.

"I'm not sure," she said. "I think Mr. Lee tried to rip the comb out of her hair."

"Do you think she let him?" Nin said.

"I don't know," Adele admitted. "I couldn't see much. They all moved away from the light." She put the wrap on the hook. "Let's get out of here, Nin."

"It can't be too soon for me," said her friend, taking her arm. "Anything to get away from that animal."

"There's something animal in the air," Adele said as they made their way slowly down the stairs. "Some kind of code we don't know about."

"It seems Miss Parnell violated every code tonight," Nin remarked. "The code of social propriety and the code of good taste."

"And the comb?" Adele asked. "I wonder what code that belongs to."

Just as they reached the bottom of the stairs, a puff of tulle collided with them and Adele found herself staring into the distressed eyes of Miss Parnell. She stared back at her, then turned and ran toward a discreet doorway which Adele guessed led to the servants' quarters. She still had her hand on the back of her head. Adele saw the comb was still there.

CHAPTER 5

Jackson was only too glad to leave the party as well. "Mr. Dilworth persuaded me to allow card tables into the other room," he said as he shifted in the driver's seat of the Beaton. "I don't know if I ought to tell Hatfield about it."

"I should think one may play poker in the privacy of one's own home," Nin remarked.

"I didn't say it was illegal, Miss Branch."

"But it is immoral?" she asked.

"Most people don't object to cards at a party, Jack," said Adele. "I suspect your attitude would be more forgiving if you were a better poker player."

"As a matter of fact, dear sister, I usually win," he said with a smile.

"You have more luck than we do," Adele sighed, leaning back. "Nin wasn't very fond of Mr. Lee."

"I had a hell of a time with him," her friend declared in her brutal way.

For once, Jackson didn't flinch at her swearing. "He seemed like a cad."

"He kept pushing me to join him," Nin said. "Some picnic on Tuesday, a boat race on Thursday and a party on Friday."

"And what about you, Del?" Jackson asked. "You and Mr. Cress were getting along rather well."

"Better than Mr. Cress and Miss Parnell," Adele said.

"Better than all of them and Miss Parnell," Nin added.

"I suspect Miss Parnell knows more about life than all three of them put together ever learned in college," Adele scoffed.

"Why do you say that, Del?" Jackson glanced at her as he rounded the corner with care.

"The way she infiltrated herself into the Dilworth family, for one," she said.

"I imagine Mr. Dilworth is away a lot with his export business," Jackson said. "His son clearly has his own life and his own interests."

"What are you getting at, Mr. Gossling?" Nin eyed him.

"Well, it stands to reason Mrs. Dilworth is left alone much of the time," he said. "So many of these wealthy women who are left alone develop filial relationships with their lady's maids."

"She has a daughter," Adele reminded him. "Not that she thinks very much of her."

"Miss Parnell has usurped her," Nin said.

Jackson grinned at his sister. "Aren't you always lecturing me about how women have never been encouraged in their ambitions and it's high time they were?"

"Only when they do it with integrity." Adele played with the strap on her bag. "Miss Parnell clearly doesn't think twice about making a promise and breaking it."

"And she slithered her way into the Dilworth family right enough," Nin added.

"Slithered!" Jackson burst out laughing.

"It's the only word for it, Jack," said Adele.

"She means to have Mr. Lee." Patting her hair, Nin repeated with more assurance, "She means to have him."

"A lady's maid and a senator's grandson?" Jackson stopped the car in front of Nin's flat. "I doubt that very much."

"Why else would he have tried to pull her hair out?" Nin asked.

Jackson was alert. "Now that is interesting."

"It was her comb he wanted to pull out," Adele said. "They were all quarreling about it." In an absent-minded way, she added, "I wonder what was so special about that comb."

"I thought it was rather too big for her head," Jackson said.

To Adele's surprise, Nin burst out laughing.

"I'm glad you find me amusing once in a while, Miss Branch," Jackson said but Adele could tell he was pleased.

"Only when you're not looking, Mr. Gossling," she said with a sparkle in her eye as she trudged up the stairs to her flat.

~~~~~

On Tuesday, Mead Building & Contract sent their workers to Adele's shop. Three burly young men with matching bright red beards and overalls appeared outside the shop at seven o'clock in the morning, loitering about and earning a glare from Mr. Raleigh, who lived above his store and saw them on the street. He was so disturbed by the sight that he called the Gossling house while Adele and Jackson were just sitting down to breakfast.

As usual, Tomas handed the phone to "the señor of the house," disregarding the fact that the house was actually leased under Adele's name. Jackson put on his deputy sheriff's face as he sipped his coffee, listening patiently while Adele could hear the roaring of Mr. Raleigh's voice on the other end. When he hung up, he said, "Did you have men coming today, Del?"

"Lord!" Adele dropped her fork. "Vera told me they would be at the shop to start the work on the new room."

"It appears Miss Mead is rather too eager at her job," Jackson remarked. "According to Mr. Raleigh, two 'bouncer types' have been pacing outside your shop for twenty minutes, probably
~~~~~

contemplating theft." He couldn't hold back a smile. "His words, not mine."

"She said they would come early, but she didn't tell me they would come *that* early!" Adele grabbed her jacket sitting on the back of her chair. "I have to go down there immediately." She ignored Tomas' disapproving look, as he hated seeing either of them leave the table before they had finished the meal.

"What about your little spy, Miss Glenn?" His eyes twinkled. "You put her to work, didn't you?"

"Bea, dear brother, still has to finish her education," Adele snapped. "Don't think she wouldn't love to escape Mrs. Wrigley's classrooms for the joys of filling ink bottles and stocking paper in my shop, but I'm seeing to it that she completes her studies like a lady."

"Rather ironic, considering you're always insisting you're anything but a lady," he said dryly.

She leaned against the back of her chair. "Would it shock you to know I have since changed my mind?"

"It would."

"When one meets expectations on the surface, one can do whatever one likes under the surface." She flounced out of the dining room, hearing him roar with laughter behind her.

The workers were soon settled and in spite of their tendency to grunt their replies, Adele managed to communicate to them what she wanted done. When Beatrice came in at noon, the sound of hammers made her face pinch.

"How are we ever to get any work done with that noise?" She sniffed.

"We pretend it isn't there," Adele said promptly. "You'll find many times in life, Bea, you'll have to pretend something isn't there."

"Something or someone?" The young woman eyed her.

"Both, and sometimes at the same time," Adele said. Beatrice laughed.

Missy Grace, the editor of the *Arrojo Courier*, hurried into her shop, her cotton hair flying around her face. She pushed back her bangs with the edge of her pencil. "Adele, what can you tell me about the body found in Virgil Riddle's conservatory?"

"What the devil are you talking about?" Adele stared at her.

"Don't use such vulgar language, Adele," Beatrice chided.

"It's no worse than your 'bum it,' dear," Missy said.

Beatrice's nose went up in the air. "I've stopped saying 'bum it.'"

"My congratulations." Missy turned back to Adele. "I'm talking about the sheriff and your brother hastening out of the police station looking very official."

"They told you there was a body in Virgil Riddle's conservatory?" Adele asked.

"Certainly not," Missy said. "You know how hush-hush they are when they're being official."

"Then how do you know about it?"

"I caught Assistant Deputy Curd having his lunch at the drugstore and wheedled it out of him."

"It doesn't surprise me you did," Adele said dryly.

"Naturally, the boy was too dense to know anything," Missy continued. "He could only tell me Mr. Riddle found a girl lying among the shrubbery in his conservatory and she was most certainly dead."

"Golly!" Beatrice sighed. "Another murder."

"I wouldn't necessarily take Assistant Deputy Curd's word for it," Adele said. "He's not the brightest of men."

"That's why I'm coming to you," said her friend. "You remember our bargain, Adele?" She looked meaningfully at her.

"I tell you what I know if you tell me what you know." Adele nodded. "Only I honestly know nothing, Missy. This is the first I'm hearing of this."

"Well then," her friend took her arm, "it's our duty as star reporter and lady detective to find out, isn't it?"

"I'm not a lady detective, you know," Adele remarked, but she took off the apron she always wore when dealing with some of the dirtier aspects of her work.

"You're leaving me to mind the shop?" Beatrice's green eyes, which had become more almond-shaped as the years passed, widened. "Golly!"

"I see you've replaced your 'bum it' with another inelegant colloquialism," Missy remarked.

"A woman may speak as she needs to be heard," Beatrice said with her chin a little up.

"You know how to handle the cash register, as I showed you?"

"No one will come in anyway," said the young woman. "They're all at lunch."

"Nevertheless, we must be ready." Adele put on her gloves. "We'll stop off and fetch Nin first."

"Has she appointed herself lady detective too?" Missy eyed her.

"You might consider her the unofficial medium for the police," Adele said as they emerged from her shop. "She's helped the police a great deal in the past, Missy."

"I don't object if she won't," she said.

Nin did not object, as she had become as keenly curious about the goings-on of the police as Adele in the past three years since they had first worked on the case of Lucy Blackstone.

"I wonder who this woman could be," she said.

"Assistant Deputy Curd also told me they're almost sure she's a working girl," said Missy.

"Perhaps she works for Mr. Riddle," Adele suggested.

"That's what makes it so intriguing," Missy said. "I also got out of Assistant Deputy Curd that Mr. Riddle is a bachelor and has only one manservant and one cook and it's not the cook."

"No maid?" Adele asked.

"He used to have a maid, but she quit a few weeks ago," said Missy.

"That's suggestive, isn't it, Adele?" Nin looked at her friend.

"It depends on why she quit," Adele said, taking her arm.

"I can well imagine why," Missy said with a gleam in her eye. "I phoned a friend of mine on the *San Francisco Bee*."

"And you found out he's a pig?" Nin asked.

"A rather unsavory way of putting it, Miss Branch, but that's essentially what he is," Missy said. "According to my friend, he's had more than one run-in with the police involving a lady. None of it was printed, of course."

They took the Beaton down Bridge Street and into the area of town where the largest houses had situated themselves on a small hill, as if determined to lord over the more even ground of Arroyo's middle class citizens.

Mr. Riddle's house was large but, as Adele would expect of a bachelor, unadorned and unimpressive. The musty scent in the hallway and the manservant taking their coats and hats reminded her of the warehouses she had visited in her work with the settlement houses. Everything was brown and leather, giving off a heavy, weighed look.

From the hallway, she heard a wailing voice. "But I don't understand! I don't understand it!" She wasn't surprised to find, when they entered the parlor, the voice belonged to Mr. Riddle, who was collapsed on the leather couch, a brandy glass raised to his shaking lips, and Deputy Dooland poised with the decanter, ready to pour out more. The young man nodded toward the open French glass doors. A dirt path led a little distance away to the glass encasement.

The ladies stepped gingerly down the path, muddy from the morning dew. The side door was open and the sheriff, Jackson, Assistant Deputy Edison, and the medical examiner's assistant Martin were there. The body of the woman was lying face down on the ground with shrubbery hanging over it.

Adele looked at it. "Who is it, Jack?"

"Miss Parnell," he said.

Upon hearing this, Nin suddenly stumbled to the corner, grasping at the wall, her face pale.

"Are you all right, dear?" Adele took her by the shoulders.

"My fault," she choked out. "My fault."

"Miss Grace, I think you'd better take Miss Branch home," Jackson said. "You shouldn't be here anyway."

"No!" Nin recovered. "I'm all right. I want to stay."

"And so do I," Missy said in a firm voice.

"I can't think how you heard about this so soon, Miss Grace." The sheriff's tone was anything but cordial.

"I have my ways, Sheriff." Her eyes were sparkling, and Adele was thankful she didn't put Assistant Deputy Curd and his loose tongue on the spot.

"You'll appreciate we've only just arrived," Jackson said, his pad and pencil poised. "We don't even know what happened yet."

"In other words, there is nothing to report, and I'd better keep my surmises to myself," Missy said. "I know it all, Deputy. I promise not to print anything the sheriff doesn't approve of."

Jackson sidled up to Adele and hissed in her ear, "You shouldn't have brought her here, Del!"

"I didn't bring her here," she said. "She brought us here."

Nin glared at him. "Maybe if you had told us you were going to investigate a murder, Mr. Gossling, we would have been more discreet."

"I didn't know then, did I, Miss Branch?" he countered. "And we don't know if it's a murder yet."

"Martin was just about to tell us that." Hatfield looked at the young man expectedly.

The assistant medical examiner, his sleeves rolled up and his glasses perched on the edge of his nose, replied, "It's murder all right, Sheriff." The man's brows knitted together. "A rather startling one."

"Why do you say that?" Jackson asked.

"The young lady was shot in the back," he said.

"So we can rule out accident or suicide," Hatfield said.

"One can hardly shoot oneself in the back." Nin agreed. "Unless one is a contortionist."

Martin laughed. "I highly doubt this woman was, Miss Branch."

"Is that what you find startling?" Missy asked. "I mean, isn't it rare to find a woman murdered by a gunshot?"

"Poison is more of a woman's weapon, though more as a murderess than a victim," Jackson said.

"It's not the murder weapon, Deputy, but the way it was used. Or the way they were used," said Martin, rolling down his sleeves.

"Speak plainly, man," Sheriff Hatfield said with a growl.

Martin grinned. "You always want one to get to the point, don't you, Sheriff? But medical examinations aren't that simple."

"She was shot with a gun," the sheriff began slowly.

"She was shot," said Martin, "three times."

"Three times?" Jackson stared at him.

"Three times!" Missy scribbled on her pad.

"Rather unexpected, isn't it?" asked the medical examiner's assistant. "The shots are a little haphazard, so perhaps the shooter didn't intend to shoot so many times, but there it is."

"Which might mean he — or she — was in a rage during the killing," said Jackson,

"Perhaps he or she had a score to settle," Nin remarked.

"We'll have to find that out, won't we?" The sheriff kept his eye on Martin, who was tidying up his medical bag. "Something bothers you about that, doesn't it, lad?"

Martin shut his bag with a snap. "Frankly, yes."

"Well, come out with it," he said.

"I can't be sure —"

"You know policework is partly clues and partly guesswork," Adele reminded him.

"It's this, sir." He turned to the sheriff. "I don't think those bullets came from the same gun."

"Three murderers!" Missy exclaimed. Hatfield gave her a sharp look and she added, "That won't go in the paper. Yet."

"Much obliged," he said dryly. "You don't think but you don't know for sure?"

"Not until we have a ballistics test done," said Martin.

"Well, then, we'll put in a request for one," said Hatfield.

"Time of death?" Jackson jumped in.

"That, I'm afraid, is another complication," said the young man, beginning to look sheepish. "Right now, I'm determining it was between eleven and midnight, but if she's been here for a while, the cooling temperature could have delayed rigor."

"It is rather chilly," Adele admitted, buttoning the top button of her jacket.

"Is there no way of knowing for sure?" Hatfield asked.

The young man shrugged. "You know how these things work, Sheriff."

"Anything else?" The sheriff studied him. "Anything else, Martin? Come, come, you're being very reluctant with this one."

"Something isn't right about it, sir," he said.

"Right about what?"

"The whole thing," he muttered. "The body, I mean."

Nin stepped to the other side near the woman's head. She bent down but, now familiar with police procedure, didn't touch the body. Her hand slowly waved over the head and shoulders and down the back. "She's been here a long time, but not all night."

"You mean she was dragged here from someplace else, just like Lucy Blackstone?" Adele asked. Missy wrote furiously on her pad.

Nin glared at Jackson standing with his arms crossed. "I expect you'll say I'm being misty, Mr. Gossling."

"Not at all, Miss Branch," he said. "In fact, I think you're right."

"You do?" She stared at him.

"This time your vision or whatever you call them is backed up by cold, hard facts." He pointed to Miss Parnell's skirt. "That green mulch, sir, and the twigs stuck to the heels of her shoes. They didn't come from here."

"A very good observation, Deputy." Hatfield was clearly pleased at the astuteness of the man he chose to assist him three years before. Jackson smiled in gratitude.

"There's plenty of such vegetation in the woods outside of town," Missy offered.

Nin shook her head. "The woods are cleaner and greener." A little shyly, she added, "I ought to know."

"Perhaps there's a part of the woods you haven't been to, Miss Branch," Jackson said.

"I don't deny it, Mr. Gossling," she said.

"An analysis would help," Martin said.

"That's not the sort of thing Dr. Rhodes would have the skill or the inclination to do," Hatfield snorted.

"What about the men who did the analysis for Adele a few years ago for the Marsh case?" Missy asked.

"Lom Brethren." Hatfield nodded. "Yes, I think he and Mr. McClure can help us a great deal here."

"I'd be happy to collect samples and take them," Martin offered.

The sheriff patted him on the back. "Good work, lad. I might make you an honorary assistant deputy one of these days." To this, Edison pouted.

The creak of the conservatory door echoed in the damp room and Adele was surprised to see Mayor Willett maneuvering his thick figure around a cluster of potted plants. He stared down at the young woman.

"Morning, Mayor," Hatfield said, clearing his throat.

"This is a bad case, Sheriff, a bad case." Adele was surprised to see the fumbling politician she and Nin had often laughed at suddenly erect and commanding.

"Every case of murder is a bad case," said the sheriff.

"Let's not beat around the bush." The man looked at him with beady eyes. "What have you so far?"

Hatfield was clearly annoyed, but related their finding, leaving out, Adele noted, any mention of Martin's theories about the three shots fired from different guns.

When he finished, Mayor Willett boomed, "Well, it's as I thought, then. Virgil had nothing to do with it if the body was, as you say, dragged here."

"We don't know that yet, sir," Jackson mumbled.

"I think we do, Deputy." He glared at him.

"May I ask why you're interested, Mayor?" Adele ventured.

He regarded her with a wary gaze. Adele returned it, as she was still smarting from the mayor having rejected Hatfield's application to make her a consultant for the police the year before. "I'm interested in anything that happens in Arrojo, Miss Gossling."

"You never came to see a body before," Nin said.

He looked away from the body lying on the ground. "Miss Parnell worked in the home of one of my best friends, who is, I might add, one of our newest and most prominent citizens."

"The latter is more important to you than the former," Nin mumbled.

"I expect you to solve this case as quickly as possible, Sheriff," the man continued, taking out his handkerchief and wiping his face.

"We always do, sir," Hatfield said.

"And with discretion." Mayor Willett gave him a meaningful look. "More than ever in this case, we need discretion."

"You just said Mr. Riddle couldn't have done it, so why the discretion for a lowly servant?" Adele eyed him.

"Any servant working for one of our best citizens reflects badly on the whole town," he snapped.

"How civic-minded of you," Nin murmured.

The mayor gave Hatfield a pointed look. "I thought we discussed this idea of the deputy's sister getting involved in cases, Sheriff."

Hatfield stiffened and his face grew chiseled. "We discussed leaving it to my discretion," he said. "I think you can count on my discretion in all things, Mayor." He gave him an even look.

"May I offer a suggestion as to where you can start looking for your killer?" Mayor Willett's tone was more appeasing.

Adele realized Jackson was grimacing but Hatfield took it with his usual mild manner. "You know I'm always open to any suggestions, sir."

"It's what we appreciate about you, Sheriff," the man said. "I realize this state of affairs looks, erm, suspicious." He glanced over his shoulder toward the parlor where they had seen the mumbling Mr. Riddle. "But I'm sure this dastardly deed was done by one of the servants."

"Why would Mr. Riddle's servants want to kill Miss Parnell?" Nin questioned.

"Not necessarily Virgil's," he said. "I mean any of the servants."

Jackson looked at him. "Can you explain further?"

"I'm sure you're aware, Deputy, that since Dilworth bought his house here, several of his — our — friends have also bought houses in Arrojo." His chest puffed out with pride. "Some of the finest men I know."

"Yes, yes," Jackson said with impatience.

"Well, we sort of have our own little society," he said. "We often have parties and picnics and other social events together and the servants know one another very well."

"And you think one of them might have done Miss Parnell in?" Adele finished.

"That is what I was getting at, Miss Gossling," he said. "It's not unlikely, is it, Sheriff?" He glanced at Hatfield.

"Not unlikely but not a certainty," Jackson said dryly.

"If something should turn up that, erm, requires even more discretion," the man looked at him steadily, "we all expect you to do the right thing."

"Including the killer if he should require more discretion?" Nin raised an eyebrow.

"The sheriff knows what I mean, Miss Branch," the man sneered.

The edge of Hatfield's mouth curved. "I'll do the right thing, sir."

"Good, good!" Mayor Willett pounded him on the back. "I knew we did right when we elected you. An honest man and a steady one, eh, Deputy?" He glanced at Jackson.

"Indeed, sir," Jackson said.

The moment the mayor had gone, Jackson exploded. "What a damned hypocrite!"

"My, but you swear so beautifully, Mr. Gossling," Nin said with a sly smile on her face.

"I apologize," he said.

"If you hadn't used the strong language, I would have," said the sheriff, straightening his hat. "Do the right thing indeed!"

"And how he's trying to throw us off with his suggestions," Jackson growled.

"His suggestion was the only sensible thing out of his mouth," said Hatfield.

Jackson studied him. "Do you really think one of the servants in the other houses did this, sir?"

"In the words of our beloved mayor, it's not unlikely," Hatfield said with amusement.

"But not a certainty either," Nin said.

"How many dead domestics have you and I seen between us

where another servant was guilty?" Jackson asked. "None that I can think of, Sheriff, and I don't recall you telling me of any."

"That doesn't mean they don't exist, Jack," Adele pointed out. "The police can't afford to rule out any possibility."

"Your sister, as usual, thinks like a lawman more than you do, Deputy," Hatfield said, amused.

"Law woman, if you please." She bowed. "You'll do the right thing, Sheriff, even if it won't be right in the eyes of Mayor Willett or his friends."

Hatfield smiled at her, looking almost like a shy little boy.

CHAPTER 6

Both lawmen bent down, gingerly spreading the skirt near the hem where it had been dirtied.

"Perhaps this will help." Adele held out the magnifying glass her father had given her.

Hatfield took it and inspected the skirt. "I see some wild grass here."

"There's certainly nothing like grass here." Jackson glanced around the conservatory.

"Mud, twigs, wild grass," Adele lamented. "It sounds like Tanner's Swamp."

"Perhaps that's where she was killed," Missy ventured.

"Tanner's Swamp would certainly be a good place to shoot someone, begging your pardon." Hatfield said the last with a bow to the ladies.

"No one would hear the noise," Jackson agreed. "Even if they did, they would think someone was out shooting ducks."

"That's not for print, Miss Grace," said the sheriff. "I believe you have all you need for your story at present."

"In other words, he wants you to leave," Nin said, not without a little nastiness.

"Aren't you going to question Mr. Riddle?" the woman inquired. "The body was found in his house, after all."

"Whether we do or don't, you'll hear about the fact in due time." There was no mistaking the sheriff's meaning as he looked at her with steady eyes.

Missy put her hand on Adele's shoulder. "You'll update me when you can?"

"With the permission of the sheriff," Adele said, glancing at him. Hatfield nodded.

When she was gone, Jackson growled, "She never should have been here!"

"I don't like her in on the first discovery," Hatfield agreed. "I realize Miss Grace is your friend, Adele, but she's also the voice of the press in these parts. That makes her a danger to our investigation."

"Missy has always been discreet, Sheriff," Adele said. "She will be this time as well."

"I've a feeling this case is going to be rather thorny, sir," Jackson said.

"Thorny or not, we have a job to do, Deputy," said Hatfield. "We haven't even had a chance to look around."

"You can start with her hands," Adele said.

"What about her hands?" her brother asked.

Adele pointed to the right hand, which was resting on the ground. "There's something in this one."

With expertise, Hatfield gently pried the piece of paper from under the flattened palm. "Strange how it's lying on the ground like that."

"You would think she was grasping it in her hand when she died," Nin agreed.

"If she wrote it," Jackson added.

The sheriff studied it, then handed it to him. "She wrote it all right."

Adele peeked at the note: *Riddle did it.*

"Riddle," Jackson mused. "Virgil Riddle, no doubt."

"A tidy accusation," Hatfield remarked. "The victim naming her killer."

"Well, it *is* his house, sir," his deputy pointed out.

"It doesn't follow that he did it, Jack," Adele insisted. "We already know the body was brought here from somewhere else."

"We don't know that," Jackson corrected. "We suspect it."

"Why would a man kill a woman somewhere else and then bring her to his house and hide her in his conservatory where it's sure to be found?" Nin asked. "It doesn't make any sense."

"Indeed it doesn't, Miss Branch," the sheriff agreed.

Adele looked at the figure of Miss Parnell whom Martin had turned over on her back when he left. She was thankful there was little blood and her lovely face was as peaceful as if she were asleep. Her lips were only slightly parted, as if she had been about to say something when her life was extinguished.

"Sheriff," she said, "do you notice something peculiar about Miss Parnell?"

"What do *you* notice, Adele?" he countered.

"She's dressed quite plainly," said Adele. "Her shirtwaist and skirt and the jacket."

"No hat," Jackson observed. "Of course, maybe it was left behind at the real scene of the crime."

"She might have been running errands," Hatfield suggested. "With all that dust on her shirt, I wouldn't expect her to be dressed for a ball."

"That's just it," said Adele. "She's dressed in street clothes but her jewelry and hair are done up."

"Like they were at the party," Nin agreed.

"I'm not sure I see what you mean," the sheriff said.

"That brooch, for example." Adele pointed to the jewel pinned neatly to the lapel of the jacket. "It's a little too fancy for a walking suit." And, indeed, the brilliant green, blue, and gold shades shone in the sunlight.

"Perhaps she was meeting someone and wanted to show it off," Jackson suggested.

"Look at her hair, Jack," Adele said. "It's the same comb she wore at the party. Remember what she said about it?"

"She only wears it on special occasions," Nin chimed in. "And it has rubies."

"It's true, Sheriff," Jackson said. "She did say that."

Adele touched the crown of Miss Parnell's head gingerly with her gloved hand. "It's not put in correctly either. Her hair is every which way."

"If she were dragged here, it would be," Hatfield pointed out.

"If she was dragged, it wouldn't be in her hair anymore," Adele argued. "It's as if someone put it in her hair after the fact."

"What for?" Jackson asked. "Not to leave a prettier corpse, surely."

"Perhaps when we answer that question mark, we'll have our murderer." Hatfield brushed the dirt from his hands. As he did so, he scooped beneath a bushy plant. "It seems the lady not only wore fancy jewelry but fancy gloves as well."

"Too fancy for a lady's maid," Jackson observed.

"Some man bought them for her," Nin insisted.

"May I see them, Sheriff?" Adele asked.

They were of a pale green-gray shade that matched the suit Miss Parnell was wearing. The material felt like silk and the lace "V" on the backs made them look both elegant and practical. She turned them over and admired the two pearl buttons on the cuffs that were used to secure them to the woman's wrists.

Peering under the flap of the cuff, she said, "Sheriff, there are some seams here."

Hatfield glanced at them. "The store label, no doubt."

"Someone ripped it off so we couldn't trace where they were bought," Jackson said. "Very clever."

"And very odd," the sheriff said. "Unless the person who killed her was the one who bought the gloves for her and didn't want to be identified."

"Doesn't it strike you that this crime has contradictory elements of forethought and spontaneity, Sheriff?" Adele asked.

"You've been reading too many crime novels, Del," her brother scoffed.

"But it's true," Nin said. "They tore the label off the gloves, but they left the skirt dirty so the police could trace where the dirt came from."

"They, Miss Branch?" Hatfield peered at her. When she gave him a questioning look, he explained, "You said 'they tore the label off.'"

"Martin said there were three shots in Miss Parnell," Adele said, trying not to shudder.

"But they might have all come from the same gun," Jackson said. "They very likely did."

"We'll know more about that when we coax Rhodes into calling the ballistics expert friend he's been boasting about." Hatfield put the gloves in a paper bag and handed it to Edison. "I believe we're finished here, Deputy."

"Shall we take the comb and brooch as well, sir?" Jackson asked. "If we're going on the theory that the gloves were bought by a gentleman of Miss Parnell's acquaintance who doesn't want to be identified, he might have bought her the jewelry as well."

"Good thinking, Deputy," Hatfield said and handed him another paper bag.

Adele glanced at her friend. "There's something you might find interesting about that comb, Sheriff."

"Oh?" He leaned against the table where the gardenia lay.

"Miss Parnell and Gene Dilworth and his friends had an argument at the party about it."

"That's true, sir," Jackson said. "Del told me on the way home."

Adele gave him a brief description of what had taken place.

"Mr. Cress spoke a lot about promises that night," she mused. "Maybe Miss Parnell made a promise about that comb and broke it."

"It wouldn't surprise me," Nin said.

"Mr. Lee actually tried to pull it from her hair?" Hatfield asked.

"I didn't think the man was a gentleman," Jackson sniffed.

"I can tell you for certain he wasn't," Nin growled.

"I wonder what she meant when she said it was all over and done with," Adele said.

"Probably some love affair where the comb was the parting gift," Jackson said. "Though why she would promise not to wear it is beyond me."

Adele glared at him. "Now who's been reading too many novels, dear brother?"

"If it was a love affair with a servant in one of Mayor Willett's tight-knit group, Jackson could be right, Adele." The sheriff held the conservatory door open for the ladies. "I see Martin sent for the proper authorities to take the body away. Just in time too."

Two young men in white uniforms and a stretcher nodded at them as they carefully lifted Miss Parnell and covered her with sheets.

Mr. Riddle was still on the couch. He was dressed in an evening suit, his bowtie undone. His hand held the empty brandy glass. Hatfield gave Dooland a sign and the young man put the brandy bottle back in the cupboard, locked the door, and handed the key to the butler, who stood waiting.

"Sheriff!" Mr. Riddle looked up, his bright eyes helpless. "You know I had nothing to do with this, don't you?"

"Nobody is accusing you of anything, sir," said Hatfield as he sat on the leather chair. "But we must ask a few questions."

"Bad business, bad business," he lamented. "And in my house!"

Just then, the two men came by with the stretcher, carefully maneuvering it between the heavy furniture so the sheets covering Miss Parnell's body wouldn't slip. Mr. Riddle groaned as he watched his servant lead them into the hallway. "Poor girl."

"You knew Miss Parnell, Mr. Riddle?" Adele eyed him.

He glared at her. "I can't think what your interest is in this matter, Miss Gossling."

"Deputy Gossling is my brother," she said.

"So the rumors about you being a lady detective are true." He looked away. "I don't fancy being questioned by a woman, Sheriff."

"Miss Gossling has my permission to ask any questions she wishes," Hatfield said in a sharp tone. "If she hadn't asked the question, I would have."

"What makes you think I knew her at all?" Mr. Riddle asked.

"I noticed you were quite friendly with one another when you were dancing at the party," she said.

"Oh, that," mumbled the man. "Well, I suppose you could say we all knew her."

"We?" Jackson asked.

"The people in our little group," he said.

"Yes, the mayor told us about that," Hatfield mumbled.

"We attend the same social functions," he said. "Arabel— Miss Parnell, well, she wasn't the sort of maid to hide behind curtains, if you know what I mean."

"She was treated like one of the family," Adele murmured, thinking of what the girl had told her when she came into her shop.

"Yes, that's it," he said.

"But I see you're distressed about her death, perhaps more so than one would think of a man in your position," the sheriff said delicately.

"Not to mention you almost called her by her first name," Nin said under her breath.

"I'm distressed, Sheriff, because a dead girl ended up in my conservatory!" he growled. "And for your information, Miss Branch, everyone in our group calls the servants by their first name. We often send our servants to help when there are lavish social functions going on."

"I suppose you're going to suggest one of the servants in the other houses killed Miss Parnell?" Jackson eyed him.

"Well, it certainly wasn't one of us," the man said. "Is that what you're thinking?"

"We don't think, sir. We dig out facts," said Jackson in a flat tone.

"Well, then, dig them out!" the man stormed. "Ask whatever questions you like, only don't make accusations before you have your facts."

Sheriff Hatfield gave Assistant Deputy Dooland a look and the young man obediently brought out the brandy again. Mr. Riddle downed a glass and leaned back on the couch. "I apologize for my rudeness, Sheriff. This has gotten me in a muddle."

"We're trying to help, sir," the sheriff said. "If it's any comfort to you, we don't believe Miss Parnell was killed in your conservatory."

The man looked up. "I assume you have reason to believe that?"

"We do," Hatfield confirmed. "But we're not prepared to disclose it."

"My, but you police can be secretive, can't you?" Mr. Riddle mumbled.

"Did you hear anything last night that was strange or alarming to you?"

The man gave the ladies a sheepish glance and lowered his voice. "I wasn't here last night, Sheriff. As a matter of fact, I had just come in and poured myself a drink when Maklin came to tell me about — her."

"You're still in evening clothes," Nin observed.

Mr. Riddle's hand flew to his loosened tie. "I am a bachelor, free to roam as I please when I please," he said with more defensiveness than dignity.

"Aren't you a little old to still be sowing your wild oats?" Jackson eyed him.

"Who said I was sowing my wild oats?" he snapped. "I merely said I was out last night."

"And what did you do, sir?" Hatfield asked.

"I don't know as I should answer that without my lawyer." He stiffened.

"Only if you have something to hide," Adele said, thinking about what Missy had told them about her friend at the *San Francisco Bee*.

The man looked sheepish again and reached for the brandy but a sharp glance from the sheriff made the assistant deputy raise it above his head and toddle to the cabinet to put it back again. "I've nothing to hide. I was merely trying to spare some unpleasantness for the ladies."

"We can stand it if you can," Nin said.

"I dined with a friend of mine at the club."

"Club?" Jackson stopped writing on his pad.

"The Orion Club," said Mr. Riddle. "I'm sure you've heard of it, Deputy."

"I've heard of it," he said.

"Then we got involved — well —"

"Yes?" Sheriff Hatfield prompted.

"In an all-night poker game," he said. "You see now why I was reluctant to mention it in front of the ladies." He gave another sheepish grin. "I've a notion they don't approve of men playing cards for high stakes."

"Neither do I, sir," said Sheriff Hatfield. "I shall have a talk with the club manager."

"And then you came home and your manservant told you

about the dead body in the conservatory?" Jackson asked. "Why did you have him phone the police instead of doing it yourself?"

"That can be explained, Deputy," he said. "I came in here for a little — pick-me-up." He glanced toward the cabinet where Dooland was now guarding the brandy bottle. "Maklin — my man — was the one who told me and asked if he should call the police."

"And you were coward enough to let him do it," Nin growled.

"Well, I didn't know anything about it, did I?" he challenged. "I didn't even go into the conservatory to look at the girl."

"You didn't even bother to look at the woman dead among your flowers and shrubs?" Adele glared at him.

"It sounds as if Miss Branch is right in calling you a coward," Jackson said.

"Deputy, that is impertinence!" the man thundered. Sheriff Hatfield gave Jackson a look and he folded his hands in front of him.

"Was Maklin the one who discovered Miss Parnell in the conservatory?" asked the sheriff.

"You'll have to ask him that." Mr. Riddle closed his eyes. "It's all been such a daze."

"We'll need the name of this friend who dined with you," Hatfield said.

With much reluctance, the man finally answered, "Mr. Donald Tupman. He lives in Caton. But I would appreciate it if you would call upon him at his office."

"So his wife won't know?" Adele raised an eyebrow.

"She disapproves of his playing cards," Mr. Riddle mumbled.

"I think you ought to know something, sir." The sheriff took out the note they had found and held it up. "I can't let you touch it, of course, as it's evidence."

Mr. Riddle's face grew pale as he read it. "But this is impossible! I didn't do it, Sheriff. I don't care what that note says!"

"We think it was written by the dying girl," Jackson said in a quiet tone. "Sometimes, when things go awry, women are apt to take revenge."

"That's hardly the handwriting of a woman scorned, Jack," Adele protested.

"There was nothing to scorn!" Mr. Riddle insisted. "I tell you I hardly knew the girl."

Hatfield motioned toward Edison, who laid the paper bags with the jewelry they had collected on the table. "Will you please look at these and tell us if anything looks familiar to you?"

Adele watched as Mr. Riddle inspected the jewelry and gloves with the care of one who was used to elegant things. "No, I can't say I do," he said at last. "Oh, wait a minute. The comb. I seem to recall seeing that somewhere."

"Miss Parnell was wearing it the night of Mr. Dilworth's birthday party," she supplied.

The man stared. "You mean you took it off the dead girl's body?"

"You don't happen to know where she bought it, Mr. Riddle?" the sheriff asked.

"I know nothing about the young lady's buying habits, Sheriff." He sniffed.

Hatfield sighed. "We'd like a word with your servants now, if we may."

"You may ask them anything you like." Mr. Riddle rose. "Now I'm off to take a hot bath and get some sleep."

The sheriff's smooth face creased. "I didn't say I was finished with you yet."

"Really, this is intolerable!" the man snarled. "I shall have a word with the mayor about the brutal practices of country police."

"Sit down, sir," Jackson said with finality.

Mr. Riddle gave him a pouting look but he took his seat on the couch, staring into the empty brandy glass.

Maklin, who proved to be a very efficient butler, had withdrawn when Hatfield mentioned the servants and entered now with a portly woman whose immaculate appearance did not hide from Adele that she was overworked.

"This is Mrs. Gregory, Sheriff," Maklin stated. "She's the one who found the girl."

"What a nasty sight it was amongst the daffodils and roses!" The woman heaved a sob.

Adele, whom the sheriff trusted to question the ladies in a case, rose and put her arm around the woman's shoulders. "It must have frightened you terribly, Mrs. Gregory."

"Indeed, miss!" The woman wiped her eyes with her handkerchief. "I was going to get the morning bouquet — the master always likes a fresh bouquet of flowers at the table —" Mr. Riddle looked almost embarrassed. "The daffodils were in bloom, too. I opened the door, and there the poor thing was!"

"Did you recognize her?" Adele asked.

"Well, not at first, miss," the woman said. "She was lying face-down, you know."

"I know," Adele said. "We saw her too."

"Oh, it weren't a sight for young ladies!" The woman looked from Adele to Nin. "You shouldn't have allowed it, if you'll pardon my saying so, Sheriff."

"I've learned, Mrs. Gregory, one does not allow or disallow young ladies anything nowadays," he said dryly.

"That's right, you're one of them New Women, aren't you?" She looked at the ladies.

"She is," Nin said stoically. "I'm not."

"When did you know it was Miss Parnell?" Adele continued.

"Maklin is the one who looked at her face, miss."

"I only lifted it a bit to see who she was," Maklin supplied. "I didn't touch anything else, Sheriff."

"That's good thinking, Maklin," said Hatfield. "Perhaps it was better your master entrusted you with such a delicate task after all." He eyed Mr. Riddle.

"Did you know Miss Parnell well?" Adele continued.

"Oh, there were a few times when the Dilworths asked me to help in the kitchen when their cook was ill," said Mrs. Gregory. "And, well, Mr. Riddle's friends are always needing extra help when they give a party."

"Yes, we heard about that," said Hatfield. "We understand the servants from one household to another know each other quite well."

"That we do, Sheriff," she said. "Miss Parnell didn't speak to any of us much. Used to go her own way when we were — talking."

"You mean gossiping," Nin said.

"I'll have you know my people don't gossip, Miss Branch," Mr. Riddle growled.

"I won't say the younger ones don't have a word now and then," the woman said. "I suppose that's why it was so odd Miss Parnell kept to herself."

"She felt above the rest of you," Nin supplied.

"Yes, miss, I expect she did," said Mrs. Gregory.

The sheriff gave Maklin a pointed look. "You look like a rather observant fellow, Maklin."

The man's face did not shift a muscle. "I try, Sheriff."

"As a butler, you would oversee the rest of the staff at these larger parties and dances?"

"Myself or another butler, sir."

"Do you agree with Mrs. Gregory that Miss Parnell thought herself above the rest of you?"

"No above *me,* Sheriff," he said in a stoic tone.

Hatfield took a step toward him. "I'm sure you have to be on the lookout for the behavior of the male staff toward the female staff at these events?"

"Look here!" Mr. Riddle half rose. "Maklin's behavior is always impeccable."

"The sheriff isn't implying it wasn't," Jackson said in a sharp tone. "Sit down, Mr. Riddle."

The man sank back into his seat.

"It's been suggested there may have been a staff member at one of the other houses — a footman or manservant, for example — who may have taken a fancy to Miss Parnell."

For the first time, Maklin's lips curved in what resembled a smile. "Some of the younger servants did find her fetching, Sheriff."

"Anyone who paid particular attention to her?" Jackson asked.

Maklin shifted. "There was one young man, as I recall. A footman with the Woods family."

"Woods?" Sheriff Hatfield snapped his fingers. "They live just up the hill on Baton Street, don't they?"

"Yes, sir," said Maklin.

"He was rather keen on her," Mrs. Gregory put in.

"His name?" Jackson asked.

"Cole. Douglas Cole."

"Any of the other maids ever speak to her?" Adele asked. "She might have confided in one of them."

"I doubt that, miss," said the woman. "They all thought her uppity, if you'll pardon my saying so."

"Because she kept to herself?" Nin asked.

"Not just that, miss," said Mrs. Gregory. "She refused to help with the serving. Thought she shouldn't have to have to, her being a lady's maid. And she never wore work clothes. She always wore fine dresses."

"I can see why they would be put off by that." Adele nodded with sympathy.

"And on a lady's maid's salary too," the woman said with a sniff.

"I imagine the maid who used to work here would hardly be

able to afford so much as a rhinestone comb even if she saved all her salary for ten years," Adele remarked.

Mrs. Gregory stared at her. "Land sakes, how did you know there was a maid here?"

"It stands to reason," said Adele. "You look as if you're taking the burden of the household duties with no one to help you." She eyed Mr. Riddle. "You really ought to hire another maid, sir."

To her surprise, the man's face softened. "I'm sorry about that, Mrs. Gregory. I realize what a hardship you have on your hands. I simply haven't had time —"

"Then let her do it," Nin interrupted in her crude way. "She's the one who has to work with her, not you." Then, with a devilish look in her eyes, she added, "Unless there's some reason why you insist on hiring the maids yourself."

Clearly irked, Mr. Riddle leapt up and, pushing Dooland aside, grabbed the brandy bottle out of the cabinet. "Mrs. Gregory, you have my permission to do what you must to get the help you need."

"Thank you, sir." The woman curtsied. "You've always been very generous."

"I think that's all for now," said the sheriff with a bow.

"Just one more question," Adele said. "This maid who worked with you —"

"Nellie," Mr. Riddle supplied.

Adele did not miss the flicker in Hatfield's eye. "Nellie. Why did you fire her?"

"Who said I fired her?" the man asked. "You assume too much, Miss Gossling."

"All right, then, why did she leave?"

"I hardly think that's any of your business," Mr. Riddle said. "In any case, she can hardly have anything to do with that poor dead girl."

"Perhaps they were friends," Adele suggested.

"I imagine she had another position." The man shrugged. "Why do these maids up and leave without any notice?"

Adele said in a low voice, "Mr. Riddle, I used to know many domestics when I worked in the settlement houses in San Francisco. They rarely left a position without notice unless they felt they had no choice."

"What the blazes are you getting at?" the man growled.

"Watch your language in the presence of ladies, sir," Jackson growled back.

"Many of them left because, shall we say, their employers' demands put them in a compromising position?" Adele folded her hands.

The man did not answer but the look on Mrs. Gregory's face confirmed Adele's suspicions.

"You may go," Hatfield said. "If you think of anything else, please let us know."

Mrs. Gregory and Maklin looked only too happy to leave and the butler silently shut the parlor doors.

"Is my sister right, Mr. Riddle?" Jackson asked.

"I suppose I can be a little particular at times." The man's speech was somewhat labored, and Adele realized he may have had too many brandies. "But I was certainly not 'demanding' and I would never put any young lady in an awkward position. I feel sorry for them really."

"Sorry?" she asked.

"They're young, no money, not much education, no young men to court them —"

"Why do you assume they had no young men to court them?" Nin asked.

He grimaced. "You have little experience with hiring maids, I see. Many of them are quite plain or they would be doing something else."

"It always amazes me how it's only men on the other side of

the apron who find a girl who has to work for her living so cheap!" Adele snarled.

"I never said I thought any maid cheap!" Mr. Riddle barked. "Really, Sheriff, this is uncalled for."

"I agree." Sheriff Hatfield looked steadily at Adele. "I don't think we need question Mr. Riddle on his feelings about servants, Adele."

"Since being a pig does not mean he's a killer too," Nin said.

"Well, I'm happy you don't think I'm a killer, Miss Branch," said the man. "Though I can't say I appreciate being called a pig. Now, unless there's anything else —"

"I'm afraid there is, sir," said the sheriff. "Do you own a gun?"

The man jumped up. "You just said it was obvious I didn't kill her!"

"Miss Branch said it," Jackson said in a quiet tone. "We must explore all possibilities."

"Including the possibility that I would shoot a girl in the back and then put her body in my conservatory?" Mr. Riddle's eyes glowed. "I may not be the brightest of men, Deputy, but I'm not so stupid as that."

"You're stupid enough to admit you saw the body well enough to know she was shot," Nin remarked.

"You also claimed you barely got a look at it," Adele added. "But you clearly got enough of a good look to see she had bullet wounds."

He shrank back on the couch. "I wasn't lying, Sheriff. I didn't get a good look at the body. But, yes, I did notice the holes through her jacket. It was ghastly!" He looked into the empty brandy glass.

Sheriff Hatfield quickly took the glass and handed it to Dooland. "I'll ask you again, sir. Do you have a gun?"

"I did have a gun," he said. "An old Civil War revolver."

"Where is it now?" Jackson asked.

The man looked foggy. "I haven't the faintest idea. Lost, probably."

"One does not simply lose a revolver, sir," Jackson snapped.

"Deputy, I have only been in this house six months," the man insisted. "It got lost when I moved my things, probably. I came from Los Angeles so it's quite a ride."

"I gather Maklin packed and unpacked for you," said Hatfield. "Might he know then?"

"Maklin started working for me after I moved into this house," said Mr. Riddle. "Before that, I had another man who did the packing and unpacking. He died just before I came here. He wasn't a very young man." The last was said in a rueful tone.

"All the same, I'd like to question Maklin, sir," said the sheriff. "Butlers usually know much more than their masters realize."

"I don't see the point in disturbing the man again." Mr. Riddle sniffed. "You appreciate you've disturbed the routine of this house enough, Sheriff."

"All the same." Hatfield rose and leaned against the back of the chair, making it clear he had no intention of backing down.

"Oh, very well," Mr. Riddle grumbled and pulled the bell cord on the wall.

Maklin appeared, looking even more immaculate than before. "I've taken the liberty of putting breakfast on the sideboard, sir," he said. "I thought the police were finished with their inquiries."

"Not by half," Nin said, smiling at the annoyed look Maklin gave her.

"Mr. Riddle tells us he used to have an old revolver," the sheriff said. "He can't seem to find it. Do you know where it is?"

"A revolver, sir? I don't believe I've ever seen one around this house," he said.

Adele did not miss the relieved look that passed over Mr. Riddle's face as he sank back against the pillows.

Nin leaned forward and whispered, "He's lying!"

"Are you sure about that, Mr. Maklin?" Adele asked.

"Positive, miss," he said. "It's not a thing one would mistake if one saw it."

"I'm sure you wouldn't," she said.

"Thank you, miss." He bowed and withdrew from the parlor with a wave of the sheriff's hand.

"I told you, Sheriff," Mr. Riddle said.

Hatfield put on his hat. "I thank you for your cooperation and your patience. I suggest you get your breakfast now and stay away from the brandy the rest of the day."

With this sage advice, they left the house.

CHAPTER 7

As they assembled into the police car with the ladies squeezed in the narrow backseat, Adele remarked, "I think you may have given Mr. Riddle too much liberty with that liquor, Sheriff."

"He was so drunk he was shaking," Nin agreed.

"Men's tongues grow loose under the influence of liquor," Jackson said with a half-smile.

The sheriff started the car. "Dooland was keeping a close eye on him. The young man's had experience with tippers. His uncle used to own a bar."

"Perhaps Jack's right," Adele admitted. "A loose tongue can help the police a great deal."

"You make us sound like vigilantes," Hatfield grumbled.

To this, Jackson's face grew somber, as his detective experience had come from eight years with the Anspach Agency, a rival to the more lavish Pinkertons and just as brutal and lawless with their ways.

"You got a few choice reactions out of him anyway," she said.

"Such as?"

"He knew Miss Parnell much better than he claims," Adele

said. "Perhaps even intimately."

"Not perhaps," Nin said in her assured tone. "There was a deep connection between them. It was like a wall of mist that surrounded him."

"I didn't see anything," Jackson mumbled.

"You wouldn't, Mr. Gossling," she snapped. "One who doesn't believe is blind."

"You deduce that because of what he said about barely having seen the body and then knowing about the wounds?" Sheriff Hatfield turned the corner. "It's a common mistake, really. People think there's something sinister about having viewed a dead body."

"And the gun," Adele continued. "He was relieved when Maklin said he'd never seen it."

"You think Maklin was lying?" Jackson asked.

"They were both lying," Nin declared. "It was written all over their faces."

"How would Maklin know his master had denied still owning the gun if he knew where it was?" the sheriff asked.

"Servants listen at doorways, sir," Jackson said. "Some are even trained to do that in case their masters need an alibi. I suspect Mr. Riddle needed a story to get out of more than one awkward situation, though not necessarily a law violation."

"More like a gentleman's violation," Nin snarled. "I'm sure he's faced a shotgun with an angry husband at the end of it more than once."

"It's almost uncanny, Sheriff," said Jackson, leaning back. "We have nearly a perfect case here. The body of a young woman found in the conservatory of a man one can imagine might have chased young domestics. A note we can assume comes from the victim who wrote it with her last dying breath to tell us who her killer was. The possibility of a liaison between them, if we can prove that."

"I think the sheriff is on the scent of a different trail, Jack,"

Adele said. "You're taking seriously what the mayor said, aren't you, Sheriff?"

"We now know there might be just cause," Hatfield defended. "We'll need to speak with this Douglas Cole."

"I still think that's a dead end, sir," Jackson said.

"So might your Mr. Riddle be," Nin pointed out.

"As you know, Deputy, a lawman puts his hound nose on all trails leading to solving the case," said Hatfield. "We'll speak with Mr. Cole and this Mr. Tupman."

"And Nellie," Adele chimed in. "She might have something to tell you about Mr. Riddle you need to know."

"And Nellie," Hatfield acknowledged. "I'd also like to take another look around that house for that gun."

"It's good you left Dooland there though I'm not sure he could see a bee if it stung him on the nose," Jackson said.

Sheriff Hatfield laughed. "I gave him instructions to watch both Mr. Riddle and Maklin with a close eye in case either of them should behave suspiciously before we have a chance to get the search warrant."

"You think they would try to get rid of the gun?" Adele asked.

"You never can tell, Adele." He stopped the car in front of the Dilworth house. "At any rate, we'll see if we can get Mr. Dilworth to tell us something Mr. Riddle didn't."

The scene at the Dilworth house made Adele's heart heave. The dining room showed the remains of an abandoned breakfast, right down to a half-nibbled sugar cube at the edge of a saucer. They found the family in the parlor. Mr. Dilworth had his arm around his wife, comforting her as she sobbed into a handkerchief. Gene Dilworth sat tightly in a chair, his mouth against his fist. Only Hazel, standing as if she had just come in, looked confused.

Hatfield said in a low tone, "I take it you already heard the news."

Mr. Dilworth nodded. "The mayor told us."

"He was here?" Jackson could barely hide his annoyance.

"He told us everything." Gene's voice was subdued.

"Arabella!" Mrs. Dilworth screeched.

"What about Arabella?" Hazel asked.

"You haven't heard about Miss Parnell?" Adele asked softly.

"We sent her upstairs when Mayor Willett arrived," said Mr. Dilworth. "He thought it best."

"I'm not a child!" Hazel snapped. "I know bad things happen in the world."

"Then you ought to know," Adele said before anyone could stop her. "The police found Miss Parnell dead in Mr. Riddle's conservatory this morning."

"Arabella!" Mrs. Dilworth sobbed. "Heaven help us!" She began to shriek and sway. Nin, with lightning speed, slapped the woman's face. Mrs. Dilworth broke down into sobs.

"Was that necessary, Miss Branch?" Mr. Dilworth looked annoyed.

"It was if you didn't want her getting into a hysterical fit." Nin put her arm around her shoulders. "Someone should get her a glass of water."

"I'll do it." Gene went out.

Hazel stared at her mother, her face like stone. "You screamed as if your heart was breaking."

"Hazel, please go," Mr. Dilworth insisted. "This is no place for a child."

"She just told you she's not a child," Nin said.

Hazel seemed to come out of her frigidity. "No! I want to stay. Maybe I can help the police."

"Dear —"

"Please, Father," she begged.

"She might be of use to you, Sheriff," Adele said.

Hatfield glanced at her and she knew he saw her sympathy for the girl. "I have no objections if Hazel stays. As she said before, she's not a child, Mr. Dilworth."

"Very well then." But the man looked less than pleased.

Gene came back and handed his father the water. "Please, Mother, don't be upset. Arabella was no longer our concern, after all."

"What do you mean by that, sir?" Jackson asked.

They were all silent for a moment as Mrs. Dilworth collected herself, her sobs subsiding and her figure still. Finally, Hazel blurted out, "Arabella left us!"

"Left you?" Hatfield glanced at Mr. Dilworth. "Is this true?"

The man nodded. "She went the day after Gene's party."

Adele caught the sharp look Hatfield gave Jackson, who was writing things down in his leather notebook. "Wasn't that rather sudden?"

Mrs. Dilworth, now completely subdued, answered, "She didn't even give notice. Just left early that morning before any of us were awake."

"Are you sure she meant to leave?" Jackson asked. "Perhaps she had to leave abruptly and only planned to be gone a short time."

"Her trunks are gone," said Gene. "Most of her things as well."

"She even left behind some of the things I gave her." Mrs. Dilworth dabbed her eyes.

"I know you relied a great deal on her, Mrs. Dilworth," Adele said gently. "And I know she revered you."

"She was very loyal." The woman sighed.

"She ought to have given us notice," Mr. Dilworth growled. "Not run off like that."

"That was rather thoughtless," Gene chimed in.

"She spoke to no one before she left?" Jackson asked.

They all shook their heads.

"How long has she been in your service, Mrs. Dilworth?" asked the sheriff.

"Two years and three months," said the woman.

"You have a good head for dates," he complimented.

The woman smiled. "I know what you're thinking, Deputy. You're not the first."

"I don't quite understand, ma'am," he said politely.

"Mrs. Dilworth means you're thinking Miss Parnell was awfully familiar with the family for just a few years of service," Adele supplied.

"I wasn't thinking that," he said.

"You would have been right if you had."

"Del!" Jackson hissed at her.

"I rather thought it a little much myself," Mr. Dilworth admitted. " but Arabella was indispensable to my wife."

"I don't doubt it," Nin mumbled.

"Men don't understand." Mrs. Dilworth turned to Adele. "I've been told you believe in rights for women, Miss Gossling." Adele nodded. "So do I. For *all* women, not just the privileged."

"You're a rare breed, Mrs. Dilworth."

The woman bowed. "Arabella was very bright, and she had the makings of something fine. I suppose that's why I allowed her more liberties than most ladies would." She added ruefully, "More liberties than many of my friends thought wise."

"She wanted more than domestic service could give her," Adele guessed.

"She wanted more than her past life could give her," the woman corrected. "Did you know Arabella wasn't her real name?" She grimaced. "It was Annie. She said she changed it because it sounded too much from the farm."

"She was a farm girl?" the sheriff asked.

Mr. Dilworth nodded. "Her family is from Fresno, I believe."

"She was a farmer's daughter but damned if she would be a farmer's wife," Gene added. "That's what she said. Didn't she, Mother?"

His mother nodded. "I don't know if I can explain it, but her people — they're good people, honest and hard-working. But they see life as something that exists, not something to live."

"They've been farmers for generations, I believe," Mr. Dilworth added.

"When one lives in a circle, one can't see beyond the rim," Nin murmured, her eyes glassy.

"Yes, it's that way with the Parnells," Mrs. Dilworth said. "Arabella had more vision, as you call it. She could see beyond that circle."

"So she left the farm to become a domestic servant," Jackson concluded.

"She left home at fifteen," Gene said.

"I'm guessing she worked her way up the ranks," said Sheriff Hatfield.

"And very quickly," said Mrs. Dilworth. "She worked for several middle-class families before she came to California and found a position as a housemaid for Nora Murphy."

"The Murphys are friends of ours in Rosa Gris," Mr. Dilworth added.

"Rosa Gris," Adele repeated. "I should think someone like Miss Parnell would have headed for San Francisco or Sacramento."

"She had an idea about that, Miss Gossling," said Mrs. Dilworth. "She said it was easier to build her experience working for big families in smaller towns than in small families in big towns."

"The big fish in a little pond," the sheriff murmured.

"Exactly," said the woman.

"So she was in service with Mrs. Murphy before she came to you?" Jackson asked. "How long was she there?"

"About a year and a half, I think," said Mrs. Dilworth.

"And why did she leave?" asked Hatfield. "I'm assuming she left and wasn't dismissed or you wouldn't have hired her."

The Dilworths looked uncomfortable for a moment as they both seemed to shift on the coach. Mr. Dilworth said, "I think it's best you ask the Murphys that question, Sheriff."

"We will." The sheriff gave Jackson a look. "We're trying to get a sense of what sort of person Miss Parnell was. That often can give us clues as to who would, well, want her dead."

"Willett told us you have a notion it may have been one of the servants in the other houses," Mr. Dilworth said.

Hatfield did not hide his annoyance. "I'm entertaining any notion for now, Mr. Dilworth."

"There was that footman who made eyes at Arabella during Kate Standon's coming out ball," Hazel offered.

"Don't be ridiculous," Mrs. Dilworth snapped. "Arabella would never allow anyone from the houses to flirt with her."

"She didn't say she allowed it," Nin said. "She said the footman was making eyes at her."

"Does he work for the Woods?" Jackson asked.

"I believe he does," Mrs. Dilworth answered.

Adele had been watching Gene during the conversation. The young man clearly looked uncomfortable. He crossed and uncrossed his legs several times and scraped at the arm of the chair with clawed fingers.

"Are you all right, Mr. Dilworth?" she asked.

"What? Oh, yes. Well —" He coughed. "This talk of who might have wanted Arabella dead —"

"Yes?" Hatfield prompted.

"I was just thinking of something I saw a few weeks ago."

"If you have information that might help the police, you must tell them, Gene," Mr. Dilworth said in a firm tone.

"I saw Arabella with — someone."

"You mean a man, don't you, sir?" Jackson eyed him.

"Well, one doesn't speak of such things in the presence of ladies," he mumbled.

"I think you'd better say what you mean, Mr. Dilworth," Sheriff Hatfield said "This is a murder investigation, after all."

"Where did you see her?" asked Jackson.

"At the Orion Club," he said. "That's the men's club in Rosa Gris."

"We've heard of it already from Mr. Riddle," Jackson said with a twisted smile.

"You really ought to join, Deputy," said Gene. "As you are Otis Gossling's son, I'd be glad to sponsor you."

"When one is fighting for the law, sir, one hardly has time for clubs," Jackson said. Adele thought he sounded as stuffy as a trophy room bird, but she was surprised to see Nin cast him an admiring gaze. "I'm more interested in hearing about these rumors."

"What would Arabella be doing at the club?" Mrs. Dilworth blinked. "Did Mrs. Butler send her on an errand?"

"She wasn't there for any errand, Mother," Gene said. "At least, it didn't look like it."

"What did it look like?" Adele asked.

"Well —" He uncrossed his legs. "Quite frankly, Miss Gossling, it looked as if she were waiting for someone at the club."

"I don't believe it!" The woman stared, her face pale.

"It's true, Mother," he said. "I didn't want to have to bring this up —"

"You were certainly quick enough to do it," Nin mumbled.

He flinched. "I want to help the police, Miss Branch."

"Go on, sir," the sheriff said.

"When Miss Parnell first came here, we caught her listening at the door when we were discussing the Orion Club."

"Who is 'we?'" Hatfield asked.

"My friends and I," he said.

"Maxwell Lee and Nathan Cress," Jackson supplied. "We met them at the party."

"We've been friends since college, Sheriff," he said.

"Go on," said the sheriff.

"As I was saying, we were discussing a billiard game for that night at the Orion Club, and we caught her listening at the door."

"That's not unusual," Adele said. "Maids and butlers like to know what's going on in the house. Even our houseman eavesdrops now and then." This made Jackson glance sharply at her.

"That night, we went to the billiard game," said Gene. "And I could have sworn I saw a woman who looked like Miss Parnell lurking outside the side entrance. You can see it from the front stairs."

"Nonsense!" his father scoffed. "What would she be doing there?"

"Well, sir." The young man hesitated. "I think she was — how shall I put it? Hoping to catch a glimpse of someone."

Mrs. Dilworth frowned. "You must be mistaken, Gene. Arabella had her work to do."

"I expect she was let off for the night, Mother," he said "She often was, wasn't she?" Adele could tell by the way he avoided his mother's gaze that he was almost accusing her.

"Is that when you saw her with this man?" Sheriff Hatfield rested his elbow on his knees.

The young man glanced at his mother.

"It's all right, dear." She patted his arm. "You must tell all you know."

"No, that was another time," he said. "Once I was called down to the club waiting room by an old friend who isn't a member and Miss Parnell was waiting there."

"Did she see you?" Adele asked.

He gave her a surprised look. "Of course."

"But you didn't acknowledge one another," she guessed

"How would you know that, Del?" Jackson eyed her.

"Wouldn't *you* like to know, Mr. Gossling?" Nin's eyes sparkled.

"I didn't want to embarrass her," Mr. Dilworth admitted. "She may have been running an errand, just like Mother said."

"But she wasn't?" Hatfield asked.

"Just as I was walking out of the room to get my coat, a man came in."

"I assume you knew the man?"

"Well, Sheriff, the Orion Club is a big place and I don't know everyone," he said.

"I think you knew this man, sir." Hatfield eyed him.

"It was —" he glanced at his father, "Virgil."

"Perhaps she was running an errand for him," Mr. Dilworth suggested.

"I could see into the room as I got my coat," said the young man. "Virgil took both her hands —"

"This is absurd!" his father growled.

"They left right away but as they went out, I heard her laughing."

"As if she were very familiar with him," Adele said.

"Well, shall we say, Miss Gossling, she didn't behave in a very reserved way," he mumbled.

"You mean she didn't behave in a very ladylike way," Nin corrected.

A groan came from Mrs. Dilworth and her husband put his arm around her shoulders. "It's all right, dear. I'm sure Gene's mistaken."

"I'm not mistaken," the young man insisted. "I can even tell you what she was wearing. A blue dress with beads down the front and a lace collar."

Mrs. Dilworth spoke in a vague tone, " Yes, she did have a dress like that. It was one of mine from a few seasons ago."

"I assume you knew nothing about this, sir?" Hatfield turned to Mr. Dilworth.

"I knew nothing of it because it didn't happen," the man insisted. "Virgil never behaved improperly toward Miss Parnell or any of our female servants in any way."

"You mean in this house, Father," said his son. "I don't need to tell you a man can be very different outside the walls of polite society."

"He can even be a brute," Adele couldn't help adding.

"He usually is," Nin said.

"A reporter friend of mine mentioned she read a few articles that were less than complimentary toward Mr. Riddle," Adele said.

"You're on the wrong track with Virgil," Mr. Dilworth insisted. "I'll admit he was a little wild in the past but now he's reforming."

Adele took note as his son turned his head away.

"You seem very sure of that, sir," Jackson remarked.

"I am sure." He leaned forward and reached for a cigar from the box on the table, then thought better of it and put it back. "Virgil is engaged to be married."

This clearly surprised both his wife and son, as they stared at him.

"He never mentioned the fact to us when we questioned him," Jackson said.

"Well, he wouldn't," he said, "because it's not actually an engagement. Yet."

"Really, sir." The sheriff was clearly annoyed. "The police don't like games."

"It's not a game, Sheriff," the man insisted. "What I should have said is he plans to get engaged very soon."

"To Mrs. Allington?" Mrs. Dilworth smiled. "I'm glad."

"Who is Mrs. Allington?" Hatfield inquired.

"A very respectable lady who lives in Sacramento," she supplied. "The widow of an old friend of Virgil's. They knew one another in his army days, then he and her husband went their separate ways as men often do after the army. They just found one another again last year."

"And he was eager to comfort the widow," Nin said with a sly smile.

"Well, yes, if you want to put it that way," Mrs. Dilworth admitted. "But I didn't know it had gone so far as an engagement." She glanced at her husband. "It was naughty of you to keep that from me, Len."

"He asked me to, dear," said her husband. "She has another year of mourning and they didn't want to appear disrespectful."

"So you maintain, because Mr. Riddle was courting Mrs. Allington and planned on proposing marriage, that he wouldn't have had a fling with a young lady below his station in the meantime?" Adele eyed him. "Come now, Mr. Dilworth, you're too much a man of the world for that."

"I didn't expect to find a woman of the world like you in this sort of town, Miss Gossling," the man said sharply. "I'm not sure that's a good thing either."

"My sister, Mr. Dilworth, has helped young ladies out of difficult situations." Jackson's voice rose like thunder. "She's well aware of how some men can abandon such young ladies to fend for themselves."

"Virgil would never do that," the man insisted. "He's the sort who would be loyal to one woman if he intended on marrying her."

"I'm sorry we've had to distress you, ma'am," Hatfield said to Mrs. Dilworth. He laid the gloves and jewelry on the table. "Do you recognize any of these?"

The woman studied them carefully. "I don't think so. They're quite beautiful, though." She reached her hand toward the brooch but the sheriff stopped her.

"I'm sorry, ma'am, but they're evidence now."

"Evidence?"

"They were found on Miss Parnell," he said in a discreet tone.

"That's not possible." The woman stared. "I knew she liked beautiful things, but this!" She stared at the brooch.

"Then you had no idea she possessed such fineries?" Jackson asked.

"Certainly not," Mr. Dilworth said. "Her wardrobe was always modest."

"Not even the comb?" Adele questioned. "She was wearing it the night of Gene's party."

"Yes, she was," Gene mumbled.

"I suppose I was too busy hosting to notice," Mrs. Dilworth lamented.

"You didn't give them to her?" Hatfield asked.

"I gave her dresses and blouses," said Mrs. Dilworth. "But that's all."

"These are very expensive items," said the sheriff. "Can you give us any clue as to where she might have gotten the money?"

Adele noticed Hazel, who had not spoken for some time, shifting in the chair so her knees pressed together.

"Arabella was always saying she was saving her pennies," Mrs. Dilworth said. "I had hoped she was saving them for — well, we spoke about her getting out of service and becoming a nurse." She covered her face with her hands.

"You had high hopes for her," Adele said kindly.

"She had high hopes for herself!" Gene snarled.

"Too high hopes," Nin guessed.

The sheriff rubbed his hands together, and Adele recognized the contemplation on his face that came when he had to put a difficult question to a suspect. Finally, he said, "Mrs. Dilworth, I'm sure you paid Miss Parnell very well, but do you think she could have saved enough pennies to buy such elegant jewelry?" He picked up the comb. "I've no conception of how much such things are, of course, but the ladies here know more than I do, and they assure me this would have cost a pretty penny."

"Easily half her salary for the year," Nin chimed in. Adele glanced at her and was surprised by the assured look on her friend's face.

"I understand what you're asking, Sheriff." The woman remained dignified. "Perhaps you're right. But where —" She left the question unresolved as she hid her face in her handkerchief.

"Oh, Mother, how naive you are!"

CHAPTER 8

This outburst came from Hazel, who had been sitting like a jackknife in the chair.

"Hazel, you'll speak respectfully to your mother or not at all!" Mr. Dilworth stormed.

"I didn't mean —" The girl put her hand over her mouth.

Adele put her arm around her. "It's all right, Hazel. You said you want to help, and the police need the truth."

"If you've something to say, Miss Dilworth, don't be afraid to say it," Jackson said. His tone was soothing and with his dashing appeal, the teenage girl warmed to him.

"She got it from — men." Her face turning red.

"You don't know that, Hazel," her mother said sharply.

"It's true, Mother," the girl insisted. "She told me."

"She told you!" Mrs. Dilworth turned white. "Arabella would never —"

"No, in your eyes, she would never." Her daughter sagged into the chair. "In your eyes, she was honorable and good."

"Oh!" Her mother let out a groan and turned away.

"Please continue, Miss Dilworth," said Hatfield.

"I'm only telling you because, just as Miss Gossling said, it might help the police," the girl said stubbornly. "She did tell me. After she finished getting Mother ready for bed, she would pass by my room. She often stopped in to boast about one thing or another."

"What did she boast about?" asked Adele.

"All the attentions she received from everyone," said the girl. "Mother and Father would have a party, and she would tell how the guests talked to her as if she were the guest of honor."

"Go on," said Hatfield.

"She would boast about the presents people gave her," she said. "She said Lavinia Murphy was always sending her little things."

"Any relation to the Nora Murphy you mentioned earlier?" asked Jackson.

"She's her daughter," said Mrs. Dilworth. Her voice was small now.

"I asked to see them and she would make some excuse." Hazel looked at Adele with sly eyes. "I don't think she ever got any presents from Lavinia. I know Lavinia and she's not the generous type."

Adele smiled. "You're very attentive, Hazel."

"Don't let anyone blind you when you grow up," Nin advised.

Hazel was clearly more at ease now. "She did show me a few things. That comb, for one. I've seen it once before."

"Did she tell you anything about it?" asked the sheriff.

"Just that a 'cordial young man' had given it to her," said the girl. "She went on and on about how he was crazy about her."

Out of the corner of her eye, Adele saw Gene stiffen.

"But she didn't say who he was?" she asked.

"If she were bragging, she would have gone all out," Nin agreed.

"She was being mysterious about it," Hazel said. "She showed me the brooch too."

"That same evening?" asked Jackson.

"No, that was later. Quite a bit later," said the girl.

"But she implied it was the same man who gave it to her?"

"She didn't say anything about that," said the girl.

Jackson's patience for the word games of young girls had clearly worn thin. "Will you please, then, tell us what she said, Miss Dilworth? We haven't got all day."

"She said a 'fine gent' gave her that," she said. "He just pulled her into a jewelry store and couldn't wait to buy it for her."

"Did she say which shop?" Adele asked.

The girl shook her head. "I wouldn't be surprised if she stole it from that jewelers on Bridge Street!"

"Hazel!" Mr. Dilworth warned.

"Did she ever show you these?" Hatfield laid the gloves on the table.

The girl shook her head. "She never mentioned them. I think they look gaudy. Just Arabella's taste."

"Hazel, that's enough!" her mother shrieked. "I won't have you talking that way about Arabella."

"And I won't have *you*, Sheriff, upsetting my wife by questioning my daughter in this manner." Mr. Dilworth shot him a look. "If it continues, I shall have to ask you to leave."

"That won't be necessary, sir," said Hatfield. "Thank you, Miss Dilworth, for telling us what you know. I think now it would be a good idea for you to go upstairs like your mother asked you to do earlier."

This time, the girl didn't argue. She walked slowly up the stairs.

"I'm rather tired too." Mrs. Dilworth twisted her handkerchief between her fingers.

"I'm sorry we have to do this, ma'am," said Sheriff Hatfield. "But we've only a few more questions. It seems as if you knew Miss Parnell best so you can help us catch her killer."

"I should like that." The woman's eyes filled with tears again. "Whatever she's done — if what Hazel says is true, that is —"

"My dear, you know how fanciful the girl can be," Mr. Dilworth said. In an almost embarrassed tone, he added, "Hazel is prone to, well, romanticizing notions."

"She reads too many French novels." Gene wrinkled his nose.

"All young girls do," Jackson said, enduring the glare from his sister and Nin.

"Young ladies have a lot more sense than people give them credit for," Adele said. "I've one working as my assistant in my shop and she's very clever."

"Hazel sounded remarkably clever herself when she talked about Miss Parnell," Nin said.

The sheriff unfolded the note they found beside the body. "I'd like you to take a look at this, Mrs. Dilworth, and tell me if you recognize the handwriting."

Adele was aware of a clucking noise echoing softly in the room. She realized it was coming from Gene, who had taken up a wooden box lying on the shelf beside him and was now drumming it against the arm of his chair.

"You mean, it's — oh!" She turned her face away but quickly recovered. "Of course, I shall do anything you ask, Sheriff." She studied it with her husband leaning over her shoulder.

"My God!" Mr. Dilworth exclaimed as he sat back. "This is madness!"

"It was found beside her," said Jackson in a quiet tone.

"And you think Arabella wrote it as she was dying?" Mr. Dilworth put his hand on his forehead. "I don't believe it!"

"Is it her handwriting, ma'am?" Hatfield asked.

"It's hard to tell," the woman admitted. "It's in print so it could be anybody's."

"Have you anything we can compare it to?" Adele asked. "A note she wrote you, perhaps?"

"Arabella had no cause to write me, Miss Gossling," said the woman.

"What about the party invitations?" she asked.

"I wrote in the names, naturally," said Mrs. Dilworth. "I always do."

"What about her parents?" Mr. Dilworth asked. "She wrote them, didn't she?" He looked at his wife.

"She never spoke of them," Mrs. Dilworth said. "I don't think she wrote them, Len."

"I didn't get the impression she was very close to her family," he admitted.

"She wrote letters to Lavinia," said Gene. "I remember her giving Lawford an envelope once when he was going down to take the letters to the post office. I saw Lavinia's name and address on it."

"We'll check with her, then," said Hatfield as he folded the note.

"Surely you can't believe Virgil is guilty based on a note!" Mr. Dilworth said. "Why, if she did write it, she must have been out of her mind."

"As I said, sir, we take into consideration all the evidence," said the sheriff. "Now, do either of you know of places where Miss Parnell spent her days off?"

"Why do you want to know that?" asked Mrs. Dilworth.

"Well, ma'am." Hatfield was clearly embarrassed. "It has to do with evidence we found that we can't disclose yet. Suffice it to say it would help us if we knew the places Miss Parnell frequented when she wasn't working."

"The Orion Club, obviously," Gene said in a dry tone. "I just told you that."

"I was thinking of remote places," said the sheriff.

"Remote?" Mrs. Dilworth frowned.

"Where she might have met someone for privacy," said Jackson.

"I know of no place Arabella mentioned where she went outside of town," said Mrs. Dilworth. "The only place I know of is the church in Caton. She went there on holidays as she said it reminded her of home." Tears filled her eyes.

Adele glanced at Nin. "Arabella went to church?"

"Oh, yes, every Sunday," said Mrs. Dilworth with a vague smile.

"I just remembered," said Gene. "Miss Parnell might have gone to the swampland in this area."

"You mean Tanner Swamp?" Jackson looked up.

"Yes, I suppose so," he said. "That general vicinity, anyway."

"How do you know this, Mr. Dilworth?" Adele asked.

He scraped the wooden box down the length of the arm. "It's rather embarrassing in front of the ladies —"

"We passed embarrassment a long time ago," Nin assured him.

He gave a laugh. "Actually, I'm surprised you don't already know."

"Enlighten us, sir," said Jackson.

"Yes, of course," he said. "That swampland has become, well, a sort of meeting place for young couples."

"Has it indeed?" Sheriff Hatfield glanced at his deputy.

"Oh, I don't mean anything immoral, Sheriff," the young man said quickly. "It's just a place where they can have a picnic or go walking without the strict eye of their parents."

"I understand completely," said the sheriff. "I had my courting days too, Mr. Dilworth."

"A handsome man like you, Sheriff, I'm sure had many courtships," Mrs. Dilworth complimented. The sheriff blushed and Adele couldn't help but smile.

"You think if Miss Parnell were stepping out with any man at the Orion Club, she would go there?" Jackson inquired.

"Oh, I didn't say that," Gene said. "I only know it's a place where young people like to go."

"Do *you* like to go there, Mr. Dilworth?" Adele eyed him.

The young man smiled. "I have much more dignified places to take the ladies who honor me with their company, Miss Gossling."

"I'm glad to hear it," she said.

"Tanner Swamp is a nasty place," Nin added. "Such foreboding plant life."

"My friend goes into the woods for her work," Adele explained.

"You work with herbs, don't you, Miss Branch?" Mrs. Dilworth smiled. "I must visit your shop one day. I've heard it's fascinating."

"I don't sell herbs because they're fascinating," Nin said stiffly.

As this made Mrs. Dilworth look down, somewhat embarrassed, the sheriff said quickly, "You say Miss Parnell left your employment just a few days before her death. She left no word where she was going?"

Mrs. Dilworth shook her head. "None." She sighed. "I wish she had."

"I never saw her again," Gene said.

"Mr. Dilworth?" Hatfield turned to him.

The man seemed to be deliberating. Then, he said, "Well, as a matter of fact —"

"You saw Arabella?" His wife turned to him.

"I thought I saw someone who looked like her going into that boarding house off the main street," he said.

"You mean Mrs. Taylor's?" Adele asked.

"Yes, I suppose that's it," he said.

"Len, why didn't you tell me?" His wife sounded distressed.

"Well, dear, she left so abruptly," he said with a condescending smile. "She was a servant, after all."

"You mean she was *only* a servant," Nin said.

"But she wasn't just a servant to you, was she, Mrs. Dilworth?" Adele looked at the woman, her heart softening a little to see the woman's genuine misery.

"No, she wasn't," Mrs. Dilworth admitted.

"We'll check with Mrs. Taylor, of course," said the sheriff. "It's quite possible she may have taken a room there until she decided what she was going to do." He rose. "I know this has been trying for you all, but I must take advantage of your indulgence further."

"What is it, Sheriff?" asked Mr. Dilworth.

"We'd like to interview your servants," he said. "They worked with Miss Parnell so they may know more about her that might be useful to us."

"Certainly, though I don't know what they could tell you," said Mrs. Dilworth. "Our servants aren't the gossiping kind."

"I'm sure," said Hatfield dryly. "And I'm afraid we must examine Miss Parnell's room."

"Oh, no!" Mrs. Dilworth covered her mouth with her handkerchief.

"The police might find something important, ma'am." Adele put her hand on her shoulder. "I'm sure you want them to find out who did this as quickly as they can."

"Of course we do," Gene said in a rough tone. "It's a distressing thing to have happened."

"For the police to go through her things —"

"But she took her things when she left you," Nin pointed out.

"Not everything, Miss Branch," said the woman. "That's why I wanted to know where she was, so I could return them."

"That's vital to us, ma'am," said Sheriff Hatfield.

Adele pressed the woman's hand. "Nin and I will be there the entire time. And the police are always respectful."

"Yes." The woman wiped her eyes. "Yes, I'm being silly. I know you must do what you must do, Sheriff."

"I'm much obliged, ma'am." Hatfield tipped his hat.

"Gene, won't you show these people to the servants' hall?" Mr. Dilworth asked. "I want to take your mother upstairs."

The young man led them through the hallway and to the back of the house where he pointed to a door. "That leads down to the kitchen and servants' quarters, Sheriff." He fiddled with the chain on his waistcoat. "I hope you find out who did this soon. I don't like to see my mother so distressed."

"We'll do our best, sir," Hatfield bowed.

~~~~~

As the hour was just after breakfast, they found the Dilworth staff finishing their meal and the table already cleared except for the coffee. Adele was surprised that, for all the Dilworths' propriety, there were only three servants. With Arabella gone, all of them were senior staff.

Lawton immediately reached for the jacket he had taken off draped on the back of his chair.

Hatfield held up his hand. "Don't bother with that, sir. Our investigations are quite relaxed."

The man sat down again.

"We could stand some coffee, though." The sheriff eyed the cook.

"Right away, Sheriff." She rose.

"I'll be happy to get it, Mrs. —" Adele smiled at the woman.

"Pinch," answered the other woman in the room who had the face of a sour cat. "We wouldn't think of it. Get these people some coffee, Mrs. Pinch, and whatever is left of the pie."

"And you are?" Adele eyed her.

"Mrs. Butler, the housekeeper." Her voice was equally sour.

Nin leaned toward Adele and whispered, "They were enemies."

Adele could imagine Arabella's vivacious ways would be at odds with this dour woman.

After they were seated with steaming coffee in front of them, the sheriff turned to Lawton. "You've been here quite some time, sir?"

The man's face shone with pride. "I've served Mr. Dilworth since he was a bachelor."

"As his manservant, I gather," Jackson said.

"Yes, sir," he said.

"And when he married, you naturally took over the running
~~~~~

of the household," Hatfield continued. Adele heard a grunt coming from Mrs. Butler.

"That I did, sir," he said.

"So you must know all the staff here pretty well," the sheriff remarked.

"Well, Sheriff," he said with a little smile, "as well as one might expect from a man in my position."

"He keeps his distance all right," Mrs. Butler mumbled.

"What did you know about Miss Parnell?" asked Hatfield. The man was silent for a time. The sheriff prompted, "Surely, man, you must know *something* about her."

To Adele's surprise, Lawton's well-worn features melted and tears gathered in his eyes. "It was a great tragedy, sir."

Jackson leaned forward. "You must have known whom she was seeing —"

Adele grabbed her brother's hand to silence him. She said in a soft tone, "Mr. Lawton, do you mind if I ask you some questions?"

"Well —" He looked at the sheriff.

"Miss Gossling has my permission to ask questions, sir," he said. "She often has a more courteous way than her brother." He glared at his deputy.

"What were your private opinions about Miss Parnell?"

"She was a shifty-eyed hussy!" This outburst came from Mrs. Butler.

"She didn't ask you," Nin snapped. "She asked him."

"She was like a daughter to me, miss," said the man.

"So you were close?" Adele asked.

"I don't know if I would say that," he said. "But I knew she missed her father, so —"

"So you became like a father to her," Nin finished. Adele could tell she was moved.

"I never overstepped my position," he insisted. "But she would sometimes chat with me while I was in the cellar choosing the wine for dinner. The thought of someone doing what that ruffian did —" His lips twisted with rage.

"Did she ever discuss people she knew?" asked Adele. "Friends from back home, other servants in other houses?"

"No one in particular, miss," he said. "She did think highly of Miss Murphy."

"Lavinia Murphy?" Jackson asked.

The man nodded. "She wrote to her often." Then, his tone deep with remorse, "Perhaps I should have encouraged her to confide in me more. I might have been of more help."

"You could hardly see she was going to be murdered," Nin said.

The man shuddered. Adele patted his hand. "We'll do everything we can to find out who did this, Mr. Lawton."

"What sort of worker was she?" Hatfield asked.

"She always went beyond the call of duty, Sheriff," he said. "She pitched in at the other houses to help wherever she could."

"She didn't hold herself above the other servants here because she was a lady's maid?" Adele asked. Mrs. Butler grunted.

"No, indeed, miss." He looked surprised.

"We heard she thought herself rather uppity."

"Some people didn't understand her," he sighed. "*I* never had any trouble with her." He gave Mrs. Butler a meaningful look.

"But you did understand her?" Adele asked.

"Miss Parnell grew up on a farm, miss, but she knew what the world was about,"

"Hm!" Mrs. Butler snarled.

"What do you mean by that, sir?" Jackson asked.

"Well, Deputy, she didn't intend to stay in domestic service all her life," he said.

"You mean she wanted to move up in the world," Nin guessed.

"And she would have," he said. "She had a mind, miss. She was pretty, certainly, but she never let people forget she also had a mind."

"So you didn't think Miss Parnell had ideas above her station," Adele remarked.

"She did and no mistake!" Mrs. Butler burst out.

"That's not true!" Mrs. Pinch, who was at the sink doing the dishes, whirled around.

"You'll get your chance." Nin waved Mrs. Butler away.

Adele turned to the woman whom she felt was anxious to talk. "She worked directly under you, Mrs. Butler?"

"She ought to have," said the woman. "But the mistress, well, Arabella had her fooled."

"I understood a lady's maid often reports directly to her mistress," Jackson said.

"She knew nothing about being a lady's maid, Deputy." The woman's dull features brightened with fury. "The mistress put her under my care so she could learn her duties. But that wasn't good enough for Arabella!"

"Why do you say that, ma'am?" the sheriff asked.

"When a young girl like that rises too quickly in the ranks, Sheriff, she takes liberties."

"What sort of liberties?" Jackson asked.

"I caught her several times using the telephone." Mrs. Butler narrowed her eyes. "Ain't none of us supposed to use it without permission."

"Maybe she had Mrs. Dilworth's permission," Nin pointed out.

"She did not!" The woman sat up straight. "The master and mistress were away at the time."

"I gave her permission, Mrs. Butler," said Mr. Lawton in a steely tone.

"You gave her permission *once*," the woman insisted. "She took liberties with the phone well after that."

"Maybe she got permission from Mrs. Dilworth before she left," Nin suggested.

"She did not, I tell you!"

Adele bit back a smile. "I'm sure you're right, Mrs. Butler. No one would know the desires of the mistress better than you."

This made the woman smile.

"Who was she calling, do you think?" Adele asked.

"Oh, some man or other," said the woman.

"Stop talking nonsense!" Mrs. Pinch whirled around again. "She was speaking to her family, I'm sure, miss. She always talked about calling them."

"They ain't got no phone out there in the country," the housekeeper snarled.

"The neighbors do!"

"She wouldn't be giggling like a silly goose on the phone to her family, would she?"

"Ladies, please, show some dignity." Mr. Lawton shrank back. "And you, Mrs. Butler, show some respect for the dead." He turned to the sheriff. "I believe Mrs. Pinch is right, Sheriff. She had a younger brother whom she was very fond of, and she said he often told little jokes that amused her."

"We've been told a footman named Douglas Cole who works for the Woods family was rather keen on her," Adele said.

"He did pay her quite a bit of attention," said Mr. Lawton. "But Miss Parnell wouldn't have anything to do with him. She told me she thought he was cocky."

Mrs. Butler snorted. "How would she know? The likes of her wouldn't even look him in the face. She was too good for him!"

"Who would she look in the face, then?" Nin asked.

"I can't say, miss, but whoever it was weren't decent."

"You seem to harbor a grudge against the girl, Mrs. Butler," Hatfield ventured.

"It's cruel, talking about the dead like that!" Mrs. Pinch said in a tearful voice.

"The police want to know what she was like, don't they?" the woman grumbled. "I'm only telling it as I saw it." She turned to Adele and began talking in a confidential tone. "Oh, she was all right when she first came. Did her work as she was told, talked about her family. A right nice girl. But I saw quickly what she was."

"How?" Adele leaned forward like a confidante.

"The way she ingratiated herself to the mistress, that's how!" the woman said. "Always popped up like a jack-in-the-box whenever the bell rang and ran up to her call."

"Well, if she were her maid, she would do that," Jackson pointed out.

"But it wouldn't take her a full twenty minutes to come back down and say the mistress wanted a hot water bottle or an aspirin or a clean handkerchief, would it?" the lady said tartly.

"That was devious of her," Nin agreed.

"I hope you spoke to Mrs. Dilworth about it," Adele said with sympathy.

"Naturally I spoke to her about it," said the woman. "As judiciously as I could. I'm a very judicious person."

"So we see," Jackson said dryly.

"Do you know what the mistress said?" She leaned toward Adele. "She said, 'I believe I can make something of her, Mrs. Butler. I aim to try.'" She wrinkled her face with distaste. "I don't approve of such things!"

"You may be right, Mrs. Butler," said Adele. "So you feel Miss Parnell played up to the family?"

"I think that's exaggerating, Miss Gossling," Mr. Lawton said.

"I think not," Nin countered.

"She was fond of the family," he insisted. "When the other servants would gossip about the families they served, she never said a word against the Dilworths."

"There were two members of the family who interested her, in my opinion," said Mrs. Butler.

"They don't want your opinion," Mrs. Pinch snapped.

"On the contrary," said Hatfield. "We're very interested in

Mrs. Butler's opinion." He sat back from the table, the plate of pie cleaned and the coffee gone.

"The mistress and the young master."

"The young master?" Jackson asked. "You mean Gene Dilworth?"

The woman nodded. "These brazen girls always have their eye on the young master. Think they're going to run off and marry them and make them a lady. Get them in trouble, more likely!"

"Mrs. Butler!" Mr. Lawton lost his temper with a roar.

"Stop!" Mrs. Pinch, who had by now finished with the dishes, sobbed in her apron.

Nin put her arms around the woman's shoulders and led her to a chair. Adele poured her a cup of coffee and placed it in her hands. "You liked her, Mrs. Pinch?"

"She was a sweet girl," the woman sobbed. "Don't believe anything that woman says! She just didn't like it that the mistress preferred Arabella to her."

Mrs. Butler, who was clearly not insensitive to the woman's feelings, bit her lip and turned away. "I'm sorry if I've upset you, Mrs. Pinch."

"I think you'd better get on with your duties, Mrs. Butler," said Mr. Lawton in a quiet but authoritative tone. "If the police are finished with you, that is."

"We're finished with both of you, sir," said Hatfield. "We don't want to keep you from your work."

Both the senior servants seemed only too glad to escape the warm kitchen.

"She was a good girl," Mrs. Pinch lamented. "She always helped me with the dinner on Saturday nights. The master and mistress often have company and at the last minute." She dabbed her eyes. "My old head don't work as good as it used to so she would come up with ideas on how to feed the extra guests and even go to the store for me."

"That was very kind of her," Adele said.

"She used to read the Bible to me every Sunday night. I can't go to church, you see, as I get dizzy spells. Comes from standing on my feet all day for twenty years." She gave a little laugh.

Adele smiled. "That was kind of her too."

"She left me her Bible when she went," said the woman. "Oh, I can't understand it!"

"Death is difficult to understand when it's sudden," Adele said with sympathy.

"I mean her leaving like she did." The woman sighed. "Simply disappeared one day."

"She didn't leave you a note?" Jackson asked.

The woman shook her head. "I expect she didn't have time."

"Why do you think she left so suddenly?" Hatfield asked.

"She once said, 'When my opportunity comes, Ivy, I shall grab it with both hands.'"

"That's just what she did, isn't it?" Nin sighed.

"And look where it got her!" Mrs. Pinch sobbed again.

"A woman must take risks sometimes to get on in the world," Adele said gently.

"But to be killed and left in some stranger's conservatory like that?" The woman blew her nose. "Oh, we've known all about it."

"I'm sorry you had to hear that," Adele said. "Mrs. Pinch, you can help us a great deal since you knew Miss Parnell so well. Do you know of any enemies she had?"

"That Mrs. Butler!" the woman choked. "She hated the sight of her."

"I hardly think she would have killed because of that." Adele patted the woman's hand.

The blood drained from Mrs. Pinch's face. "Oh, sakes, I wasn't saying — why, Mrs. Butler wouldn't hurt a lamb, except with her words."

"I'm sure you're right, ma'am," said the sheriff in a serious tone, though Adele could see he was trying to hold back his amusement at the idea that the housekeeper could have shot

Arabella Parnell three times in the back and dragged her into Mr. Riddle's conservatory.

"I don't think she had enemies," Mrs. Pinch continued.

Hatfield put the jewelry and gloves on the table. "We found these among her things."

Mrs. Pinch stared at them. "What a lovely brooch!"

"Then you've never seen them?" Adele asked.

"Oh, she talked about something like that to Miss Dilworth one day, but I thought she was only teasing," said the woman.

"Then you have no idea who bought them for her," said Jackson.

"She must have bought them for herself," she lamented.

"On a lady's maid's salary?" The sheriff eyed her.

The woman's face twisted with indignation. "She saved her money, Sheriff. She had a little piggy bank her father gave her and she put her money in there. What was left of it at the end of the month."

"Thank you, ma'am." Hatfield put the gloves back in their wrapping and in his pocket. "We won't distress you further, but we would like to see that Bible Miss Parnell left you."

"Certainly, Sheriff." She rose. "But — you will give it back to me, won't you?"

"Of course he will, Mrs. Pinch," Adele assured her, pressing her hand.

"It's precious to me now that —" And she ran out of the kitchen, sobbing into her handkerchief.

CHAPTER 9

They all sat back and took a breath. Jackson was the first to speak.

"Well, sir, we have a sphynx on our hands," he said.

"It seems there were two sides to Miss Parnell," Hatfield agreed.

"I prefer to refer to her as Arabella," Nin said. "We have intimate knowledge of her, after all."

"To some she was a church-going, considerate, and hard-working young woman," Adele mused. "To others, she was a scheming and conniving hussy who got what she wanted out of men."

"I don't put much stock in what Mrs. Butler said," Jackson said. "We know there's always jealousy amongst the servants in any house."

"Not that she didn't have good reason for being jealous," Hatfield added. "I would be too if I were a housekeeper who saw a subordinate getting into her mistress's good graces."

"Not to mention being so familiar with the mistress she had her room among the family rather than the servants' quarters," Nin said.

"I don't think Mrs. Dilworth would take it that far," Jackson said.

"We saw Arabella running up the stairs and slamming the door to a room at the end of the hall," Adele said. "I would hardly think she were going to seek comfort in an empty room."

"That is interesting," the sheriff said with a whistle.

"What's even more interesting is she left a position where everything was clearly to her advantage," Jackson said. "It's like killing the goose that lays the golden egg ."

"Maybe that's why she left," Nin suggested. "She found another goose that laid bigger golden eggs." This made Jackson smile.

"Her leaving so suddenly is mysterious," Adele admitted. "Even if she were trying to better herself. According to Mrs. Pinch, she was more considerate than that, at least to her."

"When a man asks a woman to run away with him, she hardly has time to be considerate," Jackson said.

"Is that what you think, Mr. Gossling?" Nin eyed him. "She ran off to get married?"

"Perhaps she thought the Dilworths would try to stop her," he suggested.

"I don't believe that for a moment, Jack," said Adele. "I'll admit we can't jump to conclusions, though. It's not uncommon for a domestic servant to see her way out of service through marriage."

"The easy way out," Nin added in a grim tone.

"There doesn't seem to be any evidence she was being courted by anyone," Adele said. "Anyone that would induce her to elope, that is."

"What about this 'cordial young man' and 'fine old gent?'" Nin pointed out.

"You and I know when a woman talks freely about a man, the last thing on her mind is marriage," Adele said.

"Do you think Mr. Riddle is the 'fine old gent,' sir?" Jackson asked.

"What do *you* think, Deputy?"

"It's possible," he said.

"And the cordial young man might be this Douglas Cole fellow," the sheriff said.

"Do you really think —" Jackson stopped as Mrs. Pinch came in, holding the Bible with both hands.

"A handsome thing," Adele murmured as the woman set it down. It was indeed a rather majestic book, large and thick and encrusted with silver.

Mrs. Pinch looked at it, her eyes glistening. "Thank you, miss."

"It was a lovely gift she gave you." Adele brushed her hand delicately over the cover.

"Miss Parnell clearly came from a family that took their faith very seriously," Jackson said as he admired the silver etchings.

Adele glanced at the inside page. A dedication in florid handwriting said *To our dear daughter, may God's peace follow your every footstep. "The wisest of women builds her house, but folly with her own hands tears it down."*

"I imagine this was a gift given to her when she left home," the sheriff said.

Mrs. Pinch nodded. "Arabella said it was her family's parting gift to her." Her eyes filled with tears. "For her to give me such a precious thing!"

"She thought highly of your friendship," Adele said kindly. "This Bible must have cost her family a fortune."

"She ought to have told you her plans," Nin growled. "One doesn't do such things to a friend." She glanced meaningfully at Adele.

"Oh, but she must have had her reasons," Mrs. Pinch objected. "Arabella was the sort who always did things for a reason."

"A very intentional young lady." Hatfield rose. "Thank you for giving this to us, Mrs. Pinch. I promise we shall return it to you unharmed. And now, if you'll show us to Miss Parnell's room —"

The woman obliged, though Adele could see she was still

hesitant as she led them with careful steps up the stairs they had come down and into the main house. Upstairs, all was rather too quiet and the closed doors looked apprehensive. Adele imagined Mr. and Mrs. Dilworth resting and Hazel in her room, all quietly contemplating what had just befallen them. At the end of the hallway was a small nook containing a table with a candlestick telephone. Gene Dilworth, with his back to them, had the receiver in his hand. Although she couldn't make out any words, she heard the urgency in his low tone.

The first thing Adele noted about Arabella's room was how small it was. But it was very clean and arranged well. The bed set in the corner made the rest of the room look bigger than it was. The walls were bare but there was evidence some small pictures had adorned one side at one time. The washbasin stood in one corner and a small table in the other. There was even a small closet in the room.

"Her initial intention was to stay," Adele pronounced.

Jackson stared at her. "How in the world do you know that, Del?"

"She arranged the furnishings in that way," she said.

"It does seem as if she made the most out of what little space she had," the sheriff agreed.

"It must be awful to spend one's nights, year after year in such a tiny place," Nin said. Adele knew her friend was feeling the suffocation of the small space so she opened the door. Nin, grateful, retreated to the hallway just outside of it.

"At least we won't need to spend much time here," Jackson said as he opened the closet door. "Well, look at this, sir!"

Hatfield peered inside the closet. "Adele, what do you make of these?" He put two dresses on the bed. Both were made of cotton and both were well-worn and had clearly been mended many times. Their practical shades of brown and gray made them look severe.

"You may have been right, Jack," she said.

"A nice change, seeing as you're so eager at times to prove me wrong." He grinned. "Would you care to explain how I was right so I can repeat the miracle in the future?"

She swiped at him with the gloves she had taken off with a laugh. "You said her gentleman friend must have been generous. Clearly he was."

"He was so generous, she didn't even have to take her old clothes with her," Nin agreed.

"I don't blame her." Adele fingered the straight edge of the skirt. "These must have been the clothes she brought with her when she left home. Rather grim."

"We'll verify that with her parents." Hatfield gathered both dresses and handed them to Jackson.

"Whoever he was, he spared no expense in decking her out," Jackson remarked.

"And yet, no one knows who he is," Hatfield said. "Or even if there were several men in her life."

Suddenly, Nin began to cough. It was a choking kind of cough that alarmed Adele and she escorted her friend out of the room. The hall had a small bench and also a window. She opened the window as far as it would go. The chilly air seemed to calm her friend.

"Was it so stifling in there, dear?" she asked gently.

"It wasn't that." Nin's eyes were damp but had the glassy finish of when she had an aura. "It was suddenly crowded."

"Four people in a room like that makes for a crowd," Adele agreed.

"No, more! More!"

"Are you all right, Miss Branch?" Jackson wandered into the hall, and Adele was touched by the genuine concern on his face.

"That room." Nin pressed her hand to her forehead. "Suddenly it was like there were a million people in it."

"I highly doubt you could get five in there, much less a million," he said with amusement.

"Don't mock me, Mr. Gossling!" Nin jumped up. "I tell you, there were lots of people in there. And the room reeked of cigars."

"I smelled nothing," he said.

"No, you wouldn't," she seethed. "You wouldn't smell a pan of fried bacon if it were right under your nose!"

"There is no need to get nasty, Miss Branch," he mumbled.

"If Nin says she felt there were lots of people, it means something, Jack," Adele said. "You ought to know that by now."

He shrugged and returned to the room.

"Will you be all right, dear?" Adele pressed her friend's hand.

Nin nodded. "If I could just stay here near the window for a while."

"There's no need for you to go in there again," Adele said. "I want to look for something, though. Can I leave you for a moment?"

Her friend smiled. "You're always so thoughtful, Adele."

Adele pressed her hand and returned to the room. She started poking around the floor with the end of her parasol. Glancing inside the tiny trash can, she regretted it was empty. She even looked under the mattress.

Hatfield watched her with a grin. "May I ask what you're looking for? It's clear you're looking for something in particular."

"Probably one of Del's 'ideas,'" Jackson mumbled.

"As a matter of fact, I have a very practical reason for looking," said Adele. "Mrs. Dilworth said she had no letters from Arabella. I was hoping Arabella might have left something behind here — some scrap of paper or something with her handwriting."

"Even if she had, it would hardly be enough for us to make an identification," Jackson said.

"I'm sure we can get confirmation from her parents about the note, if that's what you're thinking." The sheriff glanced around the room. "I think we're finished here, Deputy."

"We knew we wouldn't find much, sir," said Jackson. "Not

with the young woman having left the place a few days before she was killed."

"Nary a note nor a letter," Adele lamented. She slid her parasol all the way under the small bed and felt some obstruction. She pulled it out. Coated with dust was a thin piece of paper smeared with ink.

"She must have missed that note," Hatfield stooped to pick it up.

"I don't think it is a note," Adele said. Indeed, there was heavy ink with the emblem of *Ada's Millinery* on it as well as some numbers.

"A bill." Jackson studied it. "At least we know she did her shopping in town."

"Or some of it anyway," said the sheriff. "We'll certainly question Miss Stevens about this."

"Two skirts and two blouses," Adele remarked as she read the contents. "And those are Ada's most expensive materials too."

"Could they have been custom-made?" Jackson asked.

"At those prices, I wouldn't be surprised," Adele said ruefully. "Ada told me since the Lucy Blackstone case got in the papers, she's been asked to do more custom-made clothes."

"Another lady who is getting too big for her britches." Jackson sniffed.

"A woman has a right to earn her living, Jack," his sister snapped.

"But at prices like this?" He tapped the page. "That's more than what you used to pay for a dress in San Francisco!"

"And paid it was." Hatfield pointed to the PAID stamp across the bill. He brushed off the dust and put it in his pocket. "I confess, I'm more than anxious to speak with Mr. Riddle again."

"You really think he might be the generous gentleman friend?' Adele asked. "Leaving his mark in paid bills? It seems unlikely."

"Men of privilege can be careless, Del," said Jackson in a knowing voice.

"Even I know that, Deputy," said Hatfield. Jackson blushed, as if he had forgotten the sheriff, in spite of his mother having married an English nobleman, came from hard-working stock.

They went outside. Nin leaned against the open window, letting the wind blow through her hair.

"I hope you're feeling better, Miss Branch," Hatfield said kindly.

"It was an aura," she said.

"A million people in the room," Jackson remarked. "I suppose your aura didn't tell you who they were? We might have picked out the murderer among them."

The woman glared at him with her sparkling green eyes. "I don't see visions, Mr. Gossling. You know that."

"Even if you did, we could hardly convict a criminal on the evidence of a vision," said the sheriff with a chuckle.

As they made their way back to the front hall, Adele saw Gene was still on the phone. He turned when he heard them and abruptly put the receiver back on the hook.

"I see you found what you were looking for, Sheriff." He eyed the bundles under Jackson's arms.

"Nothing of importance, sir," said Hatfield.

Gene led them down the stairs. "Father asked me to see you out. I'm afraid he's a little upset about all this."

"That's understandable, sir," said Jackson. "First a former servant found dead and in his friend's house —"

"He doesn't believe Virgil had anything to do with it for a moment," Gene insisted.

"But you do?" Adele eyed him.

"I never said that, Miss Gossling." He stiffened.

"You don't like him," Nin said. "You were rude to him at the party."

"Was I?" He blinked. "Well, he was late."

"You were more than eager to bring his name up," Nin observed with her usual blunt insight.

Gene glanced up the stairs, then lowered his voice. "There's a reason for that."

"Yes?" Hatfield glanced at him. "Something you didn't mention before about seeing him and Miss Parnell?"

"Well, no, not that," he said. "You mentioned Arabella was shot."

"Indeed," said the sheriff.

"I happen to know Virgil owns a gun," he said. "He showed it to my father and me once. He's very proud of it."

"We're aware he has a gun, sir," said Jackson.

"Oh, did he tell you?" The young man looked disappointed. "Well, then, I'm sure I'm wrong. A man who killed a woman doesn't go around showing off his gun to the police, does he?"

As he helped her into her coat, Adele ventured, "Is everything all right, Mr. Dilworth?"

"This murder business is very distressing."

"I meant the phone call," she said. "I saw you on the phone when we went upstairs. Nothing serious, I hope?"

"A college chum dealing with a romantic crisis." He grinned. "Quite petty, really."

When they climbed into the police car, Adele glanced back. The young man was still standing at the doorway with his hand gripping the doorframe and an agitated look on his face.

CHAPTER 10

The next morning Adele sat at the breakfast table lost in thought while Jackson read the *Arrojo Courier* over his oatmeal. The previous day's events buzzed in her mind like bees around a hive, each bee representing a different idea: Arabella leaving the Dilworths, Mrs. Butler's antagonism, Mrs. Pinch's grief, Gene Dilworth's urgent phone call. She realized long ago what Jackson once told her about solving crimes was true — one gathered a link, then another, then another, and put them together to form an unbroken chain of evidence.

"You've been working on that same piece of toast for ten minutes." Her brother flipped over the newspaper. "You're making Tomas nervous."

Adele glanced back at the dedicated man she had employed since he had taken her wagon filled with furniture to her new house in Arrojo. His sensitive face was indeed wrinkled with worry, and he was rubbing his hands.

She smiled reassuringly and made a show of taking two more slices of toast and putting generous amounts of butter and marmalade on them. His face relaxed.

"Will you be free this afternoon?" Jackson asked.

"It depends what for," she said. "I was planning on doing some inventory on the new machines I received."

"Hatfield told me last night he wants to interview the Parnells today." He poured himself more coffee.

"They're in town?"

"Of course they are," he said. "You don't expect them to leave their daughter's body to be buried in a strange cemetery, do you?"

"I forgot about that," she said softly. "I forgot she came from Fresno."

"She certainly acquired the habits of the more worldly California girls rather quickly," he remarked.

"They want to bury her in a family plot, I imagine," Adele murmured.

"The sheriff wants to question them before they leave," Jackson continued. "He even asked Dr. Rhodes to withhold the release of the body until we've talked to them."

"You think they can shed some light on the crime?" Adele asked.

He shrugged. "She might have said something in her letters to them about some trouble she was in or there might even be someone she left behind in Fresno who wasn't pleased with her new life."

"Her new expensive life," Adele corrected, finishing off the second slice of toast.

"A modest young lady often acquires such a life when someone else teaches it to her," he countered.

"You mean some man who can afford expensive habits." Adele eyed him. "I don't imagine you've had personal experience, Jack."

He grinned. "You know me better than that." In a more serious tone, he added, "I've known quite a few men who have done just that. And they're usually middle-aged men looking for their youth in the eyes of a pretty young lady with a hankering for pretty things."

"That might describe Arabella Parnell and Virgil Riddle perfectly," Adele said, "if that was the situation."

"We're not taking anything for granted, Del." He unhooked his jacket from behind his chair, a habit that always made Tomas grit his teeth.

“Including a footman who might have lost his head and gotten hold of a gun?” Adele eyed him. “Hatfield seems to be taking the mayor’s idea seriously.”

“Too seriously,” Jackson snorted.

“He has to deal with the politics of his position, Jack, not you,” Adele reminded him.

Her brother slipped into his coat and adjusted the wide shoulders. “Hatfield requested that you and Miss Branch be there when we speak to the Parnells. He has a notion it's going to be difficult for Mrs. Parnell and having ladies around might ease her discomfort."

“Naturally, we’ll do all we can,” Adele promised.

She walked into town with Jackson and left him at the station. As she neared her shop, a feeling of apprehension rose as she anticipated the nagging she would get from townspeople for details of the crime Missy had written about for the morning paper.

But it seemed Missy, with her first-hand knowledge, had gotten the better of her, and there were only a few customers throughout the morning. Most came in to make inquiries about when she would have the new typewriter room finished. Mr. Abbott, owner of the Arrojo Finance Company and a rare customer, came in to discuss the possibility of replacing the typewriters his clerks were now using which, he admitted, were "older than Methuselah” with new ones, and she promised the moment the room was finished, he could come in and choose what he liked and she would give him the wholesale price.

In spite of the good business she did that morning, she shut the shop doors with shaking hands that afternoon. Nin, too, was jittery as they walked to the Arrojo Hotel where the sheriff, sensitive to the Parnells' reduced finances, had convinced the town council to put them up for a few nights.

"How does one tell the parents of a girl whose whole life was ahead of her that she was brutally shot in the back three times?" Adele sighed.

"We told the Blackstones when their daughter was found murdered in your backyard," Nin pointed out.

"I know, dear, but that was different," Adele said. "The Blackstones were people who knew the world."

"These people are innocents," Nin agreed. "I don't imagine they've done much in their lives except tend their farm."

"I trust the sheriff to be delicate," Adele said. "But Jack can be a bulldog sometimes."

"He does see things as too black and white," Nin agreed. "And if he starts in on an older man having courted their daughter —"

" — Mr. Parnell might pull out his shotgun," Adele finished with a smile. "I'll make sure to stomp on his foot if it looks as if he's going that way. I used to do that when we were children, and he tried to get the best of my friends." Nin laughed.

Mrs. Bell, who owned the hotel with her husband, went to them immediately. "The sheriff says to go right up, Miss Gossling," she said. "Room 281." Her voice lowered. "Right homely people, those Parnells. It's hard to imagine they could have had a girl like that."

"That's an unkind thing to say," Nin snapped.

The woman stiffened. "I thought Miss Gossling would want to know!"

But Adele was almost glad Mrs. Bell made her remark, for it prepared her when they walked into the room. Hatfield and Jackson were already there, leaning against the wall. Adele's heart went out to the couple who looked broken and deflated. Mr. Parnell's collar was too large for him as was the hat he held in his lap. Mrs. Parnell's dress, much like the ones her daughter had left behind, was made of gunny sack and hung on her like ice melting to the ground.

Neither of them looked up as the sheriff made the introductions. They only gave a soft nod of acknowledgment. Nin sat on the bed, her eyes troubled.

No one said a word for a moment. Then, Adele, clearing her throat, began. "Mrs. Pinch showed us the lovely Bible you gave your daughter before she left home."

"It was the least we could do," Mrs. Parnell said, her voice very soft.

"It must have cost you a pretty penny," Nin remarked. Jackson glared at her.

Mr. Parnell answered in a dull tone, "Nothing was too good for our Annie. She loved reading aloud to her brothers and sisters."

Mrs. Parnell gave a small sob and buried her face in her handkerchief.

"We know this is most distressing for you," Hatfield said. "But we must ask questions in cases like this."

"Cases like this?" Mr. Parnell blinked. "Then what that newspaper lady said was right? Someone — someone took our Annie's life?"

"Newspaper lady?" the sheriff asked. "You mean Miss Grace?"

The man nodded. "She came by asking questions."

"I'm sorry she did that." Hatfield's face became bull-like. "I shall have a stern word with her about interfering with the law."

"Oh, they weren't them kind of questions," Mrs. Parnell said quickly. "She wanted to know about Annie. What she liked, how much schooling she'd had, why she left the farm —"

"Why did she leave the farm, Mrs. Parnell?" Adele asked.

The woman stared at her. "I don't rightly know."

"She never told you?" asked Jackson.

"I expect she had an itch," Mr. Parnell said. "You know, like young girls get. They get an itch to see the city, and then they come back, marry some local boy, and forget all about it."

"Was there any local boy she was interested in?" asked Hatfield.

"I really can't tell you, Sheriff." The man turned to his wife. "She tell you 'bout someone, Mary?"

"There was Sam Valentine's boy she went to the fair with," Mrs. Parnell recalled.

"Land sakes, woman, she was ten at the time!" Her husband sniffed. "Don't recall seeing her with the boy after that, though."

"I can't remember anybody," said the woman.

Her husband shrugged. "She more likely would tell you than me."

"She didn't tell me nothing," his wife barked.

Adele noted the look Jackson shot the sheriff. Hatfield continued in a soft tone, "Did she ever write you about any of her acquaintances?"

"No one I can recall," said Mr. Parnell. "But then, she didn't write more than a few times."

"You mean she didn't write at all?" Jackson asked.

"As I said, she wrote a few times."

"Three times," said Mrs. Parnell. "I wish I'd kept 'em!"

"You — didn't keep the letters?" Again, Jackson shot the sheriff a look.

“She always sounded fine,” said the woman. “She was working hard but she was fine. Didn’t seem much to keep.”

"We don't have a lot of space in our cabin, Deputy," said Mr. Parnell in a defensive tone. "Ain't got the room for keeping letters."

"But there were only three," Nin said.

"Things like that aren't important to us, Miss Branch," said Mrs. Parnell, equally defensive. "I suppose that's why Annie hardly wrote. She knew we wouldn't want to clutter the cabin with papers."

"She didn't write you about anyone she had met?" Jackson persisted. "Friends, for instance?"

"Oh, friends!" Mrs. Parnell seemed relieved. "I thought you meant — you don't mean men friends?" Her eyes shifted toward the small bedside table. Adele realized she was looking at the large Bible that sat on top.

"I'm sure she had many friends," she said gently.

"She was such a lively girl!" The woman's eyes filled with tears.

"Never let the grass grow under her feet," Mr. Parnell added.

"Few women do these days," Nin said dryly.

Jackson took out his pad and pencil. "Can you give us some names of people she mentioned?"

"No one in particular." Mr. Parnell shook his head.

"She didn't mention a man by the name of Douglas Cole?" Hatfield asked. He added quickly, "They worked together sometimes."

"No one by that name," Mrs. Parnell said. Her entire face sagged off the bone. "Just can't understand why she left us!"

"She was anxious to move on to other things," Adele offered.

"Farm life is hard," Nin said, her voice sympathetic.

"She could have stayed in Fresno for that," sniffed the dead girl's father. "Sam Valentine's boy would have married her just like that."

"You said you saw her with him when she was ten," Nin said. "How could you know a thing like that?"

"He would have married her, I tell you." The man was obstinate.

His tone, though hardly raised, had the effect of silencing the room for a few moments. Adele saw the sheriff was contemplating his next move.

Hatfield took the jewelry and gloves from the bag he had brought and put them on the bed. "I don't suppose you know anything about these?"

The bewildered look on their faces deepened. Sunlight gleaming from the window struck the jewels, making them glitter, and the gloves, making the silk gleam.

"They were Annie's?" Mrs. Parnell was the first to speak.

"We found them near —" Jackson stopped so abruptly that Adele was surprised until she saw the sheriff had grabbed his arm. "We found them among her things," her brother corrected.

"She always liked fine things," Mr. Parnell said.

"That's right." Mrs. Parnell agreed. "She bought that hat once, remember, Abe? She saw it in the window of March's General Store and vowed she would get it. She saved for three years. 'Course it wasn't exactly the latest style by then, but she bought it!" The woman's face shone with pride.

There was more silence. Hatfield said slowly, "She never told you she had these things?"

Mr. Parnell blinked. "Well, I suppose friends of hers might have bought her presents. Her sisters were always giving her things they found in the woods. She was like that." He smiled vaguely. "She was sweet to people, and they always wanted to give her things."

"Yes," Adele murmured. "Give her things."

Hatfield quickly put the evidence in the bag and rose. "Thank you very much, Mr. and Mrs. Parnell. We're very sorry to intrude upon your grief."

"You don't want to ask us any more questions?" Mr. Parnell looked up at him.

"Not just now, sir," the sheriff mumbled. "I'll tell Dr. Rhodes you can take Miss Parnell home now."

"We'll bury her in the family plot," lamented Mrs. Parnell. "Got a place there for all of us. We just didn't think it would be so soon." The woman buried her face in her handkerchief.

Adele put her hand on the woman's shoulder and Nin put her arms around her as a mother might a child.

~~~~~
~~~~~

"The devil!" Hatfield growled the moment they were on the street.

"Not the devil, sir." Jackson chuckled. "Adam and Eve."

"I told you they were innocents." Nin pulled her shawl closer around her shoulders.

"That was more than innocence, Miss Branch," Jackson said. "That was sheer ignorance."

"It was painful to watch," Adele agreed. "I'm glad you didn't press them, Sheriff."

"I didn't see much point since they knew practically nothing," said Hatfield. "Certainly nothing that would help us." He sighed. "It certainly isn't the first time we've questioned a witness we thought could help us and it turned out a waste of time, eh, Jackson?"

"To think they knew absolutely nothing about their daughter!" Jackson growled.

"And they were too exhausted to ask," Nin added.

"You can't blame them, Jack," Adele pointed out. "How were they to know if she only wrote three letters?"

"She had nothing to say to them except that she was fine," Nin pointed out.

"I don't imagine she would tell them even if she wasn't," Adele said. "I expect she wouldn't want to worry them."

"More likely she knew she'd get an earful of Bible quotes if she did," Nin snarled.

Adele took her friend's arm as they walked toward the station. "That Bible they gave her made it clear they didn't trust her to behave in a moral way."

"And it seems more likely than not that they were right," Jackson said.

"Because she was finally free from the burdens of farm life and wanted to enjoy her freedom?" Adele shot him a look. "Why shouldn't she?"

"But how far did she go?" he countered. "And was it far enough to warrant her death?"

"That's what we must find out, Deputy," Sheriff Hatfield said.

"And where do we go next to do that, Sheriff?" Adele asked.

He grinned. "An old friend of yours, Adele."

CHAPTER 11

Adele had developed a kinder attitude toward Mrs. Taylor since they had encountered murder at her house three years before. The woman had come to appreciate Adele and her progressive ways and even defended her when Mrs. Faderman and her brood voiced opposition to the pounding and the dust the workers produced for Adele's new wing.

Entering Mrs. Taylor's boarding house, Adele was struck by the neatness of the rooms and the proprietary atmosphere. Mrs. Taylor came out of the dining room, a dust rag in her hand and a tart look on her face. But her look softened when she saw them.

"Why, Sheriff! Forgive my messiness." She smoothed her hair which did look more wiry than usual and brushed a smear of dust from her apron. "Lilly, that thoughtless girl, *would* be down with influenza just now, and me with a full house!"

"It's not her fault she's sick," Nin said sternly. "You ought to give her ginger tea."

"Nin will bring some around for you, Mrs. Taylor," Adele said kindly. Her friend nodded in agreement.

"I shall do just that," said the woman with a smile. "I hope nothing is wrong."

"We're here on business, Mrs. Taylor," Hatfield said.

"Don't tell me it's about this lady's maid." The woman shuddered. "I saw it in the papers, of course." She led them into the parlor.

"We heard you may have had some dealings with Miss Parnell," said Jackson.

"I don't know what you mean by 'dealings,' I'm sure, Deputy." She sniffed. "I'm running a boarding house."

"You took her in, though, didn't you?" asked the sheriff.

"Miss Parnell took a room," Adele corrected. "Mrs. Taylor did not take her in."

"Exactly, Miss Gossling," the woman said. "My boarding house isn't a charity ward, Sheriff."

"So she *did* take a room from you?" Hatfield glanced at Jackson. She knew he was thinking that one of his question marks was now answered.

"Why, certainly." The woman looked surprised. "Why, did someone tell you she hadn't?"

"On the contrary," said Nin. "Someone told us she had but no one believed it."

Mrs. Taylor pressed the back of her head again. "Well, I can tell you, she did."

"When was this?" asked Jackson.

"A few days ago," said the woman.

"Mrs. Taylor." Adele could tell Sheriff Hatfield was trying hard to hold on to his patience. "This is a murder investigation, as you well know. We need you to be as specific as possible. Can you please tell us the day she arrived and the day she left?"

"She arrived last Sunday," said the woman promptly. "As for when she left — well, she didn't really because — because —"

"She was killed before she could leave," Nin finished.

Mrs. Taylor winced. "I wish you would put things more delicately, Miss Branch."

"So she was here two days," said Jackson.

"Yes, and a surprise it was," the woman mumbled.

"Why do you say that, Mrs. Taylor?" Adele asked.

"The look on her face when I showed her the room." She sniffed. "New curtains and all. She looked at it as if she were too good for it."

"So you expected her to leave right away?" the sheriff asked.

"Frankly, I didn't expect her to stay at all," said Mrs. Taylor. "She wanted her meals sent up to her room, and I told her there was no room service in my house and everyone ate in the dining room. It's more social that way." She smiled with pride. "I thought for certain she would turn around on those high heels of hers and walk out, but she only said, 'No matter' and gave me three days' pay in advance." She looked sheepish. "Must I give the money back, Sheriff?"

"I think you ought to for the one day she wasn't here," Hatfield said, smiling. "I'll send Edison over to collect Miss Parnell's things for her parents and you can give it to him."

"It's my policy —"

"Her parents need the money, Mrs. Taylor," Adele said. "They're poor farmers with many mouths to feed."

The woman's face softened. "Oh, well, in that case, I shall give them the entire three days."

"That's very charitable of you, ma'am," Jackson said with a tip of his hat.

"'Give, and it will be given to you,'" Mrs. Taylor quoted.

"Yes, indeed, ma'am," Hatfield said politely. "Did Miss Parnell come down for meals?"

"And the evening parlor entertainments?" Adele added.

Mrs. Taylor smiled. "How nice you remembered, Miss Gossling. But, no, she never showed her face. I don't think any of the male boarders here even met her. Officially, at least."

"That's a change," Nin mumbled.

"You're certain she never came down?" Jackson asked. "She never spoke with any of the boarders?"

"I didn't say that," said Mrs. Taylor. "I saw her chatting a bit to Iona. You remember Iona Hoddle?"

Hatfield nodded. "A very amiable young woman."

"Iona has the sweetness of a lamb," Mrs. Taylor said. "Even to those who scarcely deserve it."

"She might be able to help us," said the sheriff. "It might very well be she was the last one to see Miss Parnell alive."

"Heavens!" Mrs. Taylor turned pale. "Don't you go upsetting her, Sheriff."

"We won't, ma'am," he promised. "Did Miss Parnell have any visitors while she was here?"

Mrs. Taylor's face was stiff. "You know how strict I am with my rules, Sheriff."

"Surely, ma'am," he said. "But your guests do have visitors sometimes, don't they?"

"Naturally," she said. "In the parlor with the door open."

"Very sensible, ma'am," Jackson said.

"So you would have known if she had a visitor," Adele said.

"Unless she snuck them upstairs to her room," Nin said.

"No one sneaks anybody into this house, Miss Branch," Mrs. Taylor snapped. "No one."

Adele could tell Nin wanted to remind her about the Millie Gibb case but her friend only smiled sweetly.

"You've been a great help, ma'am," Sheriff Hatfield said and Jackson closed his notepad, putting his pencil in his pocket. "One more thing. We'd like to take a look at Miss Parnell's things before Edison arrives."

"Really, Sheriff," The woman growled, "this habit you have of rummaging through a young woman's possessions —"

"Only when she's dead," Nin said.

"I know how you feel about that, ma'am," he said kindly. "But if we're to find out who killed Miss Parnell, we must be thorough."

"There might be something of importance, Mrs. Taylor," Adele said. "A letter, perhaps, or a photograph, or even a diary."

"There will be ladies present, ma'am." Jackson said.

"We'll make sure they don't look where they're not supposed to," Nin promised.

"Thank you, Miss Branch, that's very reassuring," said the woman. "Well, I suppose it can't be helped, can it?"

She led them up the stairs to the wing where the women boarders lived. As they stepped down the hall, Adele realized she was leading them to the room where Millie Gibb was found dead.

Her friend leaned toward her. "Isn't this —"

"Shhhh!" Adele cautioned.

When Mrs. Taylor left, Jackson frowned. "I see Mrs. Taylor doesn't let time slip by her."

"It's been three years," Sheriff Hatfield pointed out. "You can hardly expect the woman to board up one of her rooms."

"She has to make a living, Jack," Adele objected.

"No one needs to know a dead body was found here," Nin added.

"Well, one can't tell anything was found here," Hatfield remarked as he peered through the doorway. "It seems at least she's renewed everything."

"Compared to Arabella's things, though, the room certainly looks shabby," Adele remarked. "You were right, Jack. She left her old things because she could afford better."

"Or her gentleman friend could." Jackson turned up the collars of the dresses and jackets. "No label anywhere. The man was discreet."

"And no letters," Adele said, looking around. "Not even from her parents."

"I didn't notice Mr. and Mrs. Parnell spoke of any letters they sent her," Jackson said. "I don't imagine they would have much time for letter-writing."

"Not even to their own daughter," Adele murmured.

"Not everyone believes in the sanctity of pen and paper, dear sister," Jackson remarked.

"No letters from beaus either," Nin said. "Or she burned them."

"I don't think so," Adele said thoughtfully. "Hazel said she bragged about her gentleman friends. I find it hard to believe a woman like that would throw away letters."

"Unless they were from married men," Nin pointed out.

"You speak like the French novels, Miss Branch," Jackson sniffed.

"As I've never read a French novel, I can't say, Mr. Gossling," she answered. "I'm surprised you would know French novels, though."

Adele hid her smile as Jackson turned red. "No letters also means no letters from friends," she said. "Like this Lavinia Murphy."

"Perhaps she chose to visit the young lady," the sheriff suggested. "We'll find out when we speak with her. But first we interview Miss Hoddle."

"May I make a suggestion, Sheriff?" Adele leaned against her parasol.

"Please do, Adele," he said cordially.

"Let Nin and me speak with Iona," she said. "She's been in a rather delicate state since Millie's death, especially where the police are concerned."

"She escapes to the back of Raleigh's Store every time Mrs. Faderman mentions the police," Nin agreed.

"If you and Jack went, I don't think you would get much out of her," said Adele.

"I don't think it's a good idea, sir," Jackson jumped in. "You remember what the mayor told you —"

Adele was alert. "What did the mayor tell you?"

"To make sure you kept your interest in police business to the parlor," Jackson said with a little self-righteousness.

"Did he, Sheriff?" Adele looked at the man.

Hatfield cleared his throat. "He did stop by the station this morning to ask how the investigation was going."

"And to make sure you weren't suspecting Mr. Riddle," Nin added with a snort.

"And to make sure *you* were keeping your mouth shut after that story in the paper," Jackson added, glancing at his sister. "He thinks Missy found out the details from you."

"How stupid." Nin shrugged. "He saw her with us when you examined the body."

"Nonetheless, Miss Branch, seeing as it's the mayor —"

"You know I have my own way of doing things, Deputy." Hatfield's tone was severe.

"But he made it clear — "

"I see no harm in having your sister and Miss Branch speak with Miss Hoddle," the sheriff said. "Provided they tell us everything she said afterward."

"That means *everything*, Del." Her brother gave her a meaningful look. "We decide what's relevant, not you."

"You know I never hold anything back, Jack," Adele said with twittering eyelashes.

~~~~~

Since it was lunchtime, Raleigh's General Store was buzzing. Adele and Nin had to thread their way past clusters of people searching through the shelves and chatting with the sales girls. Adele searched their faces for Iona's pleasant though rather anemic countenance. She received mostly cold stares from the salesgirls and the boys stocking the shelves.

"I see Raleigh still instructs his staff to shun me," she remarked.

"He ought to have gotten over that long ago," Nin said. "You've been here four years."

"He's never forgiven me for taking away his stationery business," Adele said as she gave the display of envelopes and paper a
~~~~~

contemptuous look. “One could barely make paper airplanes out of those.”

Nin laughed. “He’s up in arms about your putting in that new wing.”

Adele hunched her shoulders as they passed a group of young men, most of them clerks, hovering near the manufactured ties, ogling both of them, but especially Nin with her catlike eyes and graceful beauty. “He’s already boasted about doing me one better when his son finishes college.”

“It’s all wind,” Nin growled. “He’ll never make this place anything like The Emporium.”

“He’ll certainly try,” Adele said. She saw Iona in a corner helping Mrs. Olsen choose some spools of thread. She waved to her and was relieved to see Iona ignoring the instructions of her boss and giving her a warm smile. In a few moments, she finished with Mrs. Olsen and while Nin helped the elderly woman maneuver the crowds out to the street, Adele shook Iona’s hand.

“You look as if you’re ready for lunch,” Adele said.

“It’s my time, but, with all these people —”

Adele took her by the arm. “There’s a time for work and a time for nourishment, dear. Even Mr. Raleigh can’t deny that. Can you, Mr. Raleigh?” She glanced at the man who liked to be on the floor during the busy hours, eyeing his staff.

“Can I what, Miss Gossling?” The man adjusted the jacket over his girth.

“You can’t deny a hard-working woman must have her lunch,” she said.

“You’re taking Miss Hoddle to lunch?” He eyed her. “This wouldn’t be about the death of that unfortunate young lady —”

“Oh!” Iona covered her mouth with her hand.

“Now don’t you go upsetting my workers, Miss Gossling,” he said.

“It wouldn’t affect their work anyway,” Nin said, having returned from helping Mrs. Olsen.

"I assure you, sir, we only want to take your salesgirl to lunch," Adele insisted.

He looked at his watch. "Mind you, be back in half an hour."

"An hour." Nin took Iona's other arm.

"Miss Branch —"

"You wouldn't want anything happening to her digestion the rest of the afternoon because she ate too fast, would you?" Nin smiled sweetly.

The man shuddered and Adele smiled, guessing he was remembering his own digestive troubles. "No, I certainly wouldn't."

When they were out the door, Iona's face relaxed. "A whole hour! I feel like a queen."

"Then we shall feed you like one," Adele said, smiling.

They sat at Dora's Tea Shop where Dora made sure to make a table for them and feasted on cucumber sandwiches and scones.

"You really have come to ask about Arabella, haven't you?" Iona peered at her. "I feel responsible, Adele."

"Good heavens, why?" Adele stared at her.

"I'm bad luck, you see."

"Oh, nonsense!" Nin growled. "There's no such thing as bad luck."

"I should think you would be on my side, Miss Branch," said the young woman. "When I was eight, a classmate of mine fell down a well walking home after we played together in the park. And then there was Millie Gibb —" Tears filled her eyes. "And now, Arabella!"

"She was a friend of yours?" Adele asked gently.

"Well, I wouldn't say that," said the woman, picking up her fork. "We only knew one another for two days."

"But you liked her?"

"I thought she was brave," said Iona.

"So you didn't like her," Nin guessed.

"Oh, no!" Iona dropped her fork again. "She was — well,

perhaps assertive is the word you would use. The sort who looks out for herself, only at the expense of others."

"Very well put," Adele said, smiling.

"She was very kind to me," the girl said.

Adele leaned forward. "Then you'll want to help us find who did this terrible thing to her."

"Oh, certainly!"

Did she confide in you?" Adele asked. "She left her place of employment very suddenly and without explanation —"

"Oh, but I'm sure she left for the usual reason," said Iona.

"The usual reason?"

The young woman blushed. "To get married." She straightened her shoulders. "When Arnold gets his position in the Navy, I'll be leaving too."

"I'm sorry to hear that," Adele said kindly.

"Please don't tell Mr. Raleigh." Her voice dropped. "He doesn't approve of military men."

"I'm sure he doesn't," Adele said dryly, recalling the man's deliberate movements and his slowness of mind.

"We wouldn't dream of telling him." Nin's eyes sparkled. "It ought to be a big surprise."

"Did Miss Parnell tell you she was getting married?" Adele asked.

"Not in so many words," Iona said. "She said she was going to make a man keep his promise to her." Her face grew pale. "Do you think —"

"He was less than honorable and killed her?" Adele finished. "It's possible."

"The first part is more than possible," Nin said with a smirk.

"Oh, but he bought her such nice things!" The young woman fingered a sandwich.

"What things?" Adele asked.

"Some fine jewelry," Iona said. "A man doesn't do that unless he's serious, as I'm sure you know, Miss Gossling."

"Yes, I know." Adele cringed inside as she remembered a certain butterfly brooch of violet jewels that John Bellows had tried to get her to take from him when they were courting. "Sometimes jewels from a young man can be more like a bribe than a gift."

"But Arabella had some money of her own."

"Did she?" Adele perked up.

"Her clothes were new," the young woman continued. "She must have saved months for them."

Adele exchanged a look with her friend. "Yes, she must have," she said dryly.

"More likely the same 'fine gentleman' bribed her with those too," Nin snarled.

Iona's pearl eyes regarded her with fear. "Why, I never thought of that."

"I'm sure she bought them on her own," Adele said, seeing the distress build in the young woman's face. "Iona, dear, I don't want to cause you anguish, but you might have some important information for us."

"I'm not anguished," the young woman insisted. And, indeed, she looked fresher as she ordered another cup of tea. "If you can help the police find who did this horrible thing to Arabella, just as you did Millie, I'll do all I can."

"The police think Miss Parnell was killed on Monday," Adele said. "It would help them to know her movements that day."

Iona played with a scone. "Well, I don't know. I was at work all day."

"Yes, yes," Nin said with a little impatience. "But after work?"

"Did you see her at the house?" Adele asked.

She could see the young woman was weighing in her mind her next words. "Yes. I saw her."

"You must be honest with us, Iona." Adele took her hand. "It can't hurt her now, you know."

The girl's face grew sad. "No, you're right. It can't hurt her now."

"Did she bend some of Mrs. Taylor's rules?" Nin asked.

"Only one," Iona said. "The curfew rule."

"Perhaps you ought to tell us about it," Adele said.

"You know Mrs. Taylor's strict curfew." The young woman looked at her.

Adele nodded. "Eleven o'clock, the doors are locked."

"Everyone in the house usually goes to bed early on Mondays except me." She chuckled. "I suppose I have energy left over from Sunday."

"Go on."

"I stay in the parlor to read," she said. "I don't like reading in my room. It's so tiny."

Adele remembered the tight corners of the room they had examined earlier that day.

"I was there when I heard little taps on the stairs. I thought the cat had been hiding and missed her dinner, so I got up to get her a saucer of milk. I went out into the hall and on the stairway was Arabella."

"What time was this, do you recall?" Adele asked.

"About eight o'clock, I should say," she said. "I heard the grandfather clock chiming a little before."

"Go on." Adele leaned back.

"She was all dressed up to go out." Iona's face grew red. "Like a lady dresses to meet her beau."

"I understand." Adele said.

"I asked her if she were going to meet someone." Iona's face grew redder. "I know it was none of my business —"

"You were trying to save her from being thrown out," Nin said roughly. "I'd say your good intentions made it your business."

"Thank you for saying that, Miss Branch." The girl relaxed.

"Was she rough with you?" Adele asked. "Did she say it was none of your business?"

"No, that's the funny thing," said the young woman. "She was flushed and excited. I felt like —" The girl stopped, looking down into her teacup.

"Like what?"

"Like she was dying to tell me something," she said.

Adele gave Nin another glance. "But she didn't tell you?"

"Not in so many words," she said.

"What happened?" Nin asked.

"She said, 'I won't be long.' I told her about Mrs. Taylor's curfew, though I know Mrs. Taylor made a point to tell her when she first came. 'Don't stay out past eleven,' I told her. 'You won't be able to get back in.' She said, 'Oh, I'll be back long before that.' And then she went." Iona let out a sob. "She didn't come back before eleven. She didn't come back at all!"

Adele comforted the young woman while Nin went to Dora and came back with a shot of brandy.

"Goodness, I shouldn't!" The girl stared down at it. "What would Mr. Raleigh think?"

"You're not going to get drunk on a little brandy," Nin said. "I'll give you some lavender lozenges so he won't even smell it on your breath."

Iona took the brandy, making a face. "I can't see how men like liquor."

"Neither can I," Adele said with a smile. "Thank you for telling us, Iona."

"Do you think it will help?" Iona asked.

"I think it might help a great deal," she said as they rose. "And you say she seemed excited and bursting with some news?"

"I don't know about that," the young woman said. "It was just her manner. As if she had been waiting for something to happen and now it was."

"But that something wasn't murder," Nin remarked as they stepped out of Dora's.

The young woman consulted the clock on the Arrojo Finance

Company building. "Heavens, I only have a few minutes or I'll be late!"

Adele took hold of her arm. "Just one more question, dear. Did Miss Parnell have any visitors during her stay at Mrs. Taylor's?"

The young woman shook her head. "Not that I saw."

Adele could see again she was weighing her words. "But there is something else you remember?"

Iona toyed with the fringes on her bag. "Well, yes. It was on Saturday. I remember because I could smell the ham from my room, and Mrs. Taylor always makes ham on Saturdays for dinner."

"What about Saturday?" Nin prompted.

"I was the first one down to the parlor for sherry," she said. "And I heard — you know Mrs. Taylor put in a phone only a few months ago?"

Adele nodded. "Go on."

"She hates how it rings so she put it in the corner right near the back door," said Iona. "But you can hear it from the parlor. As I went in, I saw Arabella with the receiver to her ear and she was talking very quickly."

"You didn't hear what she said?"

The girl shook her head. "I heard how she said it, though."

"What do you mean?"

"She was very angry with someone," she said. "Angry and insistent. It was in her face. She turned around for just a moment while she was talking and she saw me. Then she hung up abruptly." The girl's eyes lit up. "If she had a row with her fine gentleman, that might mean —"

"We'll look into it certainly," Adele assured her. "Now you go in for your work."

"You'll keep me posted on how things go?" She looked at her anxiously.

"Of course I will," Adele promised.

She and Nin went back to her shop where the workers, back from their lunch, were waiting for her, this time without their cigars and cigarettes. As she opened the door, a card dropped on the dusty mat outside. She read: *Would be honored if you would join me for dinner tomorrow night at Pringles. Understand if you have previous engagement. Will be waiting at the table by the palm at eight. Nathan.*

"The colossal gall!" Nin burst out as she read over her shoulder. "He acts as if you already agreed."

"On the contrary," Adele said, smiling. "He's very polite."

"You like him, don't you?" Her friend eyed her.

"I thought he was a nice man," Adele said.

"Compared to his wolf friend, he was an angel," Nin snorted. "You'll go, then?"

Adele tapped the card against her palm. "Why not?"

CHAPTER 12

Adele worked in her shop for the rest of the day, trying to ignore the sawing that had begun on the new wing. She had to speak loudly over the noise, though it seemed as if the customers didn't mind. A wagon of picnickers from the city stopped on Bridge Street and fell into her shop. She had a fair amount of business from them, though she knew they would not be coming back with Brown & Sons Stationers at their doorstep.

Jackson came to fetch her as she was closing. "Hatfield convinced Miss Lavinia Murphy to see us before dinner, and he wants you and Miss Branch to accompany us."

"Convinced her?" Adele eyed him.

"It seems Miss Murphy makes her own decisions as to whom she wants to see even under her parents' roof." He chuckled.

"And why shouldn't she?" Adele objected. "She's over eighteen, isn't she?"

"But apparently not over herself," he remarked as Nin came out.

"Who isn't?" she asked.

"Jack was telling me about Miss Lavinia Murphy," Adele said. "It sounds as if she's going to be the haughtiest of the lot."

"I wouldn't be surprised if Arabella was such a good friend of hers." Nin pulled her shawl around her shoulders.

"We'll have our chance to find out," Adele said. "We're going with the police to question her."

"The sheriff will set her to rights," Jackson said in a severe tone.

And, indeed, when Miss Murphy finally walked into the upstairs parlor of the lavish house, Hatfield said in a polite but firm tone, "Miss Murphy, you kept us waiting twenty minutes."

"It couldn't be helped," said the young woman. She had the nasal tone of someone who thought herself above her company. "I had to see dinner was properly started. Papa likes his dinner promptly at seven."

"I'm afraid dinner will be delayed," he continued. "We have several questions we need to ask you and your parents as well."

"Why them?" The woman glanced at him.

"I assume you know what this is about?"

"The death of that possum Arabella." She sounded less than pleased. "There's no need to bother Papa with that."

"Miss Parnell worked for the household, Miss Murphy," said Jackson. "They may know something that can help us that you don't and vice versa."

"Please." The woman's voice went from cavalier to pleading. "My mother isn't here. And Papa has been upset enough by Arabella. This would only upset him more, and there is really nothing he can tell you that I can't."

There was genuine distress on her face. Adele cleared her throat. "I think Miss Murphy is right, Sheriff. Shall we speak with her first, and then if you and Jack feel you want to question her father, you can do it later?"

"I would greatly appreciate it, Sheriff." Miss Murphy smiled in a way that Adele knew would warm the sheriff's heart.

Hatfield gave Adele a nod and she leaned with both hands on

the edge of her parasol. "'That possum Arabella' — do you mean that affectionately?"

Miss Murphy chuckled. "I most certainly did *not* mean it affectionately, Miss —"

"Gossling," Adele supplied.

"I can't imagine what gave you that impression."

"We've heard from a few people that you were friends —"

"Friends?" The young woman looked at her as if she were mad. "I wish I'd never set eyes on her!"

There was silence for a moment as the air seemed to settle. Then, Adele said more gently, "That's a rather harsh thing to say about a young lady who's now dead."

"Whatever she got she probably deserved." Miss Murphy fanned herself with her handkerchief and made a forceful gesture to look at her watch.

"How can you be so cruel?" Nin demanded.

"If you knew her as I did, Miss —"

"Branch."

"Miss Branch, you wouldn't be so tender-hearted," said the girl. "If you knew how terribly she upset Mama —" Her snobbish demeanor cracked and she looked away, her cheeks red.

"Has this anything to do with why you don't want the police to speak to your parents?"

The girl turned pale, nodding. "Arabella abandoning us like she did and going to Mrs. Dilworth's without a word — well, it just upset her terribly."

"Good help is hard to find," Nin said.

"It was more than that, Miss Branch," said Miss Murphy.

"It must have been if you use the word 'abandon' rather than 'left,'" Adele said.

"Mama is ill, you see," the girl began. "She's been in and out of the hospital since I was eight. She can't do very much so we hired a maid to help her."

"Why not a nurse?" Jackson inquired.

"Mama has a fear of nurses," Miss Murphy said. "She always thinks they're going to carry her off to the hospital again."

"Go on," said Hatfield. Adele could see he was warming to her even more.

"Arabella came to work for us, and Mama grew to depend on her," the woman continued. "Then Mrs. Dilworth came to see Mama one day. They chatted about the servant problem, and Mrs. Dilworth said she was looking for a lady's maid."

"And Arabella overheard," Nin guessed.

"She left the next morning without a word," said Miss Murphy. "Mama was so upset she had to go to the hospital again. She's been there ever since."

"It was a dirty trick for her to play on your mother." Nin took the girl's hand.

"No one knows Mama is in hospital," said Miss Murphy. "They all think she's in Calistoga." She looked at the sheriff with anxious eyes. "You won't let this get out, will you?"

"We won't say a word," said Hatfield.

"I can see why you wish you'd never met Arabella," Adele said. "And yet, people seem to think you and she were friends."

"She wrote me," said Miss Murphy, "but we weren't friends."

"Wrote you?"

The young woman nodded. "A month or so after she left, I started to receive letters from her as if nothing had happened."

"What did she say in the letters?" Hatfield inquired.

She gave him a disgusted look. "Do you think I would read anything that possum had to say?"

"So you threw them away unopened." Jackson's cheeks flared with annoyance.

"I wouldn't even touch them," said Miss Murphy. "I gave them to my maid to burn."

"We'd like to talk to this maid of yours," he said.

"Carmen's away at the moment," she said. "Some trouble with her father's health, so we let her go home for a few weeks."

"Very kind of you," said the sheriff. "But I'm afraid you'll have to call her back."

"But her father's sick!" She stared at him. "I can't pull my maid away from her father's deathbed."

"You said he was ill, not dying," Nin pointed out.

"You needn't do a thing, Miss Murphy," said Hatfield. "Just give us her address and we'll cable her. I'm sure she'll come back once she sees there is a murder investigation on the line."

"If you insist, Sheriff." She gave Jackson the address. "And now, I really do need to get Papa his dinner."

"We'd like to speak to your servants before we leave, Miss Murphy."

The girl sighed. "Whatever for?"

"They worked with Miss Parnell," said Jackson. "They might know something that could help us."

"Perhaps you'd like to talk to our poodle as well?" She raised her eyebrows. "He played fetch with Arabella all the time."

"If he could speak, we would," said Hatfield with a chuckle.

"Very well," she said.

The conversation with the Murphy servants was brief. The household was small, as there was only a cook and a butler about, both of them well into their seventies. They had had little to do with Arabella, and apart from confirming they knew a Douglas Cole working for the Woods, they could say little else.

"That wasn't much help, was it, sir?" Jackson asked as they made their way back to town in the police car.

"At least we know why we didn't find any of Miss Murphy's letters among Arabella's things," Adele said. "She never wrote back."

"I don't blame her," Nin said. "That sort of disloyalty doesn't inspire affection."

"It seems Arabella's ambitions may have given her a disregard for other people's feelings," Adele remarked.

"You think that's why she left the Murphys?" Jackson glanced at her.

"It's obvious, dear brother," she said. "She made it clear that day in my shop that she didn't intend to remain in service all her life. But she had ambition enough to rise as high as she could while she was there."

"A maid for an invalid is much less lucrative than a lady's maid to a family chummy with the mayor," Nin put in.

"Why on earth would she write letters to a family she had just abandoned for a better position?" the sheriff mused.

"We only have Miss Murphy's word for that," Jackson said.

"I believe her, Jack," said his sister. "I think I know why too."

"Oh?"

"I think Arabella wanted someone to look up to as a sort of model for what she wanted to be."

"And she chose Miss Murphy?" Hatfield steered to the right. "A rather unfortunate choice."

"It doesn't make much sense, does it, sir?" Jackson asked. "Writing letters to a young woman whose family she just ruined."

"She may not have realized what she'd done." Adele gazed out the window. "Arabella struck me as the sort to be so determined to reach her own end she wouldn't think much about the means to that end."

"Or who she hurt to get to that end," Nin added.

"I very much want to speak to Douglas Cole now," said Hatfield. "He might be the key to all of this."

"So might Virgil Riddle," Jackson reminded him.

The sheriff nodded and turned the corner.

~

A few days later, Adele woke up a little earlier than usual and was at the breakfast table before Jackson had come down. Tomas had put the *Arrojo Courier* and the city newspapers in Jackson's place. She picked up the *Courier* and lazily leafed through it. One of the stories made her jump and by the time Jackson came down, she was fuming, drumming the folded paper on the edge of the table.

"You look as if you're going to chop my head off." Jackson chuckled as he sat down to his oatmeal and toast.

"I ought to," she said. "Why didn't you tell me you and Hatfield ruled out Douglas Cole as Arabella's killer?"

"Because it's police business," he said promptly. "And police business is none of your business."

"Hatfield doesn't think so," she snapped as she stabbed the eggs on her plate.

"It seems you've found out anyway," he remarked as he took the paper gingerly from her hand. "Hatfield told me he was going to give the story to Missy so as to make sure she only printed the facts."

"The facts as he and you see them," Adele grumbled. "Or the facts as Mr. Cole painted them."

"He didn't paint anything, Del," Jackson insisted. "The fellow is upright and sincere."

"Did he admit he was in love with Arabella?" She held the coffee spoon in her hand like a spear.

"He admitted he was infatuated with her," said her brother. "He also confirmed what Mrs. Butler told us. Miss Parnell never even looked his way."

Adele eyed him. "He would say that if he thought he were being suspected of murder."

"He said he tried once to invite her to dinner and she refused and that was that." He then gave her a meaningful look. "You can stop trying to stab me with that spoon, Del. The boy has an alibi."

"Oh?"

"He was in Los Angeles until Tuesday," he said. "It seems the Woods' son just got married and was about to return from his honeymoon so he was sent down along with a few of the Woods' other servants to get their new house ready."

"He may have slipped away —"

"All the way to Arrojo?" Her brother looked amused. "He was in sight of the other servants the entire time, including at night. He had to share the stable boy's room in the barn because the house wasn't ready enough for all the servants."

"Well." Adele threw her napkin on the table. "That shoots down the mayor's half-witted theory, doesn't it?"

"He may have the brain of a very small bird but he has a rather large position in this town," Jackson argued. "He was trying to avoid a scandal."

"You mean he was helping Mr. Dilworth help his friend Mr. Riddle avoid a scandal." She stirred her coffee. "I'm assuming you're now investigating whether he had something to do with Arabella's death after all?"

"The fact that Miss Parnell was found in his house and people attested to her mentioning an older man is enough to include him in our investigation."

"I don't like the man," she admitted, "but I'm not sure he would go so far as to commit murder."

Jackson took another piece of toast. "And why is that?"

"He's far too self-preserving," she insisted. "Why risk killing an insignificant little lady's maid when he has the hand of a widow with plenty of money and social standing at stake?"

"Perhaps you're right and perhaps you aren't," Jackson said. "But Hatfield intends to find out. He thinks that bill you found in Miss Parnell's room might be something."

"The bill for the blouses and skirts?" He nodded. "You questioned Ada, then."

"She said Miss Parnell came into the shop and put in the order herself."

"Then how does that implicate Mr. Riddle?" she asked.

He looked at her meaningfully. "How many customers from town do you have who pay cash up front instead of putting their purchases on account?"

Adele stared at him. "She paid cash?"

"All gold coins too," he said. "Now, where would a lady's maid get that kind of money?"

"I see what you mean," Adele murmured. "Arabella wouldn't do that, but someone like Mr. Riddle would."

"And to make himself inconspicuous," Jackson added as he picked up his walking stick.

~

Later that morning, Adele was giving Beatrice some instructions regarding the new letter openers that had just arrived when, to her surprise, Sheriff Hatfield walked in. Amidst the dainty pinks and peaches and creams of her wares, he looked like a Viking.

"This is a pleasure, Sheriff," she said with a smile. "You remember Beatrice, don't you?"

"I remember Beatrice," he said in a dry tone, making the young woman turn away.

"Can I interest you in more of those fountain pens I sent you last year?" she inquired. "Or a desk set? I think the sheriff of Arrojo County deserves a more dignified desk set than the ratty one you have."

"I'm afraid I didn't come for your business," he said. "I came for mine."

Adele could see Beatrice's eyes perk up. "Bea, you can finish that in the storeroom."

"But I need to stack them —"

"You can do that later," Adele said in a firm tone. "I'd like you to go out back to check on the workers and tell me what they're doing. Mind you, I want you to watch them for at least fifteen minutes."

Beatrice gave her an even look and disappeared out the door.

"Well, we have fifteen minutes of peace and quiet anyway," she said with a laugh. "In the meantime, I have some inkwell and letter opener sets that are just fit for the county's greatest crime fighter."

His face went red. "Really, I'm not here to buy, Adele."

"Who said anything about buying?" she insisted as she led him to the middle of the shop.

He coughed. "We've located Nellie."

"Nellie?"

"Mr. Riddle's former maid," he said. "The girl is working for a Catholic family in Rosa Gris. She's quite pious, apparently."

"I can see why she would want nothing to do with Mr. Riddle." Adele took a silver inkwell with a glass stopper and a silver letter opener, both with a blue and black enamel on them. "The latest style, Sheriff."

"I'd like you and Miss Branch to interview her," he said as he absently took the items. "I don't think she would be very helpful to us if Jackson and I went."

"Pious girls usually aren't," Adele agreed.

Hatfield shifted the items to one hand and with the other, pulled a piece of paper out of his pocket. "The address," he said. "We've already spoken to the family. They're not thrilled to have us, but they know the law."

"Nin and I will be very conscientious, Sheriff," she promised.

"You always are, Adele." With one of his boyishly charming smiles, he held out the inkwell and letter opener to her.

"A gift, Sheriff."

He nearly dropped them. "I couldn't really —"

"You've kept law and order in this town for the last four

years." She smiled. "You've won everyone over, even Mrs. Faderman. I think that deserves some recognition."

"Well at least let me —" He dug into the inside pocket of his coat and started to pull out a wallet.

She put her hand on his to stop him. "I won't take a dime."

He stumbled out of the shop, holding the inkwell and letter opener to his chest.

CHAPTER 13

Nin, who never hid her contempt for the upper class, had less hesitation speaking with someone in service, and Adele convinced her they should take her new car.

"The Beaton sisters certainly have improved," Nin remarked as she sat comfortably in the passenger seat. "Not so much jumping around in this one."

"It's a luxury car, dear," said Adele.

"It must be, with a roof to keep out the rain," said her friend.

"And six cylinders," Adele added. "We ought to get to Rosa Gris in no time."

As luck would have it, they arrived just as the servants were finishing their lunch. Nellie was hardly eighteen and the ethereal beauty of her swan-like figure made her look almost like an angel.

"You worked for Mr. Virgil Riddle for a time?" Adele began.

The maid clutched the cross around her neck. "I wasn't there long, miss."

"You still might have some vital information for us." Adele glanced at Nin and, with her no-nonsense candor, her friend hurried out of the servants' hall the other servants, their expressions annoyed but obedient. The sudden emptiness and the dim light from the gas lamps added a calming effect to the room.

Nellie's gray eyes widened. "I don't know nothing about nothing."

"You read in the papers about the death of a Miss Arabella Parnell, didn't you?" Nin demanded.

The young woman shrank back. "I don't read the papers, miss. Bible's all I read."

Adele motioned for her friend to keep silent.

"I don't like to read about sins and sinners," the girl added. "My pa — he's a preacher — says it ain't right for a girl's pure heart to be tainted by the goings-on of the world."

"But the world goes on with its tainted ways, doesn't it?" Adele eyed her.

"Oh, Lord help me, miss, yes, it does!" she burst out. Then, more sedate, she added, "But a girl has to hold on to her purity, doesn't she, miss?"

"It's better she hold on to her dignity," Nin mumbled.

"That too, miss, that too," Nellie said.

"We're not here to suggest you don't have a pure heart or dignity," Adele assured her. "In fact, I suspect they're the reason why we're here."

"I don't understand, miss."

"You don't recognize the name of Arabella Parnell?" Adele studied her. "She was a lady's maid to Mr. and Mrs. Dilworth. They're good friends of your former employer."

"I might have seen her, miss," she said. "But I wouldn't have spoken to her. I never mixed much with servants of other houses. I kept to myself and my Bible."

"Miss Parnell also kept to herself," Nin said.

"As I said, I don't know nothing about her or anyone." The girl rose. "I must get back to my work."

"How long did you work for Mr. Riddle?" Adele asked.

"It doesn't matter, does it?" she said. "I'm not working for him now." She started to leave the kitchen.

"You won't help us catch the person who killed Arabella?" Adele called after her.

There was silence and then the girl came back, standing in the doorway. "Someone killed her?"

"They shot her in the back three times," Nin said.

"Heaven help us!" The girl's mouth fell open as she crossed herself.

"She was found in Mr. Riddle's conservatory," Nin added. "The police think he did it."

Adele studied the girl. "Do you think Mr. Riddle *could* have done it, Nellie?"

Nellie played with the cross around her neck. She said slowly, "Mr. Riddle was a good employer."

"Then why did you leave?" Adele asked.

"Pa didn't think it was right for me to be in service to an unmarried man." She looked at the back door as if wanting to escape.

"Why did you take the job in the first place if you knew he wasn't married?" Nin asked.

"I like Mr. and Mrs. Casper better," Nellie lamented. "They let me help the nanny with the children."

"You like children?" Adele smiled.

"Oh, yes, miss!" She breathed.

"You ought to be a teacher, then," Nin said.

"It costs money to go to teachers' school, miss," said the girl. "I ain't got no money. I keep enough for me and send money back to them that need it."

"Is that why you took the job with Mr. Riddle?" Adele asked.

The girl rested one hand on the doorframe and buried her face in her shoulder.

Adele put her hand on her arm. "Nellie, I know someone who

can help you get to teachers' seminary. But you must be honest with us."

Again, there was silence. Then the girl lifted her head and let out a sob. "He's the devil, miss!"

The cook came running into the servants' hall, mumbling protests. Nin hurried her out again.

"I know it's hard for you, Nellie," Adele said. "But you did nothing wrong. You understand that? You did nothing wrong." The girl nodded. "Why is Mr. Riddle the devil?"

Nellie looked at her with wild eyes. "Come! Come with me." She darted down the hallway. They followed her down a dark staircase to a small room next to the cellar. Nellie opened the tiny closet door and pulled from her suitcase a soiled apron. "This is why!"

Adele unfolded it. It was a linen apron with one strap torn. The pocket over the left breast was also torn.

"The fiend!" Nin growled.

"It's all right, Nellie," Adele said softly. "You don't have to tell us any more."

"It was my fault!" she sobbed.

"The hell it was!" Nin snarled.

"Pa always said a woman drips with sin whether she wants to or not," she said. "Even in church, her curls drive a man to —"

"If a man is driven to do anything because of a woman's curls, let his eyes be burned with a red-hot poker," Nin said fiercely.

Nellie stared at her. Suddenly, she burst out laughing. It was the laughter of release and she collapsed on the bed. They were silent as they let her laughter die down.

"I never did nothing to encourage him," she said, her voice low. "Even Pa believed me."

"Of course you didn't," Adele said.

Nellie bowed her head. "You see now why I left, miss." She looked wild-eyed again. "You won't let it into the papers, will you? Pa wouldn't stand for that."

"Of course we won't," Adele said in a soothing tone. "It makes me wonder if he was that way with other maids who worked for him."

"He must have been because none of them would stick," said Nellie. "Mrs. Gregory told me. There were two girls before me." She blushed. "One of them had a black eye when she left. Said she got it opening the cellar door in her face. But the cellar door opens in, not out." She looked troubled.

"I'll ask Mrs. Gregory her name and track her down," Adele promised. "We'll see she's in a good place now."

"Thank you, miss." She bowed her head again. "I ain't got no grudges against girls who work as I do. We got to take care of one another."

"Indeed we do," Adele said. "Do you think we can go back to the kitchen now so my friend can make you a cup of tea?" She glanced at Nin, who nodded.

"I think so, miss." Nellie rose and Adele took her arm. "I'm sorry I acted like a hysterical hen."

"You didn't act in any way that wasn't understandable," Adele promised.

Once settled with a cup of tea that breathed a comforting steam of lemon balm Nin had added to it, Adele continued. "I know you said you kept to yourself, but you must have seen other servants from other families. We understand they were a tight-knit group."

"Oh, yes, miss," said the girl. "Mr. Riddle often sent us to his friends to help with things. Being a single gentleman, he didn't need us all the time. And —" she blushed again, "— I once heard him boasting how he had the most efficient servants in the county."

"He wanted to make good on his boast." Adele nodded. "You must have seen how he behaved with those other servants, Nellie."

"Especially since he seems to have a fondness for domestics," Nin growled.

"I never saw him behave improperly with any of the other girls, miss," Nellie admitted. "He wasn't that kind. I mean, he was the kind —"

"To take liberties with his own servants but not with the servants of others," Adele finished. "I can believe that."

"He certainly wasn't one who made eyes at Miss Parnell," said Nellie.

"But there were others who did?" Adele inquired.

Nellie sipped her tea. "I don't know no names, miss. I was only there five months."

"Were they young or old?" Nin asked.

"Bit of both," she said. "Oh, they never did anything more than just stare at her, of course."

"The unwritten law of the well-to-do families," Adele said dryly.

"No hanky-panky in front of the wives," Nin snorted.

"But the way they stared at her." The young woman shivered.

"As if they wanted to undress her," Nin said. This made Nellie turn pale and Nin pressed her hand.

"Did Miss Parnell acknowledge they were staring at her in any way?" Adele asked.

"Oh, no, miss," she said. "She had her work to do."

Adele rose. "Thank you, Nellie." She took out the card with her friend Vanya's phone and address. "My friend can help you get the money you need to go to teachers' seminary. Then you won't have to worry about your pure heart or your dignity." She smiled.

"Oh, thank you, miss!" the girl said. "Lord watch over you both, miss."

"Lord watch over nothing!" Nin spat out as they rode back to town. "It's Mr. Riddle's next victim the Lord ought to watch over."

"I think you're right that he has a fondness for domestics," Adele agreed. "Even the pious ones."

"That rat trying to take advantage of a girl like that," Nin snarled. "I'll slip some hemlock in that brandy he's so fond of the next time I see him."

Adele laughed. "We don't want two murders on our hands, dear." She turned on the road that led to Bridge Street. "I'm beginning to think I was wrong."

"About what?" Nin asked.

"I told Jack this morning I didn't think Virgil would take the risk of going after a girl because of his courting Mrs. Allington," she said. "But just because he didn't show any affection for Arabella in public doesn't mean he didn't have affection for her."

"We'll make sure to tell the sheriff that," Nin said as she settled back onto the seat.

~

That evening, Adele dressed with more care than she had in a long time. She laid three dresses on the bed and went from one to the other, twirling the belt of her robe as she examined them.

Jackson stood in the doorway, his hands in his pockets. "I don't think I've ever seen you so indecisive, Del."

"I haven't been out in the evening for a long time," she admitted.

"This town has made an old woman of you," he teased.

She looked over her shoulder. "I came to Arrojo for peace and simple pleasures, Jack, remember?"

"Well, you got both all right." He entered the room and held up a dark brown and honey dress. "If I may be so bold as to suggest this one?"

"Why that one?"

"It's the first time you're seeing Mr. Cress outside of the party, right? You'll impress him as a collected and level-headed woman, which, dear sister, you can be when you try."

She hit him with a pillow. "I've no wish to impress Mr. Cress or anyone else and you know it."

He laughed and held the dress high so it wouldn't trail the floor. "Had I realized how much you like this fellow, I would have insisted he come to the house."

"So you could scrutinize him like you do the tramps who come into the station?" Adele snapped the clothes from his hands.

"I wouldn't do that," he insisted. "But as the head of the household, I think I have a right —"

"Head of the household!" she snarled. "I'll thank you to remember this is *my* house."

"Del —"

"You're my brother, Jack, not my father." She herded him out the door. "I'll be late if I don't get ready."

He grasped her hand. "You know I only want the best for you, Del."

She gave him a kiss on the cheek without adding that sometimes his idea of "the best" was quite different from hers.

She waited inside the entrance to Pringle's restaurant ten minutes before Mr. Cress came rushing in, full of apologies. "Dr. Miles had to perform heart surgery on a patient and asked me to assist," he explained. "It's the curse of the doctor's profession that he can never anticipate how long an operation will take." He helped her with her coat, and Adele did not miss the admiring gaze as he looked her up and down.

"I've heard a doctor's education is never done," she said as Eugene, Mr. Pringle's son-in-law, led them to their table with an elastic smile. Adele saw Sybil, his wife, sitting in a corner and groaned as the woman caught her eye and waved. She knew her evening with Mr. Cress would be broadcast in the morning to all the gossips who had been dying to see her wed.

"I'm afraid not for me," he said with a laugh. "I still have one more year to go and then my hospital appointment before I'm free."

"And after that?" Adele asked as she studied the menu.

"Father wants me to go into practice with him in San Francisco." He played with his fork and knife as the waiter poured the wine.

"But you don't, Mr. Cress?" She put her chin in her hand.

"Call me Nathan," he insisted.

"You call me Adele, then," she said.

"I wasn't sure if it would sound silly to you," he said with a blush.

"I assure you I take life very seriously," she said.

"I want to travel to China. The bubonic plague has ravaged the country, and I'd like to help save lives if I can." He added the last with a little trepidation.

"I think that's very admirable," she said.

"Perhaps in a way we're involved in the same type of work." He offered her a roll. "Saving lives, that is. Me with my medical work and you with your police work."

"I don't work for the police," she reminded him. "I'm only a lowly shopkeeper."

"I think not," he insisted. "I had a conversation the other day with Miss Grace."

"I can't imagine Missy told you I was a police woman," Adele said.

"No, but she did say you're helping the police a great deal with this horrible business about Miss Parnell's death," he said.

"Only with the human interest," she said.

He glanced at her. "I'm not sure I follow you."

"We had to break the news to the Parnells that their daughter was killed," she said, feeling the salad weighing heavily in her stomach. "Sheriff Hatfield asked Nin and me to help."

"I can't imagine that was easy." His voice was troubled. "I've only observed so far how a doctor breaks bad news to a patient or their family but I don't know how I'm going to do it."

"You have a soft heart, Nathan," she said with a smile. "Most men wouldn't admit that."

"Most men would be ashamed of it," he agreed. "I can't even kill a rabbit or a deer."

"That's nothing to be ashamed of," Adele insisted.

He laughed. "Our first year in college, Gene, Maxwell, and I went hunting in the southern part of the state one weekend. They shot their fill of rabbits, but I couldn't even shoot one. And it wasn't because I didn't have the chance."

"Perhaps you ought to have been with us when we spoke with the Parnells," she said. "Your bedside manner would have been appreciated."

"I'm glad I wasn't," he said with such force that Adele looked at him in surprise. "I mean, telling an elderly couple that their daughter was —" He looked away. "How did they take it?"

"They were bewildered," Adele said. "Nin called them innocents."

"I can believe that," he said. "And now from what I read in the paper, the police have let go of one suspect."

Adele cut into the steak in front of her. "He wasn't really a serious suspect. It was more to appease Mayor Willett."

"You mean you don't think Miss Parnell was killed by one of her own kind?" he asked.

"It's not what I think that matters," Adele said. "It's what the police think."

He lifted his wine glass. "And what *do* the police think?"

Adele felt uneasy, as she knew Hatfield was very careful about what he was willing to let others know about investigations. "I really don't know," she lied.

"The newspaper said she was found in Virgil's house," he said. "I suppose they suspect him."

"Why would you think that?" She glanced at him.

The young man wiped his mouth, sitting back as if toying with an idea. "Well, he sort of has an eye for girls of that stature, if you know what I mean."

"How do you know?"

"I don't," he said. "Not for sure, at least."

"But someone else does?"

He laughed and pushed his half-eaten plate away. "I see your brother taught you the fine points of interrogation."

She blushed, poking at the last piece of steak on her plate. "I'm sorry. I didn't mean to sound inquisitive."

"You could never do that, Adele." He put his hand on the table only inches away from hers. "One thing I liked about you when I met you at the party was your intelligence. And you're not ashamed to show it."

"According to Jack, I should hold back at least a little," she admitted.

"I'm glad you don't." Then, in a more serious tone, he added, "Gene told me he thought Virgil wasn't exactly virtuous when it came to the servant girls."

"And he knows?"

"Well, no, he only suspects," he admitted. "But Gene has more of an eye for these things than I do." He grinned. "He wants to be an advertising man so he knows how to look at things from every angle."

"I suppose it could be true," Adele said, thinking of Nellie.

"Gene said he knew Virgil was quite friendly with Miss Parnell," Nathan continued. "Oh, I don't mean — at least, Gene didn't say so." He stirred his coffee. "But you never can tell."

"No," she said. "You never can tell." She played with the sugar cube at the edge of her cup, feeling it would be too much for her coffee tonight. "Do you think he bought her that comb she was wearing the night of the party?"

It took a while for him to answer. "I really can't say, Adele. I suppose Virgil has bought such lavish gifts for girls before."

"I was only thinking maybe that's why you were so upset about it." She didn't look at him.

"Upset?"

"I saw the look on your face when she came out wearing it." She didn't mention she had also witnessed the scene on the veranda. "I thought it strange you were talking about promises that night."

He clasped his hands around his coffee cup, looking down into it. "I really don't know why I should have been upset. I don't like it when young ladies paint themselves all over with jewelry and rouge and I suppose it upset me."

"I should be glad I didn't wear my sapphire necklace tonight, then," she remarked.

He laughed. "You're not frivolous in any way, Adele."

"Another thing you like about me?" she suggested.

"One of many." He met her look.

Eugene appeared with his elastic smile. "Enjoying yourselves?"

"The pie was excellent," said Nathan. "Perhaps we ought to have your restaurant cater the medical department's banquet dinner this year."

The young man looked pleased. "We'd like nothing better, sir."

"Dr. Miles was just telling me their usual place was booked." Nathan took out a scrap of paper and a pencil from his inside pocket. "Perhaps I ought to take down your name and number and have him get back to you."

"Certainly, sir." Eugene could barely contain his joy.

When he was gone, Adele laughed. "He's been wanting to show his father-in-law he can make a success of the restaurant now that it's in his hands for a while."

"I'm glad to help an enterprising man," Nathan said as he put the pencil and scrap back in his pocket.

"You ought to have a notepad in a leather case like Jack does," she remarked as he helped her with her coat.

"Rather unorganized of me," he admitted. "I got into the habit of carrying scraps around in my pocket in school. You never know when you would run into a professor with something brilliant to say."

She laughed as he led her out of the restaurant

~

She went with Nin the next morning to the police station. Edison and two other assistant deputies were having their coffee in the interview room which left the sheriff and Jackson in the main office. She immediately felt a chill coming from Hatfield as he guided them to one of the benches. Something in his face was less at ease than usual.

"It's a shame police don't have secretaries." Adele glanced at the stack of papers on the sheriff's desk.

"We're not a business, Adele," Hatfield said. "We're here to protect the people."

"Nonsense," Nin said. "You're doing a public service, and you ought to have all the help you can get."

Jackson chuckled. "There is precious little left in the funds for such a luxury, Miss Branch."

"I assume you've come to report on your conversation with Nellie?" Hatfield looked at Adele. "Or is there something else you wanted to tell me?"

Adele grasped the handle of her folded parasol. "We had a very interesting conversation with the amenable Nellie."

"Who wasn't so amenable about Mr. Riddle," Nin snorted.

"And why is that?" Jackson asked

"Mr. Riddle was apt to take liberties with his maids." Adele gave her brother a knowing look.

His eyes widened. "Don't tell me you got her to admit that!"

"You know my powers of persuasion, Jack."

"Better than the Anspaches," he agreed.

"Then maybe the Anspaches ought to start hiring women detectives," Nin declared.

He grinned. "I wouldn't be surprised if they did, Miss Branch."

"You said 'maids,'" said the sheriff. "Are we to assume there were more than just Nellie in Mr. Riddle's employ that, erm, were compromised?"

"Almost compromised," Adele corrected. "Nellie was far too pious to let such a man have his way with her."

"Thank God!" Nin growled.

"But there were others who did?" The sheriff demanded. "We haven't got all day, Adele."

Feeling a little hurt, she continued, "Two others were employed before Nellie and left abruptly, though I don't know if they were 'compromised.'" She tried to keep the anger out of her voice as she added, "Someone ought to compromise Mr. Riddle so he doesn't compromise others in the future."

"If he's guilty of murder, he'll be compromised," the sheriff said in a harsh tone.

"If you'll pardon, sir," said Jackson, "just because a man is loose with his maid servants —"

"*Just* because?" His sister raised an eyebrow and Nin shot him a look.

"— doesn't mean he's a murderer," Jackson finished with a meaningful glance at Adele.

"But it does mean he has a 'fondness for domestics,' as Nin puts it." She smiled at her friend.

"It also might mean Mr. Riddle may not have been truthful when he told us he barely knew Miss Parnell," Jackson finished.

Hatfield looked into the window opposite his desk, his eyes a little narrow. "If we can only prove that, we might have something."

"Nellie said she never observed any wrongdoing in him when it came to Arabella," Adele admitted. "Naturally, that doesn't mean —"

"Of course it doesn't mean," Hatfield snapped.

Jackson cleared his throat. "I wouldn't be surprised if the expensive jewelry and the gloves were gifts from him."

"Nathan told me last night Gene thinks there might have been some dilly-dallying between Arabella and Mr. Riddle," Adele said.

"So you did go out with him after all?" Nin raised her eyebrow.

"And did some sleuthing on the side." Jackson snorted. "I should have known."

"I did nothing of the kind," Adele insisted. "It came up in conversation."

"Because you made sure it would," Jackson accused.

She noticed the sheriff had fallen silent. She ventured, "He couldn't be completely sure, but Gene's known Mr. Riddle for a long time."

"And disliked him, according to your observations." Hatfield's voice was tight. "Or did Mr. Cress dispel that opinion for you last night too?"

Adele blinked. "The subject never came up."

The sheriff toyed with the stopper on the ink bottle she had given him as part of the set only the day before. His hard fingers rolled it around so diligently that Adele snatched it from him. "You'll break it, Sheriff."

"Don't worry about Mr. Cress," Nin said in an assured tone. "It won't amount to anything."

Feeling suddenly nervous, she said in a cracking tone, "If you can't prove he bought Arabella the gloves and jewelry, you might have a way to snap the cuffs on him."

"Don't sound like the detective novels, Del," Jackson said.

"That is what you're trying to do, after all, isn't it, Mr. Gossling?" Nin asked.

"We only want the right man," he insisted.

"What is this way?" Hatfield asked. She was relieved his tone was more congenial.

"The gun."

"The gun?" He glanced at her.

"Maklin said he never saw a gun," Jackson pointed out.

She played with the handle of her parasol. "I watched Mr. Riddle's face when you questioned his manservant. I think he was lying, Jack."

Her brother glanced at the sheriff. "Another one of your ideas, Del? Or perhaps Miss Branch had a vision?"

"I don't have visions, Mr. Gossling," Nin snapped. "My auras are vibrations given to me from the Generous Ones."

"And were they generous enough to tell you where the gun we're seeking is?" he fired back.

"The Generous Ones only detect the darkness. They don't reveal it," she retorted.

The sheriff leaned forward. "Why do you think Maklin was lying, Adele?"

"The look on his master's face," said Adele. "Maklin knew what we were going to ask him."

"He was listening at the door." Nin nodded. "He looked devious when you called him in."

"I suspect he's used to covering up for his master," Adele continued. "He probably covered up for him on other occasions, though perhaps none so important as this."

"So you think there is, or was, a gun, and Maklin was lying when he said there wasn't?" Jackson considered this. "It's possible. I've known many butlers to be loyal enough to their masters to lie for them."

"But to cover up murder?" Hatfield shook his head.

"I don't say it was the gun that killed Arabella," Adele objected. "But if Mr. Riddle admitted to having the gun, it would mean a lot of trouble that might get out to his circle and make things, well, very unpleasant for him."

"Especially if Mrs. Allington got wind of it," Nin added. "She might reconsider what sort of man she's going to marry." With a cat-like look on her face, she added, "Not that that would be a bad thing."

"It seems rather far-fetched," the sheriff mused. "Lying to the police to avoid unpleasantness."

"You must realize, Sheriff, Mr. Riddle is a wealthy man who's had a wealthy man's life," Adele said, smiling. "To the wealthy, unpleasantness is a violence of a sort."

"A violence on their common sense," Nin snorted.

"Perhaps we ought to question Maklin again, sir," Jackson suggested. "Get him down here in more official surroundings."

Hatfield leaned back, tapping his large hand against the desk so that it almost rattled. Edison, who had returned to his place, jumped a little at the thumping noise.

"I've a better idea," he said finally. "If I can get Marland to get a search warrant, we wouldn't have to question anyone."

"We've no just cause," Jackson objected.

"The house is a crime scene, Deputy," said his superior.

"The conservatory is a crime scene," Jackson corrected. "And we've determined it wasn't even a crime scene because the body was left there."

A slow smile spread across Hatfield's lips. "You know that and I know that. Marland doesn't."

Jackson stared at him. "You mean you didn't tell him?"

Hatfield threw back his head and laughed one of his hearty roars that made Edison flinch a little but that always warmed Adele. "Like your sister, Jackson, I'm also wily in my own way."

"But why?" His deputy was completely nonplussed.

"Are you questioning the sheriff's judgment, Mr. Gossling?" Nin eyed him.

"I'm trying to understand the logic behind it, Miss Branch," he snapped. "A lawman works with logic, not judgment."

The sheriff looked at him sternly. "A lawman needs both."

Jackson shrank back a little, rolling the fountain pen in his hands. "I withdraw the question, sir."

"You've every right to ask it," said Hatfield. "We work together, Deputy. I've no secrets from you."

He said this with such bold warmth that Jackson smiled.

"I didn't tell Marland about the body being moved because I wanted to leave the door open to a search warrant," the sheriff said. "As I said before, I suspected Mr. Riddle wasn't telling us the whole truth, and I thought it best to give us the option to search if we needed to."

"It sounds like we need to," Jackson agreed.

"Then you accept my 'idea,' Jack?" Adele eyed him.

In response, he pouted his lips out at her as he used to when they were children.

"May I come along?" Adele asked. "I'm fascinated to see how you execute a search warrant."

"Rifling through someone's things." Nin shrugged. "It doesn't seem decent."

"When murder is involved, Miss Branch, decency sometimes makes way for justice," Hatfield said.

CHAPTER 14

Later that afternoon, a little before closing time, the sheriff sent word he had obtained the search warrant. Nin declined to join them, still bothered by the idea of their raking through a man's belongings without his approval.

Mr. Riddle had clearly recovered from his initial shock and horror as when Maklin showed them into the parlor, he looked much like the country gentleman Adele remembered from Gene Dilworth's party. He also behaved like one, his manner a little haughty and condescending as he nodded briefly at the sheriff and Jackson.

"How are you coming along with this business, Sheriff?" he asked.

"Murder investigations are like puzzles, sir," said Hatfield. "If one is lucky, one begins with a piece or two that belong to opposite ends of the picture. One must continue to gather the pieces where one can."

"Where one can," the man repeated. "And you think this is one of the places where you'll find the puzzle pieces?"

"The body *was* discovered in your conservatory, sir," Jackson pointed out.

"Which you yourself determined was a farce," he retorted. "You told me Arabella's body was left there by someone wanting to incriminate me."

"My brother never said that," Adele objected. "The police merely suspect it was left there for whatever reason."

He eyed her. "I see you're still in the thick of things, Miss Gossling."

"I assure you, sir, I'm not here to play lady detective," she retorted.

"Well, may I ask why you *are* here, then?" He turned to the sheriff.

To Adele's surprise, the sheriff did not slide out of his pocket the warrant right away. He leaned on one foot and regarded the man with an authoritative look. "I want to ask you one more time, sir. Do you still maintain you lost this Civil War relic of yours?"

"What relic?" The man blinked.

"The gun, sir," said Jackson. "You told us you had an old revolver but you lost it."

"Oh, that." The man put his hands on his knees. "Of course I lost it."

"A long time ago?" Hatfield asked.

The man shrugged. "I don't know exactly when."

"So long ago even your butler didn't know you had it?" Jackson eyed him.

His face grew stormy. "Look here, what is this all about?"

"We'd like another word with Maklin, if you don't mind," said the sheriff.

"I do mind!" the man growled. "Maklin is a very busy man. He doesn't have time to be pestered by the police!"

"You seem to lend out your servants to other families rather freely, Mr. Riddle." Adele crossed her arms. "Your household can't be so busy that you can't allow your butler to answer a few questions to help the police catch the murderer of a poor young woman."

The man burst out laughing. "My, but you suffragists are sentimental, aren't you?"

"That remark was ungentlemanly, sir." Jackson stiffened. "I suggest you apologize to my sister."

"Perhaps she ought to apologize to me!" he roared. "The idea that my household servants are idle —"

"I didn't say idle," Adele interrupted. "But we know you volunteer their services quite often."

He started at her. "Who the devil told you that?"

"Careful of your language in front of a lady, Mr. Riddle." Now Hatfield's tone was cutting.

"Your former maid, Nellie," Adele answered. Jackson gave her a sharp look but she couldn't help feeling a little satisfaction at the alarm on Mr. Riddle's face.

"You spoke to her, did you?" His voice was soft. "Is she doing well?"

"Quite well," Adele said. "Now that she's out of your hands, I dare say."

"Whatever she told you, it's a lie!" the man thundered.

"Right now, we're interested in your butler, sir, not your former maid," Hatfield said.

"I suppose I can't stop you from asking questions," he grumbled as he pulled the bell cord.

Maklin entered with vacant look on his face. "Yes, sir?"

"It seems the police won't leave us alone, Maklin," said Mr. Riddle with a glare toward the sheriff. "They want to ask you more questions."

"More questions, sir?" The man's voice was a little stinging. "But I've told them all I know."

"I don't think you have, Maklin." Sheriff Hatfield brought out his authoritative tone that made clear he would stand for no stalling. "Sit down."

"But, really, Sheriff —"

"Sit down."

The command even made Mr. Riddle raise his eyebrows. Adele knew the sheriff could be intimidating when he chose, and she admired him for always making it his last choice.

The butler slowly sat down, his thin knees almost creaking. "I don't know what else I can say, sir. Mrs. Gregory and I found the poor girl —"

"We're interested in the gun, Maklin." Sheriff Hatfield propped his foot on the coffee table, a gesture that clearly annoyed Mr. Riddle.

"Gun, sir?"

"Mr. Riddle's gun," Jackson said. "Where is it?"

"I never knew he had one, Deputy, upon my honor —"

"Then your honor must be as flimsy as your master's," Adele snarled, "because you're lying."

"What!" The butler jumped up. "Listen, you meddling harpie —"

"That's enough, Maklin!"

Even though both the sheriff and Jackson looked ready to speak, it was Mr. Riddle who interrupted his servant.

The man sank back on the couch.

"I'll not have you insult Miss Gossling, even if she is working with the police," Mr. Riddle said in a calmer tone. "You will apologize to her this instant."

"I'm sorry, miss." The man was clearly humbled. "I lost my temper."

"And I apologize to *you*, Mr. Riddle," Adele said, "for that remark about your honor. I can see now it wasn't entirely true."

The man gave her a crooked smile. "I assure you, Miss Gossling, I shall make it even less true in the future." Then, with a sigh, he added, "I think in light of your outburst, Maklin, it's best you leave now. I'll tell the police what it is they want to know."

"Thank you, sir." The man's face sagged as he slipped out of the room.

"You mustn't be too hard on Makin," said Mr. Riddle with a small smile. "Perhaps he ought to have been a little less loyal."

"Then there is a gun," said Jackson quietly.

"There is a gun," Mr. Riddle confirmed.

"And Maklin has seen it," Adele said.

"Naturally he's seen it," he said. "Though I doubt he would know a Civil War gun from a ladies' pistol. He's not that kind of man."

"Why did you lie to us?" the sheriff asked.

The man gave him an incredulous look. "Isn't it obvious? A dead girl is found in my conservatory, and you say she was shot. If you had known, you would have arrested me then and there."

"The police don't go around making arrests willy-nilly, Mr. Riddle," said Jackson.

"I'm aware of that," he said.

"I'm guessing you're willing to give us the gun now?" asked Hatfield.

"You mean will I 'hand it over,' as they say in the detective novels?" He gave a sheepish grin. "I promised I was working on my honor and I am." He went to the bookcase and pulled out a large volume in red leather and produced a key from a pocket on the inside cover. He then moved to the cupboard where the brandy and other liquor were stored and behind it produced a panel with a small safe. From inside the safe he produced the gun which he handed to Jackson.

"A rather elaborate hiding place," Adele remarked.

"A gentleman must be prepared for anything," he said. "If he gets into a scrape, he mustn't be caught unaware."

"Indeed he mustn't," Sheriff Hatfield said dryly. "Now if you'll be so kind as to give us the bullets."

"I don't know where they are."

Jackson glared at him. "You don't expect us to believe that?"

"It's true, Deputy," he insisted. "I only half-lied. It's the bullets I lost some time ago, not the gun."

"If that were really true, sir, you would have had nothing to fear by giving it to us in the first place," the sheriff pointed out.

"All right!" he growled. "I didn't lose them. But, honestly, Maklin and I searched the house after you had gone and we couldn't find them."

"Then perhaps my deputy and I will have better luck." At last, Hatfield produced the warrant.

Mr. Riddle's face turned white. "You had that all along!"

Hatfield grinned. "We have our ruses too, Mr. Riddle."

"But I tell you we already searched this house top to bottom!"

"Including all the hidden panels?" Jackson eyed him.

"On my honor, Deputy." Mr. Riddle put his hand on his heart. "I don't think those bullets are here anymore."

"Then you should have no objection to us looking for them." Hatfield nodded at Jackson, who opened the study doors. "I suggest you remain here."

Mr. Riddle sank into the seat on the couch his manservant had vacated as both lawmen left the room. Some of Adele's prior annoyance at the man's unscrupulous behavior melted as she saw the genuine worry on his face. She opened the liquor cabinet, which was still unlocked, poured a brandy and handed him the glass. He drank it down appreciatively.

She sat down on the chair opposite him. "Jack was right, Mr. Riddle. The police make sure they have solid evidence before they arrest anyone, even if what they find looks damning."

"I appreciate that, Miss Gossling." His tone was softer now and he no longer looked at her with hostility. "Perhaps the police ought to take you on. You're rather sympathetic."

She smiled. "I used to help young women in the settlement houses of San Francisco. I suppose one cultivates a generous amount of sympathy when one sees unfortunate victims daily."

"You see, then, I'm an unfortunate victim?" He leaned forward.

"Perhaps in some things," she said shortly. "May I be frank with you, sir?"

"You haven't held back being frank so far," he said with a sheepish grin.

"You and Miss Parnell — you weren't the strangers you told the police, were you?"

"What makes you say that?" he asked.

"Suffice it to say a friend told me different," she said. "And you're — well, rather good-looking and even dashing in your own way."

The compliments worked, as he completely softened. "Well, I may not be young anymore, but I like to think ladies find me pleasing."

She tried not to snort. "Many do, I assure you."

"To answer your question, yes, we did know one another a little, but not in the way you think." He lowered his tone. "I don't know what Nellie told you, Miss Gossling, but I swear to you I never touched a hair on Arabella's head."

"But you did know her better than you said?" asked Adele.

He leaned back with his hands behind his head. "I don't know if I can make you understand. You're an independent woman, but not every girl is like you."

"I fail to see what that has to do with anything," she said.

"Arabella grew up on a farm," he said. "I trust you know that?" She nodded. "Hers was a very large family in a small town. Striking out on her own was — well, she didn't have many friends, and sometimes a girl that young needs someone to consult."

"I'm beginning to see." Adele leaned her face on her hand.

"She saw me as a man of the world," said Mr. Riddle. "A, well, a father figure, almost."

Adele tried not to smile. "So she consulted you as a father figure?"

"Only in out of the way places," he insisted. "I mean like the gazebo in Blue Springs —"

"I never knew there was a gazebo in Blue Springs," she remarked.

"Exactly!" he said. "And the forest near Caton. We went there quite often."

"Out-of-the-way places." Adele nodded.

"I told you, it wasn't like that!" He blushed. "I knew people would think just what you're thinking if they saw us together. They wouldn't understand."

"Did you also meet her at Tanner Swamp?"

He blinked. "No, of course not. Why would we go to that filthy place?"

"I find it interesting you knew it's a filthy place," she said.

She heard the thumping of feet on the wooden floor outside.

"Do these belong to you, Mr. Riddle?" Jackson came in, holding up a pair of leather shoes.

"Certainly they're mine." The man's rigid tone returned. "Is there a law against owning leather shoes?"

"None, sir," said Sheriff Hatfield as he joined them. "But your man doesn't do a very good job of cleaning them."

"Eh?" Mr. Riddle stared.

Jackson turned the boots around and Adele saw there was mud caked on the soles.

"Oh. Well." The man struggled for an explanation. "I remember now. I played football in my youth, and our old team met last month for lunch. We decided to play a game for old times' sake. I'm afraid I wasn't very good." He chuckled.

"Was your game anywhere near Tanner Swamp?" Jackson asked.

"Of course not," he said. "We were playing in San Francisco, up there in the Misson District." His face turned red. "I don't like to talk about my humble beginnings, Deputy. Anyway, why would it matter?"

Her brother glanced at her. She knew he was thinking of the vegetation they had found on Arabella's blouse and skirt.

The sheriff held up a piece of paper. "Are you in the habit of keeping bills from millinery shops, sir?"

"When the lady in question is my cousin, I am," he growled.

"What is that, Sheriff?" Adele asked.

He handed it to her. It was a bill for a green and orange dress on delicate pink paper with *Ida's Millinery* printed on it and PAID stamped in the corner. "You say this was for a dress for your cousin? You must be very close to her."

"As a matter of fact, it was a wedding gift," he snarled.

"An odd gift for a wedding," Adele mumbled.

"Just what are you insinuating, Miss Gossling?" Mr. Riddle looked at her.

"Sheriff," she said, "I saw a green and orange dress among Miss Parnell's things."

"Yes, I remember it," said Hatfield. "That's why this bill caught my eye."

"I was told green and orange are the latest colors for ladies' dresses." He sniffed. "They must be available in every millinery shop. I don't doubt you have one yourself in your closet, Miss Gossling."

"What my sister does or does not have in her closet is none of your business," Jackson roared.

"The dress I saw had a fan of tulle thrown over the shoulder," said Adele. "That style is Ida's signature. She saw it in Paris once and took to it."

"Rather a coincidence," Mr. Riddle sat back.

Adele leaned against the cabinet with the liquor. "Ida creates only a few styles every season, and she makes only one dress of each."

"I wouldn't have expected a suffragist like you to take such interest in fashion," Mr. Riddle snapped. "It seems even the bluestockings have their vanity."

"If you insult my sister one more time —" Jackson advanced with a thundering look, but Adele stopped him.

"It's all right, Deputy," said the sheriff. "I don't think Mr. Riddle is going to say a word against Adele again. Are you?" The look on his face was more threatening than Adele had ever seen.

"It's a shame you need result to insults to avoid admitting the truth, Mr. Riddle," she said boldly.

The man fidgeted, crossing and uncrossing his legs. His eyes moved to the brandy bottle sitting on the cupboard but Hatfield conveniently moved so as to block its view. "All right. I'll tell you all of it."

"It's time you did," Jackson growled.

"I've already admitted to Miss Gossling I knew Arabella more than I said," he began. "She wanted to know all about how to behave in society, and she asked me to show her. So we went out now and then."

"You were her own private finishing school," Jackson said.

"Something like that, Deputy," he said. "Naturally, one can hardly practice being a lady when one is wearing those stiff linen skirts and blouses these young ladies wear nowadays." He gave a contemptuous glance toward Adele's smart suit. "So I bought her a dress."

A rather generous gift," Hatfield remarked.

"Did you also buy her jewelry?" Jackson inquired.

The man looked shocked. "Really, Deputy, I would never have taken it that far."

"That's why you took her to quiet places," Adele said.

He nodded. "One can hardly practice the rigors of social manners in public. It would look ridiculous."

I assume this tutelage ended at some point?" the sheriff asked.

"When I met Mrs. Allington again," he said. "About four or five months ago. I didn't want it to look like — well —"

"So you broke things off?" Adele suggested.

"I told her it was time for her to move on," he said.

"And how did she take this?" asked Hatfield.

A smirk lined his face. "With bells, Sheriff."

"Eh?" The sheriff narrowed his eyes.

"Arabella was a very resourceful young woman," he said. "She was on to something else by that time."

"Did you help her with her resources?" Adele eyed him.

"If you mean, did I give her money, I did not." He sounded almost proud. "Though, naturally, I let her keep the dress."

"All very neat and tidy," Jackson mumbled.

"Or maybe it wasn't so neat and tidy," Hatfield said. "I find it hard to believe a young lady like Arabella would settle for only a dress when she knew she could have gotten much more from you."

"I told you, I had no trouble with her."

"Or you made sure you wouldn't have trouble with her," Adele said slowly.

Mr. Riddle blushed. "All right. Yes, she realized I was interested in Mrs. Allington and she did come later and asked for some money. She knew how people would take our relationship even though it was entirely innocent."

"How much did you give her?" Hatfield asked.

"I don't remember," said Mr. Riddle. "Shall we say it was less than I'm apt to lose at a Friday poker game. And I'm a very good poker player, Sheriff."

"In other words, you compensated her for her silence," Jackson said.

The man flinched. "You make it sound like a bribe."

"It was in a way, wasn't it?" Sheriff Hatfield's stormy face showed his opinion of the matter. "That's where she had money, then. From your generosity."

Mr. Riddle sighed. "I really thought she was going to hire some retired socialite to continue her education. What a fool I was!"

"How could you be so sure she would keep her silence?" Adele asked. "She could have easily continued to ask for money."

"I told you, my dear," he said. "Arabella was a very resourceful young woman."

"Meaning?" Hatfield asked.

"As I said before, Sheriff, she had moved on to something else." With a sly tone, he added, "Or someone else."

"You have proof of that?" Jackson asked.

The man laughed. "Naturally not. Call it a feeling." Then, with a serious face, he added, "Arabella had her faults, and she wasn't a virtuous girl, but she knew what she wanted and never lingered in the past, Deputy."

"On the contrary," said Adele. "I should have thought Miss Parnell would see it as a golden opportunity."

"Then you didn't know her at all, Miss Gossling," he snapped. "Arabella fancied herself destined to be a fine woman. She wanted wealth, certainly, but she wanted respectability too."

"And I imagine being Mrs. Virgil Riddle would have gotten it for her," Sheriff Hatfield said.

There was silence for a moment as Mr. Riddle glared at him. Then, he said slowly, "What the devil are you talking about?"

"I think you know what I'm talking about," Hatfield said.

"Look here, I wasn't even at home the night she was killed!" Mr. Riddle insisted. "Damn it, man, you know that!"

"Watch your words, sir," Jackson spit out. "There is a lady present."

"Who, thankfully, doesn't seem to cringe at harsh language," Mr. Riddle said.

"We spoke with Mr. Tupman," said Sheriff Hatfield.

"Well?"

"He confirms you had dinner with him at the Orion Club," the sheriff said. "And that you did attend an all-night poker game."

"Well, then?"

"But you didn't stay all night," Jackson said. "He said you left at around ten-thirty."

"That's ridiculous!" the man sputtered.

"He also said that you both left the game to go — elsewhere." Jackson glanced at his sister.

"If you mean a house of ill repute, dear brother, why don't you say so?" Adele bit back a smile.

Mr. Riddle slumped back on the couch. "Well, perhaps we did have a bit of fun."

"What we found interesting," Sheriff Hatfield said slowly, "is that he said once you entered the house, he didn't see you again until two o'clock in the morning."

"So what if he didn't?" Mr. Riddle stared at him.

"What were you doing between eleven — that's when Mr. Tupman says you arrived at the place — and two in the morning?"

The man turned pink. "Good Lord, what do you think I was doing?"

"The medical examiner's assistant ascertained Miss Parnell was killed between eleven and one."

The redness in Mr. Riddle's face slowly turned to white like marble. "Well — well, I was — you can check with —"

"We have," Jackson said quietly. "The ladies recall you were there for half an hour or so, and then they didn't see you again until you came in at two o'clock."

The man's breath was shallow. "I can explain that."

"I'm sure you can, sir," the sheriff mumbled.

"I was a little — tipsy, shall we say — and I went out into the alley to get some air. There was a lady there. I — I don't know her name."

"We'll certainly check it, Mr. Riddle." Hatfield motioned to Jackson who stepped forward. "But in the meantime, I'm afraid you'll have to come with us."

"You mean because of this murder business?" The man looked at him steadily.

"Because of your involvement in illegal activity," said the sheriff.

Mr. Riddle stared at him. "Good God, man, there's a murder investigation going on and you quibble about a few drinks with a questionable lady?"

"Until I verify exactly what you did that night, we have every right to hold you for questioning." Hatfield nodded at Jackson again, who took Mr. Riddle's arm.

The man did not resist but there was a sly look on his face. "You realize once my friends find out, they'll get the best lawyer in the state."

"That's your privilege, sir," Hatfield said.

The man rose. "You're going to look very ridiculous, Sheriff. That I promise you."

Adele noted the disturbed look on the sheriff's face as he took Mr. Riddle's other arm.

CHAPTER 15

After they put Mr. Riddle firmly in a jail cell with Edison tending to his complaints, Hatfield said, "I think we'd better get these to Mr. Brethren, Jackson." He held up the leather shoes.

"Can Nin and I join you, Sheriff?" Adele asked. "I think Nin would enjoy a trek to the university."

"I don't suppose she has much love for McClure," Jackson remarked. "She looked as if she were ready to bite his head off during the Marsh case."

"You misunderstand, Jack," Adele said, smiling. "She has no love for scientists, but Lom and Scotty are different."

"Because they deal with organic material?"

"Because they don't treat her as if she were a witch," she insisted.

Adele could see Nin was troubled as they set out for the university in the police car. "What is it, dear?" she asked in a low voice.

"An old woman visited me," she whispered. "She had a message from my mother."

"Your mother!" Adele was alarmed, as Atha Branch had died six years before.

"She sees ghosts," said Nin. "She's not a charlatan, Adele."

"I believe you." She took her hand. "And what message did she bring from your mother?"

"Mama's lips moved, she said, although she couldn't hear her voice. 'Sordid well.' That was all she said." Her brows knitted together. "I don't know what it means."

Adele was silent for a time. "There's the well just outside of Arrojo. Do you think she was referring to that?"

"It's possible," Nin said. "But I can't think if it was a warning or a prophecy or —" She suddenly buried her face in her hands and leaned against Adele's shoulder.

Jackson glanced at them from the front seat and although Adele knew he saw Nin, he remained silent with a sympathetic look on his face. It was one thing she had always loved about him. When they were children, he would sense her moods and keep still until she went to him for comfort.

The university in Rosa Gris had the dignity of a small and exclusive establishment. The building where Lom Brethren and the more eccentric "Scotty" McClure had their laboratory was surrounded on all sides with greenery, and there were cords of ivy climbing down the side of the building where the windows looked into the gray space where they worked. The sight of the shrubbery cheered Nin, and she reached a hand to the stiff leaves, holding them to her face.

"Jade plant," she murmured. "Always a good sign."

"Let's hope it's a good sign for our investigation too," Sheriff Hatfield remarked.

The two young men they had met a few years before were now police aids as much as scientists. Though the department heads balked at first at the idea of two of their youngest researchers involved in forensics, Hatfield's influence with the district attorney, who had influence with judges and even the mayor, worked to their advantage. In the end, the professors could do nothing about it.

Both men looked up when they entered. Scotty, whose long nose was buried in his organic chemistry experiments, often sniffed at talk of bullets and blood. But Lom embraced the added responsibility gladly. Adele sensed he was bored by the benign work his degree offered him. Now he had the blue linen suit Arabella had worn draped on one of the tables.

He greeted the men with handshakes and nodded respectfully at the ladies. "You're just in time."

"You have some news for us?" Sheriff Hatfield asked.

"It looks as if you were right," Lom said.

"Half right," McClure, bent over a test tube, corrected without looking up.

"More than half, I would say," Lom objected.

"I'd be pleased to know what it is I was right about," said the sheriff, amused. "I'm not often right, you know."

"I wouldn't say that, Sheriff," Adele said warmly.

"You always answer your question marks." Nin sat on the floor in her usual manner.

"I wouldn't do that, Miss Branch." Scotty eyed her with the trepidation he reserved for ladies. "We've had some chemical spills in that area."

But Nin remained where she was, giving him a knowing look. "My ties with Sister Sun and the Generous Ones outweigh the harm your chemicals might do me any day, Mr. McClure."

The man frowned and turned back to his vial.

"You told me you didn't think the vegetation on this skirt came from a cultivated garden." Lom held up a corner of the skirt that was covered with dry mud and leaves. "You were right."

"You know that for sure?" Jackson asked.

"I know the difference between wild foliage and cultivated shrubs, Deputy," said the man. "These tamarack leaves have moss on them, which would never come from leaves in a garden tended by a gardener."

"We don't know Mr. Riddle's conservatory is tended, sir," Jackson pointed out.

"I saw a gardener roaming around when we came," Adele said.

"We'll be sure to question Mr. Riddle about that when we get back to the station," said Hatfield.

"And this." Lom pointed to a cake of mud in the fold of the skirt. "See those shreds embedded there? Those are wild mushrooms."

Nin rose from her place on the floor and joined them. "Yellow russula. Perfectly edible and non-poisonous."

"I told you!" Lom gave Scotty a satisfied look. "It was an argument between us over dinner last night."

"I'm not surprised," Nin said sourly.

"I would hardly think mushrooms would be cultivated in a garden with shrubs and flowers," Adele said. "They couldn't stand the sunlight."

"It's the sort of thing found in the forest," Nin agreed. "Only humans separate Sister Sun's beings." This earned a snort from Scotty.

"Then it's almost certain Miss Parnell wasn't killed in his conservatory," said Jackson. ""That's a point in Mr. Riddle's favor."

"That doesn't mean he didn't kill her, Deputy," Hatfield reminded him. "We need to figure out where she was killed." He looked at Lom. "Is it too much to hope you can tell us that, sir?"

"The foliage and even the mushrooms aren't exclusive to any specific location in these parts," he admitted. "they could have come from anywhere."

"Could they have come from Tanner Swamp?" Adele asked.

"They could," said Lom. "There's certainly tamarack and yellow russula in that area."

"You know that for sure?" Jackson asked.

The man smiled. "Scotty and I have a rather strange hobby, Deputy. We like to spend our free time exploring places like the swamp and Zagar Forest and the wonders of Mother Nature."

"Remember what Gene Dilworth told us, Sheriff?" Adele asked. "Tanner Swamp has become a meeting place for young couples."

"A practice I intend to stop," the sheriff grumbled.

"Mr. Riddle told me the Caton woods were one of the out-of-the-way places he and Arabella used to meet," Adele said.

Jackson stared at her. "So that's what Mr. Riddle meant when he said he told you things about himself and Miss Parnell. You've been interrogating him on your own?"

"I asked him some questions while you and the sheriff were executing your search warrant, Jack," she said mildly. "I found some very useful information."

"She always does, Mr. Gossling." Nin gave Jackson a satisfied look.

"A shame she has to meddle to do it, Miss Branch," he said, equally satisfied.

"That doesn't mean the man is guilty," Lom objected. "Sometimes things can look damaging when they're really pointing toward someone else." Adele knew he was thinking of his friend in the Marsh case a few years ago.

"Assuming it is Tanner Swamp for a moment," Hatfield said. "Since you and Mr. McClure know it well, could you identify what area of the swamp the foliage came from?"

"The swamp is rather unwieldy, Sheriff," said Lom. "These plants and the mushrooms grow in several areas."

"How many?"

"Four or five that we've found," Scotty said.

Hatfield sighed. "Well, that at least narrows it down somewhat."

"What do you intend to do, Sheriff?" asked Adele.

"A policeman's drudge work," he said with a smile.

"You mean you're going to send the assistant deputies to do the drudge work," Nin said.

Hatfield roared with laughter. "It's the sheriff's privilege to give orders to his inferiors to do work he's not anxious to do himself, Miss Branch." He looked at Lom. "I would be obliged if you would give me the list of those places where you think we ought to look, Mr. Brethren. I'll send the lads out to search."

"Search for what, sir?" Jackson asked.

"More evidence, of course," Adele supplied.

"You're very right, Adele," said Hatfield with a tip of his hat.

"I always thought Miss Gossling would make a better deputy than Mr. Gossling," Scotty said. The deputy sheriff glared at him.

"What do you hope they'll find?" asked Adele.

"A crime scene," he declared.

"Now that we know Miss Parnell wasn't killed in the conservatory, we might find some clues as to where she was killed," Jackson explained. "The killer might have dropped something, or there might be evidence someone was up to no good at least."

"I should think anyone who goes to Tanner Swamp is up to no good," Nin remarked.

"It's not a pleasant place," Lom agreed. "Rather murky and foggy most of the time."

"A shame the Tanners abandoned it when they left town," Adele remarked.

"Arrojo doesn't exactly hold fond memories for them, Del," her brother said.

Hatfield produced the shoes he had taken from Mr. Riddle's closet out of a paper bag. "I'd like your expertise on these too, Mr. Brethren."

Scotty left his vial and strolled over to the table where Lom took the shoes. "What exactly is it you'd like us to help you with, Sheriff?"

"The mud," said the sheriff. "Is it from the same place where Miss Parnell's vegetation comes from?"

"That might be difficult to ascertain," Lom said. "The makeup of the soil in this area is much the same with only some slight differences."

"It's those slight differences we're interested in," Jackson insisted.

Scotty shrugged while Lom carefully scraped some of the mud from the side of the right shoe and put it on a glass slide to examine under his microscope.

Adele noticed her friend had suddenly backed herself against a corner. She thought it was the closed windows, so she opened the door, which let in a cool breeze. But Nin's face remained vacant. She spread her arms against the wall, holding on to it as if she were clutching at a cliff. Adele noticed she was staring at the soiled skirt still on the table.

"What's the matter, dear?" She slipped beside her. "Scotty, get Nin a glass of water."

"Will coffee do?" He slid over to a contraption of bottles and burners where one boiled with black liquid.

"No, it will not do," Adele snapped. "I said water. Clean water, if you please."

"Women and their fussing," he grumbled as he left the lab with an empty cup. But he came back with a glass of cool water that Nin downed like beer.

"An aura?" Adele whispered.

Nin nodded. "Hands."

"Hands?" Adele asked. "The killer's hands?"

"Hands all over," Nin murmured.

"All over what?" Adele asked.

"Her, her!" Nin turned her face to the wall. "When she was warm."

"You mean before she was killed? But she wasn't — that is, the sheriff said they didn't find any evidence she was attacked."

Jackson's face was soft with sympathy. "Can I get you a sherry, Miss Branch? You look ill."

"I don't want anything from a vial, Mr. Gossling," she said in a shaky tone.

He gave a small smile. "I meant from a bottle. I happen to know Mr. Brethren has one hidden in the drawer of his desk."

"Nin says there were hands on Arabella before she died," Adele said.

"Hands on her," Nin insisted.

"Well, I suppose the killer had to put his hands on her to move her from wherever she was killed to the conservatory," Jackson said.

"But that would have been *after* death, Jack," Adele insisted. "Nin says the body was still warm."

"Warm and flowing with blood," Nin said.

"Don't you think your imagination is running away with you because you're upset?" Jackson asked gently.

Nin whirled around, her color back in her cheeks. "I do not imagine things, Mr. Gossling."

"I'm pleased to hear it," he said. "I'm also pleased to see your anger has given you some of your strength back." Almost with a triumphant grin, he returned to the side of his superior.

"Of all the nasty tricks!" Nin growled.

Adele couldn't help but laugh. "He played that trick on me when we were children often enough."

"I hope you kicked him in the shins for it," Nin snarled.

"As a matter of fact, I did," Adele said. This made her friend smile.

Lom put the slide in a dish and carefully laid it with the evidence they had already explored. "All I can tell you, Sheriff, is the soil here has very similar make-up to the one on the clothes. I can't testify under oath they come from the same place."

"That's all right, lad," Hatfield said kindly. "We've some direction now at least."

Adele wandered to the clothes on the table. There was something morbid about them now and she shuddered at the thought that they had been pulled off the body of a dead woman. The blouse and skirt lay as if they were waiting for a woman to fill them. The jacket was placed on the side, leaning a little, with the arms spread out, just as Arabella's had been in death. She bent over the blouse. "Sheriff! Nin was right!"

"Eh?" Sheriff Hatfield looked surprised.

"There are handprints here."

"Don't talk nonsense, Del," Jackson said.

"You can just see four fingers here and part of a palm." She pointed with the edge of her parasol, knowing better than to touch the evidence with her bare hands. "It's faint, as if someone tried to rub them out."

Both lawmen examined the blouse.

"There are some here on the skirt too, Sheriff," Jackson said.

"It makes sense there would be," Hatfield said. "If the killer moved Miss Parnell from Tanner Swamp —"

"We don't know it was Tanner Swamp," Lom pointed out.

"From wherever he or she killed her," the sheriff continued, "and if there was this sort of mud and vegetation there, it would stand to reason he would get his hands dirty." With a small chuckle, he added, "Literally, that is."

"But from both places?" Adele questioned. "Wouldn't it be more logical for the killer to drag the body from either the shoulders or the skirt?"

"If the killer was a woman," Jackson said, "she might not have been strong enough so she alternated from one end to the other to make it easier."

"I should think the weight of a dead body would be the same from the shoulders or the legs," Nin remarked.

Jackson stared down at the prints on the skirt. "Del, can I see that magnifying glass of yours?"

"I thought you didn't like them, Mr. Gossling." Nin said. "Didn't you say once they distort the evidence?"

"Sometimes a little distortion is necessary, Miss Branch," he said.

Adele handed him the glass that had belonged to their father, a delicate disc hanging from a chain encircled with gold palm leaves.

He studied both prints for some time, his nose almost touching the delicate fabric of the skirt as he bent down. Then, handing it back to Adele, he said to his superior, "It's the most extraordinary thing, Sheriff. I don't think they're the same prints."

"Eh?" Hatfield stared at him.

"I used to trail the Chicago police sometimes in my Anspach days." he said. "Unofficially, of course."

"Of course. And?"

"They were starting to use some of the more advanced methods of the French police," said Jackson. "One of those was the study of fingerprints."

"It's not so advanced, Deputy," said the sheriff with a small smile. "We'll be using fingerprinting evidence ourselves before long."

"They didn't use it for evidence, sir," Jackson said. "You know as well as I there's still a question of whether we can rely on them or not."

"Then how did they use them?" Adele asked.

"Identification," said her brother. "One thing I learned from the Chicago police is one set of fingerprints is quite different from another."

"I think we all know that, Deputy," said the sheriff.

"Yes, but they knew how to differentiate between the grooves on the fingers," said Jackson. "They taught me."

"Very good to know," Hatfield smiled. "The extension of your police knowledge never ceases to surprise me."

Jackson bowed his head, but Adele knew he was pleased at the compliment. "Naturally, I can't be sure, but the grooves on the forefinger of the prints on the skirt are quite different from those on the blouse."

Adele peered at both prints through the magnifying glass. "I'm no expert, Sheriff, but even I can see Jack is right."

"Two killers?" Scotty breathed. "Incredible!"

"Not so incredible considering the medical examiner's assistant already told us he thought there was something odd about the way Miss Parnell was shot," Hatfield said.

"But it does put a dent in your theory about Virgil Riddle," Adele pointed out.

"Unless he had an accomplice2," Nin added. "That sour-faced butler of his, maybe?"

"It's possible, Sheriff," Jackson said. "We know Maklin lied for his master about the gun. It's not unlikely he would help him with a dead body."

"Help him drag the body to his own conservatory?" The sheriff sighed. "That's one of the question marks we have to answer." He turned to Lom. "Do you have a pair of scissors handy?"

"What for?" Scotty asked.

"To get our evidence, of course," said the sheriff.

"You're going to cut through that lovely blouse and skirt?" Nin asked.

Jackson snorted. "It never ceases to amaze me how even the most progressive lady becomes fastidious at the thought of precious linens being destroyed."

"We're still women, Jack," she snapped. "And I've seen you shudder at the sight of a cake of dirt on a man's pants."

Hatfield laughed. "My apologies to the ladies for ruining Miss Parnell's clothes, but the evidence comes first."

They were able to persuade the sheriff to allow them to cut the fabric, and Nin was surprisingly delicate and accurate so when they left the lab, they had two small parcels of wrapped tissue paper.22

CHAPTER 16

Adele agreed to join the police in their visit to Dr. Rhodes to inquire after his findings on the bullets but Nin, who had no patience for the caustic medical examiner, declined and returned to her shop.

"I don't think we've ever had a case where bullets were involved," she said. "I'm anxious to see how they do it."

"It's not a pretty sight, Del," said her brother. "The bullets are likely to be misshapen and maybe even have remnants of human bone or flesh because they've been extracted from Miss Parnell."

Adele stiffened. "You know I'm not the sort to faint at the sight of blood, Jack."

"It can be rather fascinating." The sheriff pulled the police car up to the two-story building Dr. Rhodes used as his office, laboratory, and home.

"I hope you don't put the doctor on edge, Del," Jackson said. "You know how he feels about women."

"Then he'll just have to get used to seeing us more often," she said in a stubborn tone. "More women these days are going for professions men didn't think was their right in the last century. I read that some counties are even considering allowing women to be coroners and medical examiners."

"Between a woman coroner and a woman detective, I should think the former is the lesser of two evils," Jackson said with a glint in his eye, earning a shove in his shoulder from his sister.

Jackson was right. Dr. Rhodes was none too pleased to see her accompanying the police. It was also just before the lunch hour, and Arrojo's medical examiner took his mealtimes as sacred.

"There never seems to be much rhyme or reason to your visits, Sheriff," he grumbled as he snatched the folder Martin held out to him. "You come at the most inconvenient times."

"I'm sorry about that, but murder doesn't wait, as you well know." Hatfield was well acquainted with Dr. Rhodes' hostile behavior and always tried to be calm.

Adele glanced around the doctor's laboratory, as she had never been there before. She had to admit it was more impressive than the one they just left. The white marble floor and counters gleamed under the plentiful lamps and there was an abundance of beakers, burners, and slides, each in a neat little place so that nothing would get confused.

"You have quite a place here, Doctor," she complimented.

It was the right thing to say, as Dr. Rhodes' usual sour look eased a little. "It wouldn't do for a medical examiner to have a dusty little closet, would it, Miss Gossling?"

Adele saw Martin flinch, as she knew Dr. Rhodes' insinuation referred to Lom and Scotty's modest laboratory, both of whom were good friends of Martin's.

"Sometimes that's all one needs," she said shrewdly.

"True, true," the man admitted. "Examining leaves hardly requires the same sort of modern equipment as examining bullets."

"Speaking of bullets," the sheriff said, "We're hoping you have the ballistics report for us."

"*I* don't," said the man. "Mr. Samuels does."

"Oh?" Adele eyed him. "You spoke so firmly about examining bullets, I thought you were the one who did it." This earned a side grin from Martin.

Dr. Rhodes' face colored. "I'm a medical expert, Miss Gossling, not a ballistics expert."

"And where do we find this Mr. Samuels?" Hatfield was losing his patience.

"You don't." He picked up the phone. "I'll call him and ask him to come here."

"At your beck and call, is he?" Adele lifted an eyebrow.

The man gave her a seething look. "I'm thankful one thing you forward-thinking women don't expect is respect for your insolence!"

"My sister might not, but I do," Jackson said with a thundering look.

The man glared at him and dialed the exchange.

Mr. Samuels appeared within ten minutes and was, Adele was thankful to note, a more amiable man than his friend. He was, in fact, rather excited about his business. "I haven't had much work in the counties in this area since I was appointed only six months ago," he said. "Not much use in a ballistics expert in a bar fight where there are a dozen witnesses who know to whom the bullet that killed the poor fellow belonged."

"I'm glad we could provide you with some refreshment," Hatfield said dryly. "But we've a case to solve."

"I'm afraid you won't solve it with these bullets." The man took out a box where he spilled three bullets onto a clean sheet of paper. Adele felt a little ill at the thought of the bullets taken out of the flesh of a dead woman.

Hatfield sighed. "I was afraid of that."

"Were you able to discover anything?" asked Jackson.

"I can tell you very little," the man admitted. "You see, the bullets are manufactured which probably means the guns that fired them were as well. Back in the day when guns were hand-made, we could track them down to the maker. Not so with factory guns." He sniffed. "Now any old sod could go into a gun shop and purchase a revolver."

"Provided he gets a license for it," Adele chimed in.

He grinned. "You must be Miss Gossling, the deputy's brother. I've heard a lot about you."

"I can imagine what you heard." She glared at Dr. Rhodes.

"You're mistaken, miss," he said. "I approve of ladies getting the vote and all that. This country would be much better if they did."

"I couldn't agree more, Mr. Samuels." She gave her brother a satisfied look.

"So you can't tell us what sort of guns fired the bullets," the sheriff concluded.

"I didn't say that, Sheriff," he said. "There was a Colt revolver —"

"Mr. Riddle said he had an old revolver, sir," Jackson said.

"Martin!" The sheriff used the same cutting voice that he used on his assistant deputies except that Martin didn't flinch.

"Yes, Sheriff?"

"Run down to the station and ask Edison to bring the gun and bullets we picked up from Virgil Riddle's home."

"Picked up?" Dr. Rhodes eyed him. "Isn't that taking your authority a little too far?"

"We had a warrant," Jackson said.

"You should know my methods by now, Doctor," Hatfield said in a sharp tone. "I don't do anything I don't feel is necessary."

"I wouldn't say that," the man mumbled. "I can think of several instances where you were a little too diligent with your work."

"And you're not diligent enough," Adele snapped. "I'm sure you didn't even start the autopsy report on Miss Parnell yet."

"To have a report, Miss Gossling, one must first complete the autopsy," he said. "It's difficult to do such delicate work when the town sheriff and his deputy *and* his deputy's sister barge in demanding to know about bullets."

Adele turned her back to him. "Tell me, Mr. Samuels, why would someone shoot a woman in the back? Don't killers prefer to shoot in the chest?"

"I can't speak for the criminals," he said with a chuckle. "I think your sheriff would know more about that than I would."

"There's no rulebook about killing, Del," Jackson said.

"Perhaps the shooter was a coward." Mr. Samuels shrugged. "That's the usual reason for shooting someone in the back."

"The person may have been trying to escape and had their back turned to the killer," Hatfield suggested.

"Yes, I can see that," Adele said.

"At least we know what we're dealing with now," Jackson said. "A Colt with three bullets fired."

"I beg to differ, Deputy." Mr. Samuels leaned against the desk.

"Eh?" The sheriff glanced at him.

"You didn't let me finish before," said the man. "I see Anvil was right when he warned me about your rather bulldog ways."

Adele could see the anger rising in Hatfield's face, but his tone was as mild-mannered as always. "I apologize, sir."

The man grinned. "Actually, what I did find out about those bullets might help you a little. There were at least two guns used."

"Two!" Jackson glanced at the sheriff. "Martin was right, then."

"Martin?" Dr. Rhodes gave the deputy a sharp look. "Has he been making guesses in his medical examination?"

"Martin doesn't make guesses, sir," the sheriff snapped. "The boy knows what he's doing."

"Perhaps better than you do," Adele mumbled.

"Two bullets," Sheriff Hatfield lamented. "That complicates matters."

"Two or three," Mr. Samuels said. "As I said, there is still so much about ballistics we don't know."

"But you know enough to determine more than one gun was used?" Adele asked.

He nodded. "A Colt, as I mentioned. The other was a Browning."

"You're sure?" Hatfield asked.

"Oh, positive. The two guns are nothing like one another and neither are their bullets."

"And can you tell us nothing else?" Jackson asked. "Make, model?"

He sighed. "There, I'm afraid, I'm at a loss. As I said, these guns are manufactured. One looks very much like another. Nothing unique about any of them."

"You said before there were two or three guns used," Adele said. "Don't you know?"

"That's another problem," said Mr. Samuels. "Two bullets came from a Colt and one from the Browning."

"But it may not have been the same Colt," Jackson surmised.

"Exactly," he said.

"Don't different guns use different bullets?" Adele asked.

"Some do, and some don't, Miss Gossling," he said. "At any rate, I couldn't even do a full analysis on this bullet." He picked up one that looked like a wrinkled eyelid. "It's far too smashed for me to get anything from it." Seeing her flinch, he quickly put it back in the box and closed the lid.

"So we may be dealing with three guns and not two," the sheriff murmured.

Martin trailed in with Edison at his heels.

The sheriff clasped the young man on his back so hard that his glasses slid forward on his nose. "Well, Martin, you were right about the shots."

"Was I right?" The young man blinked.

"Mr. Samuels just told us more than one gun was used to kill Miss Parnell," Adele said.

"You've the makings of an expert medical examiner," Hatfield assured him. "None I've seen would have been so thorough as to detect that sort of detail."

Adele was amused at the annoyance on Dr. Rhodes' face as he didn't miss the implication.

"Edison!" The sheriff turned to him. "You needn't handle that box as if it's precious china, lad. Give it to me."

He laid the gun and box of bullets they had taken from Mr. Riddle's house on the table. Mr. Samuels produced a magnifying glass, the sort that jewelers used, out of his pocket. "Anvil, can you spare me a pair of your rubber gloves?"

"What for?" the man snarled.

His friend glared at him. "My work may not be as delicate as cutting open a dead body, but I do like to be careful."

The doctor sniffed but before he could say more, Martin produced a pair of gloves and handed them to Mr. Samuels.

"Much obliged, young man," he said. "You'll go far in this world."

Martin blushed and retreated to the corner, his glasses slipping down his nose.

After a little examination, Mr. Samuels put down the gun. "A Remington here, Sheriff."

"Mr. Riddle's old revolver isn't a Colt, then." Jackson looked disappointed.

"They're two entirely different firearms," said the man.

"Maybe he has two guns and gave us this one to throw us off the track." Jackson looked at the sheriff.

Hatfield shook his head. "We searched his house from top to bottom. Even the hidden places. What about the bullets?"

"Of course I can't be absolutely positive," said Mr. Samuels. "But I can tell you these two —" he pointed to the two bullets in the box that were somewhat intact, "— are almost surely not from a Remington."

"How can you tell?" Adele peered at them. "They all look the same to me."

Jackson smiled. "To a woman, they would, Del."

"Because women don't know guns?" Adele glared at him. "If you recall, dear brother, we met a young lady last year who was as handy with a gun as Annie Oakley."

"And who displayed her talents in a Wild West show and nowhere else," Jackson argued.

"If you'll pardon me, Deputy, your sister's quite right," said Mr. Samuels, putting his hands on the edge of the table. "Many men don't notice differences between bullets, even when they aren't so subtle."

"And these aren't." The sheriff held up a bullet from the box they had taken from Mr. Riddle. "These are almost majestic bullets compared to the two here."

Adele thought it a strange way to describe such deadly weapons, but as she studied them, she saw what the sheriff meant. The Remington bullets were large and gold-plated. In contrast, the other two bullets were small and copper-topped.

"What about the third bullet?" Adele asked.

"That I can't say," said Mr. Samuels. "It's too crushed for me to know what gun it came from."

"So it might have been from a Remington." Jackson eyed the sheriff, who nodded.

"It might have been from a pop gun." The man laughed. "I have heard tell they're making toy guns for boys these days that mimic the real thing."

"I hope not." Her brother looked genuinely horrified. "We have enough glorification of gun fights in these new moving pictures."

"Too bad *The Great Train Robbery* made such an impression on youngsters in the vaudeville houses a few years back," Mr. Samuels agreed with a grumble. "Now every little boy wants to be a bandit."

"Thank you for the information, Mr. Samuels." Hatfield shook his hand and gathered the bullets and Remington in the box.

"Take these back to the evidence room, Edison. And mind you don't lose anything along the way."

"Yes, sir." The assistant deputy scurried away.

~~~~~

Adele had arranged to meet with Vera Mead to discuss the progress of the new wing to her shop and go over a few concerns she had. The meeting took all afternoon and it was dark by the time they finished. Vera insisted on taking her to dinner at The Soaring Eagle, which had begun to acquire more of a crowd since it opened the year before.

While she and Vera were gathering their coats and hats, she felt a tug on her arm. Mayor Willett stood with a nervous look on his face, his lips as round as his face.

"May I have a word with you, Miss Gossling?"

Adele glanced at Vera, who smiled and gave a tip of her hat to the mayor. Mayor Willett put on his politician smile though Adele knew he had no idea who she was or that she did not live in Arrojo. She mumbled that she would wait for Adele outside and pushed open the door.

The mayor took her to a corner table near the front which she knew was always reserved for him. "I wanted to prevail upon you to use your influence." His voice was low.

"I thought you were opposed to my using my influence anywhere but my shop," she said.

"Really, Miss Gossling, there is a time and a place for everything," he hissed. "I understand Virgil Riddle has been arrested."

"I wouldn't say that —"

"I think we know how this works, Miss Gossling." He leaned back, a suddenly sly look in his eye. "He's taken Virgil in because he has no other suspect at the moment. Isn't that right?"

"If you mean did your idea about Miss Parnell being killed by 'her own kind' prove true? It didn't," she said.

"Exactly!" He put both hands on the table. "Now, Miss
~~~~~

Gossling, we both know the sheriff is — well, shall we say, rather unpolished."

"You seem to forget his mother was married to a lord," Adele said shortly.

"A duck is born a duck, not a swan," Mayor Willet mumbled.

"But a duck can wag its feathers just as well as a swan," she countered.

"Virgil is entirely innocent," he insisted. "A victim of circumstance."

Adele slowly rose. "Then he has nothing to fear, has he?"

"The sheriff may not see it that way." He looked at her. "Your vision, on the other hand, isn't clouded by your position in the community."

"Aren't I lucky to be the town outcast?" She couldn't help but feel amused. "I wish you would get to the point, Mayor. Jack has no idea where I am, and I don't want worry him by staying out too late."

"It's as I said before, Miss Gossling. Use your influence."

"With whom and for what?"

"Why, the sheriff, of course," he said in a smooth tone. "He listens to you. If you could convince him —"

"You want me to talk the sheriff into letting Mr. Riddle go?" Adele stared at him.

"Nothing of the kind," he insisted. "Merely to educate him on the virtues of people like us when it comes to horrendous matters as these —"

Adele stiffened and pulled her hat over one eye. "Mayor, I am not 'people like us.' I am a working girl who trusts the police to do their job."

"I never said I didn't!" His voice squeaked. "I only say I don't want the sheriff to make a mistake."

"He hasn't made any serious one yet, has he?" Adele asked. "I won't keep my friend waiting any longer."

"Then you won't intercede?" Mayor Willet gave her a hard look.

In answer, she walked out of the restaurant.

She took her time getting home, letting the cool night air calm her down. She hadn't been entirely truthful to the mayor. Earlier, she had phoned and asked Tomas to let Jackson know she wouldn't be home for dinner. Jackson was in the parlor reading the paper when she came in. She dropped into her favorite spot on the couch, still seething.

"I take it your dinner with Vera didn't go well." He eyed her.

"It wasn't the dinner," she said. "It was the dessert. A large dose of Mayor Willett."

"What did he want?" Jackson poured her a cup of coffee.

"Only for me to sweet-talk the sheriff into letting Mr. Riddle go."

"Good Lord!" He stared at her.

"He thinks Sheriff Hatfield doesn't understand how 'people like us' feel about such 'horrendous matters as these.'"

"The sheriff understands only too well," Jackson said in a harsh tone.

She sighed and took her knitting in her lap. "It does seem as if the idea about Mr. Riddle might fall through with two guns killing Arabella, unless Maklin has a Colt hidden somewhere."

He sniffed. "May I remind you that you're not a police consultant?"

"Yet," she snapped. "The sheriff promised to try again in another six months when the mayor has calmed down." She sighed. "Somehow, I don't think the mayor is going to be very amenable to the idea now."

Her brother reached for his pipe. "I wouldn't be so sure, dear sister. You have the sheriff wrapped around your little finger."

"Nonsense, Jack." She propped another pillow behind her lower back, as the chairs at the Soaring Eagle were hard. "Was it really so surprising to hear two different guns shot Arabella?"

"Why do you ask?" Jackson glanced at her.

"I got the feeling you've seen something like it before," she said.

"As a matter of fact, I did once, with the Anspaches," he said thoughtfully. "A man whose employer suspected him of embezzling. We got the evidence and the police were all set to prosecute when the man went completely insane. He shot his wife, his brother and his sister-in-law so they couldn't testify against him and escaped."

"And he used three different guns?" Adele stared.

"He was a very crafty fellow," Jackson insisted. "The guns were borrowed from three different men. He later told the police he was sure it would confuse them."

"But it didn't," she pointed out.

"It confused *them*, but not us," said Jackson, not without a little pride in his voice. "The Anspaches had their faults, but one can't say they don't think of every angle, even the most highly improbable ones."

"But would Mr. Riddle have enough foresight to think of using two or even three different guns to shoot the same person?" Adele folded her hands. "It seems unlikely, Jack."

Her brother shrugged. "If a man is desperate and has the means, Del, he's liable to do anything that strikes his fancy."

"If that's so, why didn't you find the other guns in your search?" She pointed out.

"If that's indeed what happened, we will," he insisted. "Firearms are not so easy to get rid of."

"If he did get rid of the other two guns —"

"We don't know there were two other guns," Jackson point out. "Remember, Mr. Samuels said there might have been three used to kill Miss Parnell."

"All right," she said, "if he did get rid of the other gun or two, why would he keep the Remington if he also used it to shoot Arabella?"

"Sentimental value," her brother said. "He said it was a relic from the Civil War."

"Really, Jack," she sniffed, "I doubt a man would keep a memento he had just used to kill a woman!"

He chuckled. "Perhaps you're right. Hatfield isn't drawing any conclusions until he's secured more evidence that he can bring to Marland."

"What about the search at Tanner Swamp?" Adele asked.

"That's at least one question mark answered." Jackson lit his pipe. "Miss Parnell was killed at the swamp, no doubt about it."

Adele looked at him with surprise. "I don't think I've ever heard you be surer of anything in a murder case."

"Lom went with us," he said. "He pointed to places where the vegetation he found on the clothes grows, and we combed the area as well as we could." In an almost rueful tone, he added, "Of course, you can take that with a grain of salt since we had to rely on those bumbling assistant detectives to help us."

"Don't be unfair, Jack," she said. "Edison has helped a great deal with these cases and so has Dooland."

"Dooland seems to have all the luck finding things," he said. "He found a piece of cloth we know belonged to Miss Parnell caught on some thorns of a bush."

"From her suit?"

He shook his head. "We compared it to one of her dresses — the Parnells were kind enough to give them back to us before they left on the train — to the piece and it fit like a puzzle piece right on the inside skirt."

"That means she was there not just on the night of the murder." Adele stared at the low flames in the fireplace. Tomas bounced from his corner and began putting more logs in the fireplace.

"That's Hatfield's theory," said Jackson. "I wish the man, whoever he was, had left a spot of his clothing."

"That still wouldn't make your case," she insisted. "From what we've been told, Arabella saw a number of men."

"But did she meet all of them regularly at the swamp?" Her brother questioned. "And did she meet them at night?"

"How do you know she met anyone at night?" Adele asked.

"Because a candle holder with a pile of wax was set down on the ground."

Adele grinned. "Another one of Dooland's finds?"

"Edison's this time," said Jackson. "It seemed a very womanly thing to do, to take a candleholder with the candle —"

"It's a smart thing to do," she countered. "You can't very well drive a candle in the ground like a stake or you set the entire swamp on fire."

Jackson laughed, bowing his head. "We checked with Mrs. Taylor to see if one of her candlesticks were missing and it was. The one we found was an exact match. So was the candle that had burned down."

"Then Arabella took the candlestick and candle to her meeting that night," Adele said.

"We don't know it was that night for sure, of course," Jackson said. "But from what we gathered of Miss Parnell's short stay at Mrs. Taylor's, it's the only opportunity she had to go out at night."

"Where did you find it?"

"By the twin tupelo trees." He smiled. "You remember it?"

"I remember when we first came that it was a peaceful place before the swamp crept in." She sighed.

"Well, it's not so beautiful now, Del," he said.

"Now it's a site for a murder," she agreed with a shiver.

CHAPTER 17

The next day, two businessmen from the East came into her shop with desperate looks on their faces. They were traveling and the car they rented got stuck in a ditch just outside of Arrojo. Adele kindly roused Mr. Duncan, the postmaster, who used the post office phone to call someone he knew in Rosa Gris to the car and driver stranded by the ditch.

In chatting with them while they waited, she discovered they both owned mid-sized businesses in Vermont. By the time their car was fixed, she extracted two large orders from them and a dozen slips for the wholesalers to deliver within the next few weeks.

Exuberant, she hurried to the police station at noon, intending to take Jackson out for a celebratory lunch. When she entered, she immediately felt a somber air blanketing the usually bustling station.

Both her brother and the sheriff were in the interview room with Mr. Riddle. The man looked furious, his scruffy appearance contrasting with the polished man she had seen the night of Gene Dilworth's party.

Both lawmen caught her eye and Jackson rose, coming out to her.

"You look as if you discovered a mummy in the closet," Adele remarked, her jubilance tamed by concern.

"I wish we had," he mumbled.

"What happened?"

"We're questioning Mr. Riddle."

"I can see that," she said.

"We weren't exactly prepared for it," he said. "The district attorney forced our hand."

"I'm anxious to hear the rest." She pulled off her gloves, put her parasol aside, and marched into the interview room, in spite of her brother's protests.

She thought for a moment Hatfield was going to send her out, but he pulled out the only other chair in the room and motioned for her to sit.

"This whole thing is ridiculous!" Mr. Riddle barely gave her a glance.

"We have further questions for you, sir, and it's our right to ask them," Hatfield said. "Lawyer or no lawyer," he added.

The man gave a sly smile. "I take it you've had your orders."

"No one gives the sheriff orders," Jackson snarled. "Not your friends or the mayor himself."

Adele's stomach tightened. "The mayor?"

"I warned you, didn't I?" Mr. Riddle's grin was like the devil. "I warned you not to push me too far."

Ignoring this, the sheriff asked, "Where did you go when you went with Miss Parnell to Tanner Swamp?"

"I never went to Tanner Swamp with Arabella or anyone else." He gave the sheriff an incredulous look. "Did someone say they saw us?"

"Was she ever dressed in a peach and tan evening gown?" continued Hatfield.

"Why, did someone say they saw her wearing a dress like that when she was with me?"

"We ask the questions, sir," Jackson said. "Don't be impertinent!"

"You're the one being impertinent, Deputy," the man shot back. "I believe the detective novels call it 'fishing for evidence.'"

Hatfield tried again. "We know your gun is a Remington revolver."

"Did that bullet expert the mayor sent over say the bullet that killed Arabella was from a Remington?" To the sheriff's surprised face, he grinned again. "Oh, yes, I know about that."

"It seems you know more than you're entitled to know, sir," Jackson mumbled.

"Let's put our cards on the table, shall we?" The man leaned forward. "You brought me here because of a writ and you had no choice. Now you're trying to badger me into confessing something I didn't do." He grinned. "Am I right?"

Hatfield took out of his pocket the wrapped tissue paper package that contained the samples of the skirt and blouse and laid them on the table. "Do these look familiar, Mr. Riddle?"

"Why should they?" the man asked.

"Instead of asking rude questions, why don't you look at what the sheriff is showing you?" Jackson snarled.

Mr. Riddle glanced down at them. "Isn't that blue material the same as what Arabella was wearing when —" he gulped, "when we found her?"

"Do you see what's on them?" the sheriff asked.

Mr. Riddle glanced down again. Adele could see that his attention was now more fully absorbed. "Good Lord!"

"Handprints," Hatfield said.

"Why the blazes didn't you notice them before?"

"Because they were on the front of Arabella's clothes," Adele supplied. "We found her face down."

His look was genuinely excited. "Why, this could be the whole key to your case, Sheriff."

"It could be," said Hatfield mildly. "Did you touch the body when you found it, Mr. Riddle?"

"I didn't find it," the man reminded him. "My man Maklin did."

"But he called you as soon as he found it," Jackson objected.

"Of course I didn't touch the body." He looked almost squeamish. "Do you think I would lay a finger on a stone-cold girl like that?"

Adele studied the man. She realized for all his bravado he had the backbone of a snake. "I think he's telling the truth, Sheriff."

"Did Maklin touch the body?"

Mr. Riddle snorted. "Maklin is a very discreet fellow, Sheriff. He knows better than that." His eyes regarded the sheriff with a beady look. "I see what you're trying to do. Now you're going to say those prints are mine." He gave him a sly look. "I don't know as Mr. Angus Rand is going to like that, Sheriff."

Jackson let out a whistle. "Angus Rand. All the way from San Francisco!"

"You know the man?" He glanced at him.

"My sister and I are well acquainted with him," he said. "He was a colleague of our father's."

"Otis Gossling was indeed a formidable defender," Mr. Riddle said, his tone admiring. "It's a shame he isn't alive, or the mayor would have called him in."

Adele felt a tingle of pain in her chest at the thought of her beloved father, who always had a laugh ready to fall from his lips, now dead for six years. As if by instinct, she reached inside her bag and pulled out the white handkerchief with *O.G* initialed on it and held it to her eyes.

Mr. Riddle watched her and said softly, "I'm sorry if I've upset you, Miss Gossling. I didn't mean it in a flippant way. I know your father was the best criminal lawyer in the city and, as the sheriff has made clear, I'm going to need one. Temporarily that is."

"That was the district attorney's doing, sir, not mine," Hatfield mumbled.

Mr. Riddle rose. "Since you clearly have nothing on me, I'm free to go?"

"For now." Hatfield eyed him.

"Good," he said. "It will be a relief to go to Lake Cuyamaca for some fishing and forget this whole business."

"I meant you're free to go home," said the sheriff with a stern look. "But you're not to leave town, Mr. Riddle."

He glared at him. "But you've nothing on which to hold me."

"There's still the hearing, sir," Jackson said. "The hearing your lawyer instrumented, may we remind you?"

"And when will that be?"

Hatfield rose slowly. "You'll have to ask Mr. Rand that. Deputy, I believe Scott is around here somewhere? Will you ask him to see Mr. Riddle home in the police car?"

He said it so cordially that Adele had to hide her laugh. Even Jackson bit back a smile as he replied, "Certainly, Sheriff. I'll be glad to."

"No thank you!" Mr. Riddle buttoned his coat. "I prefer to take myself home."

"You're still in a sense under my care, sir," Sheriff Hatfield said. "I wouldn't want your lawyer to visit you in a jail cell because you broke custody. Ah, Scott!" The young man, whose attempt to grow a beard had made it an unwieldy shade of gold, poked his head inside the doorway. "See that Mr. Riddle gets home, won't you, lad?"

"Right away, Sheriff," he said in a breathless voice.

With a snarl in his direction, Mr. Riddle stomped out of the room, following the assistant deputy out the door.

The moment he slammed the door, all three of them collapsed with laughter.

"You're a devil sometimes, Sheriff," Adele said. "In the best possible way, of course."

"It will make my day thinking about a policeman escorting him to the door while his high-and-mighty neighbors watch," Jackson said, his grin deeper than Adele had seen in a long time.

"There are ways of making men who believe they're above the law understand they're just like everyone else when it comes to crime," Hatfield said as he sat down, clearly pleased with himself.

"He'll probably have Rand try to slap you with a violation of rights," Jackson said. "Rand's the type."

"There are some places, Deputy, where police authority still counts." Hatfield pushed the chair under the table. "Even in the face of a habeas corpus."

"We should have expected it, sir," Jackson said.

"What exactly is a habeas corpus?" Adele asked.

"We now need to come up with irrefutable evidence to charge Mr. Riddle," Hatfield said. "The writ requires him to attend a hearing where we present this evidence to either charge him formally or release him from all charges."

"Hence the questioning." Adele nodded.

"I thought Mr. Riddle would stew for a little bit until we could find something," grumbled the sheriff. "I didn't expect he would get a lawyer so quickly."

"He didn't," Adele said. "The mayor did." She felt her anger rise. "I'll bet he had him reserved already when he made his appeal to me last night."

"I heard about that," said the sheriff. "I'm glad you refused, Adele."

"It got you into a mess, though," she said.

"It's a mess I've been in more than once." The sheriff put on his hat. "Join us for lunch?"

"I don't mind if I do." Adele took the sheriff's arm with one hand and Jackson's in the other. "I was going to ask Jack to lunch but now I have the privilege of lunching with two handsome men instead of one."

"Don't believe her, Sheriff," Jackson said as they left the station. "She once told Elsie I had the face of a frog when I was a baby."

Their jolly mood continued as they walked toward the Hatfield house where the sheriff often ate with his mother.

"Do you really still suspect Mr. Riddle, Sheriff?" Adele asked. "Tell the truth now."

"He's fighting it awfully hard, Sheriff," Jackson pointed out. "A man doesn't hire one of the best criminal lawyers in San Francisco if he's entirely innocent."

"Unless he wants to make the police look foolish," Adele said. "Or he has the protection of the town mayor."

"We still have reason to suspect him," Jackson pointed out. "That smashed bullet might be from his Remington. It was gold-plated, after all."

"We also know Miss Parnell had ideas about connecting herself with a high-society man," Hatfield said. "And we know Mr. Riddle is bent on marrying Mrs. Allington.

"A woman who, if she has any dignity at all, would hardly accept a man who has a shadow in his past involving affairs with domestics," Adele added.

"I think the sheriff meant that if Mrs. Allington found out about him and Miss Parnell — whether it was a familial relationship or not — it's likely she is, as you said, Del, a woman of dignity and would never have consented to marrying him," Jackson said.

"The handprint evidence seems to have fallen by the wayside," Adele remarked. "I was comparing them to Mr. Riddle's hands while he spoke. There is no way they would match."

"I noticed that," the sheriff said. "We still have other evidence we need to explore. The note, for example."

"If we could prove Miss Parnell wrote that note, it might be enough for the hearing," Jackson pointed out. "The murder victim incriminating the murderer is strong evidence."

Adele pulled a leaf from a low-hanging tree as they passed. "Yes, that would help, wouldn't it?"

Sheriff Hatfield sighed. "Our already complicated case just got more complicated, Deputy."

"It always does when politics is involved," Jackson growled.

They entered the gate of the Hatfield house. It looked almost like an English cottage with its sloping roof and colorful front garden. Mr. Dunham, the handyman, waved at them from the shed.

"It was very kind of you to take in that man after the McCarthy case," Adele reflected.

"He probably would have been long dead if you hadn't," Jackson agreed.

"I wouldn't underestimate people's endurance, Jackson." Hatfield fumbled for the key to the door. "Mr. Dunham has been a great help to us with the house. There are things Ma can't do and with me away all day —"

"It's good to have a man about the house." Adele gave her brother an appreciative look.

"Aren't you the one who's always harping about how women can do anything men can do?" Jackson teased.

"Of course they can!" This came from Lady Augusta, who had wheeled herself to the hallway.

"We were just talking about how Mr. Dunham is a great addition to the household, Ma." Hatfield gave her a large kiss on each cheek.

"Because I'm so helpless?" She glared at him. "You're far too protective of me, Horatio. Why, I was scaling mountains like a billy goat while you were in my belly."

"I'm sure, Ma." His face glowed red as he hung up his coat. "You don't mind the extra guests for lunch, do you?"

"Don't be daft!" his mother scolded. "Haven't I always told you to drag that deputy of yours here for a meal? Not to mention those young men you're yelling at all the time."

"I didn't think you wanted a brigade at your table, Ma." Hatfield grinned as he pulled a chair out for Adele.

"They'd eat us out of hearth and home if they all came." Rowena, who acted as both Lady Augusta's companion and housekeeper, shuddered.

"And what if they did?" the woman declared. "I like to see young men eat hearty."

"You certainly taught me to have a large appetite," the sheriff remarked.

The woman brushed aside Rowena's attempts to help her with her napkin. "Did you get that formidable Virgil Riddle to confess, dear?"

"We don't try to get anyone to confess, Ma," her son reminded her. "They have to confess on their own."

"Well, did he confess on his own?"

"Naturally not," the sheriff said. "Not yet, anyway."

"He has a prominent San Francisco lawyer working for him now," Adele said.

"I'm not surprised," Lady Augusta snorted. "Horatio will get around him, don't you worry."

"At the moment, I can't even get around this soup." Hatfield looked down distastefully at the orange liquid.

"Carrot soup, dear. It's good for you," his mother said. "Don't tell me you've run out of ideas already."

"Mr. Riddle might be innocent, Lady Augusta," Jackson said.

"Innocent or not, he hasn't been honest," Adele said.

"How do you know that, Del?" Her brother eyed her.

"I don't buy for one moment that he and Arabella were like father and daughter," she said.

"A man of forty does not treat a pretty young girl of twenty like a daughter," Lady Augusta agreed with disgust.

"Nor does he take her to private places to teach her social graces," Adele said.

"Social graces!" When Adele told her Mr. Riddle's story, the woman threw her head back and laughed. It was the first time Adele noticed her laughter could be as deep as her son's.

"What poppycock!" said Lady Augusta.

"Until we prove that, Ma, Mr. Riddle doesn't have a motive," Hatfield said.

"I believe what Nathan told me," Adele said.

"And who is Nathan?" the elderly woman questioned, dipping her bread in her soup.

"A friend of the Dilworths'," Adele said.

"And a friend of yours too, I see." Lady Augusta eyed her.

"In a way," Adele mumbled, glad when the pork chops were served so she could concentrate on something else.

"Mr. Cress has no proof of what he says and neither does Mr. Dilworth." The sheriff's tone was brisk.

"If there was proof, it would certainly help your case, wouldn't it?" Adele asked.

"*If* there was something to connect Miss Parnell and Mr. Riddle that was, erm, compromising —" Jackson coughed.

"Then you could tell the mayor and this fancy city lawyer to go stuff their habeas corpus where no one can see it," said the elderly woman.

Adele turned to the sheriff. "What are you going to do?"

Hatfield took some time to answer. He seemed intent on dressing his meat perfectly around the edges and getting his string beans to lay one next to the other.

"Horatio!" His mother tapped the side of his shoe with her cane. "Answer the woman."

"I was thinking, Ma," he said. "We know from what Mrs. Dilworth told us that Miss Parnell liked beautiful things but her salary hardly allowed her to buy them."

"Yet we found some expensive dresses in her wardrobe, not to mention gloves and jewelry," Jackson said.

"It stands to reason someone, probably a man, bought them for her," the sheriff continued.

"I came to that conclusion a long time ago, dear," said his mother. "Really, Horatio, sometimes I think your mind isn't on your work with this case."

He blushed. "Perhaps it isn't, Ma."

"That man might have been Virgil Riddle," Adele offered.

"Perhaps she had several gentlemen friends," Jackson said. "Remember, sir, we found several different prints on the clothes."

"You're assuming, Jack," his sister snapped. "Even if Miss Parnell did step out with more than one man, that doesn't mean she accepted gifts from all of them."

"A woman with plans for herself usually elevates one man of many as the special one," Lady Augusta agreed. "She knows accepting gifts from the others will put their minds in the wrong direction."

"With all due respect, Lady Augusta, I've met women who have no qualms about putting a man's mind in the wrong direction for all she can get out of him," Jackson said.

"And so have I," the elderly woman countered. "But from what the town gossips say about Miss Parnell, I don't think she would have wasted her time courting a dress here or a pin there from many men."

"She wanted respect and status," Adele agreed.

"The question is, who did she go after to get it?" Hatfield lamented. "Mr. Riddle or someone else?"

"It all goes back to the gloves and jewelry." Jackson fished another potato from the platter on the table.

"We have to find out where they were bought and by whom," his superior agreed.

"It's not going to be as easy as you think," Adele said. "Salesgirls would hardly remember who bought one trinket or another."

"They likely sell dozens of them." Lady Augusta nodded. "Rowena, take this away and tell the new cook we asked for rice with lunch, not rice pudding."

"The woman can't see worth a hill of beans," Rowena mumbled as she took the platter away.

The sheriff speared a wedge of cantaloupe from the fruit plate. "I hardly think there are a dozen of those ornate combs lying about."

"Let us hope not," Jackson mumbled.

"The same with the brooch," Hatfield said. "And even the gloves. Someone will remember who bought them."

"They don't look like Moffitt's style," Jackson said. "He tends to be much more conservative."

"You're not starting in Arrojo?" Adele stared at him. "Surely, if the affair was clandestine, the man would hardly risk being identified by locals."

"He may not have had any idea of murder on his mind when he bought those things, Del," said her brother.

"But he would have his reputation on his mind," Lady Augusta insisted. "If he was indeed a man of wealth, he wouldn't risk any gossip leaking out about town that could reach his social circle."

"We have to start somewhere," Hatfield pointed out.

Jackson picked up his coffee cup. "So we start with Moffitt's Jewelers?"

The sheriff nodded. "Then we go to Watts Fine Jewelry in Rosa Gris and a few other places there." He finished his coffee and rose. "Delightful lunch, Ma, as always. Even with the rice pudding." He winked and kissed her cheek.

Adele took her hat from the rack, playing with the rim for a moment. "Sheriff, may I make a suggestion?"

"You know I'm always open to suggestions from you, Adele," he said in a warm tone.

"Let Missy print an advertisement in the paper about the missing jewels and gloves," she said.

"Are you crazy, Del?" Jackson glared at her. "They're our leading clues."

"You don't have to mention them in connection with a murder case," she said.

"I know you have no objection to telling lies during an investigation, but we as lawmen have to stick to the truth!" Her brother was indignant.

"I don't tell lies, Jack," she snapped. "I tell stories sometimes to get at the truth."

"Sometimes a story is worth the truth, Deputy," Lady Augusta, who had accompanied them to the door said sharply. "Horatio! Tell him I'm right."

"Ma's right, Jackson," he said. "A little white lie might gain us a pound of truth."

"And what little white lie do you want us to tell Missy?" Jackson put on his hat.

"You believe some items might have been stolen from some shops here, and you're looking for any information about them," said Adele.

"She'll relish that," Jackson mumbled. "She's been dying to print about the gloves and jewelry since this case began."

"But she hasn't," Adele said. "She's stuck strictly to what the sheriff has allowed her to say."

"She's a responsible journalist, Horatio," said his mother.

Hatfield eyed Adele. "You really think we'll get a lead from a silly advertisement?"

"You got a lead about Miss McCarthy's jewels when you put one in the paper, didn't you?" Adele pointed out.

"I don't think it can hurt, Horatio," Lady Augusta said.

"It would let whoever did buy the jewelry for Miss Parnell know we're looking for him," Jackson objected. "It's like tipping our hand."

"Not if you advertise it as a public service," Adele said.

The sheriff propped his foot up on the doorstep. "It could give us a few tips, Deputy."

"I doubt people shopping in a jewelry store would have eyes for anything but the jewelry," Jackson said.

"That's exactly the point, Deputy," said the sheriff. "They'll remember the brooch and the comb which would at least help us narrow down our search of jewelry shops." He brushed a few leaves that had fallen on his shoulder.

"Well, at least don't mention the gloves," Jackson insisted. "They're too unique to be mistaken for theft. The killer will spot them instantly."

"Fair enough." Hatfield nodded. "We'll visit Miss Grace tomorrow so she can get them in the afternoon paper."

"Let me tell her, Sheriff," said Adele. "She and I understand one another when it comes to evidence."

"We have a band of sly women on our hands, Sheriff." Jackson grimaced.

"And God bless them all!" Lady Augusta held her cane to the sky while Adele laughed.

CHAPTER 18

Adele returned to her shop where the workers were loitering outside, puffing on their cigarettes. She frowned, as she had asked Vera the day before to ask them not to smoke while working since the heavy scent discouraged customers. In her annoyance, she ordered them to put out their cigarettes and sent them down Bridge Street for a ten-minute stroll to get rid of the scent. They obliged begrudgingly as they had learned from their stern employer that it was useless to argue with a businesswoman.

Nin watched the exchange from the doorway of her place. When they left, she came out with bottle of lemon oil, sprinkling generous amounts around the front entrance of Adele's Stationery. "That ought to get rid of the stench," she said.

Adele gave her arm an affectionate squeeze. "You're a treasure, Nin."

The woman looked embarrassed. "What are friends for?"

"For some, friends are for gossiping." Adele looked down the street. "Mrs. Faderman and her brood are up to their tea party again."

The procession was a familiar one to her by now. Mrs.

Faderman came first, her back straight and her iron-gray hair neatly tucked under her hat while two of her maids scurried behind her carrying baskets of crockery and cakes. Mrs. Lynn, Mrs. Abberton, and the others followed. Dora always stuck her head out and grunted as they passed because they did not buy their tea and cakes in her shop. One of the other shopkeepers then set a table outside for them and was usually rewarded with some business. This time, it was Allen Brier, owner of Brier Groceries, which made Mr. Raleigh glare at him through the window of his general store. His reward was Mrs. Faderman sending one of her maids to buy bottles of fresh milk for the tea.

Adele grumbled, "I was going to go speak with Missy."

"About what?" Nin asked.

"Something Hatfield asked me to do regarding Arabella's case," Adele said. "But if those hens see me going into the newspaper office, they'll be flocking around wanting to know what it's about."

"Best to wait until they've gone back to their coops," Nin agreed.

Beatrice came walking down the street. She glared at the ladies as she passed and when she reached Adele's shop, snorted, "Bum it, they make my stomach turn!"

"You promised you would stop saying 'bum it,'" Nin reminded her.

"The other day, Mrs. Leighton came in and spoke to me as if I were a dumb child," the young lady said as she put on the apron Adele always made her wear so she wouldn't soil her dress with ink. "I made her take two boxes of nibs instead of one for it."

Adele laughed. "I'm glad to see your temper is doing me some good business."

"Of course she only came in to try and get out of me what you said about this business with Miss Parnell."

"And you played the innocent," Nin sneered.

"I really don't know anything." Beatrice looked at Adele accusingly.

"And you won't for the time being." Adele took her friend's arm. "I've changed my mind, dear. I think we ought to join them."

"Must we?" Nin frowned.

"I'll go!" Beatrice reached behind her to untie the apron strings.

"You will not," Adele said. "I need you here watching the shop."

"No one will come in with those hens out there," Beatrice protested.

"The first rule of a good businesswoman, Bea, is to stay open under any circumstance, even a cyclone or an earthquake," Adele said. "Besides, I want people to get used to seeing you here." She pressed the girl's shoulder. "I intend for you to help me build the shop."

Beatrice smiled and put her apron back on.

"Why the sudden interest in their squawking?" Nin asked.

"It's better to know what they're saying," said Adele. "They might have something valuable to tell us."

"Their talk is worth about one wooden penny," Nin snarled but she let Adele lead her across the street.

"Ah, Miss Gossling!" Mrs. Faderman motioned to one of the maids to prepare two more cups of tea. "You knew the dead girl, didn't you?"

"I'm assuming by 'dead girl' you mean Arabella Parnell?" Adele took the teacup.

"Why, is there another dead girl about?" Mrs. Cricket asked, shoving a cream puff into her mouth.

"Not that we're aware of," Nin said.

"I didn't exactly know her, Mrs. Faderman," said Adele. "She came into my shop once, and we saw her again at a party."

"But you've been making the rounds with the police," Mrs. Abberton said, her false curls shaking with disapproval. "I would have thought, with this new addition to your shop, you would be preoccupied with more practical matters."

"On the contrary," said Nin. "They keep banging and sawing away so she has to leave to hear herself think."

"We were just this minute talking about Miss Parnell," said Mrs. Faderman.

"I'm sure you were," Adele mumbled.

Mrs. Faderman studied her. "Do you know Henry Wadsworth Longfellow, Miss Gossling?"

"Only what my governess made me memorize," Adele said.

"Then I'm sure you know his poem about the little girl." She took a deep breath and recited,

When she was good,
She was very good indeed,
But when she was bad she was horrid.

"I'm afraid I don't see your point, ma'am." Adele felt as if someone had punched her in the stomach.

"I think you do." The woman looked at her with shrewd eyes through her pince-nez.

"Oh, well, really, Irene, aren't we all like that?" Mrs. Lynn asked. "When we're good, we're good, but when we're not very good, oh, indeed, we can be trying!"

"But *we* have good breeding, Carolyn," said the woman. "That makes all the difference."

"People who knew Miss Parnell said she was kind and thoughtful and went to church," Adele said.

"Really, Miss Gossling." Mrs. Cricket gave a condescending smile. "One may sit in the pews and ignore what the preacher is saying."

"You speak from experience, I presume?" Nin asked. Mrs. Cricket looked infuriated and turned her back.

"Even church-goers are not saints," Mrs. Faderman pointed out. "Though I'm sure there are some very God-fearing people out there in — where did she come from again?"

"A farm near Fresno," Missy, who was standing in the crowd, pencil and pad in hand, supplied.

"Everyone goes to church in a farming community," the woman continued. "They're so isolated, it's the only real social engagement they have."

"But when young people leave the farm and come to the city, what trouble they get into!" Mrs. Abberton added. "I knew a girl once who left the farm in Wisconsin and — well, never mind." She blushed.

"And you assume Miss Parnell was one of those?" Adele asked.

"We don't assume, Miss Gossling," said Mrs. Faderman. "Like you, we gather evidence."

"And who was the obliging person who gave you this evidence that Arabella was horrid?" Nin questioned.

"I had tea yesterday with Lavinia Murphy."

"Did you really?" Adele and Nin exchanged a look.

"She was hardly complimentary about the girl," said Mrs. Faderman.

"Did she tell you Arabella was the reason for her mother's nervous breakdown?" Nin asked. Her rough words caught Missy's attention but Adele gave her a sign and she kept her pencil still.

"Is that why Mrs. Murphy —" Mrs. Fournier's eyes were wide.

"Poor Nora," Mrs. Lynn sighed.

"She told me Miss Parnell left abruptly with no explanation and made it difficult for them all," Mrs. Faderman said. Adele had to admire her judiciousness and quick-witted grasping of the situation.

"Oh, my, it's always difficult when a maid leaves so suddenly," Mrs. Lynn lamented.

"Miss Parnell may not have been a pillar of society but she didn't deserve to be murdered." Adele's anger was rising.

"I didn't say she did," said the woman. "I merely say one can be blinded by appearances. I don't doubt she presented herself as a virtuous, churchgoing young lady of the lower classes, but you know how *they* are. They just don't have the moral fiber to —"

"That's not true, you goat!"

The cry came from a young woman whom, Adele realized, had been standing inside the doorway of Briar Groceries with a box in her arms. She wore plain clothes that had the rough look of having been hand-washed too many times. Her wiry hair was tucked underneath a hat with no ribbons or adornments on it.

Mrs. Faderman glared at her from above the pince-nez. "I'm not accustomed to being called names by strange girls."

"You're not accustomed to the truth, then," Nin mumbled.

"My name is Carmen," said the girl. "I'm Miss Lavinia Murphy's maid."

Adele grabbed her friend's arm.

Missy sidled up to her. "If you might spare me a few moments of your time, come into the *Arrojo Courier* and I'll take your picture."

"Oh!" Carmen stared at her.

"I assume you knew the young lady in question?" Mrs. Faderman asked with a smirk.

"I don't know what you mean by young lady." The girl stiffened. "There's lots of young ladies I know, and they're all respectable."

"Miss Arabella Parnell, of course," Mrs. Abberton said with her condescending smile. "That *is* who we were talking about. You do realize she's been murdered?"

The girl flinched. "Of course I know she was murdered! Oh, it was awful!"

"Naturally it's awful," said Mrs. Faderman. "But when a girl has a questionable reputation —"

"That's not true!"

"You knew her, then?" Mrs. Faderman repeated, again peering at her through the pince-nez.

"Well — not to speak to, but yes, in a way."

"You're very confusing, my girl." Mrs. Cricket waved her away with a fork.

"She wasn't what you said," the girl insisted. "She was brave!"

Adele put her hand on the girl's shoulder. "How was she brave, Carmen?"

"She had courage," the girl said. "She had excitement in her life!"

"That sort of excitement, my dear, I'm sure most of us can do without," said Mrs. Faderman dryly.

The girl turned red. "You don't know what a servant girl's life is like. None of you do." With a surprising tone of virtue, she continued. "They're always at you, all the time — "

"Who are at you?" Mrs. Abberton asked.

"Everyone!" the girl said. "The cook, the butler, all the other servants. And the mistress and master, of course."

"Well, it's your duty to serve them, my dear," said Mrs. Faderman in an instructive tone.

"But I'm human too!" she screeched. "And so was Miss Parnell. So don't you go playing judge and jury on the dead!" She turned on her heel and flounced down the street.

"Well!" Mrs. Abberton sniffed. "What do you make of *that,* Irene?"

"They all stick together, of course," said the woman.

"Just like all of you stick together," Adele said.

"I don't know what you mean, Miss Gossling."

"I'm sure you don't." Adele turned to Missy. "I suspect you don't need the young lady's picture with this juicy bit of gossip."

"I'm doing a human interest story, Adele," Missy insisted. "On the hardships of domestic service, to be exact."

"You ought to print about their employers' paws all over them," Nin said. "Including Lord Calpurnia."

"Whatever do you mean, Miss Branch?" Missy asked.

Adele laughed. "She means Mr. Riddle. Calpurnia was Cesar's wife."

"Oh, I see," Missy said. "So Mr. Riddle is not above reproach when it comes to servant girls?" She scribbled on her pad.

"He dallied with one of his maids," Nin said. "Why couldn't he have dallied with Arabella as well?"

"Really, Miss Branch." Mrs. Faderman almost blushed. "I don't say such things don't happen, but Miss Parnell could have easily been killed by some butler or chauffer or footman."

"The police ruled that out," Adele reminded her.

"Well, it could still have been someone of a lowly status," said the woman in a stubborn tone. "I'm sure the sheriff will see reason and let Mr. Riddle go home where he belongs very soon."

"He already has," Adele said.

"Has he?" Missy's eyed widened as she scribbled on her pad.

"I knew you knew more than you were telling us!" Mrs. Cricket gave her an accusing look.

"You're always complaining how she shouldn't get herself involved in police business," Nin said. "But when there's something to tell, you're all ears."

"You mean he's been released?" Mrs. Faderman asked.

"The fancy lawyer made him do it," Nin put in.

Missy gave Adele a grateful wave as she rushed down the street toward the *Arrojo Courier* office.

"That's as it should be." Mrs. Abberton drained her teacup and thrust it out to the maid with the teapot for a refill. "My husband and I have known Mr. Riddle for years and he's no — well, he wouldn't do that to a young lady."

"Because he's wealthy?" Nin eyed her.

"Because he's an upstanding citizen of this community!" the woman growled.

"I agree with Hester." Mrs. Faderman motioned to her maids, who began to gather the teacups and cake plates. "Mr. Riddle comes from a gentleman's generation. It's the younger generation we need worry about."

"What do you mean?" Adele stared at her.

The woman gave a patronizing smile. "You progressive ladies conveniently forget that if you have your liberty, so do the men who chase you."

"No one's chasing us," Nin said fiercely.

"I meant it in general terms," said the woman. "Young men these days take even more liberties than the women."

"And that's our fault?" Adele asked.

"Not entirely," Mrs. Faderman concurred. "These young parents don't raise the girls to be as modest as they should."

"Oh, yes, indeed, I remember Miss Brianna Barton —" Mrs. Lynn began.

"We don't want to hear it, Carolyn," said her friend.

"I'm interested, Mrs. Lynn," Adele said.

"Miss Barton was a school friend of mine," she began. "She had the loveliest skin —"

"Well, Carolyn?" Mrs. Faderman crossed her arms.

The woman hunched her shoulders a little. "I was only going to say one of the footmen at the Jacoby house was quite taken by her —"

"I'm sure he was," Mrs. Cricket snorted. "Taken by her jewels and her father's bank account more likely!"

"Oh, but they left without a penny."

"Left?" Adele asked.

"They ran away and got married," said Mrs. Lynn with wide eyes. "He used to appear from behind the apple tree when we took walks and walk alongside her, talking about his uncle's livery stable in New York City. I thought it was ever so bold!" The woman's face twisted with disapproval.

"Yes, well, those things happen even in the best of families," Mrs. Faderman said as she signaled the maids to finish packing up the tea things. "I must get the rest of this milk in the icebox"

Adele watched, lost in thought as the two maids carefully laid the remaining plates and cups inside the baskets, making use of every corner. She thought of Gene Dilworth's party and the air of lightness and excitement on the dance floor from all the young people, the flirtations she had seen in the corners of the ballroom. She thought of the Dilworth housekeeper's claim that Arabella "made eyes at the young master" and "talked on the phone with men."

"I suppose the younger generation is a little loose in regards to the opposite sex," she admitted.

"You talk as if you're an old woman," Nin said.

"Compared to Arabella, I am," said Adele, taking her arm. "Compared to Gene Dilworth and his friends, we're both old women."

"I would rather be a bear than a cub," Nin declared as they returned to Adele's shop.

"What happened?" Beatrice was upon them. "I saw that girl shouting at Mrs. Faderman."

"She was not shouting." Adele took out the account book. "She was defending her friend."

"What friend?"

"Arabella Parnell," Nin supplied.

"If that was her friend, I don't think much to her taste," Beatrice snorted.

"No worse than your friends," Nin said.

"My friends, Miss Branch, are respectable young ladies," she said.

"That's exactly what Carmen said," Adele said. "Respectable young ladies and disrespecting young men—" Her mind raced as she tapped the pencil. "Bea, do any of your friends know Hazel Dilworth?"

The young woman patted the back of her head as if to make sure her bun was straight. "Rachel knew her brother, I think. I remember she mentioned the Dilworths."

"Anyone else?"

Beatrice shrugged. "I doubt Mary would know her. She's with her aunt in Maine. Her parents thought it would be an eye-opening experience for her." She snorted. "She keeps writing about how they're buried in snow and her uncle is mean so he won't buy coal for the fire."

"That is unfortunate," Adele said kindly. "And among the younger girls?"

"Oh, they might." Her face was beginning to perk up. "You want me to ask them?"

"Of course she wants you to ask them," Nin snapped. "That's what she's been getting at."

"I want you to do one better." Adele opened the cash register and took out some bills, handing them to Beatrice. "Do you think you can arrange a picnic with this?"

Beatrice smiled. "I can arrange a feast with this."

"Good." Adele smiled. "Invite as many of the Wrigley girls as you can, especially those who are Hazel's age. Do you think you could worm an invitation to Hazel as well?"

"I'm sure I could." Beatrice eyes were aflame. "Do you want me to ask her if she knows who the murderer is?"

"Lord, how you're dying to play the police woman," Nin mumbled.

"I want you to instruct the girls to chat with Hazel in the most casual way," said Adele. "I want to know if she ever saw Arabella with any young men, either from her own class or Hazel's."

"The liberal generation." Nin studied her.

"I also want you to find out if she knows if Arabella had any beaus," Adele said. "Any young men she saw regularly."

"She might have even been engaged," Beatrice put in.

"She might have at one time," Adele agreed.

"If she had been, wouldn't he have come forward?" Nin asked.

"And get himself accused of murder?" Beatrice looked at her as if she were mad.

"Tell the girls to be conversational," Adele said. "Since they all come from similar backgrounds, they might talk about the servants in their homes and get to her that way. She didn't like

Arabella, so any complaints about servants might be a good opportunity."

"Leave it to me, Adele," Beatrice assured her, gathering her hat.

"And Bea," Adele caught her arm, "don't do anything foolish."

"I don't know what you mean." The girl's eyelashes fluttered.

"You know exactly what she means," Nin snarled.

"The sheriff thought you took too many chances last year with the Barry Circus case," she said. "The last thing we need is for you to get yourself into trouble."

"Oh, bum — oh, all right," said the girl begrudgingly as she toddled out the door.

CHAPTER 19

The moment the girl left, Adele snapped the key from the peg. "We have a call to make."

"To Carmen Skiffens?" Nin eyed her. "I saw the light appear around you when she was speaking."

"Your auras are always right," Adele said as she locked the door. "I want to get to her before Missy does."

"Missy could make a clam slam shut," Nin agreed.

"We'll see Miss Murphy first," Adele said. "I have a few questions I'd like to put to her without the police present. I've a feeling she might be more forthcoming with women of her kind."

"We're not of her kind," Nin said. "We're shopkeepers."

"I'm the daughter of a well-known San Francisco criminal lawyer and you're Atha Branch's daughter," Adele insisted as she opened the door of the Beaton for her friend. "She'll see that as her kind all right."

"Get to the maid through her mistress?" Nin sniffed. "I'd rather go to Carmen directly."

"Carmen is the sort that wouldn't say one word if it weren't sanctioned by Miss Murphy," Adele said.

"Misplaced loyalty," Nin remarked.

"I don't know as I'd say that," Adele said. "It's been difficult for Miss Murphy, and even the haughtiest chatelaine rewards her servants for their loyalty."

"But do the servants reward the chatelaine with genuine loyalty?" Nin challenged. "It doesn't seem as if Arabella did."

"I don't think Arabella even thought of loyalty." Adele pulled her veil closer around her face to keep out the dust. "When a woman is determined to move out of her station, she sometimes has to disregard charity and thoughtfulness."

Nin glanced at her. "Is that what you learned from your settlement house experience?"

"I don't say I agree with it," Adele insisted. "But when one is faced with survival or kindness, survival always wins."

"Do you really think Carmen knows something about this whole business?" Nin questioned.

"Miss Murphy said she gave Carmen those letters to burn," said Adele. "What if Carmen didn't burn them? Or what if she read them before she burned them?"

"I wouldn't blame her if she did," said Nin.

"Neither would I," Adele said. "Her mistress must have been hopping mad when she received them. Any maid would be curious as to what made her employer so angry."

"Or she would want to know what not to say to get out of harm's way," Nin added, making Adele laugh.

Adele was right. Miss Murphy was amiable as she invited them in. "The police are so bothersome," she said. "Asking questions in that harping way of theirs, as if you're a criminal yourself!"

"They don't mean to," Adele said. "They have a job to do."

"And they don't have time to waste," Nin added.

"Neither do I, Miss Branch," said the woman evenly. "May I offer you tea?"

"As a matter of fact, we just had tea," Adele said.

"Oh?" The woman unfolded her handkerchief. "I didn't

think a common town like this knew about the practices of tea time."

"We're quite civilized here," Nin said in a sticky tone. "We even refrain from throwing the sherry glasses in the fireplace after dinner." Adele could barely hide her smile.

"Oh, you'd like some sherry?" the woman asked in an absent tone.

"That would be lovely," Adele said. "It's really the ladies who have tea sometimes. You know the ladies?"

"Those gossips who came to Gene's party last week?" she asked.

"Their children came to the party," Nin corrected. "It was the younger generation of gossips."

"I don't recall seeing you at that party," Adele said.

"I was out of town," she said as she poured three sherry glasses. "I told Gene I would be, but he insisted he could only have the party on that day."

"He couldn't very well move the date of his birth to suit you, could he?" Nin asked.

The woman handed around the glasses. "Shall we make a toast?"

"Why not?" Adele held up her glass. "Here's to catching Arabella Parnell's killer."

Mrs. Murphy seemed far from eager to toast this but she drank.

"It's a shame you weren't at the party," Adele said. "I understood from Mr. Dilworth that you and he were friends."

The girl looked almost eager. "He said that?"

Adele picked up immediately on her hopeful tone. "He said you were very good friends, in fact," she said. "He clearly has a high regard for you."

The woman leaned back with a wide smile. "Do you really think so, Miss Gossling?"

"Adele is always right about that sort of thing," said Nin. Adele noticed she was keeping whatever pre-knowledge she may have had from her Generous Ones to herself.

"Mr. Dilworth is very worried about this whole business," Adele continued. "It's a blemish on his family's name, you know."

"You mean Arabella being murdered?" The woman looked surprised. "The Dilworths had nothing to do with that."

"No, but their good friend Mr. Riddle is still under suspicion." Adele watched the woman's face. "You don't disagree with the police suspecting him?"

Miss Murphy played with the edge of a cushion. "It's not for me to say."

"But someone else said it," Nin said. "Someone you want to get close to you."

"I don't know what you mean, Miss Branch," said the woman quickly. "Another sherry?"

"I got the distinct impression Mr. Dilworth isn't very fond of his father's friend," Adele said lightly.

"Well, no, as a matter of fact, he isn't," Miss Murphy admitted. "He thinks the man is a cad."

"He's very discerning," Adele said.

The girl stared at her. "What do you mean by that?"

"Mr. Cress told me —"

"Oh, you've been seeing Nathan?" The girl perked up. "Well, I must say, Miss Gossling, you have more astute taste than I thought. You might come to be one of us after all."

"Don't worry, you won't," Nin said softly in her ear.

"Mr. Cress was telling me Mr. Dilworth thinks his father's friend and Miss Parnell — well, may have been acquainted."

She studied the young lady's reaction but there was no salaciousness on her face. "It wouldn't surprise me one bit," she said.

"He is rather advanced in years," Adele remarked.

"That wouldn't make a bit of difference to Arabella," said Miss Murphy.

"Nevertheless, I should think a girl as pretty and lively as her would have hunted for a dashing young man," said Adele. "Do you recall her mentioning a young man when she was employed with you?"

"Didn't the police ask me that already?" She looked blankly at her. "You're not working on this business, are you, Miss Gossling?"

"We don't work for the police," Nin said. "We work on our own, and if we find something the police might like to know, we tell them."

"Well, you can tell them I don't recall any mention of a man, young or otherwise," said the girl with finality. "You really must have another sherry before you go."

"Thank you." Adele accepted the glass but Nin gave it a menacing look and the woman set the bottle down. "I don't want to offend you, Miss Murphy —"

"I'm not as much of a mouse as you think, Miss Gossling," said the girl, amused. "You may ask me anything. I'm rather enjoying all this."

"Murder amuses you?" Nin eyed her.

"Not really, but it does give me something to tell Mother about when I see her," she said. "Especially as it involves the woman who ruined her life. There's a certain satisfaction in it, you see."

Nin sat up. "What makes you think you have a right to be cruel to the dead?"

"When the same dead person was cruel to one who only offered her kindness in life, one can be cruel to her in death," said Miss Murphy. "Ask anything, Miss Gossling."

"Were there any young men in your circle who — well, had some regard for Miss Parnell?"

As promised, Miss Murphy didn't bat an eye. "Oh, some of them looked her way, but they would never have taken it further."

"Perhaps one did," Adele suggested. "Perhaps she wrote about him in her letters to you."

"I told you, Miss Gossling, I never read those letters," said the girl.

Adele paused, repositioning herself. "We were wondering if you would let us speak to your maid."

"Speak to Carmen?"

"She may have looked at the letters," Adele said as delicately as she could. "Maids are often curious about other maids."

"Carmen wouldn't do such a thing," Miss Murphy insisted. "She knows I would have fired her right away if she had."

"She might have spoken with Arabella before she left," Adele suggested. "They might have exchanged maid's talk."

"Maids often talk about the young men they serve with," Nin added.

"I see you do know something about our ways, Miss Branch." Miss Murphy sounded almost approving. Nin flushed and turned away.

"If she spoke with her, she might know something that might help the police."

"I don't think she knows anything," said the woman. "She wasn't here more than a few days before Arabella left."

"Nonetheless," Adele insisted, "a few days is enough for servant's gossip."

"I don't approve of gossip, Miss Gossling, and Carmen knows it." Miss Murphy rolled her eyes.

"Yes, I noticed you weren't interested in the gossip about Miss Parnell just now," Adele said. "I admire that."

The woman looked pleased. "Carmen's a rather stupid girl anyway. Even if Arabella did tell her something, I doubt she would remember it."

"It's worth a try," Nin said.

"Well, if you think it would help." Her manner suddenly softened. "I don't want you to think I'm so cruel I don't want to help you find a beast who killed Arabella. None of us are safe until he's caught. He might be lurking about anywhere."

"He certainly might," Adele said, though she doubted anyone would want to approach someone as overbearing as Miss Murphy.

The woman rose. "I'll ring for Carmen."

Adele jumped up, pulling her friend up with her. "We would prefer to see Carmen in the servant's quarters."

"Whatever for?" Miss Murphy was clearly nonplused.

"She would talk more in familiar surroundings," Nin said.

"Are you sure about that?"

"As you said before, I do know something about your ways." Adele stared at her friend, her tone and the shape of her face changing to rival the majesty of Lady Augusta. They worked to humble Miss Murphy as she stepped aside and let them pass into the hallway.

~

Unlike many homes of that size Adele had visited, the downstairs was as lavish as the upstairs. There was no narrow hallway, no seedy servants' hall or cramped quarters. The hall was wide with small windows that peeked out onto the backyard. She and Nin passed by rooms clearly belonging to the staff that had fine furnishings and bright curtains. They reached the kitchen which, Adele had to admit, was as large as her own.

A woman in a cook's uniform was beating eggs with a whisk, mumbling to herself. Her expression was so fierce that even Nin held back a little as they glanced at one another.

Adele cleared her throat and the woman whirled around. "At last! Oh!" The woman's voice immediately softened. "I beg your pardon!"

"You remember me, don't you?" Adele struggled to remember the woman's name. "I came with the police to ask you about Miss Arabella Parnell."

"I remember," said the woman in a cordial tone.

"We'd like to see Carmen," Adele said. "She wasn't here the last time we came so we couldn't ask her questions."

"She won't know nothing, miss," said the cook.

"Let us be the judge of that," Nin said in a harsh tone.

"You'll find her in her room down the hall, miss. Shall I call her?" She wiped her hands on her apron.

"No, don't bother," said Adele. "We'll go to her." She paused for a moment. "You're —"

"Mrs. Hopkins, miss." She gave a quick bow.

"You're here alone?" Adele let sympathy fall in her voice.

"The other two are down with 'flu."

"I'm sorry to hear that," Adele said. "I heard it's been going around some of the households in town."

"Soak some echinacea flowers in some elderberry wine," Nin advised in an authoritative voice.

"Well, I never!" Mrs. Hopkins stared.

"My friend knows about healing herbs," Adele put in, taking Nin's arm. "I suggest you follow her advice."

"Well, I never!" the woman repeated.

"You'd better start or you might end up sick yourself," Nin remarked as they left the kitchen.

As they neared the room at the end of the hall, Adele could hear sobbing. Glancing at Nin, she knocked on the half-closed door.

"I'm coming, Mrs. Hopkins!" came the sniffling call from inside.

Adele opened the door all the way. "It's not Mrs. Hopkins, Carmen."

The girl stared at them. "You were there with those nasty women today, weren't you?"

Adele smiled as she sat down at the end of the bed. Nin took her place on the floor, which made Carmen's mouth open. "We help the police sometimes."

"I've heard about you." Carmen seemed now to have recovered, though she turned her face a little as if trying to hide the few tears left in her eyes. "You must be brave!"

"Why must we be brave?" Nin asked.

"To go chasing after murderers and such." The girl was quiet for a moment. "You're helping the police find the person who — who —"

"Murdered Arabella?" Nin finished.

The girl let out a sob and buried her face in her pillow. Adele gave her friend a cautious look.

"We admired the way you spoke up to the ladies," Adele said.

"I had to say something." The girl wiped her face. "They were being so spiteful!"

"They need a good kick in their petticoats once in a while," Nin added.

This made Carmen laugh.

"We both can appreciate how you defended your friend," Adele said.

"Arabella wasn't my friend," she said.

Adele tried not to look surprised. "But you spoke as if you'd known one another for years."

"Oh, no!" Carmen said. "I only saw her for two days before she left. And even then I didn't speak to her. Only when we sat down to eat."

"And yet, you spoke up for her when the ladies hinted that she deserved what she got," Nin said.

"Oh, that was different." Carmen went to the basin sitting on the dresser and washed her face. "Maids stick up for one another."

"Always?" Adele eyed her.

"Well, maybe not always, but it's the right thing to do, isn't it?" She peered at Adele through the mirror.

"If the maid's done nothing wrong, it is," Adele said. "And you knew she'd done nothing wrong, didn't you, Carmen?"

"Why, miss, what do you mean?" She patted her face with a towel.

"You knew about her because you read her letters," Nin prompted.

Carmen did not answer at first. She smoothed her uniform and adjusted her cap. Then, she sank into the only chair in the room. "You won't tell Miss Lavinia, will you?"

"As far as Miss Lavinia is concerned, those letters were burned unopened," Adele promised.

"Arabella — Miss Parnell — wrote to her all the time," she said. "Miss Lavinia didn't like that. She made trouble for her mother, you see." She blushed.

"We know about that," said Nin.

"Miss Lavinia was very bitter about it," said Carmen.

"Go on," Adele said.

"Miss Lavinia used to go into an awful state whenever one of those letters came," Carmen said. "She was smart, Arabella — Miss Parnell."

"You should call her Arabella," Adele said, smiling. "If you've read her letters, you're as intimate with her as we are."

The girl fiddled with the string on her apron. "She wouldn't even look at the letters. She'd say, 'Carmen, take that filth out of here and put it in the servants' fireplace where it belongs.'" She shrugged. "I suppose she felt it was too dirty for her to put in her own."

"But you didn't put them in the fireplace," Adele guessed.

"I felt sorry for her, miss," said the girl. "She wrote so often, and I really think she thought Miss Lavinia was reading the letters."

"Even after what happened with Mrs. Murphy?" Adele stared at her.

"I don't think she thought she was doing anybody any harm," said Carmen.

Adele took hold of the woman's wrist. "You realize it's important that we know what was in those letters?"

"You mean give them to the police?" The girl shrank back. "I'd lose my job!"

"I didn't say we would give them to the police," Adele said. She felt Nin stare at her. "Those letters made you like Arabella, didn't they?"

"Or at least admire her," Nin put in.

"Indeed, miss." Carmen's cheeks glowed. "She used such fancy language, and she had such adventures!"

"You want to help us find out who killed her, don't you?"

"I hate to think of her cold and dead!" She shuddered.

"The dead are always cold," Nin said abruptly, earning a cry from the young maid.

"If we could see the letters, they might give us a clue as to whom she was seeing," Adele said.

"Oh, she didn't mention any names, I'm sure of it!" the girl declared. "Not a one."

"You must have memorized those letters to know that," Nin said dryly. The girl blushed again.

"They could still tell us something," Adele insisted. "Won't you please show them to us?"

Carmen looked down at her lap, silent for a moment. "You won't give them to the police?"

"Not unless we have to," Adele promised.

"And you won't — do anything to them?"

"They're precious to you, aren't they?" Adele's heart went out to her.

"It's silly, isn't it?" She blushed. "I never really knew her, but I feel as if she wrote them to me."

"In a way they were since your mistress wanted nothing to do with them," Nin said.

Adele smiled. "She wrote them to a woman whom she thought had a sympathetic ear. You're more that woman than Miss Lavinia, Carmen."

The girl looked at her with wide eyes for a moment. "I never thought of it that way."

"We have sympathetic ears too," Adele said. "Miss Branch and I fight for justice for every woman, especially the dead ones. They can't fight for themselves."

"Oh, I see what you mean, miss." Carmen's trepidation was gone, and she went to the bureau, unlocking the bottom drawer. "I know they'll be safe in your hands." She handed her the packet tied with a piece of twine.

"Thank you, Carmen." Adele rose. "We've got to take these for a while but I promise you we'll return them to you."

"Keep them as long as you wish, miss." She gave her a wan smile. "It's worth it if it will put the man responsible in jail."

"Poor girl," Adele sighed after they had left the Murphys. "It's a shame she and Arabella never got to be friends."

"She could use a friend," Nin agreed.

They went to Dora's Tea Shop which they knew would be nearly empty at that time of day. In a quiet table in the corner, they examined the letters.

"Carmen was right," Nin said. "Arabella was cautious."

"No names," Adele agreed. "But my idea was right."

"Your idea about the young man?" Nin asked. "I thought that's what you were getting at this afternoon."

"I don't doubt Arabella wanted everything," Adele said. "Not only wealth and generosity, but youth too."

"She was going for the moon, not the stars," Nin agreed. "She keeps saying 'the city, the city' in this one. Apparently, they took her to some excursion in 'the city' for a day."

"They?"

"She doesn't name names," Nin said, the disappointment clear on her face.

"She was being prudent," Adele agreed. "No mention of names in these either, just as Carmen said." She put her chin in her hand. "One has to wonder why she was so prudent."

"It's a contradiction, isn't it?" Nin asked. "She bragged about the men that were interested in her, yet, she never proved her claims by giving names."

"She was smart, Nin." Adele opened another envelope. "These young men — and I see now they were young, not Mr. Riddle's age — must have been from very prominent families for her to be so discreet."

"Or she merely wanted to make Miss Murphy jealous," Nin pointed out. "She was insistent that the young men of her social circle did nothing more than glance at Arabella."

"Yes, she was very clever indeed," Adele mumbled. Her eyes scanned the letter in her hand. When she turned the page over, she nearly dropped it. "Nin! Look at this!"

She handed the page to her friend. In the round and clear hand Adele felt certain Arabella had practiced over and over again to make it look so aristocratic, the dead woman had written:

I have found my gentleman at last! He's so dashing and intelligent. He takes me to the grandest places. Do you remember that restaurant you told me about? Ever since you mentioned it, I've been meaning to go there. I did a little sweet talking and he took me there last evening! He borrowed a Rolls (heaven knows where he got it!) and the road was so bumpy, but of course I pretended I had been in an automobile before. He gave me his sister's dress, a lovely gown of red and gold silk. I felt positively scandalous in it! I ate a tiny bit of everything just like you once told me, though I was so starving when I got home, I had to steal a chunk of cheese and loaf of bread from the pantry. Not that Mrs. Pinch would mind. She would have insisted I sit down to a meal of eggs and bacon if she had known. She's such a trusting soul.

"Trusting soul," Nin growled. "She took advantage of every person who was fool enough to like her."

"This proves my idea even further," Adele said.

"About the young man?" Nin asked.

"It looks as if there were several young men," Adele said.

Nin watched Adele carefully as she tied the twine around the letters again. "You're thinking of someone in particular, aren't you?"

"When we spoke to Mrs. Butler — she's the Dilworth housekeeper — she insisted she had seen Arabella 'making eyes at the young master.'"

"You mean Gene Dilworth?" Even Nin was dumbfounded. "She was a fresh one! The son of her employer!"

"It would stand to reason," Adele said. "Gene has a bright future ahead of him. He's the heir to the Dilworth fortune."

"And the Dilworth stand high on the social platform," Nin added. "It's a shame the police can't find out. They could trace that restaurant in the city if they knew what restaurant and what city."

Adele played with the edge of the packet, flipping through the envelopes like a deck of cards. "We're not going to tell the police about this just yet, Nin."

"Not tell them?" Her friend blinked. "But they've nowhere to go now with Mr. Riddle out of jail."

"There are too many question marks yet," her friend insisted. "I'm going on an idea Gene was involved somehow but we're still not sure."

"You really think Gene Dilworth killed Arabella?"

"I'm not sure of anything right now, dear," Adele said. "But if he was somehow involved, it wouldn't do to have the sheriff pursue it."

"Because he's high society?" Nin studied her. "You were the one who disregarded propriety with the Blackstone case, remember? They were high society too."

"Which is why whatever high society there is now in Arrojo will have its back up," Adele pointed out. "They know Sheriff Hatfield isn't going to be taken by social standing, no matter what the mayor or even the governor threaten to do. We don't want to risk his job if there's nothing in it."

"But you don't believe there's nothing in it, do you?" her friend asked.

"I don't know," Adele admitted. "But if there is, you and I are in the best position to find out. Gene likes us, remember? Even his friends liked us."

"I remember that all right." Nin said. "I still feel that worm's hand on the small of my back when we danced."

Adele put her arm around her shoulders. "He won't be laying a finger on you anymore."

"You bet he won't," Nin said fiercely. "I'll chop it off if he tries!"

Adele laughed just as the bell above the door rang, letting Beatrice in.

"It's all settled," she said, a large grin on her face. "Sandra is going to ask Hazel."

"Sandra?"

"Her mother and Mrs. Dilworth are friends." She took off her hat and hung it on the rack. "You'd be surprised how many friendly conversations ladies exchange at the salon."

"Yes, I know," Adele said dryly. "Bea, there's one more thing I'd like the girls to find out."

"What's that?" Beatrice leaned forward with an eager expression.

"Have them talk to Hazel about clothes and find out if she has or has ever had a red and gold gown."

"Surely you're joking!" Beatrice stared. "Red and gold? At fifteen?"

"I know it sounds bold," Adele admitted.

"Maybe she bought it without her mother knowing and hides it in her closet," Nin pointed out.

"I don't think Hazel would do that," Bea said. "I might, but she wouldn't. She's too much of a coward."

"You're not the only brazen young lady in the world," Nin snapped. Adele hid a smile.

CHAPTER 20

When Adele closed her shop for the evening, she noticed the lights in the *Arrojo Courier* office. She imagined Missy flitting about, her assistant Carla looking on with worried eyes as the newspaper woman cranked out sheets for the evening edition.

She went upstairs to Nin's apartment. "We're bringing Missy dinner," she announced. "She's working late, and you know how she is about food when she's getting the paper out."

"Plus, you have that errand to run for Hatfield," Nin reminded her.

They went into Dora's Tea Shop and bought sandwiches and cakes, and Dora allowed them to take one of her pots of tea.

The office was buzzing but without the mess that had haunted it before Carla became her assistant. The girl looked relieved when they came in with the basket and teapot. Missy was hidden behind the press machine and the noise was deafening.

"Can't you turn that thing off?" Nin shouted, covering her ears.

Carla, who had gained a little more confidence working with Missy, yanked the plug, and all was suddenly quiet.

Missy appeared from behind it, annoyed. "Of all the —" She saw them and smiled. "Oh, well, that's all right, I guess."

"It's more than all right," Adele said. "It's dinnertime and the presses stop."

"Carla, get some cups from the shelf downstairs, dear," she said. When the girl was gone, she gave Adele a meaningful look. "Why did I have to hear about Virgil Riddle being released from the gossips?"

"Because that's how people hear about things in Arrojo," Adele said dryly.

"You know what I mean." The woman watched her lay out the dinner on the table. "I thought we had an understanding, Adele."

"We never had an understanding we would come running to you every time the police made a move," Nin snapped.

"That's not what I mean," she said crossly. "I thought we agreed last year after the circus murder."

Carla came back with cups, and Adele poured the tea. "I wasn't holding something back, Missy. Hatfield just released Mr. Riddle a little while before the tea party made its appearance."

"You could have told me before you told them," Missy objected.

"You know how those ladies are," Adele said. "They don't give a breath of air to one once they get hold of you."

Missy sighed. "I suppose you're right. But can't we be more helpful to one another from now on?"

"You know we can't do that." Nin glanced at Carla who made no secret of her fascination with crime since the circus case the year before. The girl was leaning with her thin face forward like a mask on a wall, her eyes bulging.

"Carla, I won't need you anymore tonight," Missy said. "Go on home. Your brothers need you."

"But the type setting —"

"It's nearly done," Missy said. "You know, I did get out a newspaper before you came to work with me without your help."

"Oh, yes, miss, but —"

"Go home!" Nin snarled. The girl scurried out of the office.

"Her ears are getting too big," Adele observed.

"So is her mouth," Missy grumbled. "I found out she blabbed all over town about Mr. Lyman's promotion last year, and he was getting congratulations before it even appeared in the paper."

"I'm sure he was thrilled about that," Adele said.

"He was, but Mr. Abbott wasn't," Missy said. "You know how he likes to make a ceremony of everything." She tore the crust off the sandwich and discarded it in the trash near her feet. "I don't see why we can't be honest with one another when we're all working for the same end. Justice."

"Justice or sensationalism?" Nin eyed her.

"You know I'm not a yellow journalist, Miss Branch," Missy snapped. "But no journalist is worth her name if she doesn't chase down a good story."

"Nin only meant Hatfield is very cautious about what evidence he wants known to the public," Adele said. "We've always told you what we can, but we can't go over his head."

"I'm not asking you to!" The woman put her cup down. "Didn't I keep quiet about evidence in this case because the police told me to?"

Adele pressed her hand. "Of course you did. Hatfield himself said you were a very responsible journalist."

"Well, then." Missy leaned back. "When you come to me with anything, I'll print it only as you and the police allow it. How's that?"

Adele heard Nin whispering in her ear, "Be careful!"

"Here's something you can print," she said. "Hatfield wants you to put an advertisement about Arabella's jewelry."

"Advertisement?" Missy stared at her.

"Pretend advertisement," Nin said.

"He doesn't want people to know the brooch and comb are hers," said Adele. "But we need to find out where they came from and, if possible, who bought them for her."

"What makes you think she didn't buy them for herself?" Missy already had the arched eyebrows of her trade.

Adele gave her an even look. "Because a maid's salary would hardly allow her to buy glass, let alone diamonds."

"Yes there is that," Missy admitted. "So the police think the man who bought them for her might be the one who killed her."

"We didn't say it was a man," Nin said sharply. "It might have been a woman with money who took pity on her.

Missy snorted. "From what we know about Miss Parnell, it's hardly likely any woman would take pity on her!"

"Put in the advertisement like you did Miss Murphy's ruby necklace," Adele instructed. "He wants people to think they were stolen and he's trying to find them."

"Very clever," Missy said.

Adele took a sip of tea to clear her throat. "You didn't take photos of the jewelry that day we went to Mr. Riddle's house, did you?"

"How could I with your brother shooing me away every time I lifted the camera?" Missy grumbled.

"I think it's time you took those pictures." Adele felt Nin's eye on her. "And take a picture of the gloves too."

"You mean it?" Missy sat up. "Oh, that would be grand!"

"They're not for print, Missy," said Adele. "Not yet."

"Oh, I meant it was grand purely from a vanity standpoint," Missy said, smiling. "I just got the new Kodak folding Brownie, and I haven't had a chance to photograph more than Mrs. Wrigley's new daffodils for the social column. But why take them if I can't print them?"

Adele folded and unfolded the edge of her napkin. "We want to borrow those photos."

"What for?" Nin burst out.

"Because, dear, we'll be going to San Francisco tomorrow and we need them."

"Are we going to San Francisco?" Her friend's nose wrinkled.

"Is this one of your ideas, Adele?" Missy glanced at her.

"One of my unprintable ideas." She gave her a meaningful look.

"All right, one of your unprintable ideas," her friend said.

"The police are betting on a local jewelry store for that brooch and comb," Adele said. "Nin and I are betting on a shop in San Francisco."

"That's not a bet. That's a long shot," Missy said with a smile.

"Not such a long shot," Nin objected. "If Arabella was having a liaison with a man who's capable of killing her, he would hardly want it known he was stepping out with a maid."

"That might be true," Missy admitted. "But there must be dozens of millinery shops and jewelers in San Francisco. I know you grew up there, but even you can't know all of them." Missy glanced at her friend's plain blouse. "And from what I know of your taste, I can hardly imagine you frequented such shops."

"I didn't," Adele admitted. "But I have plenty of friends who did. That's why the pictures would be useful. If I could show them the photos, some of my friends might recognize the style."

Missy smiled. "I'll give you a set of prints even if it takes me all night to develop them, and without telling the police." She added the last with a glance at Adele. "That is what you want, isn't it?"

Adele gathered up the paper from the dinner and threw it in the trash. "We'll have to go now to get them."

"Hatfield won't be in the office," Nin said. "Neither will your brother."

"Exactly what I'm counting on," Adele said, taking her friend's arm.

~

The police station was quiet since both the sheriff and deputy had gone home for the day as well as most of the assistant deputies. Since they took turns minding the station overnight, the only ones there were Dooland and Carson. It was clear Dooland was teaching Carson the filing system, as they were standing over a stack of folders with Dooland's rotund figure bent over the twiggy young man, his hands behind his back and his face stern. Adele held back a smile at the way the deputy assistant was trying to mimic the sheriff.

"Good evening, Assistant Deputy Dooland," she sang out as they entered.

"Good evening, miss." Carson remained silent, gaping at the camera in Missy's hands.

"How is your father's Ford holding out?" Adele asked. The young man told her last year he convinced his family to buy one of the new cars.

Dooland's face brightened. "Oh, splendidly, miss! It's got a sixteen-horsepower engine."

"Faster than my new Beaton," Adele admitted.

"Well, I imagine that wouldn't disturb you, miss," he said. "Beaton's a nice car for a woman."

"A woman don't need to go fast," Carson said in his squeaky voice. Nin glared at him, and he ducked his head.

"We won't disturb your work, Assistant Deputy," Adele said. "We just came in to get some pictures of evidence from the Parnell case."

Dooland's stern expression returned, and he looked like a statue standing in front of the desk. "I can't let you do that, miss."

"Oh, don't be an ass!" Nin snarled.

The young man's hand went to his badge. "If you'll pardon, miss, the sheriff is very particular about removing evidence."

"We're not going to remove anything," Missy said. "We're just going to take some photos."

"The sheriff wouldn't approve of that either, miss."

"Not approve?" Missy snarled. "He wants me to put something in my paper about the jewelry."

"So let us see it, you buffle head!" Nin gritted her teeth.

This only made the young man more determined. "You'll have to get the sheriff's permission, miss."

Adele could feel her temper rising. "We *have* the sheriff's permission, Assistant Deputy. Sheriff Hatfield told me I could view evidence from any case whenever I wanted."

"Yes, miss, but you don't deny you have a habit of pilfering evidence —"

"Pilfering!" Nin stepped forward, a Medusa look on her face, which made Carson hunch in his seat.

But Dooland stood firm. "I'm sure the sheriff wouldn't mind you phoning him at home. He seems —" the young man coughed, "— rather partial to your requests, miss."

Adele felt her face redden. "Sometimes you do your work a little too diligently, Assistant Deputy."

The door opened and Edison came in carrying three dinner buckets from The Soaring Eagle. "Oh, good evening miss!" He bowed to Adele.

"I've just been telling Miss Gossling if she wants to view evidence, she has to call the sheriff and get his permission," said Dooland with a grin that puffed up his round face.

"Of course she doesn't have to ask his permission!" Edison put down the buckets a little too hard, and the clatter made Carson jump. "Don't be a fool, Dooland!"

"But the sheriff —"

"The sheriff told me we ain't — aren't to deny Miss Gossling anything she wants to see." Edison's tone lost its boyish hesitation. "He said he wants Miss Grace to put the advertisement in about the jewelry as soon as possible." A keen look appeared in his eyes. "Imagine what he would say if he knew you were turning Miss Grace away from doing her job."

"I suggest, Assistant Deputy, that you sit down, have your dinner and let Edison handle things," Adele said firmly. "Assistant Deputy Edison and I have always had an understanding." She gave the young man a knowing look.

"The sheriff said I'm in charge when he and Deputy Gossling are away, didn't he?" Edison gave him a satisfied look.

"I suppose he did," Dooland mumbled as he lost his stern look and slunk behind his desk, grabbing one of the dinner buckets as he did so.

Edison led the ladies to the evidence room. "I'm sorry about that, Miss Gossling."

"It was more an annoyance," Nin said. "We would have just kicked him aside."

Edison grinned and lowered his voice. "I almost wish you had, miss. Dooland thinks far too highly of himself."

"It seems we've quite a few people in town lately who are guilty of that," Adele murmured, thinking of Arabella.

"You can see anything you like, miss." He glanced at Missy. "Though the sheriff didn't say nothing — anything about pictures."

"We'll let that be our little secret, Assistant Deputy," Adele said.

"I won't be printing them until the sheriff lets me," Missy promised. "You know I always keep my word, Assistant Deputy."

"Oh, of course, miss," he said, blushing. "I never thought you wouldn't."

"I'm glad you trust me," Missy mumbled.

The young man hedged. "I'm afraid there is one thing, miss. You'll have to sign a book."

"Oh, for pity's sake!" Nin growled.

"Just your name and the date, miss," Edison said. "I'll fill in the rest." He took a leather book from behind the cabinet.

"A new procedure?" Adele asked as she signed it.

"It was my idea, miss." The young man could not hide his

pride. "Oh, not because you took out evidence all those times. That's all forgotten. But I thought, well, this way, we always know who's looking at the evidence and when."

"That's very enterprising of you, Assistant Deputy." Adele smiled as she handed him the fountain pen. "A police station ought to be organized and, the sheriff is, shall we say, not very strong on that point."

"Indeed not, miss." The young man laughed, then looked embarrassed. "He's the best sheriff we've ever had, though."

"He is indeed." Adele smiled. "We'll overlook his faults just as he overlooks ours." She shook hands with Edison and he went out, closing the door behind him.

CHAPTER 21

The next day the advertisement appeared in the *Arrojo Courier*:

The police are looking for any information about certain jewelry stolen in the area. This paper received anonymous reports that jewelry has gone missing, including a diamond brooch, a ring of crossing olive branches, a pair of pearl earrings, and a large ruby comb. As the reports failed to identify any details, even the shop names, if anyone has any information, please contact the Arrojo Sheriff's Office.

Jackson slammed the paper down. "Of all the absurd fabrications!"

"What do you mean?" Adele buttered a slice of toast.

"Hatfield never told her to make up that lie about the ring and earrings," Jackson said. "He also didn't ask her to say she had anonymous reports." He looked so cross that Tomas, ever keen on the family's moods, slipped beside him and pushed the vile oatmeal he had for breakfast every morning to the far side of the table, as if afraid Jackson might going to throw it against the wall.

"How else are people going to come forward with the information you want?"

He eyed her. "This was your doing, wasn't it, Del?"

"Don't be silly," she said. "Missy is only trying to help the police, Jack."

"She won't help us by telling lies!"

"Not lies, just a little story to get people to act," Adele insisted.

"We'll have every jeweler in the county nervous." Jackson rose, shaking out his jacket. "And Moffitt will probably give us the third degree about why we didn't let him know there was another thief in town."

"Because there isn't." Adele unhooked her parasol from the rack.

"I'm glad you take crime so lightly, Del." He opened the gate for her. "I only hope the sheriff will too."

Adele hurried to her shop. Nin was waiting for her with the paper in her hands. "She didn't print the photos."

"I know," said Adele. "Jack was in a state about her story-telling, though."

"I think it was clever of her." Nin followed Adele into her shop. "Someone is bound to remember the brooch and comb weren't stolen and go to the sheriff."

"Let's hope he or she does," Adele said with a sigh.

Nin unfolded the newspaper and Adele saw the envelope. "Missy left this with me this morning, since you weren't in."

Adele smiled. "The photographs. I wonder if she really was up all night developing them."

"She's as bitten by the crime-solving bug as you are," Nin remarked.

"And as *you* are," Adele teased. "Now we can go to the city tomorrow."

"Why should we?" Nin asked.

"We're going on a treasure hunt," Adele said. "And we're paying the Blessings a visit."

"Because of the letters?" Nin asked.

"The letters, yes. And this." Adele took out of her bag the note the police had found near Arabella's body.

"Adele!" Nin stared. "You stole evidence again."

"Borrowed," Adele insisted.

"I hope it's for a good reason," her friend said.

"It is," Adele assured her.

~~~~~

The day was quiet, and there were hardly any customers. In a way she was grateful because the workers were especially noisy. They brought two more saws with them and the scraping made her jumpy. She was glad to get away to Nin's for lunch even though the echo of the saws followed her through the thin walls of Nin's shop.

Near closing time, she was not surprised when Mrs. Faderman entered to buy a box of pencils for her husband. She expected the woman to accost her with question about the advertisement in the paper. But surprisingly, Mrs. Faderman was silent on the matter.

Just before she left, Adele found out why. In an almost offhand tone, Mrs. Faderman said, "You may tell Sheriff Hatfield I think he's going about getting his information very well."

"I don't understand, ma'am." Adele put on her coat, her keys in hand.

The woman smiled. "It's rather obvious. There's not a word of truth in what Miss Grace put in the paper about thefts in the area, is there?"

"If the sheriff says there are thefts, I imagine he knows," Adele said vaguely as she locked her front door.

"Please, Miss Gossling." The woman shuddered. "Arrojo is not a town where criminals lurk in every corner."

"True," Adele admitted. "Though we've had a few murders in the last years."

"That is not the same thing," Mrs. Faderman insisted. "What I mean is he's looking for information about that jewelry Miss Parnell was wearing the night she was killed."

Adele dropped the keys in her hands. She bent down in the
~~~~~

darkened doorway to look for them. "How in the world did you know that?"

The woman looked as sly as a cat. "I have my sources too, Miss Gossling."

"I hope your sources aren't spreading gossip about it all over town," Adele snapped as she pressed her hands against the ground, feeling for the key.

"Don't do that, dear," said the woman. "You'll spoil your gloves. I'll get a candle from Raleigh's."

"Don't bother," Adele said. "I found them."

"My sources are as discreet as yours." The woman shifted the basket with the rest of her shopping to her other arm. "It was Vanessa, if you must know. She recognized the description of the comb."

"How could she —"

"You were at that party too, weren't you?" she asked. "You saw Miss Parnell wearing it."

Adele put her hand to her mouth. "Lord, I forgot about that!"

"Don't use blasphemous language, Miss Gossling," said the woman. She patted her shoulder. "Don't worry, dear. I'm sure no one noticed it except Vanessa. She's partial to such details."

"I'm sure she is," Adele mumbled.

But the conversation remained in her mind through the evening and kept her awake half the night. Early the next morning, she left a note for her brother as she always did when she went to the city and met Nin at the train station. She knew her friend had a keen sense of people's moods even when her gift was dormant and she felt Nin's cat-like eyes observing her as she chatted on about some gossip she had heard from Mrs. Jessel about her trying to form an organization for women business owners in Rosa Gris.

When they settled in the passenger car, her friend said, "You're worried about something. There's a sheet of black all around you."

"And I tried so hard to wear my brightest suit today," Adele said with a nervous laugh.

"Don't try to make light of it, Adele," said her friend with unusual annoyance. "You sound like your brother."

"Jack does try too hard sometimes to distance a situation with logic," Adele agreed. "Ever since he was a child —"

"Now you're trying to change the subject." In a rare moment of affection, Nin took her hand. "It's something to do with this case isn't it?"

"Nin, I think I made a mistake."

"So you made a mistake." Her friend shrugged.

"You don't understand," Adele said, playing with the fringes on her bag. "This mistake might cost Arabella the justice she deserves."

"We're going to the city to chase down information about the rogue who killed her, aren't we?" Nin asked. "I don't consider that shirking justice."

"I mean about the advertisement," Adele said. "I had a visit from Mrs. Faderman yesterday."

Nin snorted. "That woman blows a lot of wind out of her mouth but it never settles anywhere."

"It settled in my mind," Adele said. "She knows the real purpose of the advertisement."

"How can she?"

"She put two and two together," Adele said.

Her friend sniffed. "Mrs. Faderman couldn't put a teapot and a lid together."

Adele smiled in spite of herself. "Vanessa recognized the description of the comb," she said. "Mrs. Faderman knows the police are looking for information about Arabella's death."

"Probably many people recognized the description," Nin said. "I saw a comb very similar to that gaudy thing Arabella wore that night in Moffitt's window a few years back."

"But that was a few years back," Adele objected. "How many

people were at that party or read about it in the social column of the *Arrojo Courier* and remember it?"

"Who remembers what they read in the paper last night, let alone last week or last month?" Nin insisted. "Don't waste your worry on that."

"If Mrs. Faderman recognized the description, ambiguous as it was, the killer would certainly recognize it."

"Criminals aren't that smart," Nin insisted. "He might not even be in Arrojo anymore."

"But he might be scanning the local papers to find out what's going on with the case," Adele said. "I'm afraid, Nin."

"Of what?"

"Maybe Jack was right," she said. "If the man who killed Arabella realizes the police are looking for information about who bought her those things, he'll get out of town."

"The police would catch him anyway," Nin said. "There are police cars nowadays, don't forget, and telephones. They would get the word out."

"Nonetheless, it means we have less time than I thought to get our information to the police," Adele said.

"What is our information?" Nin asked.

"Nothing yet, but I think we will have something by the end of the day," Adele insisted.

"Well, then, that would narrow the investigation for them, wouldn't it?" Nin asked. "If we're going to hunt down the man who bought Arabella that jewelry in the shops in San Francisco, we ought to get a good description of him, right? So even if he's escaped town, the police will know who to look for." She eyed her friend. "And if it's Gene Dilworth, he won't get very far, will he?"

"I never said I thought Gene was guilty," Adele said.

"But that's what you're thinking, isn't it?" Nin asked. "I saw your face when we read the letters."

"I was thinking more along the lines that any *young* man might have killed Arabella," Adele said.

"So you think the police are looking in the wrong direction with Mr. Riddle?" Nin asked.

"I just don't think the pieces fit," she mumbled.

"But the pieces fit for Gene?" Nin eyed her.

"It would be an awful cliché," Adele insisted. "A wealthy young man gets involved with his mother's lady's maid, then when he tries to get rid of her, he finds murder is the only solution. It's like a story in the melodramas."

"Things like that do happen," Nin pointed out.

"Someone went to a great deal of trouble to put the finger on Virgil Riddle," Adele said.

"He does hate the man," Nin pointed out. "Mr. Cress told you that."

"But that doesn't mean he would kill his mother's lady's maid just to incriminate him," Adele said.

The train reached the city and both women threaded around the crowded platform, catching a hackney to Oak Street where the Blessings lived.

Elsie welcomed them with the affection of a long-lost cousin. Her athletic figure had thinned which, Adele knew, was from worry over her father whose health had been declining over the years.

"I finally convinced Papa to reduce his days at the university," she said, her voice low as she helped them out of their coats and hats. "He gripes all the time, of course, but it's done him a world of good."

"I'm glad," Adele smiled. "And have you reduced your days too?"

"My days?" Her friend blinked.

"With the Lilith Crusade," Nin supplied.

Elsie stiffened. "I promised Papa to ease up on radical politics if he stayed home more and I'm keeping my promise."

"You always do, Elsie." Adele pressed her hand.

"That's not to say I don't know what they're doing." Her voice lowered. "There's a demonstration at Wells Fargo tomorrow. They let go of all their women clerks with some excuse of tightening their belts, but they were quick to put men in their places after the women left. They've written letters to the management and the mayor and gotten nowhere."

"So you think throwing stones through their windows will get them their jobs back?" Nin asked. "Or are you going to rob the bank?"

"That might not be a bad idea, Miss Branch." Elsie smiled. "At least we could compensate those poor women for the sixty percent less pay they were getting over the years than those male clerks."

"Elsie, don't start anything that will mean your father's health," Adele begged.

"She won't," Nin said with the confidence of her gift.

"As I said, I know what they're doing but I'm not participating. Worst luck." Elsie grabbed each of their hands and marched them into the parlor.

Adele was relieved to see that, although Dr. Blessings still looked less robust than he had when she had consulted him about the Blackstone case, his health had not deteriorated since last year when they visited him at the university. He still gave them a warm smile and spoke in a jovial tone.

"I suppose Elsie told you she has me living like an old man now?" he asked as his daughter adjusted the pillows against his back. "Don't fuss so, Elsie!"

"People say people make much more of their lives in their old age," Adele insisted.

"Lady Augusta has more energy than her son and he's the sheriff of Arrojo," Nin added.

Dr. Blessings laughed. "Well, perhaps I ought to pay her a visit and learn her secret." He sighed. "I can't do anything but look out the window."

"It's better than straining your eyes in the dark laboratory, Papa," Elsie insisted. "And it's time for your tea anyway, so it's just as well we have visitors."

"Tea!" the man spit out after his daughter left the room. "Elsie's taken to gentile practices since I'm tied to this chair." He slapped the arms. "Tea and luncheon and bridge games —" He took a breath. "And me with a smaller salary!"

"Your health is worth more than a few extra coins," Nin insisted.

He patted her hand. "It's good to know someone else thinks so." He was quiet for a moment. "She's been getting money from somewhere for all these trifles, Adele. I don't know where."

"I shouldn't worry," Adele said. "I wouldn't be surprised if Elsie is washing dishes for some establishment in the Tenderloin to earn extra coins while you sleep."

"She's not afraid to do muck work when necessary," Nin said. "She's not like other well-to-do young ladies who won't dirty their hands and run up debts on silly things."

"Of that you're quite right, Miss Branch." The man looked more relaxed. "Elsie has always been resourceful. I suppose I'm worrying too much." He stretched his feet out. "Will you be so kind, Adele, as to get me a cigar from behind that row of *Universal Cyclopaedia*?"

"Don't you dare, Adele!" Elsie came in with the tea tray. "He's not to have more than one cigar a day, and he's already had it."

"Elsie, dear —" Her father looked annoyed.

"And don't give him the bowl of sugar either," she continued. "The doctor put him on a strict diet."

"For heaven's sake," the man grumbled. "No cigars, no sugar in my tea. I'm not dead yet!"

Elsie kissed his cheek. "I mean to see that you stay on your feet until I'm well under mine."

"Considering you used to outrun me even when you were a child, I may be as old as Rip Van Winkle by that time!"

"Not as old as that." Nin's eyes becoming like two lamps. "But you best follow your daughter's orders."

Dr. Blessings looked at her for a moment with alarm and sipped his unsweetened tea.

"What do you need help with now, dear?" Elsie asked.

"How do you know we've come for help?" Nin challenged. "We wanted to see how your father was doing."

"If you'll pardon, Miss Branch, Adele might come for a social call but I hardly think you would."

"What a thing to say." Nin looked entirely innocent.

"Come, dear, I'm not a newborn." Elsie leaned back, crossing her legs. "I know you don't like me."

"It's your own fault for calling me a country mouse," Nin grumbled.

"I've changed my mind about that," Elsie said. "Papa and I might take ourselves to the country when the university gives him his pension."

"Is that what you really want?" Adele eyed her.

Dr. Blessings laughed. "I do. Elsie is a different story."

"You know I'll go wherever the doctor says is best for you, Papa," she said with affection.

"He must be a miracle worker to make you so complacent," Nin remarked. "This doctor, I mean."

"This doctor is a she," Elsie said roughly.

"That explains it, then," Nin said.

Adele laughed. She took out the letters Nellie had given them and the note from the evidence box. "As a matter of fact, we do have something we'd like you to take a look at."

"What's the case this time?" Elsie leaned forward.

"Something even you could sympathize with," Nin said. "A domestic servant was found dead in a rich man's conservatory."

“Then why do you need Papa if you already know who did it?” Elsie looked disappointed.

“It’s likely the man didn’t do it,” Adele said. “At least, the police have no evidence so far.”

“And is this part of the evidence they do have?” Dr. Blessings glanced at the papers.

“Part of it is,” Adele admitted. “They found this note next to the girl’s body.”

“‘Riddle did it.’ What kind of riddle?”

“Not what. Who,” Nin said. “Riddle as in Virgil Riddle.”

“He’s the man who owns the conservatory,” Adele said.

“Well, then, there you are!” The woman leaned back. “Really, Del, I have heard of detectives making things complicated when everything is there right in front of them.”

“I’m not a detective, Elsie,” Adele snapped. “Detectives work with their feet more than their heads.”

“I doubt Jackson would appreciate that.” Elsie smirked.

“You say the man has been proven innocent?” Dr. Blessings asked.

“Not really proven,” she said. “But there are circumstances that make it unlikely he is guilty.”

“Then you think this note is a forgery,” he concluded.

“Or the dead girl was trying to blame Mr. Riddle for some unknown reason,” Adele said.

“And dragged herself into his conservatory before dying so the police would think they had a complete case?” Elsie looked at her. “I suppose anything’s possible.”

“But not probable,” Nin said. “She had three bullets in her back.”

“Miss Branch, please.” Elsie flinched.

Nin snorted. “You’d slash the mayor’s face to pieces with a broken bottle but you can’t think of a woman being shot!”

“I’m guessing you want me to compare the handwriting on

the note to these letters, then?" Dr. Blessings asked, finishing his tea.

"You know me too well by now." Adele smiled. "These are letters Arabella — the dead girl — wrote to her former employer's daughter."

Elsie fetched her father's bag of tools and he went to work. Within a few minutes, he leaned back, rolling the magnifying glass he had been using in his hand. "It's difficult to tell, Adele."

"It's difficult or you won't commit yourself?" Nin asked.

"It's difficult, Miss Branch. You see, this note is like a child's."

"How so?" Adele asked.

"It's printed, for one. And the letters are carefully traced so as to make them unidentifiable."

"I see what you're saying," Nin said slowly. "When children learn to write, they trace letters until they find their own style."

"Very well said, Miss Branch." He smiled. "I'm glad to see some of my expertise has rubbed off on you." Nin blushed and played with the silver spoon.

"It was deliberately done, you think?" Adele asked.

"Oh, no doubt," he said. "Even when one writes the most neutral hand one can, one can't help but leave their mark. It's as much a part of us as breathing."

"But there's no mark here?" she asked.

He shook his head. "The person who wrote it was too careful."

"Then it couldn't have been Arabella," she surmised.

"A dying woman would hardly take the time to be careful with her handwriting," Nin agreed.

"I didn't say the writer was careful," said Dr. Blessings. "There are a few things I can tell you about this." He tapped the note with the magnifying glass. "For one, whoever wrote it did have some emotion."

"What do you mean?" Adele asked.

"He was agitated or nervous or even excited," he said. "You see the jagged lines here on the edges of the 'n' and 't'? The pencil smeared because he pressed too hard."

"I can hardly imagine Arabella being nervous telling the police who her killer is," Nin observed. "She was the sort who would shout it from the rooftops if she could."

"Who is this Mr. Riddle?" Elsie asked.

"A wealthy man who claims to have had a filial relationship with the murder victim," Adele said.

"The police think he was having a love affair with her," Nin said.

"And Riddle is his last name?" Elsie inquired.

"His full name is Virgil Riddle," Adele said.

Dr. Blessings glanced at his daughter. "Just what are you getting at, dear?"

"If they had a warm relationship — filial or something else — and if she were trying to tell the police he killed her, she would have written 'Virgil did it,' wouldn't she?" Elsie asked.

"I think you're right!" Adele said

"He might have told her to hide their relationship," Nin pointed out.

"But even then, Miss Branch, she would have written 'Mr. Riddle did it,' and not 'Riddle did it,'" Elsie said.

"And how do you know so much about what a young lady would call a man in her warmest regards?" her father asked in a teasing voice and she grunted at him in reply.

"Anything else you can tell us about the note, Dr. Blessings?" Adele asked.

He narrowed his eyes, looking into the unlit fireplace. "I don't know, but I have a feeling it was written on impulse."

"Well, it would be," Adele pointed out. "I don't think one plans to write who one's killer is."

"I don't know if I can explain it," he said. "You remember Mr. Arnow, Adele?"

"I do indeed," she said. "John Bellows was always trying to convince him that he needed a woman to take care of him."

"He would," Nin snorted.

"John was only trying to marry off his Aunt Nina so he wouldn't have to pay for her house," Elsie agreed with a sniff.

"Mr. Arnow has been a foursome for our bridge games in the last several weeks." Here, Dr. Blessings gave his daughter a wary look. "The man is absolutely obsessed with bridge."

"He's a keen player," Elsie agreed.

"He told me he always carries a bridge pencil with him in his coat pocket so he's ready for any game. Remember, Elsie?"

"'Got to be ready for anything, m'dear,'" Elsie mimicked, making them all smile.

"I think I see what you mean." Adele pressed her head back against the cushion on the sofa. "The person who killed Arabella suddenly got the idea to incriminate Mr. Riddle and so he took out a pencil he had in his pocket and wrote the note."

"Provided he had paper on him too," Dr. Blessings chimed in.

"I'm assuming there's a reason why you say 'he,' Papa?" Elsie asked. "Other than the fact that only a brute with a beard could have killed such a girl."

Dr. Blessings glanced at his daughter. "I will remind you, my dear, Adele has told us many stories about women killers from her exploits with the police?"

"One ought never to underestimate the deadliness of a woman," Nin echoed.

"Be that as it may, there is a reason," he said. "The more I look at it, the more I'm fairly certain this note was written by a man."

Adele exchanged a meaningful look with her friend. "You're sure of that?"

"The strokes here are wide," he said. "And the 'o' and 'e' are more boxy than round. There's no doubt."

"You mean you're actually committing yourself?" Nin stared at him.

"On that point, Miss Branch, I have no hesitation," he said. "Your Arabella did not write this note."

"And certainly not on her deathbed," Elsie added. "If Papa says so, then it's true."

"I have no doubt whatsoever," Adele said as she put the letters and the note away.

CHAPTER 22

Dr. Blessings' strength gave out after he supplied them with what they needed and begged to rest, insisting he would have his lunch later. Adele, seeing the anxious look on Elsie's face, the tenderness that softened the usually solid features as she helped her father up the stairs touched her heart. She knew it touched Nin's too, as she saw the woman's eyes moisten.

"It's difficult when one's beloved parent is ill," Nin whispered. Adele knew she was thinking of her own mother who had died by her own hand after months of melancholic existence.

"Yes, it is," she echoed, thinking of her own father. "We mustn't leave her alone, Nin."

When Elsie came down, Nin sat at the dining room table and asked, "Are you going to feed us or not?"

This brought a smile to Elsie's face. "You always refuse."

"We're hungry," Nin insisted.

"Indeed we are." Adele followed her friend's lead and settled herself on a chair.

Elsie brought out a colorful spread of cold meat, cheese, thick brown bread and sliced vegetables. "I rarely eat rich foods anymore," she admitted, spearing an olive. "Papa can't have meat and cheese like this, you know."

"We won't tell him, then," Adele said with a wink.

"If you're making it, you ought to reap the rewards," Nin added.

"I don't mind housekeeping for Papa," Elsie said. "It's the wolfish man who expects to have his stew under his nose the moment he gets home that I object to."

"You may find yourself willingly serving a wolf one day, Elsie," Adele said. "But he won't be a wolf. He'll be an educated, cultured man."

"That will be the day," Elsie snorted. "Don't tell me you've found one of these educated, cultured men in that dusty town of yours?"

"I wouldn't call the sheriff educated and cultured," Nin said. "But he's a good sort all the same."

"Oh, it's the sheriff, is it?" Elsie raised her eyebrows.

"He's sweet on her but she isn't sweet on him," said Nin. "She's now interested in a medical student from a rich family."

"I'm not interested in anybody," Adele insisted. "Nathan and I are friends." She spread butter on a slice of bread. "And he's not a medical student. He's almost done with school."

"So the sheriff is out?" Elsie asked.

Adele felt her face grow hot as she tore into the salad. "It's business only, Elsie."

"And when your business is finished?" Elsie grinned.

"But it isn't," said Nin.

"You've more letters for Papa?" Her face became worried. "I don't think he has the strength right now Adele."

"Not letters," said Adele. "We're going on a hunt."

"For evidence?"

"In a way," Adele said. "We're hunting up a pair of gloves and some jewelry."

Elsie nearly spit out her coffee. "Aren't you the same woman who once told me you'd rather wear an elephant around your head than a tiara?" Nin smiled.

"Not for us," Adele said, laughing. "Arabella had some rather expensive accessories on her when her body was found and the police think —"

"The police think some wealthy miscreant bought her gloves, lavished her with jewels and then killed her because she expected too much of him," Elsie finished. "They would think that."

"And what do you think? She diligently saved her money to buy them?" Nin sniffed.

"In spite of my being a professor's daughter, Miss Branch, I do know something about working women's salaries and their struggle to survive." Elsie was clearly hurt. "I've done work in the settlement houses just like Adele."

Adele expected her friend to snap back, but she looked genuinely ashamed. "I'm sorry. I've no cause to talk. I don't know anything about it."

Elsie patted her hand. "Don't give it another thought, dear." She slapped another slice of cheese on the already piled slice of bread. "You realize there are at least dozens of milliners and jewelers in this city?"

Adele took out the envelope Missy had left for her. "We're starting with these."

"Oh, the evidence," Elsie said dramatically as she examined the photos. "Well, that ought to help some."

"Milliners and jewelers leave their mark in their style," Adele agreed. "All we have to do is find the signature style."

Elsie bent down to the photographs. "Adele, can you get me the bag Papa left in the parlor?"

"Don't tell me you're taking up the handwriting analysis business," Adele teased.

"I find those magnifiers he has useful once in a while," Elsie said, clearly distracted by the photo.

Adele fetched the bag and her friend used the magnifier that her father had used only a short time ago.

"What is it?" she asked.

"These gloves," Elsie murmured. "Are they leather or doeskin?"

"How should we know?" Nin asked.

"You saw them, didn't you?" Elsie countered. "I'm assuming you touched them as well?"

"They were very soft, now that you mention it," Adele said.

"Probably doeskin," her friend surmised. "Mrs. Rochefort's Fashion House on Sacramento Street is always advertising her doeskin gloves are the best in the city. These pearl buttons look like her style."

"Good work, dear!" Adele pressed her hand.

Elsie picked up the photograph of the jewelry. "Distinguishing marks, you said?"

"It's not much, I agree," Adele admitted. "But there was nothing on the jewelry to indicate where they came from." She watched as her friend scrutinized the picture. "Rather hideous, isn't it?"

"Like a plate of fruit no one wants to eat," Nin agreed.

"It shouldn't be too difficult to find a jeweler who makes everything look like it belonged to our mothers," Adele said, smiling.

Elsie tapped the photograph. "I think I know who made this!"

"Elsie!" Adele stared at her. "You hate such fineries as much as I do."

"Nonetheless, dear, one is forced to take them in now and then," she said in a breezy tone. "You notice the stones in the center have a chain pattern?"

"Like manacles," Nin snorted.

"Exactly," said the woman. "We had an auction last year and women from the Hera Society made some donations." She rolled her eyes. "They condescended to join us to raise money for the children's foundling home because 'the poor little dears have no mothers, after all.'"

"Go on." Adele sat up.

"One of the ladies — Mrs. Walton, you remember her?"

"She claims to have a sister who's a duchess," Adele said to Nin. "The comb would be exactly her style."

"She donated a pair of earrings and a necklace. She said she was 'tired of them.'"

"At least the foundlings got them," Nin said.

"And you know at what jewelry shop she bought them?" asked Adele.

"Not exactly," Elsie admitted. "I do remember Mrs. Thomas asking her about them and she mentioned a jeweler who 'still knows what women's fashion is all about' on Post Street."

Adele jumped up and gave her a tight embrace. "That helps us enormously!"

"We'll make a detective woman out of you yet," Nin said, smiling for the first time.

"Heaven forbid!" Elsie rolled her eyes.

~

Mrs. Rochefort's Fashion House was a large establishment at the corner of Octavia and Sacramento Street. Its ornate wooden arabesques hanging over the display windows that stretched the length of half the block made it a force to be reckoned with.

Almost subconsciously, Adele tucked in her stomach and tilted her hat at a fashionable angle, putting on what her brother had once teasingly called "Del's aristocratic face." She glanced at her friend and noted Nin seemed to be aware of her own inherited refinement and looked nearly as haughty as Lady Augusta.

The young lady behind the counter closed the novel she was reading and hid it on a shelf behind her. "May I help you?"

"We'd like to see Madame Rochefort," Adele said.

"Have you an appointment?"

"We're not here for clothes," Nin said.

"I'm sorry, but —"

"She'll want to see us," Adele said. "It's very important."

The girl looked from one to the other as if weighing whether the argument she anticipated from them was worth the effort. Adele tried to look as if she were about to make a scene, and the girl finally said, "Please take a seat, and I'll see if she's in."

"She'd better be in," Nin said with a growl and the girl looked frightened.

As they settled on an overstuffed couch, Adele said, "I see she's been well trained."

"And well deprived," Nin added. "That suit she had on didn't come from this shop."

A woman with the face of a badger came out. "What is this all about?" The woman's spoke in a throaty voice and had an exaggerated French accent.

"We're sorry to disturb you, ma'am," Adele began.

"I do not see ladies who do not buy." The woman's eyes gained some focus. "Michelle told me you are not here to buy."

"We're here to ask about someone who did," Adele said.

"You'd better talk to us if you don't want the police here," Nin said.

"Police!" The woman's face turned white.

"Sit down, Madame," Nin said in such a brutal way that the woman sank into a lounge chair.

Adele took out the photo of the gloves. "Is this your design, Madame Rochefort?"

The woman hesitated before answering, "I do not know."

"Look again," Nin said.

The woman sighed. "I do not need to look again. Yes, it's my design."

Adele could see Madame Rochefort was truly alarmed and she realized why. She imagined the woman had left her country, perhaps even a ghastly situation, by sneaking on a boat to San Francisco without papers. She said in a gentle tone, "We don't intend to bring the police if we don't have to. But we need your help."

The woman relaxed. "What is it you want to know?"

"We're looking into the death of a woman we knew," she said. "We think she might have bought these at your shop." She took out the photograph Missy had taken of Arabella after they found the body.

The woman's confidence returned. "What a strange picture."

"She's dead," Nin said.

The madame gasped and took out a handkerchief. "I can't say, Miss —"

"Gossling."

"I can't say, Miss Gossling." Some of her conceit returned. "You appreciate I wait only on the best in the city."

"Arabella was definitely not the best," Nin remarked.

Adele looked at the girl behind the counter. "And you, miss?"

"I don't know what you mean." The young woman was instantly alert.

Adele rose and held out the photograph. "Michelle, that's your name?" The girl nodded. "You can help us a great deal. You see all the ladies who come in here, don't you?"

Michelle grimaced. "Can't help it, can I?"

"Did you see this one?"

She peered at the photograph. "She looks something like —"

"Yes?"

"Oh, we salesgirls called her the braggart."

"That sounds like Arabella," Nin said dryly.

"Michelle! Do not talk that way about customers," her employer warned.

"Well, Madame, she's dead, isn't she? It don't matter much now."

"Please!" The woman held her handkerchief to her face again.

"Why did you call her that?" Adele asked.

"She always came in showing off her latest jewelry," Michelle said. "Shaking her wrist with a new bracelet or pulling forward her ears with new earrings."

Adele took out the photographs of the jewelry." Any of these?"

The girl nodded. "I've seen that brooch before."

"Did she say where she got it?" Nin asked.

"No, miss. Just that she could get more where that came from anytime she wanted." She snorted. "As if we couldn't do the same if we were willing —" She shrugged.

"Willing to let a gentleman buy them for you?" Adele eyed her.

"Well, it ain't like we could get them for ourselves with what —" her voice lowered. "with what Madame pays us."

"How do you know a man bought them for her?" Nin asked.

"Oh, not *a* man, miss. Several men." The girls' eyes sparkled. "She was very clear she had 'generous gentlemen friends.'"

"Did she ever come in here with a man?" Adele asked.

"Only once, miss," Michelle said. "Are you really investigating a murder?"

"Who said anything about a murder?" Adele asked. "I said she was dead, not that she was murdered."

"Why else would you want to know if she bought the gloves here?" The girl stiffened. "Got to be murder. Wouldn't surprise me if one of her 'generous gentlemen friends' did it."

"Did she come in here with one of them?"

"Not inside the shop, but a man waited outside for her once," Michelle recalled.

Adele leaned against the counter. "Can you describe him?"

"Not really. He stayed outside the whole time," said Michelle.

"Was he old or young?" Nin asked.

"I'm not sure," she admitted. "I couldn't see well from the window. And he had his hat over his eyes."

"Was he tall, short, thin, fat?" Nin prompted. "You must remember *something*."

The girl gave a sly smile. "We get more ladies coming in with gentlemen who prefer to remain inconspicuous than Madame will admit. They're always dressed fine, always have hats over their eyes and collars up to their necks."

"Blast it!" Nin snarled.

Adele returned to Madame Rochefort and shuffled through the photographs until she came to one in particular. "Madame, can you tell me what this piece that was cut out of the gloves would have been?"

The woman looked almost scandalized. "Somebody ruined my design!"

"The killer had to get rid of something," Nin said.

"We want to know what that something was," Adele said. "Was it a label with your shop name on it?"

The woman shrugged. "Ladies prefer not to have labels showing on their gloves, Miss —"

"Gossling," said Adele.

In her conceited tone, Madame Rochefort added, "I make the designs, you appreciate, but my workers make the garments. You appreciate I only make the dresses —"

"For the best ladies in the city." Nin rolled her eyes.

"May we speak to your workers, Madame?" Changing her tone, Adele added, "It may have something to do with her death."

"If you don't tell us, you'll have to tell the police," Nin added.

Madame Rochefort's lips twisted with fear, and she nodded at Michelle. The girl disappeared behind a curtain and came back with three young ladies, their sleeves rolled up.

"Did any of you make these gloves?" Adele handed them the photographs.

After a few minutes, the girl on the far left said, "I think I did, miss. I remember the color."

"Then that green-gray shade isn't typical?" Adele asked.

The girl shook her head. "The lady was very particular. I had to go to my artist friend to get the right shade. But I got paid extra for it." She curtsied to Madame Rochefort in gratitude and the milliner nodded.

"It was a special order then," Adele said in a low voice to her friend.

"Damn lucky for us," Nin answered.

"Can you tell us what was on this part of the glove that was cut off?" Adele pointed to the photograph.

The young lady answered without hesitation, "Why, the initials, miss."

"Initials?"

"The lady wanted them embossed in silver," said the girl.

"And do you remember what the initials were?" Adele held her breath.

"An A and a P, miss," she said. "Sort of stuck together, you know, so the leg of the 'A' touched the 'P'."

"A.P," Adele murmured. "Arabella Parnell."

"Very good, ladies." Madame Rochefort clapped her hands. "You may go now."

The workers retreated to the back room.

"That will keep the police away from here, yes?" The milliner looked hopeful.

"They may come with a few photographs of their own," Adele said.

"When they have a suspect for the man," Nin added.

"That's all they'll need." Adele gave the woman a meaningful look. "Nothing else, Madame."

The woman relaxed. "*La pauvre fille!*"

"Yes," Adele murmured. "The poor girl."

They went outside into the sunshine.

"We've something definite to tell Hatfield now," she said.

"There *was* a man who bought Arabella expensive clothes," Nin agreed. "Whether Virgil Riddle or someone else. It's maddening that girl couldn't remember anything about his looks."

Adele laughed. "Maddening, perhaps, but not surprising. When you've lived among the socially sensitive, they know well enough when to show themselves and when to hide."

"The cad!" Nin grumbled.

As they passed by the alleyway, Adele felt someone grab her arm. "Miss!"

She turned around and realized it was the young seamstress who had identified the gloves.

"Is it true?" she asked, out of breath.

"You'll catch cold," Nin said, as the young woman had rushed out with only a shawl.

"Is it true?" the girl repeated.

"Is what true?" Adele asked.

"About Miss Parnell — that she's dead?"

Adele glanced at Nin. "Yes, I'm afraid it's true."

The girl's face froze. "When?"

"About a week ago," Adele said. "You were friends?"

"Well, not exactly, miss." She glanced at the open doorway of the milliner's shop.

"But you spoke with her enough to like her?" Adele guessed.

"In a way, miss," she said. "She wasn't like the other ladies. They think little elves make their clothes."

"You mean she went in the back to see you," Adele said, smiling.

"She appreciated there was someone working hard on her gloves," Nin said.

"That's it, miss," said the girl. "That's just the way to put it." She slipped a rough linen handkerchief from her pocket, and Adele realized she had tears in her eyes.

"What's your name, dear?"

"Shirley Frances," she said.

"Miss Frances, I don't want to upset you, but Miss Parnell's death wasn't accidental."

Miss Frances stared. "You mean she committed suicide? Oh, she wouldn't do that, miss! She was so happy and — well, she had people who appreciated her."

"You mean people who gave her things." Nin eyed her.

"It's the same thing, I reckon," said the girl in a stubborn tone. "At least it is in our eyes."

"You mean the working girl's eyes," Adele said softly. "Yes, I can see how you would see it that way." In a more official tone, she asked, "Did you see the man who bought Miss Parnell the gloves?"

"I was always in the back, miss," she said. With a sniff, she added, "I know what the other girls said about her, but it wasn't true!"

"What did they say about her?" Adele asked.

"That she was sweet-talking men into buying her things," said Miss Frances. "But, really, miss." She lowered her voice. "I think it was the man who was at fault."

"Of course it was," Nin said. "The man with the money always has the advantage."

"No, I mean she was being taken by him, not her taking him," said Miss Frances.

Adele leaned on her parasol. "Why do you think that?"

"She came here one day looking all down. I asked her what was the matter, and she said a man who had been teaching her how to be a lady suddenly dropped her."

Adele glanced at Nin. "A man named Virgil Riddle?"

"She didn't say his name," she said. "She only said he was better than her own father but now he was afraid people would think —" She breathed. "Then she said, 'The irony is I'm not the least bit interested in him in that way. I've someone else in mind.'"

"But she didn't say who?" Adele asked.

The girl shook her head. "But whoever it was, he took advantage of her all right. Oh, she was more innocent than everyone thinks, miss."

"How do you know?" Nin asked.

"It was the way her eyes were like two stars every time she came into the shop," said the girl. "Like she couldn't believe what she was seeing. That's how it was when she came into the workroom too and saw the dresses." She sighed. "She came in one day all in a flutter because this man had bought her a bracelet with diamonds!"

"A woman's first diamonds are always a treat," Adele said, smiling. Then, she added with a laugh, "I threw mine across the room in a fit one night."

"Oh, you shouldn't do that, miss!" she said. "Miss Parnell, she treated 'em like they were baby birds still in the nest. She said they were Kelly & King's, the best to be had."

"Kelly & King Fine Jewelers?" Adele felt a twinge in her stomach. "Of course!"

"I been there only once," said the girl with a sigh. "I mean, I looked through the window. Then a salesman gave me a dirty look, and I had to move on." She blushed. "I was just coming home from work, and I suppose I looked pretty dingy."

"You're not dingy," Nin said firmly. "You earn an honest living."

"Nice of you to understand, miss." Miss Frances smiled. "Not many people do."

Adele reached for a handful of bills from her pocket and slipped them into Miss Frances' hand. "Buy yourself something nice with this."

The girl looked embarrassed. "D'you mind if I put it in my fund? I'm saving to get married, you see."

"Do with it whatever you like," Adele said, pressing her arm.

Miss Frances had barely time to thank her when Madame Rochefort appeared in the doorway, and she had to rush down the alley. Adele saluted the milliner and turned on her heel as she and Nin walked down the street.

CHAPTER 23

"Well, we learned one vital piece of information," Adele said.

"That Arabella may have been taken advantage of by the men she sought?" Nin guessed.

"We knew that already," Adele said. "I'm talking about Kelly & King."

"Who are they?"

"Only one of the most exclusive jewelry shops in the city," Adele said. "And they're on Montgomery Street."

"Just what Elsie told us." Nin's lips spread in a slow smile.

"Now we know where to go." Adele opened her parasol, as the sunshine had begun to sear her eyes.

"With our luck, the mysterious 'gentleman friend' decided to remain incognito there also," Nin grumbled.

It took some time to weave their way through the busy streets to reach Montgomery. After the sparsity of a small town, Adele felt the invigorating air of people walking past them, involved in their own conversations or hurrying past with their own thoughts, lifting packages or bags to their chest to avoid hitting others. It was nearly dinnertime, and the scents coming out of the open restaurant doors filled her head with meat and onions and rising bread.

Her friend held on tightly to her arm. Nin, unlike her, was unused to crowds, and her apprehension toward people in general made her anxious.

They found the façade with a sign reading *Kelly & King Fine Jewelers* off of Sutter Street. The entrance looked so plain with only two small display windows that Adele felt disappointed. Her wealthier friends had praised the shop's elegance and variety so much that she expected something grander.

"Not much to look at for one of the finest jewelers in San Francisco, is it?" Nin echoed her thoughts.

"Better for us." Adele straightened her shoulders. "A smaller place means better memory for faces."

However, when they entered the store, Adele was surprised to discover it ran deep and wide with rows of display cases between marble pillars. Plentiful electric lights showing in just the right angles made all the jewels sparkle.

"I don't think we should tell them the truth here, do you?" Nin whispered.

"I doubt they would be very forthcoming if they knew we were inquiring after a murder," Adele agreed. "We'll have to try something else."

"Leave it to me," said her friend with surprising confidence.

A young man with a curling mustache dressed as if he were going to the opera approached them. "May I help you, ladies?"

Before Adele could say a word, Nin slid forward, adjusting her small height so as to stand regally. In a voice Adele had never heard before, she said, "I'd like to see a selection of brooches."

"Certainly, miss."

"Ma'am," she corrected. "My husband is Mr. Jackson Gossling, son of Mr. Otis Gossling. You've heard of Otis Gossling?" She regarded him with the look of a spider on a fly in its net.

"The famous criminal lawyer." The young man's smile

widened. "I'll be happy to show you anything you like, Mrs. Gossling."

"This is his sister, Miss Gossling." Nin took her friend's arm. "We want something set in white gold with diamonds. A lady always has a use for diamonds. Isn't that right, dear?" She glanced at Adele.

Adele, too bewildered to answer, only nodded.

"Indeed, ma'am." The young man rubbed his hands as he led them to a display in the middle of the shop. "I have some fine brooches here. You've heard of our lion pin, no doubt?" He reached underneath the glass and brought out a brooch shaped like a red lion with two diamond eyes.

"I'm not a child, sir," Nin said with emphatic annoyance.

"Oh, I didn't mean —"

"It's rather lovely, dear." Adele recovered her voice. "But I think we're looking for something a little tamer."

"Indeed, we've had enough of wild cats to last us a lifetime," Nin answered and Adele hid a smile, knowing she was speaking of a case involving a charlatan and his golden cat the year before.

"I was wondering —" Nin began.

"Yes?" The young man perked up.

"A friend of ours raved about a brooch her husband bought her not long ago." Nin snapped her fingers at Adele and she, taking the cue, took out the envelope with the photographs Missy had taken of the jewelry. Nin fumbled through them and slapped the two with the brooch on the table. "It's such a lovely piece, we can only assume it came from you."

The young man's eyes were keen. "Why, of course! Our Sea Breeze pin! Oh, but that was last year's model, ma'am."

"Last year?" Adele perked up.

"Last summer, to be exact," he said. "A one-of-a-kind piece, to be sure. If I may show you —"

"If it's one of a kind, then you must remember her and her husband coming into the shop," Nin interrupted.

"Well, ma'am, I'm afraid I wasn't the one who sold it to her," he said, ducking his head a little.

"Then we'd like to see the young man or woman who did," Nin said. "My taste is very similar to hers, and I'm sure the shop person who sold her the brooch wouldn't waste my time showing me children's pieces." Adele had to turn her back so the young man wouldn't see her laughing.

"I'm terribly sorry, ma'am." The young man's politeness didn't hide the fact that he was miffed. "I'll try to find the shop person for you, if he or she is here, that is."

"See that you do, young man." Nin settled her elbows on the display case. "We'll wait right here for you."

When the young man left, Adele did not contain her laughter. "Nin, you're awful!"

"It'll do him good," Nin insisted. "These salesmen get as pompous as their clientele. They need to be taken down a few pegs."

The young man returned with a salesgirl who, Adele was relieved, looked less formal in her linen suit. "This is Miss Goode, ma'am. I believe she can help you." With some relief, he retreated to the front of the shop where a couple had just walked in.

"You sold this piece to a friend of ours, I believe?" Nin asked.

"Oh, ma'am, I'm so sorry!" The girl gushed.

"Sorry?" Adele asked.

"Why, I saw it in the papers," she said. "That young lady who was killed last week, isn't it?"

Adele exchanged a surprised look with Nin. "You know about that?"

"It was in the Rosa Gris papers, wasn't it?" she asked.

"How did you get hold of the Rosa Gris papers?"

"Oh, not me, miss, my beau," she said. "I remember it clear as day. He showed it to me as sort of a Sunday conversation piece, you know, and I took one look at that picture of the girl and, wouldn't you know it, I said to him, 'Why, that looks like the young lady who bought the Sea Breeze brooch from me last year!'"

Adele led the girl to a quiet corner with a few plush chairs. "Miss Goode, may we be honest with you?"

"Naturally," said the girl.

"We're not here to buy any brooch," she said. "And the woman in question wasn't a friend of ours."

"Not really," Nin added.

"Her name was Arabella Parnell, and we're looking into her death," said Adele.

"Oh, a terrible thing it was," said the young woman breathlessly. "Three bullets in the back, it said in the papers. Can you imagine dying like that? Why, a glass of wine with hemlock would have been better! At least you don't know what hits you then."

"Hemlock is a very frightening way to die," Nin said with authority. "But not all species are poisonous."

"Oh, miss, please!" The girl clutched her stomach.

"We don't want the shop owners or the other salespeople to know why we're really here." Adele lowered her voice. "Shops that serve the wealthy tend to be very closed-mouth when a police inquiry is involved."

"They wouldn't like it here, no, indeed," Miss Goode agreed. "We had a couple make some kind of a row — it turns out they were getting divorced and wanted witnesses — and, oh, you should have seen the face of Mr. Weaver." She nodded toward the young man who had approached them. "You'd have thought *he'd* just witnessed a murder!"

"I can imagine," Adele said. "Is there somewhere we can talk privately?"

"There's the storeroom," she said. "A bit musty, but I expect it's better than being overheard. They eavesdrop all the time, these fresh young men." She gave a vicious look toward Mr.

Weaver as she led them to the side of the shop and up a flight of stairs. The room was indeed dusty but definitely quiet.

"Now," Adele said, "we want to know everything about Miss Parnell's visit to the shop and the purchase of that brooch."

The girl pressed her hands together. "She came in on a Thursday. I remember because it rained all day Wednesday, and I was just telling my ma that same morning how it was lucky I had to go to work after the rain and not during."

"Go on," Nin prompted.

"She came in around lunchtime," she continued. "She wore a dress in that lovely peach shade that was so in fashion last year."

"Yes, yes, go on," Nin snapped. "We don't need to know that many details."

"Was she with a man?" Adele asked.

"Come to think of it, yes, she was," she said.

Adele squeezed her friend's hand. "Can you tell us anything about him?"

"He was trying to hide, of course — they always do — but I got a glimpse of him under that big hat all the same," said the girl. "He had light features and sort of reminded me of an ostrich. His knees were knobby."

"You mean long and bony?" Adele murmured. She recalled Gene's extended neck. "Are you sure?"

"Oh, certainly," said the girl. "He was trying to make an impression on her, encouraging her to choose the most expensive brooch on the tray."

"Did she refer to him in any way?" Adele asked. "Maybe even a name?"

"I believe I heard her call him 'sweet' once, but I can't be sure," she said. "I was concentrating on the sale, you see. They're very strict here about you selling so many pieces a week or you get written up and I was short that week by just one piece. I didn't want to lose my job, as I've been written up twice already —"

"It's good Miss Parnell was able to keep you your job," Nin said quickly.

Adele shifted through the photographs and found the few that Missy had taken of the comb. "What about this piece?"

"Oh, that's one of ours too," said the girl with pride. "'The Crown of Thorns,' it's called. The designer, I forgot his name, well, his father was one of those farmers who went wholeheartedly after that fellow William Jennings Bryan, and he went crazy over that speech of his —"

"'You shall not press down upon the brow of labor this crown of thorns. You shall not crucify mankind upon a cross of gold,'" Adele recited. "Yes, it was very powerful."

"I didn't understand much of it myself, but I know it was about gold and silver and all that." The girl fanned herself with a linen handkerchief. "That's why the designer named it that. It has gold and silver, see?" She pointed to the arc of the comb on the photograph. "Oh, I suppose you can't see a thing in these pictures!"

"We've seen the real one," Nin said.

"Miss Parnell just adored it." The girl rolled her eyes with a sigh. "She said she would feel like a queen in it!"

"Was it the same man who bought it for her?" Adele asked.

"Oh, no," said Miss Goode. "It was the other man."

"Other man?" Adele glanced at Nin.

"The redhead."

"Redhead?"

"A carrot-top, I suppose you'd call him. Oh, nothing clownish about him, though. He had a nice face."

"Can you describe his face?" Nin was now leaning forward.

"Rather long, I should say, with a sort of square jawline and a broad forehead," said Miss Goode. "Nice green eyes too. Not really handsome, but, well, a nice face all the same."

"You have a good memory, Miss Goode," Adele commended her.

"Call me Bernice, won't you?" The young woman smiled.

"You call us Adele and Miss Branch, then," Adele said.

"I ought to remember. *He* wasn't trying to hide like the other gentleman," she said.

"Perhaps he didn't hide his name either?" Nin asked hopefully.

"I'm afraid I didn't catch that," she said. "But I think he knew that other man."

"Why do you think so?" Adele asked.

"It was really my fault." She hung her head.

"Why would it be your fault?" Nin asked.

"When I saw Miss Parnell walk in with the young man, of course I went right up to her. We're encouraged to wait on the same people, you see, since we get to know their taste and we can suggest things —"

"— and get them to buy more than they intended," Nin finished.

"Well, it *is* our living, Miss Branch," she defended.

"I wasn't judging," Nin insisted. "The more you can squeeze out of those high-handed 'gentlemen' who bring their paramours in for a trinket, the better."

Bernice giggled. "I sort of see it that way too."

"Go on with your story, Bernice," Adele said.

"So I said to her, 'Nice to see you in again, Miss Parnell. Are you enjoying the Sea Breeze brooch?' She looked ever so embarrassed. I should have known better." Again, she hung her head. "We see some ladies come in with different men all the time, and they look mortified when any hint that they might have been in the shop before with someone else —"

"You didn't do anything wrong," Nin assured her.

"The young man gave her a strange look and took Miss Parnell aside. I couldn't hear what they were saying, but I could see she was trying to calm him, being all smiling and sweet. He just kept getting redder and redder."

"He was jealous?" Nin asked.

"Oh, he simply turned beet red," Bernice said. "But I guess what she said finally worked. He was smiling again when they came to my counter." She sighed. "I was so relieved! I thought I was going to lose the sale for a minute there. You can't imagine how many times a gentleman has walked out of here in a huff."

"So this man was sweet on her?" Nin prompted.

"Cow-eyed is more like it," Bernice said with a smirk. "The gall of him questioning *her* when she told me later she had to practically drag him in with the last of his savings in his pocket!"

"So he wasn't a rich man?" Adele asked.

Bernice shook her head. "Poor as a church mouse, she told me." Her face grew somber. "But he looked so nice and oh, what a tragedy!"

"Tragedy?" Adele asked.

"She told me all about it when she came in the last time," said Bernice. "To think of her — of both of them —" The girl really did look remorseful.

"Tell us about the last time she came in." Adele put her chin in her hand.

"It was just three or so weeks ago," said Bernice. "She came in alone."

"With a check signed by some man," Nin guessed.

"Oh, no," said the girl. "She wasn't in to buy, just to look, she said. To cleanse her eyes from m'lady's satins and silks which she could never wear, she said." She looked confused. "I can't imagine what she meant."

"She worked as a lady's maid for a prominent society woman in our town," Adele supplied.

"Oh, well that explains it, doesn't it?" Bernice twirled a curl that had fallen out of her bun with her finger. "I've done that myself. Once we had Miss Crabtree come in with furs hanging all down her shoulders. The manager tended to her, of course, but, oh, she left our tongues hanging out with that fur!"

"What else did Miss Parnell say?" Adele asked. "I expect you and she were quite friendly by this time."

"We were, as a matter of fact," Bernice said. "I suppose it was bold of me, but I asked her which of the young men's presents she liked the best."

"That was bold of you," Adele said, smiling.

"But very useful to us," Nin added.

"She said, 'I like men who don't have to spend the last of their father's allowance on just one trinket.'"

"So she preferred the ostrich to the redhead," Adele concluded.

"I don't think she preferred either of them," Bernice said. "I think she had her eye on someone altogether different."

"Oh?" Adele raised her eyebrow.

"She said to me, 'You know, Bernice, they say there are many fish in the sea, but for my taste, it's the quality of the fish that matters, not the quantity. Why settle for herring or even trout when you can get striped bass?'"

"So the redheaded man was definitely not striped bass," Adele murmured.

"And neither was the ostrich," Bernice assured her. "Or if he was, he was overly cautious about it. I've seen a lot of gentlemen opening their wallets to pay for a trinket and you can always tell the trout from the bass by the wear on them. The bass men have old-looking wallets from opening them up so much!"

Both Adele and Nin laughed and Adele clasped Bernice's hand in hers. "You're a bright woman, Bernice."

"A shame there are no police women, isn't it?" The girl's eyes sparkled. "I would have made a very good one."

"I'm sure you would have," Adele said. "You mentioned a tragedy connected with the redheaded young man. What was it?"

Bernice's face became grave. "That was so sad. But, you know, I don't think Miss Parnell was very sad about it."

"About what?"

"Well, the young man killed himself."

Adele was stunned and even Nin's eyes widened. When she found her voice, she asked, "And Miss Parnell wasn't sad?"

"She did call him 'poor boy' and cried into her handkerchief," Bernice admitted.

"This was the last time she came in? Three weeks ago, you said?"

"Oh, no, it was months before that," said Bernice. "Three weeks ago, she came in. She'd been in a few times before that and we — well, we sort of became acquainted." She smiled. "She even met Ma once when she came to pick me up. Ma didn't like her very much. Said she had the eyes of a fox."

"She wasn't far wrong," Nin mumbled.

"Then what happened three weeks ago?" Adele asked.

"She came in to look," said the woman. "It was lunchtime, so she invited me to lunch."

"That was nice of her," Nin remarked.

"We went to *Fior d'Italia*. Best ravioli in town." The woman beamed.

"I know," Adele said with a smile. "Did she talk about this young man who killed himself?"

"Oh, we talked some about him," said Bernice. "She said he was weak, and he killed himself for love of her." A sly look came into her eyes. "I think she was just making that up, like a lot of ladies do to cover up how they feel about a tragedy."

"But you said Miss Parnell wasn't sad," Nin pointed out.

"She wasn't sad, but that doesn't mean she wasn't sorry about it," said the girl. "She even said, 'I'm glad I have something to remember him by, poor boy.'"

"Yes," Adele murmured. "Poor boy."

"He was born Irish, you know," said Bernice. "His father owned a grocery store in North Beach. But she said he never had the proper manners, and he would never inherit something like a big estate. She made it clear she wanted that." She sniffed. "I read about these big estates and they cost so much to keep up. I wouldn't want to have to pay hundreds of dollars a month to a gardener just to keep the dead leaves off the trees."

"It does seem such a waste," Adele said, though her mind was on something else.

"Dead leaves help keep weeds away," Nin said.

"I expect you're right." Bernice glanced at the door that had just opened, admitting a man in a starched coat and bow tie. "Oh, that's the manager! I must be getting back or he'll get annoyed."

Adele rose and took out her coin purse. "You've been such a great help, Bernice." She looked around the store. "It's lucky you were in such a position to know things."

"Oh, this is a nice place with nice people." The girl was pleased. "You ought to come see us when we move to Post Street in the spring." Her voice rose with pride. "We'll have three floors in an earthquake-proof building!"

Adele laughed. "Perhaps we will."

The girl clasped her hand over the open mouth of the purse. "Don't, please. I'm not that sort of person."

Adele smiled. "No, you just want to help."

The girl's eyes suddenly appealed to her. "Find who killed Miss Parnell. She wasn't a good girl, I know, but that doesn't mean she deserved to be killed!"

"If every girl who wasn't a good girl deserved to be killed, there would hardly be any women left in the world," Nin said.

"Only if those who judge what's good and what isn't were deciding," Adele insisted as they left the shop.

CHAPTER 24

Safely settled on the train back to Arrojo, Adele's mind felt clear like the blue sky and grassy fields outside the train window. "Now we begin to put the pieces together."

"Arabella was definitely interested in more than one man," Nin observed. "She enticed at least two of them to buy her jewelry."

"And one of those we know," said Adele.

Her friend eyed her as she adjusted her jacket around her shoulders. "I wondered whether you would guess who the man with the light features and knobby knees was."

"I ought to," Adele said. "I spent an evening with him."

"So it wasn't Gene she was interested in after all," said Nin. "It was Nathan."

Adele looked out the window, her brow wrinkling. "He didn't seem like the type."

"Maybe you didn't want to see him as the type," Nin said shrewdly.

"No, really, dear, he didn't strike me as the sort who would swoon to the coarse charms Arabella possessed," Adele said.

“All men are blind to sense when a pretty girl points her arrows at him,” Nin snorted.

“I should have thought Gene was more susceptible to that type,” Adele continued.

“Or Maxwell,” Nin said. “He’s the sort who would always be one step ahead of someone like Arabella.”

“I wonder who the second man was,” Adele mused. "The redhead.”

"It definitely wasn't Mr. Riddle," Nin said.

"No, I would hardly call him a redhead,” Adele said, laughing. "The more I think of it, Nin, the more it seems clear Arabella's killer must have been a young man." She sighed. "I wish we knew who that redhead was."

“Some poor working sod she met through one of her last employers,” Nin suggested.

“It’s possible.” Adele nodded. “We know he didn’t have the sort of money Nathan has.”

“And we know he killed himself for love of her.” Nin sighed. “What a waste!”

“We only have Bernice's word for that,” Adele pointed out.

“You mean we have Arabella's word for that," Nin snorted.

Adele smiled. “Jack would say you’re drawing conclusions just like a policeman.”

“I don’t draw conclusions,” Nin said stubbornly. “I go by what I feel.”

“I can’t deny it would certainly suit a woman like Arabella to want people to think men would kill themselves for her,” Adele admitted. “It would also suit a girl like her to be shot by three different bullets.”

“Why do you say that?” Nin glanced at her.

“I don’t know,” said Adele. “The thought just came to me.”

“If I’m absorbing your ideas, you’re absorbing my feelings,” her friend defended.

"Perhaps I am," she said. "I think we know what we're looking for now."

"Are you going to interrogate Nathan or are you going to let the police do it?" asked her friend.

"Neither," she said.

"Surely, Adele, you have to tell the police now," Nin objected. "They still think Mr. Riddle did it."

"I don't think they think that anymore." She took her friend's hand. "Look, dear, if my idea is right, we're looking at a very tricky crime."

"Murder is always tricky," her friend said.

"But some murders are trickier than others," she said.

Nin stiffened. "You mean when they involve the upper classes?"

"It's a fact we can't ignore," Adele said. "Remember the sheriff almost lost his job with the Marsh case."

"That was just hot wind," Nin insisted. "The town council knows it won't get a better man than Hatfield."

"But this involves friends of the mayor," Adele said. "At the very least, I want to find out what Beatrice has to tell us."

"What could the chatter of schoolgirls have to contribute to this case?" Nin snorted.

"It's certain chatter I'm looking for," said Adele. "I'm hoping Hazel's contempt for Arabella leads to some of the truths we're looking for." She leaned back. "We must tread very lightly until we have strong evidence to bring to the police."

"Personally, I would rather stomp all over the mayor's face with what we have now," Nin snarled. "It might even make him look sincere for once."

Adele laughed and retired to looking out the window, but her stomach churned with a troubling sensation.

The train pulled into the Arrojo station, and they were glad to get out and feel the air against their backs.

"To the police station?" Nin inquired.

"I want to stop at the shop first," said Adele. "Beatrice should be there, and I want to hear about their picnic with Hazel."

"If they didn't spoil everything," Nin cautioned. "You know how indiscreet they can be."

"Beatrice knows what she's doing," Adele assured her as they descended the wooden steps of the platform onto the street.

"She'll beat them with a stick if she has to," Nin agreed and Adele laughed.

She was delighted to find not only Beatrice but Rachel and Sandra, whom she hadn't seen in a long time. The girl was sixteen and looked even more mature than Rachel, though she still retained the delicate skin and hair of her childhood. Her voice was also still childlike as she greeted Adele warmly.

"What have you been doing?" Adele pressed her hand.

"She's been getting herself engaged," Beatrice intervened. "They both have, the blockheads."

"There's nothing blockheaded about marrying a good Catholic boy," Rachel objected.

"He'll bury you in house and babies before you've had a chance to stick your nose out the door and see the world," Beatrice snarled.

"How you do think yourself so progressive, Bea," Sandra snapped. "The only reason you're not engaged is because all the young men we've introduced you to are scared silly of you."

Adele bit her lip to keep from smiling. "I hope you'll both come see me once in a while after you're married."

"Oh, you're invited to the wedding!" Rachel insisted.

"I don't think Mama will invite you," Sandra said in a small voice. "She thinks you've been a bad influence."

Adele stared at her. "Is that why you haven't been to see me?"

The girl nodded, then burst into tears, throwing her arms around Adele's shoulders. "Oh, but I don't agree with her, Adele! I told her you were marvelous, always giving us presents and standing up for us when Mrs. Wrigley got in one of her moods."

Adele patted her back. "It's all right, dear. I'm not offended. I've had plenty of disapproving looks come my way in this town since I came."

"Now you can spit at them," Beatrice said. "Even they can't deny there would still be murderers on the loose if you weren't here to help the police."

"I'm sure the police are quite capable of catching criminals without my help," Adele said, amused.

"But it would take them years instead of weeks or months," Beatrice pointed out, laying her jacket on the stool and sitting down on it as she always did.

Adele shut the door as she saw Mrs. Abberton and Mrs. Cricket emerge from the bakery. "How was the picnic?"

"Hazel brought the most delightful chicken sandwiches," Sandra said. "Mama always said the Dilworths had the best cook."

"We even had beer," Rachel added. "Not that I partook in any."

"We can imagine whose idea that was," Nin said, eyeing Beatrice.

"I wanted to make sure a jolly time was had by all," Beatrice said in a sweeping tone. "Jolly people talk a lot." She gave Adele a knowing look.

"Hazel was glad to come," Sandra said.

"Her mother treats her like she's a moth," Beatrice declared.

Rachel turned pink. "Really, Bea, you ought to remember a lady doesn't speak that plainly."

"Then I'm not a lady." Beatrice sounded proud of the fact.

"Bea's right," Sandra said. "If Hazel had been treated properly, she would have excelled."

"I didn't say she wasn't right." Rachel sniffed. "I only said her manner was unladylike."

"Oh, bother!" Beatrice said.

"What do you mean, treated properly?" Adele asked.

"Her mother doesn't like her," Sandra said with a shudder. "Imagine a mother not liking her own daughter!"

"That's very astute of you, Sandra," Adele said.

The girl beamed with pride. "Bea thinks she's the only one who notices things. I notice things too."

"She treats her like a stray dog that was left on her hands," Rachel chimed in. "Something she has to feed and clothe but no more than that."

"Very good, Rachel." Adele smiled. "I thought as much when I met her."

"And don't think Miss Parnell didn't know it," Bea said. "You ought to have heard the words Hazel used when she spoke about her."

"Prompted by your colorful imagination, no doubt," Nin said dryly.

"I gather getting her to talk about troubling servants wasn't a problem," Adele said.

"Oh, she was dying to talk about Miss Parnell," said Sandra. "Mrs. Page — that's our cook — she's an older cousin to Maria Summers, the Dilworths' maid."

"So they had something in common," Rachel said. "We let Sandra do all the talking."

"Very smart of you," Adele complimented.

"She told me how Miss Parnell would always rub it in her face that her mother thought of her more as a daughter than Hazel," Sandra said. "I never liked Mrs. Dilworth, if you want to know the truth. She treated my brother Bob as if he weren't good enough to be friends with Hazel."

"The sort who thinks no one is good enough for her." Beatrice nodded.

"Hazel said she would say things like, 'I'll bet I have as many pretty dresses as you have,' and 'Your mother said she would buy me a dog if I wanted one.'" Her eyes grew narrow. "That really hurt poor Hazel. Hazel always wanted a dog."

"But Hazel didn't let things just go," Beatrice said. "She got Miss Parnell back all right."

"How?" Adele leaned over the counter.

"She would put frogs and things in her bed," Rachel said with a shudder. "Oh, it makes me ill just to think about it!"

"Better frogs than a snake," Nin said.

"That was rather childish," Adele remarked.

"Well, it would be, wouldn't it?" Beatrice defended. "She was only a child at the time."

"And when she wasn't a child any longer?"

"She would try to find out things," said Sandra. "Listen in when Miss Parnell was using the phone."

"She shouldn't have been using it at all," Rachel said in a prim tone. "She told us Miss Parnell wasn't allowed."

"She said Miss Parnell was making dates to go to Rosa Gris or Tanner Swamp with boys all the time," said Sandra.

"Did she make any dates with them in Caton?" Adele asked.

"No, she never mentioned that place," said Sandra.

Adele gave her friend a knowing look. "Did Hazel know any of the boys she was meeting?"

The girl shook her head. "No names were ever mentioned."

"Wasn't that crafty of her?" Rachel asked.

"But rather unfortunate for a murder investigation," Beatrice said. "I'm sure the police would love to know who those young men were."

"We're leaving the police out of it for now," Adele said. "You're sure they were *young* men?"

"Oh, absolutely," said Sandra. "She said they sounded Gene's age."

"She even threatened one of them!" Beatrice said with shining eyes.

"Is that her word or yours?" Nin raised her eyebrow.

"Hers," Sandra insisted.

"She was very agitated," Rachel added. "Snarling into the receiver."

"Snarling?" Nin questioned.

"Her word, not mine." Rachel sniffed.

"Is that why Hazel thought she was threatening the man?" Adele asked.

"Oh, no," said Sandra. "She heard her say, 'You know you'll be sorry.'"

"If what?" Nin leaned against Adele's shoulder with an eager expression.

"She didn't hear," Beatrice said. "Her mother came into the hall, darn it."

"So she must have seen Miss Parnell on the phone," Adele pointed out.

"Mrs. Dilworth sees only Hazel when Hazel is around," Sandra said.

"Did Hazel say if there was any one young man she spoke with more than the others?" Adele asked.

"Only toward the end," said Sandra. "I mean — the end of her life." She gulped.

"Hazel has no idea who it was, I take it," Adele asked.

Rachel shook her head. "No names, but she did say the last time she listened, Miss Parnell spoke to a man in a desperate tone."

"Desperate?" Adele stared.

"She didn't know why," Sandra said. "She thought maybe — she thought —"

"She thought Miss Parnell might have been in a family way," Beatrice said.

"Bea!"

"Did she say that?" Nin asked.

"Well, no, but it's what all of us were thinking." Beatrice sniffed. "Why else would a girl be desperate to a man she knows if she wasn't in a family way?"

"It would be so awful if she were desperate in that way and he wouldn't marry her," Sandra said. "I don't care if she was an evil girl."

"A man ought to be made to marry a girl he gets into trouble," Beatrice agreed in a rough tone.

"You'll be happy to know Miss Parnell was not in a family way," Adele said. The three of them breathed a sigh of relief. "Did Hazel observe any young men from her own set who had their eye on Miss Parnell?"

"She knew only one, but that was last year," said Sandra.

"Did she know his name?"

"Oh, certainly," said the girl. "He was a friend of her brother's."

Excitement went through Adele's veins. "Who was he?"

"A boy called Troy," said Sandra.

Adele pressed Nin's arm. "What did she say about Troy?"

"She had a lot to say about him," Rachel said.

"I think she was stuck on him," Beatrice said in a sly voice. "No girl knows that much about her brother's friends unless she's stuck on them."

"He was a friend of Gene Dilworth's?" Nin asked.

"I gathered it was one of those alliances college boys make," Sandra said thoughtfully. "You know, they meet young men who are of a different background than they are but they become friends nonetheless."

"Troy certainly was of a different background," Nin remarked.

"Oh, you know about him?" Sandra looked disappointed.

"We heard the name mentioned," Adele said.

"Poor, of course," the young woman continued, taking on a throaty tone Adele had no doubt she learned from her mother. "Good student, a scholar even. But no money to speak of."

"Such a shame," Rachel sighed. "She made him sound so nice."

"She would if she were stuck on him," Nin said.

"Hazel said Arabella absolutely turned his head," Sandra continued. "She said the first time Gene invited him to tea, and he saw Arabella sulking over the teapot — that's how Hazel put it, as Maria was ill that day, so she had to help with the serving —

his mouth gaped open, and his gaze wouldn't leave her for a moment while she was in the room."

"Men behave so idiotically when they're taken by a pretty girl," Beatrice growled.

"I think we can all agree on that," Adele said. "And how did Arabella act, according to Hazel?"

"She spent the time standing against the wall 'sizing him up,'" said Rachel.

"Sizing up his bank account, more likely," Nin said.

"Oh, that goes without saying," Sandra said in a serious tone. "It's what we're all told to do. While we chat with the young man, watch for his manners, look at how polished his shoes are and how lint-free his clothes are, whether he has a gold watch or a silver one —"

"Good heavens, your mother told you to do all that?" Rachel stared at her.

"I never did it," Sandra insisted. "I take my fiancé Victor for what he is, not whether he wears boots or shoes!"

"I'm pleased to hear it," Adele said. "But it seems as if Miss Parnell had other ideas."

"I can't think where she learned them," Sandra lamented. "A lady's maid!"

"Probably from watching Miss Murphy at garden parties," Nin muttered.

"And did she like what she saw?" Adele asked. "Miss Parnell, I mean."

"I don't know about that." Sandra shrugged. "But he certainly liked what he saw. Hazel said he came to the house every week after that, sometimes twice a week. Not that she minded."

"He always had a pretense, but he managed to catch a glimpse of Arabella and exchange a few words with her," Rachel added.

"A man will do anything to capture his conquest," Beatrice said.

"It doesn't sound as if he was successful in capturing Miss Parnell," Adele suggested.

"Hazel said it was disgusting the way she treated him," Sandra said. "He used to bring her presents, little things that didn't cost much."

"It probably cost him his lunch for the week," Nin snarled.

"Hazel thought so too," said Sandra. "She said one day she'd had enough. She marched right into Miss Parnell's room and told her she oughtn't to accept the small gifts because they came out of Troy's weekly allowance."

"She knew that from Gene," Rachel supplied.

"And what did Miss Parnell say?" Adele asked.

"The insolence!" Rachel sniffed.

"She said 'That's all you know. He's asked me to marry him already — twice.'" Sandra patted the short strands of hair over her forehead. "Poor Hazel. She said she prayed that night —" She stopped.

"Prayed what?" Nin prompted.

"That something bad would happen to her." Sandra's cheeks turned red. "Oh, but she didn't mean it!"

"It was just a schoolgirl's silly fancy," Rachel added.

"I know, dear," Adele said. "We all have fancies sometimes where we wish someone we didn't like would get hurt."

"She would never do anything to Miss Parnell," Sandra defended.

"Where would Hazel get hold of a gun anyway?" Beatrice chimed in. "She certainly wouldn't have enough courage to shoot someone."

"Nobody thinks for a moment she did such a thing," Adele assured them. "I suppose Miss Parnell had no intention of marrying Troy?"

"He was too poor for her blood," said Rachel. "That was obvious."

"She should have been honest with him from the start," Beatrice snapped. "Then what happened wouldn't have happened."

"Now, Bea, nobody said she was to blame," Rachel chided.

"What happened?" Adele asked, though she knew what was coming.

"Hazel said they were having Easter dinner when the news came. One of Gene's friends who also knew Troy stopped by and took Gene aside." Sandra shuddered. "Hazel said Gene was sobbing. She'd never seen her brother sob before."

"He was dead," Rachel said, her voice sorrowful.

"He was more than dead," Beatrice said. "He took his own life."

"This was last Easter?" Adele asked.

The girls nodded.

"I'm sorry to hear that," she said in a soft tone.

"Did he leave any note?" Nin asked.

Sandra shook her head. "Nothing. Not a word to anyone. Maxwell — that's the friend who came to tell Gene — invited Troy to have Easter dinner with them and when he didn't show up, he went to the flat he shared with two other young men. They said Troy told them the day before he was going to the stables out of town — he often went there to ride."

"Maybe he had an accident," Adele suggested.

"Oh, it was suicide all right," Rachel said and shuddered. "They didn't see him after that but they knew he was going to Maxwell's for dinner so they assumed he went straight from the stables to his house and changed there."

"They found Troy hanging from a rope." Sandra's face was grave. "He'd been dead for hours."

"His face was all blue and bloated —" Rachel covered her mouth with her handkerchief.

"Don't think about it, dear." Adele put her arms around the girl's shoulders. "Hazel must have been devastated."

"She cried when she told us," Sandra said. "She said Miss

Parnell didn't shed a tear. She looked more annoyed than anything."

"I can imagine," Adele murmured.

"She's the sort who would never have understood how someone can die for love of someone else," Sandra contemplated.

"That's very astute of you, Sandy," Beatrice complimented.

"It is indeed," Adele said. "One more question before I let you go — did you ask Hazel about the green and orange dress?"

"Hazel said she didn't have any dress with those colors," said Sandra. "She thought she'd seen a dress like that on someone's sister."

"Someone's sister?" Adele asked.

Sandra nodded. "One of her brother's friends. The one who came to tell them about Troy."

"Mr. Lee," Nin murmured.

"Why is that important?" Beatrice's shrewd eyes were on Adele.

"Adele knows why it's important," Nin snapped.

"Indeed I do," Adele said softly.

CHAPTER 25

Rachel and Sandra departed soon after that with a more somber step than they had entered. Adele left Beatrice to look after the shop as she took Nin's arm, leading her out on the street.

"I think it's time we spoke to the sheriff," she said.

"I thought you'd see it that way," Nin said. "It's all three of them, isn't it?"

"Why do you think that?" Adele stared at her.

"The dress," said her friend. "I know why you wanted to know if it was Hazel's. You thought the man in the letter was Gene and the dress he gave Arabella as a lark was Hazel's."

"I thought it might be a possibility," Adele admitted.

"But it belongs to Mr. Lee's sister," Nin concluded. "I'm not surprised he would kill Arabella."

"We don't know the killer was Mr. Lee," Adele pointed out.

"You may not, but I do," Nin said with a shudder. "That man is the biggest fiend I've ever come across."

They started to walk down the dusty street. "You know, Nin, I think this murder was more complicated than any of us imagined," Adele lamented.

"How so?" Nin asked as they nodded at Dora standing in the doorway of her tea shop.

"I think the man who murdered Arabella had the help of his friends."

Nin stopped. "You mean Mr. Lee killed Arabella with the help of Gene and Mr. Cress?"

"Or Gene killed Arabella with the help of Nathan and Mr. Lee," Adele said.

"Or Mr. Cress killed Arabella with the help of Gene and Mr. Lee." Nin eyed her.

"I think that's the least likely," Adele said.

"I vote for the first," Nin said. "Mr. Lee has the morals of a reptile."

"I don't think we can rule out the other two," Adele said. "That's for the sheriff to decide."

The police station was quiet, and Adele realized why as she rested her parasol and bag on one of the benches. Both Hatfield and her brother were absent.

"Have they gone to lunch, Assistant Deputy?" she asked.

Edison shook his head. "They're in Caton, miss."

"Looking for evidence in a secluded forest?" Adele asked.

"Miss?" He leaned forward.

"Never mind," Adele said, smiling.

"That advertisement in the paper —" he began.

"Someone answered it?" Nin stared at him.

"Yes, indeed," he said. "Some fellow from Caton is in town to see Mr. Abbott about some bonds of his —"

"Yes, yes," Nin said impatiently.

"He happened to see the paper and came right in." Edison grinned. "Talked like the devil — sorry miss." He blushed.

"He knows something about the jewelry?" Adele glanced at Nin.

"He said he saw a girl who looked like Miss Parnell in some jewelry store there. He couldn't remember if she was with a man or not." He looked at her meaningfully. “Frankly, I thought he was drunk."

"Why is that?"

“He was walking unsteady-like," he said. "But the sheriff said it ain't — isn’t — for me to judge and to mind my own business."

"They have to follow up on every tip," Nin pointed out. "You know that."

"Oh, certainly, miss," he said. "Only it's an awful long way to go for a drunken tip."

The door opened and Hatfield and Jackson came in. They moved slowly, hanging their hats and coats on pegs. Adele's heart went out to them.

"Don't look so defeated, Jack," she said. "We knew that advertisement was a long shot."

"It was a waste of a good afternoon," Jackson snarled. "I'm beginning to think Edison was right, sir."

"A drunken tip," Edison repeated with a satisfied look.

"I gather it was a wild goose chase.” Adele sat at the edge of the desk.

"The jewelry store owner said he never saw Miss Parnell, with or without a man," Hatfield sighed. "I'm beginning to think we're barking up the wrong tree."

"That's because you are," Nin said. “We took a chance too and ours wasn’t a wild goose chase.”

“Oh?” He glanced at Adele.

“I asked Missy to take photographs of the jewelry,” she began.

“You what!” Jackson fired out.

“Edison!” Hatfield shouted without even looking at the young man. “Is this true?”

“Well, yes, sir, Miss Grace did bring her camera,” Edison said meekly.

“Why the devil didn’t you tell me?” the sheriff snapped.

“She didn’t print any of the photographs, sir,” Edison said in a squeaky voice. “Miss Gossling made her promise not to.”

"That doesn't mean we didn't need to know about it," Jackson snarled.

"They were my request, Sheriff," Adele said sharply. "I needed them."

"It's against the law to take photographs of evidence without the permission of the police," Jackson said.

"You quote the policeman's manual very nicely, Mr. Gossling," Nin snapped. "But we aren't policewomen and we had permission. Assistant Deputy Edison gave us permission."

Hatfield, as usual, reacted much calmer than his deputy. "And why, may I ask, did you need the photographs so badly you were willing to swear my assistant deputy to secrecy to get them?" Edison ducked his head.

"Because I knew it would take me months to find out where they were bought and who bought them if I didn't have something to show the jewelry stores." Adele gave her brother a sharp look. "In spite of what you think Jack, there is method to my madness."

"What made you think the jewelry was from San Francisco?" Jackson asked.

"How did you know we were in San Francisco?" Nin asked.

"Mr. Brent said he saw you at the train station this morning when he went to open the drugstore," Jackson said.

"Are you making the townspeople your spies now, Mr. Gossling?"

"When one's sister is apt to stick her nose where it doesn't belong, one must use all one's resources, Miss Branch," he snapped back.

"Was the jewelry from San Francisco?" Hatfield asked. His slightly annoyed look was replaced by interest.

"The jewelry and the gloves." Adele told Hatfield and her brother about their visit to Mrs. Rochefort's Fashion House and Kelly & King Fine Jewelers.

When she finished, Hatfield was sitting back in his chair, his hands folded on his stomach. "So a young fellow bought her the gloves and the jewelry, eh?"

"Several young fellows," Nin said.

"You said his face was hidden at all times," Jackson pointed out. "It could have been a man of any age."

"According to the story Miss Frances told us, Mr. Riddle was telling the truth about his relationship with Arabella," Adele insisted. "He was also telling the truth when he said he broke things off with her and she moved on to someone else."

"We'll certainly verify that with Miss Frances," Hatfield said. "But I think we can rule out Mr. Riddle as a suspect for the time being."

"The mayor will be pleased," Nin mumbled.

"I couldn't give a hoot about pleasing the mayor," Hatfield said with a chuckle. "But we did get a tip from that advertisement."

"Oh?" Adele's face perked up.

"It seems while your brother and I were in Caton, Edison had a visit from a young lady who works at a jewelry shop in Rosa Gris." He threw his head back. "Didn't you, lad?"

"Yes, sir." Edison could barely contain his pride.

"He even had the post master in Caton interrupt our lunch to tell me about it," the sheriff remarked, making the pink pride on his assistant deputy's face turn beet-red.

"The young lady was most insistent, Sheriff," the young man defended.

Hatfield laughed. "You did right, Edison. It was a very enlightening piece of information."

"What did she say?" Nin asked.

"She saw a young lady wearing that comb walking down Adams Street arm in arm with a red-headed man," said Hatfield. "The young lady matched Miss Parnell's description. She looked in the window at a pair of butterfly earrings he had on display but they didn't go in." He added, "The salesgirl thought the young man looked worried when he saw her admiring the earrings but when they went on, the worried look turned into relief."

"He didn't want to go another month without lunch to buy them for her," Nin snorted.

"Now we know who the young man was." Jackson propped a knee against the edge of his desk. "A fellow named Troy, according to your girl Bernice."

"I think Troy is the key to the whole business," Adele insisted.

"A wave of troubling breeze," Nin murmured, getting a faraway look.

"Death always leaves trouble in its wake," Jackson said.

To Adele's surprise, her friend gave him a grateful look. "Indeed it does, Mr. Gossling."

"By all accounts, he was in love with her." Adele rolled her folded parasol across her knees.

"But to kill himself because of that?" Jackson looked dubious. "I don't see she was worth it, to be honest, sir."

"No woman is worth a man's strangled neck," Nin said harshly.

"To us, perhaps not," said the sheriff. "We know who she really was. A man in love sees the woman he loves differently." He coughed with embarrassment.

"It might very well be servant hall gossip," Jackson insisted. "We only have Miss Parnell's word for it."

"Hazel said as much too," Adele said.

"Hazel? Gene's sister?" He stared at her.

"We had Beatrice and her friends interrogate her," Nin said.

"Not interrogate, dear," Adele corrected. "Conduct an enlightening conversation."

Hatfield burst out laughing. "How you do color things, Adele!"

"What would Hazel know?" Jackson asked. "She's only fifteen."

Adele stiffened. "And that makes her head as empty as a gourd?"

"If Hazel were a boy, you wouldn't say that," Nin snapped.

"You probably think the assistant deputies are smarter than she is." To this Edison sniffed.

"I agree with Adele," said Hatfield. "Miss Dilworth struck me as a sensitive and attentive girl when we spoke to her."

"And inclined to exaggerate like most young ladies before they come of age," Jackson added, giving his sister a meaningful look. She made a face back at him.

"Miss Dilworth must have had plenty to say about Miss Parnell," the sheriff remarked. "I had the impression she didn't quite like her."

"Why should she?" Nin asked. "Arabella took her place as the daughter of the family."

"In Mrs. Dilworth's eyes at least." Adele nodded. "Hazel said Arabella didn't turn a hair when she discovered Troy was dead but her brother did."

"Cried like a baby," Nin added.

"Well, he would be upset if they were friends," Jackson said.

"But a young man that age weeping over the death of a friend?" Hatfield lamented. "I've known many young sailors who lost their comrades at sea and were melancholy about it for weeks but never shed a tear."

"Sadness breeds resentment sometimes, doesn't it?" Adele asked.

"What are you implying, Del?" Jackson eyed her. "Gene killed Miss Parnell because she rejected his friend?"

Adele tilted her head, looking at the sliver of sunlight through the curtains on the window. "Remember when we went to the theater on my fourteenth birthday, Jack?"

"Only because you forced me to sit next to Elsie," he said. "What has that to do with anything?"

"The play was Shakespeare's *Measure for Measure*," Adele said. "Those words came back to me as we were on the train."

Hatfield smiled and recited, "'Haste still pays haste, and leisure answers leisure / Like doth quit like, and Measure still for

Measure.'" To her curious look, he added, "Ma used to take me to an open theater where they played Shakespeare all the time when I was a boy."

"Sounds like a jolly show, sir," Edison said with enthusiasm but a withering look from his superior put his nose back in the papers he was looking over.

"You think that was what this was?" Jackson looked at his sister. "Justice for justice?"

"I think it's the only explanation that fits," she insisted. "Why else would there be more than one bullet?"

"You mean all three of them shot her?" Nin stared.

"One or two of them shot her, more likely," Adele said. "Remember Mr. Samuels couldn't confirm the third bullet was different from one of the other two."

"Two men using three bullets?" Jackson frowned. "It doesn't make sense, Del."

"She doesn't want to believe the third bullet might have come from Mr. Cress," Nin said.

Adele stiffened. "I never said that."

"I've held many men in high regard who ended up being killers," Hatfield said in a soft tone. "It isn't pleasant. Less so when the man in high regard might not deserve that regard." He glanced at her.

"Whether Mr. Cress fired a shot or not, I believe he wrote the note," Adele said.

"Why is that?" Jackson inquired.

"He always has a pencil and scraps of paper with him," Adele said. "He used them to write down an address for Mr. Gardner after we dined." She caught the sheriff stiffening from the corner of her eye. "He said he got into the habit of carrying them around when he was in college."

"That doesn't mean he wrote the note," Jackson pointed out.

"I think they were trying to incriminate Mr. Riddle," Adele said.

"Gene hates him," Nin pointed out. "I don't blame him."

"They did a rather sloppy job of it," Hatfield remarked. "Leaving the body in his conservatory like that. They also probably knew he had an old gun and we would suspect immediately that gun was used to kill Arabella."

"And the note wasn't even written by a woman," Nin added.

"Who told you that, Dr. Blessings?" Jackson asked.

Adele slid the piece of paper they had found near the body. "As a matter of fact, he did."

"Adele, for God's sake!" Jackson exploded. "Haven't you learned your lesson by now?"

"It's not as if she were sneaky about it this time," Nin said. "It's all in the book."

"What book?" Jackson sighed.

"Assistant Deputy Edison's book." She looked at the young man expectedly.

"Miss Branch is right, Jackson," said Hatfield. "I knew Adele took out the note."

"It was a good idea to have the book, wasn't it, sir?" Edison prompted.

"Yes, yes, lad, very efficient of you," Hatfield said. "I should have guessed the reason you took it out."

"So that was why you went to the city," Jackson said. "You went to see Dr. Blessings."

"And Elsie," Nin said with a sly smile. "She sends you her regards." When he gave her a wary look, she giggled.

"Not just that, Jack," said Adele. "We got hold of some of those letters Arabella sent Miss Murphy."

"Did you now?" Hatfield eyed her.

She took the packet out of her purse and put it on his desk. "For the evidence box, Sheriff."

"Should we ask how you got hold of them?" Jackson eyed her.

"It's not important," Adele said. "Dr. Blessings compared the handwriting in the letters to those on the note and said they weren't a bit similar."

"Well, they wouldn't be, if Miss Parnell were scrawling her killer's name to the police with her last dying breath," Jackson said.

"My, how you do dramatize crime, Mr. Gossling," Nin said. "Almost as much as a fifteen-year-old girl exaggerates."

Jackson looked away.

"But it wasn't scrawled," Adele pointed out. "It was written very carefully in printed writing a child would use."

"I think I see what you're getting at," Hatfield said slowly. "I remember a case back in my San Francisco police days of a man incriminating another with a note. He wrote it with his left hand so the police wouldn't be able to match it to his handwriting."

"Exactly," Adele said. "And just as Nin said, Dr. Blessings told us the handwriting on the note could only belong to a man."

"He was even almost willing to commit himself," Nin added.

"That is a rarity indeed," Jackson said dryly.

Hatfield slapped his hands on his desk. "Well, Deputy, I think we have enough to bring the three young men in for questioning."

"We can at least find out the truth about their involvement with Miss Parnell and this Troy business," Jackson agreed.

"Edison!" The young man rose, giving a salute. "As you're the only one here, it looks like you're going to have to play the scout." Edison grimaced. "Go to the Dilworth house and fetch Mr. Gene Dilworth. Go with him to find Mr. Cress and — who's the other one, Jackson?" He leaned his head toward his deputy.

"Maxwell Lee," Jackson said.

"Go with him to get Mr. Cress and Mr. Lee and bring all three to the station," the sheriff instructed. "And mind you don't let them intimidate you with cries of lawyers. They can call their lawyers if they want to once they get here."

"Yes, sir." Edison grabbed his hat from the rack.

"Wait!" Adele screeched.

While Sheriff Hatfield had been dispatching his orders, her mind had been racing. She remembered the dinner she had with Nathan, their conversation echoing in her mind.

"What now, Del?" Jackson asked.

"I don't think that's going to work with these boys, Sheriff," she said.

"What won't work?" Hatfield asked.

"Questioning them," she said. "If they really did seek justice for justice, their answers will be so logical they'll only put your investigation on the shelf."

"People who do something to pay someone else back think they had every right," Nin agreed. "They won't see they did anything wrong."

"That will raise a red flag for us, then," Hatfield said.

"It might raise a red flag, but you need evidence to lower it," Adele reminded him. "If you question them, you'll not only get useless answers but you won't have a chance of getting your evidence."

"We can get search warrants," Jackson insisted. "We can search their homes for any firearms and match the bullets to those in Miss Parnell's back."

"You really think they haven't gotten rid of the guns by now, Jack?" Adele looked at her brother.

"We don't know if it was any of them at all," the sheriff said.

Adele leaned forward. "Sheriff, these are young men who grew up with privilege. If their fathers didn't get them out of a mess, they learned to be wily enough to get themselves out so their fathers wouldn't know about it."

"Murder is a little more than just a mess, Adele," Sheriff Hatfield said firmly.

"I agree," Adele said. "But that doesn't mean they and their families won't use the influence they have." She eyed him. "Mayor

Willett will get Mr. Rand to slap three writs on your desk and you'll lose them, Sheriff."

"I don't give a hang what the mayor does," said the sheriff with a fierce tone. "Law and order will be done in spite of any political or social influence."

"But you won't be the man to do it," Nin said brutally. "They'll get some straw man to take your place."

"Nin's right, Sheriff." Adele looked at him steadily. "Is that what you want?"

Jackson was now looking at his superior. Hatfield rose and made a small circle around the desks in the center of the room, his hands in his pockets. His usually smooth countenance was wrinkled at the brows and his boyish appearance looked suddenly wise like an old man.

Edison suddenly burst out, "I wouldn't want to work here if you weren't, sir!"

The pensive look on the sheriff's face eased, and he put a heavy hand on Edison's shoulder. "Thank you for saying that, lad." He returned to his desk, his quiet authority restored. "What do you propose instead, Adele? I assume you have an idea?"

"Take it with a grain of salt, sir," Jackson cautioned.

"The sheriff always does what he thinks is best, Jack," Adele reminded him.

"And he's never been wrong yet," Nin said.

"Thank you for that vote of confidence, Miss Branch." Hatfield bowed his head. "Coming from you, that is a compliment indeed." She turned away, looking a little hurt.

"I think I can get Nathan to talk," said Adele.

"What do you mean, talk?" her brother asked.

"She means a confession," Nin said.

"Really, Del," Jackson sniffed. "You're sounding just like the detective novels."

"I know Nathan," she said. "He's not like his friends."

"If he committed cold-blooded murder, he's worse than his friends," Hatfield reminded her.

"I don't believe he did," she insisted.

The sheriff played with the fountain pen Adele had given him on his desk. "Don't you think your feelings for Mr. Cress are getting in the way of your judgment, Adele?"

Adele's temper rose. "I may not have been a San Francisco policeman or a Wells Fargo detective, Sheriff, but I do know how to discern good and evil in someone."

She immediately regretted saying it, as she saw the features on his face harden.

"I wouldn't question Del's judgment, sir," Jackson said quietly. "If she believes Mr. Cress didn't kill Miss Parnell, there are good reasons."

Adele pressed her brother's hand. "Thank you, Jack."

"If he didn't commit the murder, why do you think he will talk?" Hatfield asked, his tone brisk.

"Because he has scruples," she said. "He told me he wants to help people in China with his medical work."

"That is admirable," Nin admitted.

"He also told me about a rabbit hunt he went on with his friends once," she said. "He couldn't shoot one. He didn't have the heart."

"And you think just because he didn't shoot a rabbit and wants to go to China, he's going to confess to murder?" Jackson chuckled.

"My point, dear brother, is a man who wants to help others less privileged than himself and wouldn't shoot a helpless creature has a conscience," she said in a severe tone.

"A man with a conscience can't shoot a woman without feeling guilty about it," Nin chimed in. "Even you ought to know that, Mr. Gossling."

"At the very least he knew what one or both of his friends had done," Adele argued.

"And what makes you think that?" Hatfield eyed her.

"Because when I mentioned seeing Miss Parnell's parents, he looked very disturbed," she said. "Gene or Maxwell would have shrugged it off. He didn't."

"So you think he felt guilty about her death?" Jackson asked.

"He would feel guilty about not going to the police if he knew who killed her."

"*If* he knew," the sheriff said.

"I think I can find out," Adele said. "Let me have a conversation with Nathan — a conversation, not an interrogation." She gave her brother a meaningful look. "If I get nowhere, then you can haul them into the station, lawyers and all."

Hatfield was silent, tapping the pointed edge of his fountain pen on the blotter.

Jackson folded his arms. "I don't like it, sir."

"I don't like it either, Deputy," he answered.

"What's not to like?" Nin insisted. "You're both being silly!"

"Silly are we?" Jackson glared at her. "Has it occurred to you, Miss Branch, that if Mr. Cress did kill Miss Parnell or was involved, he won't hesitate to do what he feels is necessary to make sure no one finds out about it?"

"You mean he might try to kill me?" Adele asked. "Oh, nonsense!"

"I'll be there to make sure he doesn't," Nin said in a seething tone.

"And how will you do that?" Jackson was now amused. "Hold a shotgun to his back during the entire conversation?"

"If need be," Nin retorted. "It might interest you to know, Mr. Gossling, I was taught how to shoot straight by a fur trader's wife when I was eleven."

"Heaven help us!" Jackson threw up his hands and even Edison shuddered.

Hatfield roared with laughter. "It's a shame we didn't know that before, Miss Branch, or we might have had use for you when we dealt with those horse thieves last year." In a more serious tone, he said, "Your brother is right, Adele. It's too dangerous to let you go alone to meet with this man."

"She's not going alone," Nin said. "She's going with me."

"I don't think even your straight shooting could deter a desperate man, Miss Branch," Hatfield said. "And make no mistake — if Mr. Cress was involved with this crime and made some kind of pact amongst his friends, he will be desperate."

"Boyhood bonds are strong," Jackson said. "Even if he didn't do the actual killing, he'll do anything to protect his friends from being hanged."

"I'll take that risk, Sheriff." In a lower tone, she said, "A lot of people have passed judgment over Miss Parnell. They think she deserved what she got."

"Mrs. Faderman and the hens?" Jackson asked.

"Not just them, Jack," she said. "Suppose the boys evade justice even with the evidence, and you close the case as unsolved. People will think they were right, and she deserved what she got." She suddenly took the sheriff's hand in hers. "It's vital we see the killer or killers are brought to justice in spite of what social or political pull they might have if only to prove Miss Parnell wasn't as evil as people think. Don't you see?"

Hatfield looked at her with wide eyes. She felt the powerful grip of his hand. Then, all at once, he dropped hers.

"May I use my brotherly privilege, Sheriff, and ask you to forbid Del to do this?" Jackson spoke up.

"Nobody forbids me anything, Jack," she snarled. "You should know that by now."

"When police business is involved —"

"I make the final decisions, Deputy," the sheriff said. "With your consultation, of course." He turned to Adele. "I'll make a compromise. You may have your rendezvous with Mr. Cress on two conditions. First, that Miss Branch indeed goes with you — without the shotgun," he added with a crooked smile. "And second, Jackson and I aren't far away in case something does happen."

"What could happen?" Adele sniffed.

"He could pull a pistol on you, for a start," Jackson said. "He might have a knife on him. He might —"

"We get the idea, Deputy," Hatfield said.

"It's going to be difficult to be inconspicuous in a restaurant or theater, sir," Jackson said.

"I wasn't going to meet him in a closed space," Adele said.

"What were you thinking of, then?"

She tapped the edge of her parasol against the wooden floor. "Tanner Swamp."

"Tanner Swamp!" Jackson stared at her.

"Oh, not the scene of the crime," she assured him. "Not exactly, that is."

"There are too many deserted areas there, sir." Jackson turned to his superior. "It will be even more dangerous."

I think your sister knows what she's doing, Jackson," said Hatfield. "All right. Let us know when and where, and we'll be there hiding among the bushes so no one will see us."

"Del hasn't said she agrees to your conditions, Sheriff," Jackson said. "She's not one to comply without her own conditions."

"You know me too well, Jack." She pinched his cheek playfully. "I have no objection to the police being in the vicinity. But you must do something for me, Sheriff."

"And that is?"

She picked up the note. "Let me keep this a little longer."

"What for?" Jackson asked.

"That's my business," she said. "Agreed?" Hatfield nodded. She turned to Nin. "And a favor from you, dear. I have to meet him alone."

"Because Nathan is sweet on you?" Nin sniffed. "Don't tell me you reciprocate."

"He'll be more open if it's just me and him," Adele said.

"I can hide with the posse, can't I, Sheriff?" Nin looked at him.

He chuckled. "I wouldn't exactly call us a posse, Miss Branch, but you may join us if you wish."

"It might still be dangerous, sir," Jackson objected.

"You give me that shotgun, Mr. Gossling, and you won't be in any danger," Nin assured him, earning a roaring laugh from Hatfield.

CHAPTER 26

Persuading Nathan to meet her at Tanner Swamp proved easier than she had anticipated. Adele sent him a note on her prettiest stationery inviting him to lunch with her in "the most private place in town." She gave him instructions of where to meet her. When Mr. Duncan delivered the mail that same evening, the note she received from Nathan expressed delight in the meeting the next day.

She had Ruth pack a very special picnic basket which she instructed be kept in the icebox until she came by in the afternoon to take it with her.

"Señorita has a young man?" Ruth's eyes sparkled.

"Señorita does not have a young man," Adele said emphatically. "Don't make more of it than there is, Ruth."

"Sometime, Señorita get married," Tomas said with a knowing look at his wife.

"Some time," Adele said. "But definitely not today." She went out of the kitchen, smiling at his somber look.

The sky was a blue-gray as she set out for the swamp, though the temperature was surprisingly pleasant for that time of year. Her way took her beyond the park and into the rim of town, though not quite the outskirts. The further away from town she got, the quieter it became. Vegetation seemed greener and more robust and the air was cooler and denser.

As she entered the swampland, the mild weather changed to a nippy cold, and she was glad she decided to take her coat. The chill went through her leather gloves, and she held the basket closer to her. Although it wasn't dark in the swamp area, the trees and shrubs were now clustered together, and the dark green gave a tint of more gray than blue to the sky above. The raw scent of murky water filled her lungs.

She was relieved to see Nathan waiting for her. She held back a moment but she heard or saw nothing that indicated the police or her friend Nin. She had no doubt Hatfield and the assistant deputies were somewhere nearby, and she knew whatever happened, Jackson and Nin would not fail her.

But Nathan looked hardly dangerous. He wore a gray suit with a striped bowtie and a straw hat. His hands were shoved in his pockets, and he was whistling a tune she could hear only vaguely in the crowded air.

She sang out, "I hope I'm not late!"

"I was early." He took the basket and blanket from her. "It's an annoying habit of mine. When I'm not called into last-minute surgery, that is." He chuckled.

"I don't think punctuality is annoying." Adele shook out the blanket tucked under the handle of the basket. "I don't see any ants around here, do you?"

He took out his handkerchief and wiped his neck. "Maybe we ought to go somewhere else. It's a little muggy."

Adele caught sight of a flash of silver and knew it belonged to Jackson's gun. "How about a little over there beside that patch of purple wildflowers?" She directed him a little to the left so they would be out of sight of the flashing gun but still within range.

"If you wish" he mumbled.

She laid the blanket on a carpet of clover. "Maybe we'll find a four-leaf. I'm feeling lucky today."

"I'm the lucky one," he said with a shy smile. She noted he relaxed once they were further away from the crime scene.

"I've never been here, you know," she remarked.

He eyed her. "I thought you would know it quite well."

"Because this is the place where the courting couples meet?" She laughed. "I should think you would know that better than I!"

"Why?" he asked, his tone a little jerky.

"Oh, young men like yourself do a lot of courting at college," she said as she laid out the plates and food.

He exhaled. "I was never that sort of young man, Adele."

"You thought I was that sort of young woman, though," Adele said. "You thought I knew the swamp well."

"I didn't mean to insult you," he said. "I only meant — well, you're so lovely and accomplished, I would have thought —"

"You're very sweet," Adele said. "But I've always shied away from clandestine meeting places."

"I wouldn't consider this clandestine," he said.

"Your friend Mr. Dilworth told me it was," she said.

"Gene?" He blinked. "Gene isn't the type — I mean, he never hides his —"

"Affairs?" She gave him a sly look. "I suppose our generation is bolder about those things than our parents were. The older generation still believes that affections between a man and a woman should be private in public."

He laughed. "That's a charming way of putting it."

"Is it?" She kept her eyes on the water glasses she was filling up. "I didn't get the impression Mr. Riddle would have found it charming. According to the police report, he used to meet Miss Parnell in Tanner Swamp."

"Well, he has a reputation to maintain," Nathan pointed out.

"I hardly think he's worried about his reputation when he courts Mrs. Allington," she remarked.

"Oh, but she's a respectable widow and Arabella was —"

"A cheap maid?" Adele eyed him.

He clasped his hands around the water glass. "Must we talk about such sordid things as murder?"

"But we're not talking about murder," Adele said. "We're talking about the life of an innocent girl."

"Innocent girl!" This spat out into the quiet air, releasing a flock of birds that had been perched in one of the taller trees a few feet away.

"I met a very interesting young woman in the city recently." Adele adjusted her skirt around her ankles. "You might not think much of her either. She makes fine dresses for a millinery."

"You should know me better than that," he said. "I'm a working man myself."

"She knew Miss Parnell," Adele continued. "She thinks the man who shot Miss Parnell dazzled her with talk of wealth and social standing and then betrayed her."

Nathan put the sandwich down. "Now we are talking about sordid murder."

"I'm sorry." Adele hung her head. "I just find it so fascinating."

"Considering you've chosen to involve yourself in your brother's work, I can imagine," he said. "Doesn't it ever irk him?"

"Jack is used to me getting interested in his pursuits," said Adele. "When we were children, my father bought him a toy gun for his birthday. I used it more than he did!"

He laughed. "I should make sure there are no guns around if I upset you, then!"

"I do try to help the police when I can," she said. "Some things a woman can discover better than a lawman."

"Such as?"

She helped herself to more chicken salad. "Nin and I took a trip to San Francisco to search for the jewelry."

"What jewelry?"

"The police were looking to find out who bought Miss Parnell certain pieces of jewelry they found on her person," Adele said. "They were rather ingenious about it."

"Were they?" Nathan asked. She noticed he had not finished his sandwich. "I suppose they have to be."

"It was really my idea to put the advertisement in the paper." She glanced at him from the corner of her eye.

But his face remained impassive. "I try to avoid reading the papers too much. They get in the way of my medical books."

"I can imagine they do." She tried not to show her relief that he had not seen the advertisement.

As if he had realized his lunch was half-finished, he bit heartily into the sandwich. "Was this jewelry business so important they had to be devious about it?"

"They thought if they could prove Mr. Riddle had been the one to buy her the jewelry, they could prove some kind of affair between them and a motive for murder."

"And did they?"

"No, but we found out a great deal more."

His hand stopped midway to reaching for another sandwich. She saw the fingers were uneven. "We?"

Adele felt like she was stepping her foot into an icy river. "Miss Branch and I. We spoke with a young woman named Bernice Goode from Kelly & King."

"What is that, a lawyer's office?"

"It's a jewelry shop," Adele said. "Don't tell me you didn't know that, Nathan."

"I'm not in the habit of buying jewelry for ladies," he snapped.

"Oh? I heard differently."

The offhand tone hit its mark. His figure was almost like a jack knife, reclined on the blanket with stiff legs and arms. "Is that what this Bernice told you?"

"She couldn't describe the men who came into the store and bought Arabella jewelry, as a matter of fact."

"Look here, Adele, do the police really think they can find a killer by finding out who bought Arabella trinkets?" He snorted. "I understand they want to have something solid against Mr. Riddle, but I should think a man of his standing would be — well, discreet about a brooch he bought his best friend's maid."

"How did you know one of the jewels she sold Arabella was a brooch?" Adele gave him a sharp glance.

"Why, every woman has at least one brooch, doesn't she?" He tapped the pin on her lapel. "Case in point."

"Kelly & King pride themselves on their one-of-a-kind pieces," said Adele. "There was no mistaking where it came from and the woman was certain about the fact that a man bought it for Miss Parnell."

He looked at her. "Well, doesn't that prove Virgil could have been the one?"

"She was quite certain it was a *young* man." Adele watched him carefully.

He reached his long hand into the grass and began picking through a patch of clover. "I'm determined to find you that four-leaf clover. Maybe our luck will change."

"I wasn't aware I was unlucky," she said. "Are you unlucky?"

"I'm not sure," he said in a low voice. In a louder tone, he said, "I wouldn't put much stock into what this Bernice says, Adele. How could she remember if the man was older or younger?"

Taking a chance, Adele said, "The police are planning on making a trip to San Francisco to Kelly & King and showing Bernice a photograph of Mr. Riddle to see if she can identify him."

"Oh?"

"It makes sense, don't you think?" Adele began wrapping up the remainder of the sandwiches and putting them in the basket. "I'm disappointed, Nathan. You hardly ate."

"It's this place," he growled. "It doesn't give one much of an appetite. I wish we could go somewhere else."

"But you promised me a four-leaf clover," Adele said in a coy tone.

"I'm not sure I'll be so lucky now," he murmured. "What will the police do if Bernice doesn't identify the person as Virgil?"

"They might show her photographs of other men in Miss Parnell's circle," she said. "Just to clear the field, so to speak."

"And prove some gentleman with money took advantage of her like your friend thinks?" He looked at her sharply.

"It's what the police think too," she said.

"And what do *you* think?" He sat up, pulling a handful of clover with him. "Adele, what do you think?"

She weighed her words carefully. "I think it's possible she was taken advantage of by some ne'er-do-well young man, even one from a good family." She glanced at him. "I've known young men like that, and I'm sure you have too."

"I don't make it a habit of associating with ne'er-do-wells." His tone was vicious.

She laid her hand in his. "I'm sorry, Nathan. I know you're a good man with a good heart and a conscience."

"It's very gratifying to hear you say so, Adele." She felt him squeeze her hand. "But maybe the police should consider some women take just as much advantage of men, whether they are ne'er-do-well or not."

"I never said Arabella was an angel." She unwrapped a large square of crumb cake. "Care for half of this?"

"Can the police really be that concerned about one brooch?" Nathan's hand shook as he tossed aside the clover in his hand.

"They're concerned about a comb someone bought her too," Adele said.

A caw filled the silence. Adele, who was cutting the cake in half, jumped at the sound.

"Are you all right, Adele?" Nathan grabbed her wrist, turning her hand upward. Adele heard a shuffling in the bushes.

"Perhaps I should let the good doctor examine it," she said quickly.

"I don't know that I'm good yet," he said with a modest smile. "But I can heal cuts and bruises." He examined her hand. "I don't think there's any damage here." He took the knife from her hand. "You mean that hideous thing she was wearing the night of Gene's party?"

"Yes," Adele said. "The police are now looking for a young man with red hair whom Bernice says bought it for Arabella. They think his name is Troy."

He stared at a bush near them which had needle-like leaves scraping the ground in the wind. "I knew a man named Troy."

Adele felt her heart beating fast. "Was he one of your fraternity boys in college?"

His face grew limp. "No, he wasn't in the fraternity."

"Bernice got the impression he was quite taken by Arabella." Adele tried to make the remark sound incidental.

Nathan grabbed both her wrists, his face as wild as the needles on the bush. "All right, Adele, stop playing games!"

She heard another shift in the bushes farther away, and this time she could see the edge of Jackson's rifle.

"I'm not playing games, Nathan," she said in a calm voice. "I'm trying to get at the truth. I know you value the truth as much as I do."

"You want to know about Troy, don't you?" he asked. "The police sent you here to find out about him so they can accuse him of murdering Arabella."

"No one sent me here," she said in a soft tone. "I came because I wanted to." At least here, she was telling the truth.

"Well, you can go back and tell the sheriff Troy couldn't have committed murder or any other crime. He's dead!" He began to laugh, his head shaking. "He's dead!"

In almost a whisper, Adele said, "I'm sorry."

"Do you want to know what Arabella was, Adele?" Nathan's voice was uneven. "What she was really?"

"What was she, Nathan?" she asked.

"She was a predator," he said. "She stalked her prey, caught him, and when he was of no use to her, she left him behind to die!"

She felt his hands squeezing her wrist bones and her heart beat even faster. "Tell me about Troy, Nathan."

The young man dropped her wrists and fell back on the blanket. His face was marred with distress. "He was good. Always cheerful and loyal. He didn't play around like so many of us. He worked hard. He wanted to be somebody."

"And he fell in love with Arabella," Adele said.

"It was supposed to be only a bit of fun," Nathan spat out. "We all knew that."

"We?"

"The four of us," he said. "We shared everything. Class notes, exam answers, beers at the pub. Why shouldn't we share Arabella too?"

Adele tried to swallow but nearly choked. "I see."

He was breathing quickly now, his words tumbling out. "The way he went around like a puppy dog, talking about her as if she were a queen! And giving her every penny he had. Sometimes we had to feed him because he didn't have money for even a loaf of bread."

"I'm sorry," she said.

"She played with him like a cat plays with a butterfly," he lashed out. "She enjoyed seeing how earnest he was in his affection. She even let him kiss her!"

"I see."

"We told him he was making a mistake when he got the ring," Nathan continued. "We knew she would laugh in his face. But we didn't think she would stomp on him as if he were an ant that dared to get in her way."

"Did he get in her way?" Adele asked.

"Oh, she had her eye on someone else by then," he said. "And Troy — he was so sincere, so kind-hearted. He couldn't imagine a girl could be so sweet and soft for months and then suddenly turn into a witch!"

"What happened to him, Nathan?" Though she knew already, she wanted to hear it from his own lips.

"He couldn't cope when she rejected him." Nathan began to choke with sobs. "He took his own life."

"And so you took hers," she said.

He raised his head a little, facing the prickly bush. "We had to do it. I know we had to do it. But, God, why did someone have to die?" he sobbed.

"Two people died, Nathan," Adele said quietly. "Both were innocent."

"No!" he tore out. "Only one was innocent! The other deserved it."

"Did she?"

He looked at her with wild eyes. "I shouldn't have told you. You'll tell the police."

Although Adele's heart was nearly bursting through her chest with fear, she said in a calm tone, "I'm not going to tell the police, Nathan. You're going to do it."

"Are you mad?"

"You're going to tell them because you're not a killer," she continued. She saw Hatfield emerge slowly from behind a cluster of trees with Nin, motioning with a wave of his hand where a few assistant deputies came out from their hiding places. But he put up a hand to stop them and all were silent. Nathan, who had his back to them, seemed not to notice.

He grabbed her wrists again. "I took a gun to a woman!"

"I don't believe you did, Nathan," she said slowly.

"But I did!" His voice raced up and down, frightening the last of the birds in the trees. "I wrote the note! I wrote it!" With each word, he shook Adele. She felt the grip of his hands on her wrists, the back of her head tossing back and forth as if it were going to unhinge at any moment. "I can't let you tell the police! We made a pact, I can't —"

His eyes grew misty, and he dropped one of her wrists, only to pick up the knife she had used to cut the crumb cake. Its sharp blade glared at her where the sun hit like a malicious eye.

Jackson rushed forward, aiming his rifle at Nathan's temple. "Let go of my sister, Mr. Cress."

Nathan's gaze rested on Adele. He collapsed, letting go of her other wrist and the knife. He fell to the ground with a sob. Hatfield let the sobs go for a few moments before he motioned to Jackson, who took the handcuffs out of his pocket.

CHAPTER 27

Adele was so shaken after the scene at Tanner Swamp that Nin had to walk her home. Taking charge, she shooed Ruth out of the kitchen and created a concoction of skullcap, lemon balm and chamomile and made Adele lie down, commanding her to drink it. She then closed the curtains and through a misty sleep, Adele heard her giving Tomas orders that if anyone, including Jackson, attempted to disturb her friend, she would come at him with an ax. She couldn't help but smile in her fatigue at the image of Tomas' face at these words.

The next day she felt better, but her friend came again and in her commanding way, convinced Adele to stay in bed, promising her she would tend her shop and get Beatrice to help. That evening, Adele felt well enough for Nin to help her down the stairs. She was pleased to see Hatfield and Lady Augusta sitting in the parlor with Jackson.

"I've told Horatio to make my infamous rum punch, dear." The elderly woman wheeled forward to meet her.

"I don't know if I'm up to it," Adele said with a small laugh.

"Nonsense!" said Lady Augusta. "It will put some spark in your heart."

"I don't think Del's heart needs more spark than it already has," Jackson said with a smile.

"You mean my tongue, not my heart, dear brother," she said with a wink.

"But do try one, Adele," Hatfield said. "Ma's punch is marvelous."

Tomas handed the drinks around on a tray, his expression showing disapproval. As if Lady Augusta sensed this, she took a glass from the tray and thrust it at him. "Try one, my good man. I think you need a little spark in you, though I should argue it ought to go elsewhere than in your heart!"

Tomas gave her a dubious look, and they all laughed as he left the room.

"I'm sorry I was so put out," Adele lamented. "It isn't like me at all."

"No, it isn't," Jackson agreed. "Usually you're like a buffalo in a china shop."

"I believe the expression is 'bull in a china shop,'" Adele said stiffly. "If you're going to tease me, Jack, at least get it right."

"It's understandable," said Hatfield. "This has all been a terrible ordeal."

"I was there," Nin announced, "when they confessed."

"Which one killed her?" Adele asked. "I'm not asking out of morbid curiosity. I really want to know." She played with the napkin, her stomach like lead.

"You liked Nathan quite a lot, didn't you?" Nin asked softly.

Adele looked into the dark fireplace. "Yes. I liked him quite a lot." She heard a sound and realized it had come from the sheriff.

"He seemed like a nice young man," Lady Augusta offered. "A shame he was caught in such circumstances."

"He wasn't caught in circumstances, Ma," Hatfield said in a growling voice. "He's as much a killer as his friends."

Adele's hands felt cold. "So he killed her after all?"

"They all did," said Jackson.

"All?" Adele echoed.

He grimaced. "For once your idea was wrong, Del."

"Only partially wrong," Nin corrected. "They were all involved. That much is true."

"We couldn't guess they all pulled the trigger," the sheriff said. "We can't even know which bullet killed Miss Parnell."

"And that's what they were counting on," Jackson said. "A juvenile idea, but an effective one."

"Not as effective as they would have liked," Sheriff Hatfield pointed out. "Their confession will be enough to hang them all."

Adele felt her stomach turn and she grasped the pillow in her lap with both hands. "They're so young."

"It's not up to us, Del," said Jackson, reaching for her hands. "It's up to the district attorney."

"I don't imagine they will hang, dear," Lady Augusta said. "Horatio uses harsh words sometimes but he'll lobby for life imprisonment as hard as their own lawyer."

"I expect so, Ma," Hatfield mumbled.

"Measure for measure," Adele murmured. "They thought they were getting justice."

"Not the sort of justice we have in this country," Jackson insisted. "This is no longer the Wild West where men can carry out vigilante justice. Not even the Anspaches."

"They confessed they shot Arabella because they see her as Troy's murderer?" Adele asked.

"Not just that," Nin said. "She was blackmailing Maxwell."

"Blackmail!"

"That phone call Miss Parnell made the day after Mr. Dilworth's party," Jackson said. "She was threatening to take Maxwell to court for breach of promise."

"You mean he proposed to her?" Adele blinked.

"I always said the man was vile," Nin said. "He admitted to making the promise in writing."

"We have to find those letters first," Hatfield said. "Miss Parnell must have hidden them well."

"It was her trump card," Jackson said.

"I think she really was in love with Mr. Lee, Jack," Adele said. "Remember what Shirley said, Nin."

"Her eyes were two stars, like she couldn't believe what she was seeing," Nin recalled. "He dazzled her with his wealth."

"They were waiting for an opportunity to kill her and she put it right in their hands," Hatfield said.

"I didn't think it was a spur-of-the-moment thing," Adele said.

"Why do you think that, Del?" her brother asked.

"The guns," she said. "They wouldn't have a Colt or an American Eagle just lying around, would they?"

"Your sagacity, as always, astounds me, Adele." Hatfield smiled. "You're right, of course. They bought the guns about a year ago in Sacramento. I've got Sheriff Hill working on the gun shops there. He'll soon find out where they were bought."

"The impertinence of the young men wasting precious police resources," Lady Augusta grumbled. "They ought to have told you themselves."

"It's the way of arrogant criminals, Ma," her son explained.

"But if they're going to be hanged," Nin pointed out, "why not tell the police everything?"

"It's because they're going to be hanged they don't tell everything, Miss Branch," Jackson said. "They want to torture us as they see us torturing them."

"They were only waiting for the right moment to use those guns," the sheriff said.

"All very logical and heartless." Lady Augusta shuddered.

"Most pre-planned murders are, Ma," he said and kissed her hand.

"You remember the scene you and Miss Branch witnessed on the balcony with the comb?" Jackson asked.

"They were furious at her for wearing it." Adele nodded. "It makes sense now. They didn't think she had the right to wear a gift given to her by a man they believed she had killed."

"Well, it was in rather bad taste," Jackson remarked.

"What a way of putting it, Mr. Gossling!" Nin shivered.

"I'm sorry if I sounded flippant, Miss Branch." He bowed in apology.

"The incident with the comb sparked a chain of events," Hatfield continued. "I gathered from the boys no mention had been made by Miss Parnell of Troy Gallagher for some time before that."

"Gene said they even believed she felt sorry for Troy's death," Nin chimed in.

"I suppose her parading the comb in her hair that night proved them wrong." Jackson shrugged.

"Arabella threatened Maxwell with blackmail because he made a fuss over the comb?" Adele gave her brother a dubious look.

"It wasn't the comb," Nin said, her voice soft. "It was me."

"Don't be absurd, Miss Branch," Lady Augusta snarled.

"It's true, ma'am," she said.

"Why would you have anything to do with it?" Adele took her hand.

"Mr. Lee was flirting with me that night," said Nin. "Arabella didn't like that. She called his bluff."

"She would if she believed Mr. Lee would eventually marry her," Adele said.

"That's yet to be proven," Jackson pointed out. "I'm sure once his lawyer gets hold of him, he'll swear up and down he never promised her anything."

"We'll know when we find the letters," the sheriff said.

"According to Mr. Lee, Miss Parnell was always watchful of his interest in other ladies," Jackson said. "He thinks his flirtation with Miss Branch may have brought things to a head."

"And so she phoned him from the Dilworths and said if he didn't marry her, she would take him to court." Adele nodded.

"That sort of thing would ruin a man's reputation in such a close-knit society as the Dilworths," Jackson said.

"That's why she left the Dilworths' so suddenly," Adele continued. "She was confident she was going to marry Mr. Lee."

"She also phoned him from Mrs. Taylor's," Jackson said. "She demanded he meet her at the swamp to bind the agreement with some papers she got from a lawyer."

"That needs to be verified too," Hatfield said.

"I've no doubt she was telling the truth," Lady Augusta remarked.

"That's what led them to act," Adele said.

"I don't think it's that simple, Del," Jackson said. "They acted because they wanted justice for their dead friend. The threat opened the door."

"Murder is rarely simple in a case like this," Hatfield agreed. "A man who kills another in a bar room brawl is acting on animal impulse. But three men who shoot a woman in the back —" He shrugged, helping himself to another rum punch.

"From there, it was a matter of planning," Jackson said. "Maxwell arranged to meet Miss Parnell at the swamp. They met there quite often."

"She had no idea what was waiting for her?" Adele murmured.

Jackson shook his head. "We know she took the candle and holder, but I expect she thought she was meeting one man, not three."

"Shall we finish the story over dinner?" Lady Augusta wheeled back her chair. Tomas, taking the cue, grabbed the handles on the back of the chair.

In the dining room, Adele felt better with the flowers giving out a sedate perfume and Ruth's tomato soup, hot and creamy just as she liked it. "Tell me the rest of it."

"It's rather sordid, Del," her brother said.

"Tell me."

"The young men met at the foot of the swamp," Hatfield said. "Mr. Lee brought the wagon with him padded with India rubber. It seems his father owns stock in some company that uses them, and he bribed one of the workers to let him borrow the wagon."

"Without any consideration of how the worker might be blamed for his wagon being used as a transport vehicle for a murder victim." Lady Augusta shuddered. "Some men!"

"They were desperate, Ma, as most killers are," her son said. "Not that that's any excuse."

"Go on, Sheriff." Adele held her wine glass with both hands.

"They put the wagon in some overgrowth near the meeting place," he said. "Very near to where we were, I imagine."

"The other boys hid while Mr. Lee spoke with Arabella," said Jackson. "He claims he had every intention of trying to reason with her."

"Bunk!" Lady Augusta snarled.

"I agree, Ma," said Hatfield. "They came there to kill her, and kill her they did."

"All at the same time," Adele murmured.

"You ought to have seen their faces when they told us, Adele," Nin said. "They were so proud of their plan!"

"They didn't plan on shooting her in the back." Jackson took another piece of meat loaf, one of his favorites. "She tried to run."

"Why did they take the trouble to drag Arabella's body to Mr. Riddle's conservatory?" Adele asked.

"They knew Mr. Riddle's relationship with Miss Parnell was more than paternal." Jackson coughed. "We were right about that even if we couldn't prove it."

"Horatio would have found the evidence eventually." Lady Augusta patted her son on the shoulder.

"I expect so, Ma," he said. "They thought we would prosecute him when they found out he had something at stake — Mrs. Allington's hand in marriage."

"Public opinion would be against him," Jackson agreed.

"But just in case the police missed anything, they wanted to make sure they had Mr. Riddle on their list, so they wrote that note," Nin said. "Of course, you proved that to be all hogwash."

Hatfield grinned. "You were right about Mr. Cress, Adele. He does have a conscience." He said this with some trepidation. "Or at the very least, his conscience isn't altogether obliterated. He admitted to writing the note and copied it for us — using his own scrap of paper and pencil, both of which have now gone to the lab to be matched to the note."

"I take it the fingerprints we found on Arabella's clothes matched theirs?" Adele inquired.

The sheriff nodded. "They matched Mr. Cress and Mr. Dilworth." He sighed. "One thing I do have to admire is Mr. Lee could have easily allowed his friends to take the blame for the killing since his fingerprints weren't anywhere — he was taking care of the wagon and he wore gloves — but when the prints matched theirs, he confessed like the others."

"Poor Arabella." Adele shook her head.

"Poor Arabella!" Jackson stared at her. "She was going to blackmail a man into marriage, Del. You're really taking your sympathy for the cause too far."

"She paid the price for it, Mr. Gossling," Nin insisted.

"It must have been terrible for her to be faced with three guns pointing at her," Lady Augusta agreed. "And they shot her down like a doe."

"She was no doe, Ma," her son said. "But they were certainly hunters."

"Now it will be her turn to receive justice for justice," Adele said. "I only hope you'll get justice for doing your duty, Sheriff."

"Eh?" The sheriff stopped midway to reaching for another piece of pie.

"It won't be easy explaining all this to the mayor," she pointed out. "Remember the boys' fathers are friends of his."

"Mayor Willett already knows," said Jackson. "After we brought you home, we went with Nathan to his office. He made his confession to him and the district attorney. They both agreed the boys had to be arrested."

"Not that he was happy about it," Nin chimed in.

As they finished their dessert and retired to the parlor for coffee, Adele noticed her brother's face was disturbed, his brows gathered like a gray storm. She heard him ask Hatfield, "Sir, do you really think those boys will be found guilty?"

She did not hear the sheriff's answer but when she entered the parlor, Jackson's brows were still gathered.

~~~~~

Author's Note

Hello reader!

Thank you for reading Book 6 of my Adele Gossling Mysteries (which I assume you did if you're gotten this far!) I hope you enjoyed this book, as it turned out to be one of my favorite books to write (so far).

Why? Because it's based on a true crime that happened in the early 20th century. A crime that's never been solved!

In the summer of 1908, the body of a young woman was found floating face down in Teal Pond, which is located near Sand Lake in upstate New York. The woman was later identified as Hazel Drew, a maid to a prominent citizen of Troy, New York. Her killer or killers were never found.

There are so many aspects of this case that are intriguing: Why was Hazel killed? What was she doing near Teal Pond, an eerie kind of place, when she had told friends and family she would be
~~~~~

somewhere else for the weekend? Why did she suddenly leave her employer just before she was killed without the usual notice? Why did friends see her on a train bound for Albany, New York the day before her death?

But for me, mysteries aren't just about the crime. They're about the victim too. It's not for nothing Agatha Christie makes her super-sleuth Hercule Poirot always say that you can learn a lot about the crime by knowing the character of the victim.

In this case, the victim was an enigma. To her family and friends, she was a loyal, conservative, church-going young lady. But the investigation revealed Hazel Drew might have had another side to her. For example, she was known to love trips to New York City, expensive jewelry and clothes and fine dining — all things a domestic servant's salary could ill afford her. There were also letters found in the suitcase she left at the train station the morning of her death from many different men, most unidentified, and some promising undying love and devotion.

So perhaps the real mystery here is not "who killed Hazel Drew?" but "Who was Hazel Drew?"

Can't get enough of Adele Gossling? Read on for an excerpt from a novella about Adele's exploits helping the police recover a ruby necklace!

Happy reading!
Tam

FREE NOVELLA INFORMATION

When a jewel and a girl go missing on New Year's Eve...

Eleanor McCarthy, a lovely though somewhat flighty debutante, has graced the tiny town of Arrojo, California, with her presence. One of Arrojo's prominent ladies throws a New Year's Eve shindig to introduce her to Arrojo's high society — whatever little of it there is. Naturally, the daughter and son of one of San

Francisco's influential lawyers, Adele and Jackson Gossling, are invited.

But screams replace popping champagne corks when Eleanor's priceless ruby necklace is discovered missing. And soon, so is Eleanor!

In this historical cozy mystery set in the early 20th century, follow Adele Gossling, stationary store owner and amateur sleuth, and her clairvoyant sidekick Nin Branch as they search for a ruby necklace that may or may not have been stolen and a young woman who may or may not have run away.

Want to read an excerpt from this book? I got you covered! Turn the page.

FREE NOVELLA EXCERPT

"Coffee!" Miss McCarthy laughed. "Heavens, no! I haven't had my first taste of champagne yet." She flung her hand out to her brother. "Bring me a bottle of champagne, my good man."

"I don't mind," he said.

Before he could saunter out the door, Mrs. Abberton jumped up. "I'll get it."

"I really think we ought to get coffee," Mr. Abberton mumbled.

"She wants champagne," Mrs. Abberton was almost stern. "It's a celebration, after all!" She practically fled from the room.

Adele followed her and caught her arm. She spoke in a soft tone. "Mrs. Abberton, why did Miss McCarthy faint?"

"She just told you, didn't she?" The woman gave a shrill laugh. "Albert said we ought to open some windows, but it was such a windy night, I —"

"It wasn't the windows," said Adele. "Or the corset."

"Of course it was!" The woman examined some bottles on the floor. "I never could read these labels."

"You were staring at Miss McCarthy as if something that wasn't there."

"What an imagination you have, dear." The woman said.

"Miss McCarthy had her hands on her throat when she fell," Adele continued. "You kept looking at her throat."

"Nonsense," the woman hissed.

"Miss McCarthy wasn't wearing her ruby necklace," Adele declared.

Mrs. Abberton tore through a row of bottles lying on a table. One rolled onto the floor with a crack and the bubbly drink spilled across the marble. She sunk into one of the chairs. "You're too observant, Miss Gossling."

"You saw it too."

"Just before the lights went out," she said. "But Eleanor is one of those girls who gets easily flustered with her jewelry. She says it weighs her down."

"If that's true, why were you so alarmed just now?" Adele said.

"I wasn't," the woman insisted. "She locks that necklace in a box. Albert tried to persuade her to put it in our safe at the finance company, but she refused."

"That's rather unusual," Adele said.

"Eleanor's a lovely girl, but rather flighty," The woman said in a harsh tone. "I expect Celestine spoils her."

"If the necklace is missing, there might be a theft involved," Adele suggested.

Jewelry goes missing all the time. But does that mean theft? And why is Mrs. Abberton so nervous?

How can you get your hands on a copy of *The Missing Ruby Necklace*, not available in any bookstore? Simple. Go to this link: https://landing.mailerlite.com/webforms/landing/l2u0c3. What else will you get when you get this novella? How about fun facts about women in history and true crime classic mysteries, which are just as fascinating, if not more so, as contemporary true crimes?

WAXWOOD SERIES INFORMATION

Did you know I also wrote a historical coming-of-age series about a Gilded Age debutante's journey to womanhood?

"This is historical fiction at its best" – Whispering Stories Book Blog

One woman's journey to self-discovery in the Gilded Age could destroy everything she's ever known.

Meet the Alderdices:

Vivian, the daughter, whose coming out as a woman sets in motion the slow unveiling of family secrets and lies.

Jake, the son, whose search for a father figure leads him down a path of sin and redemption.

Larissa, the family matriarch, whose obsession with Nob Hill's rigid social proprieties could destroy both of her children.

Book 1: *The Specter* - In 1892 San Francisco, Nob Hill's finest gather to mourn the death of Penelope Alderdice. When an uninvited guest shows up claiming to have known Mrs. Alderdice under another name, the Alderdices are shocked. Is it possible she had another identity beyond the generous philanthropist and celebrated socialite? Her granddaughter Vivian must journey back to Waxwood to find out.

Book 2: *False Fathers* - Jake has none of the virtues of the Gilded Age masculine ideal. Where he should be aggressive, he is contemplative. Where he should be ambitious, he is wayward. Where he should be money-driven, he is artistic. Jake must decide his future during his family's summer trip to Waxwood. While there, he befriends a man who becomes a father figure, promising to mold him into the Teddy Roosevelt ideal, shaping him into the man he's meant to be.

Book 3: *Pathfinding Women* - At the close of the nineteenth century, Vivian Alderdice is twenty-six and unmarried with no prospective suitors. Her brother's tragic plight the year before left her and her mother on shaky ground with Nob Hill's blue bloods. The only way they can re-establish their social position is to win the heart of Monte Leblanc, a wealthy Canadian looking to become a member of the exclusive Washington Street society. But a young man on the train tells Vivian things about her grandmother that shake her to the core. Even as she is pursued by the debonair Monte Leblanc, Vivian can't avoid ghosts from the past who send her on a journey she is reluctant to take.

Book 4: *Dandelions* - For Vivian Alderdice, the 20th century begins with a new start. Now a working girl and progressive reformer, she has forsaken the Gilded Age opulence of Nob Hill for the humbler surroundings of Waxwood's commercial district. Harland Stevens, the man who ruined her brother two years before, appears like another specter in Vivian's life, and, in spite of herself, Vivian is compelled to help him escape from a hell of his own.

Read this historical coming-of-age series set in one of the most turbulent cities during the last tumultuous decade of the 19th century.

How about an excerpt from Book 1, *The Specter*? Coming right up! Turn the page.